THE LOST

The Second Coming
BOOK ONE

Eric Johnson

Broken Table Press

Copyright © 2021 Eric Johnson,

All rights reserved. This book or any portion thereof may not be reproduced or used in any manner whatsoever without the express written permission of the publisher except for the use of brief quotations in a book review.

First printing, 2021.

Broken Table Publishing
Belchertown, MA, 01007

www.ericjohnsonwriter.com

To Bob and Lee,

Your unwavering support made this possible.

Acknowledgments

This book would not have been possible without all the help and support I received from my family and friends throughout the years. My wife, who put up with my long hours of disappearing into the words that I create and who patiently listens to my excited non-sequiturs about characters and events she'd never heard of. My children, equally patient with my writing hours, inspire me to be the best that I possibly can. Bob and Lee, my folks, have supported my passion for writing for as long as I can remember and are probably my biggest fans. I love you all.

I want to give Chris a special thank you for being the one to both introduce me to the joy of reading horror and inspire me to begin this journey.

THE LOST

THE LOST

ONE

"They say there's a place in the woods where you can see the face of the devil in the coals of a dying fire– That spooky enough for you, Jackie?" Mikey glanced sideways at Jackie, the mischievous glint in his eyes.

He'd been ribbing her about it all day. Jackie had gotten this book from someone and called Mikey up. He called me, and we went to pick up Jeff and Jackie at her house. Now here they were, bouncing down the old dirt track headed to some run-down shack in the middle of the woods that Mikey's sister used to go drinking at. Jackie nodded and glanced back at Jeff sitting next to Geoffrey in the back of Mikey's Ford Ranger. Geo didn't really know Jackie and Jeff too well, they never talk to me at school, but Mikey and Geo go way back, preschool way back. He became popular, and Geo– Geo went on to have an embarrassing crush on Mikey's sister. Geo still didn't know why, but Mikey never let their friendship go.

"What d'ya think, Geo?" Mikey asked.

"Sorry, what?"

"Dude wasn't even listening," Jeff said, punching me lightly in the shoulder, "some backup you are."

"Lay off," Mikey said, "without him, you'd never have made it through Harris's English class."

Eric Johnson

"Why are you even here, Geo?" Jeff wasn't really one for subtlety. "You could listen once in a while."

"You're one to talk jerk-off," Jackie chimed in.

"Besides," Mikey continued, "Jackie said four." He shrugged and turned his attention back to the dirt road as the clearing with the cabin came into view. "We're here."

Calling the thing a cabin was being generous. A shack or shed would have been better, but it was common knowledge around town that this place used to be home to some recluse hunter until he finally lost it and blew his brains out on his cot. The county had taken what was left of the corpse leaving the cabin deserted. Now it was a hangout for high schoolers who wanted a place to drink, that the local cops left more or less alone.

The walls showed the wear of Virginia weather, but they were still standing and the windows, though broken, were more or less there. Over the solid stone stoop, the door hung a little off-kilter but not enough to see inside. The area around the shack had been tramped down by years of high schoolers sneaking off to throw back some beers or smoke up. Jeff and Jackie swung themselves out of the truck almost before it had stopped and immediately started to gather wood to start their fire. Geo just stood there, leaning against the side of the truck, watching them moving around in the gathering darkness. Mikey cut the engine and came around, leaning his elbow on his shoulder.

"Place always gives me the creeps no matter how many times I've been here," he looked at Geo and smirked. "You have been here before, right?"

"Not really much of a drinker," Geo couldn't take his eyes off the door.

"You've smoked some, though."

THE LOST

"Ya, I normally go up to the lookout with Steve for that," Geo felt a shiver run down his spine despite the warm night. "So, you think he really did it?"

"Don't know," Mikey said, pushing off the truck and giving his shoulder a pat, "mattress is gone, so could be."

"Wait," Geo followed him toward the shack, "you've gone inside?"

He looked back at Geo and shrugged as his response, then shot a quick look at Jackie and smirked again. Geo just rolled his eyes and shoved his shoulder as he went by, figuring to make himself useful and start setting up the fire. All those years of boy scouts were going to buy him some credibility here; maybe then Jeff would lay off being an ass. Probably not, but at least he'd have pulled his weight.

The fire started quickly, probably because it hadn't rained in a couple of weeks at least. But soon, they were all sitting around the small fire that they'd wanted, Geo assumed because he was told to keep the fire small to avoid lighting the shack on fire, but it turned out that they wanted it to burn down into coals. So they sat there in the darkness, the intermittent light of the coals casting weird shadows on the trees around the clearing. The fog slithered through the trees; Jackie and Jeff sat close with their heads in some book, earnestly flipping through the pages and mumbling to each other.

"So man, nice work on the fire," Mikey leaned back on his arms and looked at the star-lit sky.

"Thanks," Geo couldn't figure out why Mikey still hung out with him. Mikey was relaxed, popular, and confident. Geo was—well, Geo was just not.

"Scintillating conversationalist as usual," he laughed.

Eric Johnson

"What are we even doing here?" It took all his courage to ask this, but it was the question he wanted to ask since Mikey'd asked him to come along. "What's with this whole book thing?"

"Got it," Jackie's head whipped up. The smile on his face made Geo shift a little uncomfortable in his seat.

"Just wait," Mikey sat up and leaned forward, looking at the coals of the fire, "you'll see. Watch this."

Geo watched the fire with Mikey while Jackie and Jeff read something from the book in what sounded to his untrained ears like Italian or Latin. The heat from the coals seemed more substantial than they were before, but Geo shrugged that off as nerves. He looked around the clearing again, noticing the fingers of the fog had begun to lace around the truck. He could see through the slight crack in the shack's door from where he was sitting around the stoop as the fog seemed to billow from the floor.

"You see that?" Geo grabbed Mikey's shoulder, pointing to the edge of the woods behind Jackie. "I swear something moved through the fog."

"Don't worry about it," Mikey didn't take his eyes off the coals, "just your imagination."

"I don't like this."

"It's fine," Mikey glanced up at him smiling, "just chill for a bit, you'll see."

Jacki and Jeff were still mumbling something from the book, Geo couldn't make out their words exactly, but he was beginning to think it was probably for the better. Mikey's face was pale when he tugged on Geo's sleeve, staring as he pointed to the fire with a quivering hand. Geo watched in confusion as the burning coals moving and rearranging themselves into what he can only guess would be the face of the devil.

THE LOST

The door slammed open, and the same fog creeping through the woods oozed from a crack in the cabin's floor. Geo could only see a corner of the room beyond the door, but that was enough. Inside, he could see creatures that defied description, hundreds of them, crawling all over each other, all seeming to materialize from the fog, then disintegrate into it again as it swirled around the room. It moved as if pushed by some unknown wind held only by the rotting walls of the shack. The smell coming from the small space was a mix of rot and sulfur, and Geo had to cover his mouth with his hand to keep from throwing up. The fog had wholly enveloped the clearing, hiding Mikey's truck from where Geo sat, and the moon's light glowed green through the vile-smelling vapors that surrounded them. He stood up and looked around the clearing, trying to see over the fog.

A howling from the woods startled him, and he stepped backward, tripping over the coals of the fire and stumbling through the door. The cabin smelled like old gym socks and mold, and the floorboards were spongy. He searched around quickly for something to defend himself with. Sticking into the floor a little bit away was a hunting knife. Prying it out of the rotting wood, Geo held the knife in his right hand and pulled the door open slowly with his left.

"Mikey," Geo called out, his heart thumping wildly in his chest. "The fuck, let's get out of here." Silence met his words, and he was about to call out again when he heard the low guttural huffing, animalistic and hungry, from the edge of the clearing behind him. "Shit Mikey, I'm getting out of here."

As if on cue, Mikey's truck roared to life, and the headlights tore through the darkness of the clearing. Hopping to find the other three and get away from whatever this was, Geo sprinted toward the hazy outline of the truck. After only a few steps, the toe of his right foot caught something heavy and threw Geo sprawling to the ground, his hand splashing in a warm puddle. He rolled over to look at whatever caught his foot and gasped as he stared at Jeff's outline in the fog.

"Jesus, Jeff," he started standing up and going over to check on him, "stop fucking around. You scared the shit out of me." He reached for Jeff's shoulder to shake him and turn him over, but his hand slipped off on something that felt slimy. "What, no jab about tripping me this time?" Wiping his hand on his own pants, Geo grimaced. "Dude, get up." Geo grabbed Jeff's arm and flipped the significantly heavier boy over. Even in the poorly lit clearing, Geo knew instantly why Jeff hadn't responded with a barb about his clumsiness. There was a pained grimace on Jeff's face, but it was the eyes that made everything clear. Jeff stared up at Geo with eyes the color of the gathering fog. He realized then what the warm puddle was and shivered in revulsion, barely keeping himself from throwing up the spaghetti his mom had cooked for supper.

Geo backed away, scrambling over the fallen leaves and dirt, got up, and started running toward the truck again, knife clenched in his hand, the sound of bugs crunching beneath his feet as he neared it. When he reached for the handle, something brushing against him as it went in the direction of the town. Geo wrenched the door to the truck and threw himself into the cab slamming the door behind him. He closed his eyes, set the knife on the seat next to him, and took a deep breath.

It took a few seconds for the smell inside the cab to register, but as soon as it did, Geo gagged and went into a coughing fit. He put his hand on the dashboard to steady himself. It felt warm and wet as his hand slipped across. He leaned back, putting his sleeve over his nose to keep from smelling, and looked at the dashboard. Hundreds of strange bugs, like a swarm of

THE LOST

ladybugs, shone red in the moonlight. He looked to the driver's side and saw the same bugs crawling in and out of the side of Mikey's head.

"Fuck," Geo coughed into his arm as his brain tried to sort out what was happening. He fumbled for the handle of the door behind him, unable to take his eyes off of the teeming wound in the side of Mikey's head, but the bugs seemed to be everywhere, and he didn't want to touch them knowing where some of them might have been. Sliding the back window open, Geo pulling himself through. He couldn't get a grip on anything as he climbed through the window and ended up tumbling face-first into the truck's bed. His face hit something soft and moist, and his right hand was tangled in something sticky. Pushing himself up, and Geo tried to look around.

Closer to the shack, a wolf-like animal was eating something on the ground, and strange creatures from inside the shack spread into the trees. The truck was covered in blood, and Jacki's body lay on her back, staring up at the stars, a smear of blood on her chest from his face, her hair matted and pulled across her face from when Geo had reflexively pulled his hand away from the sticky tangle. He jerked with a start, rolling onto his back away from what used to be Jacki. His hand landing on a book of some kind, the leather cover seemed to wince as his hand struck it. He pulled his hand away and read the title through the smear of blood that it left. The golden letters seemed to darken as the cover absorbed the blood; the words *The Book of the Second Coming* glowered at him through the receding stain.

Rustling from near the shack brought Geo's eyes up to scan the clearing once more. He couldn't wrap his mind around everything that was going on. He'd come out here, expecting fire and maybe a beer, but nothing like this. Not seeing his only friends torn apart. The wolf-like thing wasn't there. He scanned the clearing again, hoping to see it slinking off into the woods, but the sound of groaning metal made him stop. Geo held his breath and counted to three trying to slow his heartbeat, then he stood up to look back toward the cab only to see the wolf on top of it. The hair on its muzzle matted with blood, and its eyes glowing like the moon through the fog. The wolf let out a howl, so angry and powerful that Geo lost his footing and slipped, falling on Jacki again.

Geo just had time to put his arm out in front of himself before the wolf was on him. Its strong teeth slipped easily through Geo's skin, and he cried out in pain, barely able to stay conscious. Searching with the arm that wasn't in the wolf's mouth for something to defend himself with, his hand landed on the book. Grabbing the binding, he took one second to register the weight before he swung it at the growling head looming before him. When the book made contact, the wolf winced and loosened its grip on Geo's arm. Taking the seconds this gave him, Geo pushed himself off of Jackie and lunged for the still open window in the back of the cab. The wolf snapped at him, grabbing his left ankle and pulled him back into the bed. Kicking frantically with his right leg, Geo landed his heel on the snout of the animal. It whimpered and opened its jaws to snap again, but Geo pulled with this arms and dragged his skinny frame through the window before the animal could bite a third time. The wolf pawed at the open window for a minute before it leaped from the truck. Taking a deep breath, Geo put his hand on the steering wheel after wiping away the bugs and leaned over to open the driver's side door.

"I'm sorry, man," he said as he reached over Mikey's body for the handle in the driver's door. The side of Mikey's face was a swathing mass of red bugs. Geo got the handle and shoved Mikey's body from the truck onto the ground, moving into the

THE LOST

driver's seat as he did it. Pulling the door shut, he turned the key. The truck lurched forward and stalled. He looked at the floor and found the clutch. Wincing at the pain from the bite to his ankle, Geo pushed in the clutch; he could hear the popping bugs as he pushed the pedal to the floor. He turned the key again and started the truck.

Putting it in first gear, he pressed the gas leaving a trail of dust behind. He heard Jacki's body slide along the bed of the truck and fall to the ground. The truck bounced over the dirt road that led back to town, and Geo didn't stop until it ran out of gas three towns later.

The truck rolled into the parking lot of a gas station, and with what little strength he had left, Geo stepped from the cab and limped into the office. His left arm, the one the wolf had bit, hung numbly at his side. It had been useless for a while now, and he'd felt the bugs feeding inside it. The heat had bothered him at first, but Geo stopped minding after a bit because since they had begun, the pain had subsided, and he felt almost like he was floating.

The trip across the parking lot was laborious due to the damage to his ankle. Each step, just like each time he'd had to press the clutch in, sent searing pain through his whole body. It seemed like an hour before he reached the office, but as Geo leaned against the glass door to open it, the clerk looked up as if he'd startled him.

"Help you with something?" the clerk, probably not much older than Geo, asked lazily.

Geo furrowed his brow at the kid behind the counter, wondering why he'd asked such a dumb question. Obviously, he needed help. He looked down at himself to draw attention to his condition and drew in a slow and even breath. Instead of hanging lifeless by his side as expected, his left arm held an unsheathed hunting knife down by his side. He rotated his wrist; nothing hurt. Looking down at his ankle, it looked fine, and when he put more weight on it, there was no pain. His clothes were still covered in blood, but every trace of the wolf's bites had been wiped clean away.

"Hey buddy," the clerk must have noticed the knife because his tone had clearly changed, "either buy something or get out. I don't want any trouble."

Geo tilted his head to the left slightly and thought for a moment. The truck was out of gas, and that sulfury smell of those bugs was getting to him. He smiled at the clerk, then, without a word, turned around and pushed back through the glass doors and started walking. He was amazed at how calm he was, near-death just moments before, driving like mad to get away from something that seemed to be wrong, and now— now he walked calmly down the side of the highway, back toward the same town that it all started in. Something pulled him back, back to the beginning, back to the cabin in the woods.

The clerk must have called the cops because about three miles from the station, red and blue lights blazed behind him, and the glaring white spotlight stretched his shadow out for what seemed like miles, and for a brief moment, Geo thought that he could see something moving along the edge of his shadow.

Two

The room they'd left him in was cold, and Geo shivered in the thin orange jumpsuit they'd given him after taking his clothes. At least Matt was apologetic when he did it, benefits of family, he supposed. Geo shifted in the cold, metal chair and rolled his shoulders, tightening against the unnatural position the cuffs put him in. His reflection, a dirt and blood-smeared face, his right eye swollen from where the arresting officer had elbowed him getting the knife; all in all, things didn't look as bad as he'd expected. Unfortunately, the apologetic look was about all that family got in here, he thought, leaning his head back against the top of the chair. There were no windows in the room, but he was sure that it was probably close to sunrise at the earliest, and it had really been a long night.

"Fuck Geo," Officer Matthew Bedrin said as he walked through the only door in the room, "this better not be what it looks like, or your mom's gonna kill me."

"What does it look like exactly?" Geo asked to the ceiling, his eyelids dragging closed.

"What does it look like?" Bedrin closed the door and turned the chair opposite Geo's around before he sat down, leaning his arms on top of the back. "Looks like you killed your friends."

Eric Johnson

Geo's head snapped up at the accusation. His mouth gaped, trying desperately to form any of the thousand words swimming in his brain. His friends were dead that he was sure of– but killing them, that was another story.

"Look, man," Bedrin started, "forensics is still out on that blood, but look at yourself, not so much as a scratch." He held his hand up to quiet Geo as he was about to talk, "Yah, you have bruises, but bruises don't bleed. We found the truck where you ditched it, and that was a lot of blood in it. The bed, the cab, shit man, if I'm honest with you– doesn't look good."

"But I–"

"You sure you want to start talking without a lawyer present?" Bedrin produced a small recorder from his coat pocket. "If you wanna, I'm gonna record it. Cool with that?"

Geo thought for a moment; recording the story, getting it out now, would look good for him. It'd make it look like he was cooperating. That always worked out for people on those Law and Order reruns his mom liked to watch. He nodded at Matt, feeling happy that it was him. He knew Matt, holidays and all that. Even though he was only his mother's second cousin, he was sure a distant relative wouldn't try to screw him over.

"Can you please say your name for the record?" Matt said after he moved the tape recorder between them and pressed the red button.

"Geo Hollon."

"You full name Geo."

"Geoffrey Sebastian Hollon."

"Well, Geo, can you explain why you were covered in blood when we picked you up?"

"Yes."

"Do you know where you are now?"

"Sheltham Police Station."

THE LOST

"Good, now can you tell me what happened last night?"

Geo took a deep breath and felt a calmness wash over him, he was usually nervous around authority figures, but this time he felt like he was in control, handcuffed. "So we're going to the shack, you know the one, some of the other kids go there to drink?"

Matt nodded his head and gestured for Geo to continue. The gesture annoyed him some, and Geo felt restless. He shifted in his seat before he continued to explain the events that lead up to his getting picked up on the highway just over the town line.

After Geo finished his explanation, Bedrin was quiet for a moment before he stood up and walked over to the mirror, shaking his head and watching Geo in the reflection. He spoke without turning around. "Christ Geo, you expect me to believe that?"

"It's the truth, I swear it," Geo was struggling to control his temper as he watched Bedrin's back. He'd figured, of all the cops in the town, Matt would've been the most likely to believe him. He didn't like the fact that Bedrin seemed to be casting doubt. "One minute they were reading from this book, the next we're being attacked by wolves. I swear. I don't know what happened exactly because I was running for my life." Geo cringed as he remembered pushing Mikey's body out of the driver's seat. "I was– shit man, you gotta believe me. The book, I think I had it in the truck when I got to the gas station. It's proof that my story is true. Find the book." The last words echoed in his brain, becoming a mantra and imperative. Something clicked within him, and he knew, in no uncertain terms, that book needed to be found.

"If this is the truth, then where's the book?" Matthew Bedrin turned around and looked at Geo, sympathy clearly written across his face. "You didn't have the book when we found you, but you did have a knife. Quite a bloody one too."

"I don't know what to tell you, Matt," Geo said. The soft look in Matt's eye's confirmed that he could manipulate the situation, but somewhere in the back of his mind, he could hear himself begging for help, "that's what happened. Find the book." *The book.* The phrase took on preternatural importance that was consuming him.

"Now Geo," Matt said, standing over Geo's metal chair looking like the typical small-town cop; old, bored, tired, mean, and in way over his head in this. Half the town would be down his throat about this, three kids missing, and one, no one to account for his whereabouts, was mysteriously found wandering the highway, covered in blood. "Shit, man, you have one hell of an imagination, but you can't expect me to believe that?"

"It's the truth," Geo pleaded, his old insecurity resurfacing, knowing there is no way to escape the suspicion, "I know it's far-fetched, but it's the truth." He looked Matt in the eye, trying to convince him of his sincerity.

"If this is true, then where's the book?" Bedrin let the question hang in the air as Geo looked around the room. "And explain the fucking knife. I want to believe you, I do, but you got to give me something other than wolves."

Damn-it, Geo thought, I know that I had the book in the truck when I got to the gas station. It was in the bed of the truck. He remembered the sound of Jackie's body sliding out of the bed. A shudder shook through his frame, shaking him out of a nightmare into a waking world not much better; the book could have slid out then too. Where else could the book have been? Or, he wondered, did he have it when he left the truck? When they grabbed him, it could have dropped, must have. Maybe they didn't notice it. That was a good thing, he thought, because if

THE LOST

they couldn't find the book, then they couldn't take it. It really is an excellent-looking book. "I must have dropped it," he said in a distracted tone. He was miles away, trying to remember where the book went.

The conversation continued, but the outcome really didn't matter to Geo anymore. The book was all that mattered. They must have found it, he thought, and they don't want him to have it; they want to keep it—the bastards.

"You hear me?"

"What?" Geo's leg started to bounce. He could almost picture it sitting on some shelf in a police evidence room.

"How do you explain the knife? Or, for that matter, where the other kids are? We have six witnesses that put you leaving town with them, and we found the truck at a gas station on eighty-five over in Peamont."

"I didn't have a knife, and you know it, you're not getting the book." Geo leaned back in his chair. The unusual confidence in the face of authority came back with a vengeance when he thought about getting his hands on that book again.

Matt turned his chair back around, pulled it closer to the table, sat down, and leaned forward, "Now Geoffrey," he lowered his voice, "I don't think you understand the gravity of the situation."

"You have nothing on me. You're only holding me here because you want me to tell you about the book, how to use it," Geo blurted out, accusation filling his voice. Matt drew in a short breath. "You might as well just give the damn thing back because you couldn't use it if you wanted to."

It occurred to him what he was saying, all of it. He couldn't believe that he was talking to a cop like that, especially Matt. Closing his eyes and shaking his head slightly, he tried to clear the storm of emotions rising inside. The thoughts swirled around like a hurricane, and at the center, the calm center, was that book. It was terribly important that he got it back. His eyes started to burn, and he wanted to rub them.

A knock at the door brought Matt to his feet to answer it. He left the room, leaving Geo by himself. He couldn't get up because they had cuffed him to the chair, but looking at his unblemished face in the mirror, he went back in his mind to the side of the road where they had picked him up and tried to remember what it was that he was looking for. He had pulled the knife from the side of the shack because he'd needed to pry something up. The floorboards, what he was looking for was under them, he couldn't place it? He began to wonder if Bedrin was right. Had he killed his friends, hiding them under the floor of the shack, they had wanted the book too, hadn't they?

"The lab results just came back," Matt was saying. Geo hadn't even noticed him come back in carrying a computer printout. "Apparently, the blood on the knife is yours. Where'd you cut yourself?"

"Cut myself?" Geo searched his memory, unsuccessfully trying to remember cutting himself. He looked at his hands and saw a large gash in his left arm that was still bleeding. Blinking his eyes, Geo looked at the floor beside the chair. A small pool of blood formed below his arms which had been dangling at his side. He stood up and twirled around, looking for the cuffs they had used to chain him to the chair, but they weren't there. He tried to remember when Bedrin had taken them off, but he couldn't. He was sure that he hadn't been able to move them a moment ago and panic started to course through his system.

"Let me get someone to look at that," Matt sounded concerned. "It looks pretty deep," he moved toward Geo, but Geo leaned back, trying to avoid him as he reached out. "It's okay Geoffrey, why didn't you tell me when I brought you in?"

THE LOST

The room spun around him, and Geo tried to put his hand on the table to steady himself. The blood on his palm made it impossible to get a solid purchase on the edge of the table, and the last thing Geo remembered was the corner of the table rushing toward his head. Next thing he knew, he was on a gurney, white blurring past him. The fog, the clearing. He could see the creatures out of the corner of his eye. They sat watching from the white surrounding him, laughing at his confusion. Geo felt his stomach clench, and he gagged, wanting to throw up to get some strange toxin out of his system. The room was spinning again, and there was a lot of noise, high-pitched beeps, and yelling. Everything was a blur of white, a swirling fog. The only thing that he could see clearly were those things out of the corner of my eye, but whenever he looked directly at them, they would disappear into the flood of white. Then everything went silent.

Three

The place reeked of cheap cigarettes and cheaper whiskey. It was bustling for Thursday night at eleven, but the grey-haired man at the end of the bar didn't care. He'd been there since six, and he was still trying to forget why he had come in, the same way he did every day. He would stay here until closing time, then go home and finish half the bottle he had in his car, the one he bought before coming here, the same as he did most Thursdays. He'd make sure he only drank half of the bottle. That way, there would be enough to get him through tomorrow morning until the package store opened.

On Saturdays, he made sure that he had enough to get through the next day. To him, the worst day of the week because it would always remind him of what once was. He hoped that God would forgive him for his transgressions, but he was getting to the point where even that didn't matter. So here he sat, fifty-three, grey-haired, alone at the end of the bar in a dive out on sixty-two east, a mile out of town; it was a little solace that at least he owned the place. People were talking, it hurt, but there was nothing to be done about it. He was Jonah, sitting in the whale's stomach, wishing himself dead.

"Want another Father?" the bartender came over, interrupting his self-pity. A young kid, about twenty-three, she'd been working for him for the past two years. He'd known the kid

THE LOST

her whole life, Marissa Hail, her parents, even longer than that, back in the good old days.

"Thank you, Marissa," the old man said, "I think I would."

Marissa poured the whiskey into the old man's glass and walked away, leaving him the bottle and his own thoughts. She'd had some trouble in her teens, rebelled like any other teenager with strict Catholic parents, a little anger and a little drinking, nothing too unusual. The old man remembered how happy her parents were when Marissa had gone to talk to him without being asked. But that was all before, before the accusations against him, before her breaking and entering charges. At this point, her parents barely spoke to either of them, but she had served her time, and he was happy to help give her a second chance.

He took a long drink from his glass, the ice sliding against his red nose before he put the glass down and refilled it. He felt the warming sensation of the cold whiskey as it traveled down his throat and closed his eyes, trying to hold on to the feeling as if to convince himself that he was alive. He hated thinking about the past, but no matter where he went, there was something to remind him. At home, he wouldn't even go into the library he'd loved because everything he wanted to forget was kept in that library. He tried not to listen to the television or the radio; they carried with their waves the wake that destroyed his life.

After all, how could one believe in and support a religion whose very spokesmen would do such horrible things? He remembered his sermon the day the first charges were announced; he wanted to comfort his congregation. He knew there would be those who would wonder if he was like the others, the wolves in sheep's clothing. He had labored about what to say all that night, and in the end, he still didn't feel like he was doing it justice.

Eric Johnson

"The disciples asked Jesus, who is the greatest in the kingdom of heaven, and Jesus replied by calling the little children to him and sitting among them he said, 'Whosoever, therefore, shall humble himself as this little child, the same is greatest in the kingdom of heaven. And whoso shall receive one such child in my name shall receiveth me. But who shall offend one of these little ones which believe in me, it were better for him that a millstone was hanged about his neck and that he was drowned in the depth of the sea.

"'Woe unto the world because of offenses! For it must need be that offenses come; but woe to the man by whom the offense cometh! . . . Take heed that ye despise not one of these little ones; for I say unto you, That in heaven their angels do always behold the face of my Father which is in heaven.' This does Jesus say to his disciples in Matthew chapter eighteen verses four to ten."

He had been in tears delivering that one, talking about how wrong it was, what had been done, and how the Church would never stand for such vile treatment of the children. He said he would be surprised if those priests were not defrocked immediately, and surprised he was. Surprised and ashamed. He likened them to the men of Sodom and Gomorra, who wanted to have their way with the angels when they were staying with Lot. He prayed daily that God would punish the transgressors; he railed fists in the air at the television and radio that blamed The Church for covering it up all these years. But in the end, every night, he cried for the children who had to suffer the atrocities.

When nothing came of it when the priests were moved around to other parishes, when they were promoted, when they were exonerated, he began to lose steam. His sermons became sloppy, thrown together at the last moment, and he knew the parishioners could tell. Attendance was down, the choir had been

THE LOST

halved, and people had stopped calling on him late at night if they had a problem. His Church, which had been his true love since he entered the ministry at twenty, was dying, and he didn't have the heart left to do anything about it. That's when he turned to the bottle, just a little nip before bed, to help calm him down.

The final recognition came when the bishop sent over a new priest, Father Joseph Maria, to "help out" with the parish. The old man realized what was happening then. He was letting his congregation down, people he had been a father to, people he had led, as a shepherd, down the path to God. His flock had not gone astray; he had. It was that realization, along with the presence of young Father Maria, which had led to his leaving the Church.

Now his days were filled with forgetting, oddly enough, that proved to be a difficult job for him. He refused to leave the area, not that anyone wanted him to or would stop him if he tried, except maybe Marissa, but forgetting would have been easier without all the places to remind him of what life was. There was something about this town he'd noticed when he first had come here, a sort of easiness that seemed to welcome you home after a long day. His first day in front of the congregation had been the happiest day of his life; he loved the people because they'd made it easy to love them.

He took another drink and refilled the glass again. He knew that Marissa would be back down in a bit, making sure that the old man was all right. The poor girl hadn't understood when he had left the Church; Marissa had come over to his house in tears. She had to have been eighteen or nineteen at that point, begging the old man to come back. Saying that he had helped so many people, let them help him now. But the old man wouldn't have it, pride some would say, but Marissa refused to give up. She disapproved of his drinking, but there wasn't much that could be done about it. He blamed himself for her stints in prison; he felt he'd let her down by not going back to The Church, but the young are often nieve; The Church wouldn't have taken him back anyway. By the second time she had gotten out of prison, he knew he had to do more to help her, so he'd used his savings to buy the dive on the way out of town and hired her to run the place. She's convinced the old man to do his drinking here at the Local Eights, figuring at least then she could keep an eye on him, and if he needed a ride home, make sure that he got one.

"Hey there," a voice said from the next stool.

The old man hadn't noticed when someone had sat next to him. Looking over, he squinted through the smoke-filled air at a burly man with a grizzly beard. The hair on both his head and his chin was a wild light grey, and the man's cheeks were a rosy pink. His smile seemed to come easy, but you could tell from the way he looked that this wasn't someone you would mess with. He was wearing a blue mechanic's work shirt with a name patch that read Carl.

Extending his hand, he said, "Hope you don' mind me sittin' here, looked like we both drinkin' the same shit, so I figured I'd split a bottle wichou," his white teeth bright against the smoky background. "Name's Carl if you didn't read it already, pleasedtomeetcha." He ran the last few words together with an almost lazy speed common to some people.

"I can't say that I would mind terribly," the old man smiled meekly, "but I can't guarantee I'll be much company." He motioned to Marissa to bring another glass. "My name is Peter." Carl's grip was firm and hearty, in contrast to Peter's weak, unsure hand, a difference Carl didn't seem to notice.

"Ah man, I really 'ppreciate you lettin' me squat here wichu. It's been hell for me this week. Fuckin' had to haul a load of cows cross-state, and the goddamn cops stopped me causin' he

THE LOST

said I was speedin', then all that construction, I mean shit, hows you spose to drive with all dat, you know?"

Marissa came over and placed another glass down in front of the two men. "Anything else you need, Father?"

"No, Marissa, I'm fine, thank you."

"Let me know, okay?" She headed back to the other end of the bar, chatting with some young men who had just come in, presumably trying to figure out what to get, either that or how to get her number. He smiled at that despite himself. They had no shot.

"She your kid?" Carl asked.

"Nope." Peter was hoping not to have to explain that as he silently scolded Marissa for calling him Father.

"Didn't she call you . . . ohh," Carl's face went flush. "Oh shit, eh I mean . . . sorry 'bout all dat cussin', I means I don't know."

Peter sighed, so much for that not coming up.

"What's a priest doin' in a place like this?"

"I'm not a priest anymore," there was a sadness in his voice that he was getting used to. "I left the church."

"Oh," Carl seemed uncomfortable.

So much for the easy-going smile, maybe after a few more Peter, though. He hated how this happened. Someone sat down, seemingly at ease, then they find out you were a priest, and they try to be on their best behavior. He picked up his glass and, trying to change the subject, made a toast.

"Here's to better roads," he said as he took the Collins glass like it was a shot and poured himself another.

"I'll drink to that," Carl said with a laugh and took a sip of the whiskey.

"Where are you from?" Peter asked. "I'm guessing that because I haven't seen you around before, that you are not from around here."

"Actually, I'm from Huston, Carl Hetridge at your service."

"Well, nice to meet you, Carl Hetridge from Huston. I am Peter McMurray from Massachusetts."

"Well, you quite a ways from home. What you down this way for?"

"Not that far from home, I moved down here to—well to work, and just stayed. There's a nice town about a mile west of here. You probably passed through it, Sheltham?"

"Ya, I did," Carl stopped in the middle of his sentence. He seemed like he was trying to figure out how to say something. "Wasn't those three kids that was killed from there?"

"What?"

"Ya, those three that gone missin' in the wood. Still haven't found the bodies, said the kid who did't's a real whack job," Carl was trying to soften it as much as possible. "'Sall over the radio."

Peter took another long swill and stared into his glass but didn't answer.

"You knewed 'em?" Carl asked, sensing a change in his companion's demeanor.

"Yes," Peter sighed, "I baptized them."

Carl exhaled hard, "Sorry, man, gotta be rough. No wonder you in here."

Peter finished off his glass and motioned to Carl's, "More?"

Carl nodded, and Peter filled it up and then poured the rest of the bottle into his glass.

"Last call," Marissa called out over the din of the crowd.

THE LOST

"Well, least they in heaven now, right?" Carl said smiling, "I mean kids an' all, right?"

"Heaven?" Peter could feel his pulse quicken and tried to stop himself, but the whiskey got the better of him. "What is heaven anyway? Where was God when they were being attacked? Where was His love of children when their attacker had his hands on them, tearing at them," he could hear his voice getting louder, but he didn't care. "Where was He when they were being tortured? His love of the children, what the fuck use is it when The Church can't even love children? What a fucking farce all of this religion shit is, love thine enemy," people were looking over at him, and Marissa had started to move in his direction, "I'll tell you what, if I ever see that sick little bastard who did that to those kids I'll tear him limb from limb. I'll cut off his damnable offending member and throw it to the fires, then I'll throw him to the fucking wolves."

"Father McMurray," Marissa whispered, reaching over the bar to put her hand on Peter's shoulder, "calm down."

"Don't you dare tell me to calm down," he yelled, getting up so quickly that the stool he had been sitting on tumbled over, crashing to the floor. He pushed Marissa's hand away, causing the empty bottle to topple over and smash on the floor. "I'll scream to the fucking heavens what I think, and there's nothing those fucking pedophiles can say about it."

He could feel the tears beginning to stream down his face, warm even against his flush cheeks. He backed up until he felt a post at his back, and then he slid down to the floor, his head in his hands, silently sobbing.

He could hear Marissa jump over the bar and tell everyone that it was time to leave. Most people went willingly, a couple complained that they hadn't finished their beers, but when she poured them out on the floor and said they were now, they got the hint.

"Father?" Marissa was kneeling next to him, her arm around his shuddering shoulders. "Come on, let me take you home."

The old man nodded his head and allowed himself to be helped up, and led out the bar's back door to Marissa's old blue Chevy pickup. They drove in silence past the Church, where several people had gathered outside with candles in what seemed to be an impromptu vigil for the three kids. Geoffrey was probably in the crowd somewhere, as were Marissa's parents by all estimates. One of those kids was her brother, after all. Marissa turned down Morning Rose Ave. and stopped in front of Father McMurray's house.

She helped him in and got him settled into bed, set the timer on the coffee pot for twelve-thirty, figuring the Father would need some coffee when he woke up, checked in on him one last time, and drove back to clean up the bar.

As Father Peter McMurray lay on his back and watched his ceiling spin, he closed his eyes and cursed God for letting such horrible things happen to such good kids. His stomach gurgled, and he went into the bathroom to throw up.

FOUR

The morning was the same as it always was, head pounded, and the coffee sounded like a jackhammer as it percolated in the other room. McMurray had found his way back to bed last night and fallen asleep, but this morning it certainly didn't feel like it. He had a dry mouth and could feel his stomach sloshing around; he wanted nothing more than to take a shot of the bottle he had bought. Moving the curtain aside, the bright afternoon sun seared his retinas, causing him to flinch back behind the curtain. He let his eyes adjust to the sun once more and peered out. One look out to the empty driveway told him that there was no chance of that. Thinking back through the fog of last night, he wondered how he'd gotten so bad.

In the kitchen, the clock on the coffee machine read twelve thirty-three. Getting the Friday paper from his doorstep, Peter looked blankly at the morning headlines, although he already knew what they'd be. This murder had been the top story all week. Things like that just didn't happen here. The newspaper was loving it, sells papers they'd say, not that they were asked.

How far we have fallen, Peter scoffed to himself from the glory that we were made in. Some glory. This mistake of creation won't need to be destroyed. We'll do it just fine all by ourselves.

The coffee machine growled away as McMurray stumbled into the kitchen, his clothes wrinkled from sleep. The sun glared down at him from a clear blue sky, scolding him for losing it last night. In the bright sun, his fog burned away, and he remembered the truck driver, Chuck or was it Chet, didn't matter. Hopefully, he wouldn't run into him again. He'd been such a fool last night, let the whiskey do the talking, and the morning sun now shone down on a hypocrite. Such self-righteous crap he had been spouting, but nothing hides from the morning sun.

The doorbell screamed from the front room dragging McMurray from his self-loathing and back to the moment. Standing still before the sliding glass door in his kitchen, bed ragged and red-eyed, the doorbell rang three times before he realized what he was hearing, and one more still before he moved. It was the post-drunken stupor that retarded even the best of reflexes that had settled around him during his too-short sleep. By the time he reached the front door, the person on the other side was banging loudly against the door. At least, he thought it was loud, but it could just be his splitting headache that gave the impression.

"All right, all right, I'm coming," Peter said to his side of the door. "Calm yourself."

The open door revealed a young man with a smiling face and a football jersey. His blond hair was close-cropped and neatly styled. His eyes looked through McMurray, not at him, the way some of the teens had done in catechism class. In his hand, he held a big white book emblazoned with the word Coupons. Over his shoulder was a bag that looked heavy with those books. When he smiled at McMurray, his teeth shone white against his tan face.

"Hey, we're doing a fundraiser for the Sheltham High Raiders," he said in an overly cheerful voice. "The football team."

"Are you kidding me?" McMurray asked, looking around to see if anyone else was on the street. The pounding in his head was putting him in a bad mood, and the last thing he wanted was

THE LOST

for some kid to be knocking on his door asking for money. "Go bother someone else," he groaned. "Besides, shouldn't you be in school?"

"I signed myself out because I have a study. If you get one of these books, you can save hundreds—" the kid tried to press on.

"I said get lost." McMurray felt a little ashamed for treating the guy like this, any other day but today, he said to himself. "I don't want to have to call the cops."

The kid looked at him with confusion in his eyes, "C'mon, man," he insisted, "you don't have to be an asshole. I thought you were a man of God?"

"God is dead." McMurray slammed the door in the kid's face and went into the kitchen to pour himself some coffee, fuming and slamming cupboards as he went. The nerve of that kid, he grumbled. Bugging me in my home like I was some sort of charity.

Taking a few deep breaths and sitting at his table, McMurray calmed himself and took a sip of his coffee which he nearly spat across the room when he heard the doorbell ring again.

"What the hell," he said, slamming his cup on the table, causing a small pool of coffee to spill over the edge. He could almost picture that kid standing in his doorway smiling with those absurdly white teeth like some demented Cheshire cat saying how everyone should just get along.

"I thought I told you to get off my damn porch!" McMurray yelled as he threw open the door. Standing on the front steps was a somewhat confused-looking Marissa.

"If I did," she asked, "how exactly were you planning on getting your car?"

"Oh, Marissa, I'm sorry I thought you were a kid that was here before. Come in, come in."

"Is everything okay, Father?"

"I'm fine, a little hungover," McMurray blushed slightly. "I hope that I didn't cause too much trouble last night."

"Nothin' I couldn't handle."

"Was I that bad?"

"A little."

"Want some coffee?"

"Sure."

Father McMurray walked over to the coffee maker. Marissa's check-in visits were getting far too regular, and his drinking was a little too frequent, a little too much. Marissa took good care of him, though that could be part of the problem. He couldn't remember much of the night before, but there were a few foggy images that made him feel that he had caused some trouble in the bar—something about the murders.

The trucker's voice rang in his head: *You knew 'em, didn't you? Tough the way it goes like that.* The memory of that conversation was pounding on the edges of his migraine. McMurray knew that he'd let her down again, knew that she probably had dealt with the breakfast crowd by herself again. He stared into the deep blackness of his coffee and sighed. Sitting in silence, each in their own thoughts, McMurray sipped his coffee. The bitter juice soothed her aching stomach and calmed his nerves. Marissa rotated his coffee mug on the Formica tabletop, watching the sun reflect off the white porcelain.

"Father," she didn't look up as she spoke.

There was no answer. McMurray just sat there looking at the black eye of his coffee, taking the occasional sip to break the singular reflection. There were too many things that were swirling in his mind, too many questions, too much guilt. And here was Marissa, having lost far more than he did, and she was looking to him for guidance, guidance that he didn't even have for himself.

THE LOST

She waited until it was apparent no response was coming, then dropped what she had wanted to say and started again with more confidence. "I think it's time to get your car, I've gotta get back to work for the lunch crowd, and I still have some errands I need to run."

"Oh," McMurray reacted quickly this time, his own thoughts being pushed to the back of his mind for the moment. There'd be time for them after he lost himself in the bottle; whiskey makes a great counselor. "If you need to get going, let me just grab my coat."

"I don't mean to rush you," she backpedaled, "if you need more time, that's fine."

"Marissa, you have a life that you need to get back to. No sense wasting time with an old codger like me," McMurray smiled despite himself, knowing that if he didn't, she would be able to tell something was wrong.

It was a silent car ride to the bar. McMurray's thoughts wandered to the kid from earlier; something about him was troubling, something familiar that he couldn't place. He searched his memory for the boy's face, trying to see if it was one of his old parishioners or one of their kids more likely. The thought made him blush slightly, but he couldn't be sure. All he could remember were the teeth, so white in the tanned face and his own headache. As the town flew by outside, the silence grew heavy inside the cab of Marissa's old pickup truck, cut only by the low drone of Garth Brook's, Live Like You Were Dying, coming through the speakers.

"Father McMurray?" Marissa asked as she pulled up next to his car. This time she didn't wait for an answer. "Geo didn't have anything to do with it."

"What?" McMurray was still lost in his own thoughts.

"The killings," she didn't look at him, "Geo didn't do it."

Eric Johnson

McMurray didn't know what she was talking about. Geoffery Hollon had been the only one of his friends to return from the woods, but yesterday afternoon that was all the news was saying. He was sixteen, so the new media couldn't report his name, but in a town as small as this, you hear things. This was a new one.

"No one said he did," McMurray was only half-listening, his mind still clouded by his hangover.

"It's all over the news. Even though he's a minor, the cops say there's enough evidence, and he's been charged. They're gonna try him as an adult. He didn't do it. I know him," Marissa was almost pleading with him. "You know him, Father. He's a good kid. Bedrin's probably just trying to end this before he actually has to do any work."

McMurray didn't know how to respond. This was the first he'd heard about the charges, and he hadn't had a chance to clear his head enough from yesterday. "Marissa, be nice." he thought about what she said for a moment, then continued, "I'd always thought he was, but if they charged him, there must be evidence that we don't know about."

"But Father, you have to do something. He didn't do it."

"How do you know?"

"He was Mikey's best friend since elementary school. He's not like that."

"He wasn't a bad kid when I knew him, but that was years ago. Things change. People change."

"Not that much."

"You're young still Marissa," he looked at her for the first time since last night. Her eyes looked tired and red, definitely out of character for her, and it somehow made her look older. "People change, some people more than others."

THE LOST

"I can't believe you," the look in her eyes changed. "You, of all people, have written him off. Didn't you teach us to forgive; didn't you teach us to love each other?"

"Apparently, I didn't teach him well enough."

"No, I refuse to believe it," Marissa bit his lower lip. "And if you won't do something about it, then I will."

"Marissa, calm down. Don't do anything that's going to get you in trouble. You've done so well in controlling your temper lately, accomplished so much, don't let it get the better of you now."

"What do you care?" Her words cut through the air. "You'll just write me off like you did, Geo."

"You don't know people like I do," McMurray could feel his own ire rising. "You haven't lived enough. You haven't seen how depraved man can be."

"I haven't seen depravity?" she asked, looking at him with a fury he hadn't seen in her eyes for a long time. "Don't you remember where I've been, what I was?"

"You're too young," McMurray insisted, "you can't see the big picture."

"Big picture?" Marissa was losing her typical calm, "I see the big picture better than you think. I know people can change. I changed. I know it's possible, but it doesn't happen overnight."

"It can."

"Not like this."

"You're too young."

"There you go with that again, too young. That's bull shit, and you know it. I'm sorry, Father, but it is."

"Don't."

"Don't what?" Marissa snapped, her eyes burning towards McMurray.

Eric Johnson

"I'm not a priest anymore." McMurray's voice trailed off as he undid his seat belt and opened the door. The sounds of the highway flowed in with the cool afternoon air, and with it came the reality of his words: Real-life, the murders, the futility. Marissa didn't answer; she simply stared at the steering wheel, biting her lower lip as he got out of the cab.

"Let it go," McMurray's concern was genuine. He felt bad for snapping at Marissa like that. She certainly did have a good idea about how unfair life could be. She was a good kid, meant well. His concern went unanswered.

Marissa didn't move as McMurray closed the door and climbed into his own car. The bottle was peeking out of the plain brown paper bag from Lorence Package Store, enticing him to take a drink and drown his aching heart. The feeling was well known, one he had fought and lost many times, and he knew this time would be no different. The drive home was consumed by thoughts of that bottle, thoughts of the burning liquid coursing through his stomach, and hope that it would soothe the scorching words that echoed through his thoughts, *I'm not a priest anymore.*

He didn't deserve to be, hadn't for years. How could he save his parishioners from their demons if he couldn't save himself from his? God was dead; he'd proven that years ago when the allegations first came out. He watched as one by one his heroes fell, first in New York, then Massachusetts. They all fell, from grace, from honor, from God. That was bad enough, but when the Church started covering for them, making excuses, he couldn't take it anymore. On some level, he knew then that it was over. It wasn't until the accusations turned themselves on him that he admitted it was over. He remembered the day it came, the letter informing him that someone had filed allegations against him. He remembered how his flock had looked at him that day, a traitor, he had let them down, despite his innocence, and that was the end.

The Church was willing to cover for him, but he wouldn't have it. It would have done no good. He saw his conviction in the parishioners' eyes; that was all he needed to see. He had sent a letter that week to the district's Cardinal and resigned his position. They didn't argue, simply accepting his resignation as an admission of guilt and settled with his accusers. They had abandoned him, left him with a small severance package that was just enough to keep a roof over his head and whiskey in his stomach. He was satisfied with that, drinking himself into oblivion and damning the God that left him long ago.

McMurray pulled his car into his driveway. Once this house was full of hope and life, people would come and sit with him on his porch. The community's children had helped him do his yard work; he'd paid them, of course, but they would have done it anyway. Once the accusations had hit the newspapers, people stopped coming by. They wouldn't let their children stop by either. He had gone from shepherd to wolf in days. The house had gone through a similar metamorphosis; the once populated porch sat empty, the pillars turning gray with age. The lawn was choked with weeds and the tree, from which used to hang a tire swing, was now gnarled and foreboding.

He turned off his car and looked at the facade of his house. It was as cracked and wrinkled as the old man who lived there. Not that it mattered, there was no one left to enjoy it. He didn't count for anything. Grabbing the bottle violently out of the passenger seat, McMurray trudged along his broken sidewalk; accustomed to the roots that had taken over the once-beaten path, he didn't even have to pay attention to them anymore.

FIVE

"Officer Matt Bedrin, at your service. I just wish it was under better circumstances."

"Well, Officer Bedrin, it seems that these are the circumstance, poor or not, so how about you fill me in on what I need to know," she hated moments like these. These small-town cops were always so nervous when it came to the feds, they had their preconceived notions pulled from the movies. Television shows painting the state cops as an elitist set who felt entitled to everything. Sure, she knew there were people like that in the department, but they weren't all like that, and she resented the insinuation.

"It's like this Detective . . ." Matt stopped short. "I didn't get your name?"

"Detective Magdalena Dias."

"So, Detective Dias, it's like this. We first got wind of this through a missing person's report. Four to be exact: Mike Hail, Jacquelyn Sorin's, Jeffery McMasters, and Geoffrey Hollon. Their folks came in together to file 'em. Then we get a call from the next precinct about a truck that matched the parents' description. They had it cordoned off but hadn't moved it. Said we needed to see it."

"Where's the truck now?"

THE LOST

"Well, after we saw what they were talking about, we had it towed to the station to go over it."

Magie looked at him quizzically, but he didn't seem to notice or didn't care to explain yet. By the wry smile on his face, he seemed to be enjoying his story.

"You have to understand that we're not used to handling this kind of thing. We had our best men working on it."

"Okay," she urged, "so that's why you called us."

"We're not that hopeless. We tried to figure it out ourselves first."

She hoped her frustration was not apparent on her face, but one look at the officer in the blue uniform told her that he probably wouldn't notice if it was. His green eyes looked glazed with either exhaustion or stupidity, and his facial expressions were like a child whose stupid grin was beginning to piss her off.

"There were plenty of fingerprints, DNA, and that stuff," his use of stuff made her wince. "Most of it belonged to Geoffrey Hollon, blood and prints. It seemed that he drove the car to a gas station a few towns out and abandoned it when it ran out of gas."

"You said most of the blood and prints."

"You noticed," he smiled again as if hiding significant evidence was something clever. "There were some prints from Mike Hail, as well as some of the blood in the cab. Most of the blood in the truckbed seems to be from Jacquelyn Sorin's, but there's a smear on the window leading into the cab from Geoffrey."

"I don't know what the problem is. It seems like an open and shut case. Just pick up this Hollon kid and book him. Have you found the bodies?" She was beginning to feel like this was a waste of her time.

"Well, that's just it."

"What is?"

Eric Johnson

"We've already picked up Geo and booked him. He confessed to being with them, told us where they went, told us that he took the truck, and told us that they were all dead."

"Everything but a confession," she saw less and less of a reason to be there. "I still don't see the problem."

"The bodies weren't there," Mike looked at his feet, the smile gone from his face; he looked instead like a kid waiting to be reprimanded for losing his house key. "We scoured the area, but like I said, we aren't used to this stuff. We found no trace of blood, no signs of a struggle, and nobodies."

"Maybe the kids weren't dead."

"He'd said one had a slash across his chest deep enough to see his ribs, and another had a hole through her side big enough for his hand."

"What?"

"That's when we called you."

"Because he lied?" she was incredulous. It felt like they had been wasting her time with this ridiculous incompetence. "Where's this kid now? Has he lawyered up?"

"Not exactly, but we can't get any more out of him."

"I can fix that," she felt that familiar sense of anticipation. The thought of outsmarting a twisted little fuck like this kid brought life to her. Just watching people like him break made her week.

"You don't understand," he shook his head slowly. "It's not that he won't talk, and it's not that he keeps repeating his story. He's catatonic. We hadn't noticed a gash on his arm when we brought him in, but once I pointed it out to him, he seemed surprised. He just lost it. Started talking about some book and saying that we couldn't use it, yelling it. Just not like him. Normally he's a good kid, quiet."

THE LOST

She knew that it wouldn't last. This guy's business-like detachment was too good to be true; these small towns just breed nepotism. She'd heard it countless times during her time with the department, being sent from town to town. "He's a good boy," "she'd never do anything like that," "we never thought"; the last one was her favorite, it was the truest at least. She'd expected it to come out sooner than this, but it was inevitable, like the rain.

"There wasn't any book. We found a knife with the kid's prints on it in the cab of the truck, but the blood on it was his."

"It's a ploy," she'd seen it before, "he's setting himself up for an insanity plea. Don't let them fool you; kids today know the score."

"I'm not sure."

"So you want help convicting him without the bodies or a confession. A crime scene on wheels and a knife with only his blood on it."

"No, I want you to help us find out what happened. Something about this seems funny."

"That's where you're wrong," the look on his face when she said this seemed a mix of shock and anger; he obviously wasn't used to hearing that he was wrong. Nepotism. "This is pretty much an open and shut case. I'll look around for some more evidence, but you already have the killer in custody. It's just a matter of proving it."

"You didn't listen, I said . . ."

She didn't want to hear it. "I heard you, and I know your wrong. Look, your heart is in the right place, but it's getting in the way of the facts. The last person to see them alive? This Geoffrey kid. The last person to be seen in their truck? Geoffrey also. The last person found, covered in blood with a knife? Geoffrey. The answers are all the same. There's only one left to ask. Where are the bodies?"

Eric Johnson

"We don't know that. This might all be some weird coincidence."

"In my line of work," Magdalena turned to walk out of Mike's office, "there are no coincidences."

She knew he was watching her leave, and she knew he was pissed. It gave her a perverse pleasure knowing, although he had called her in, she was now in complete control. Maggie sauntered across the precinct to her make-shift office; she needed to go through the evidence if she was going to find what she needed to convict the boy. She needed to see what they had missed.

The file was thin, too thin for a triple homicide. Maggie methodically reviewed each piece of evidence one by one: the missing person reports, the pictures of the knife, the photos of the car, the transcript of Geoffrey's interrogation, and a small tape from one of those mini recorders. Most places had switched to the digital recorders some years ago, but some of the more backward precincts still used the tape deck. She looked around for a tape player, taking it off the desk next to her, she played the tape.

The introduction of the tape seemed like standard procedure; date and time of the interview, the person doing the interview, topic. When the questions started, she followed along on the transcription. She hoped something in the voice would give the kid away, though a video would have been better.

Officer Bedrin: Can you please say your name for the record?
Geoffrey Hollon: Geo Hollon.
Officer Bedrin: Well, Geo, can you explain why you were covered in blood when we picked you up?
Geoffrey Hollon: Yes.

THE LOST

Officer Bedrin: Do you know where you are now?

Geoffrey Hollon: Sheltham Police Station.

Officer Bedrin: Good, now can you tell me what happened last night?

<static>

She fast-forwarded the tape to get through the static and pressed play again. More static. She kept fast-forwarding until she could hear another voice.

Officer Bedrin: Christ Geo, you expect me to believe that?

Geoffrey Hollon: It's the truth, I swear it, <static> I was— shit man, you gotta believe me. <static>

Officer Bedrin: If this is the truth, then where's the book? You didn't have the book when we found you, but you did have a knife. Quite a bloody one too.

<static>

Maggie pressed stop on the tape player, rewound it, and played it again. It was the same. Every time the kid was supposed to say something, there was nothing but static every time he said on the transcript. She leaned back in her chair and listened to the rest of the tape, it was all like that until the end when Officer Bedrin asked about the cut, and Geoffrey's answer could be heard plain as day, a scared child.

<*Knock on the door. Sound of muffled voices*>

Eric Johnson

Officer Bedrin: The lab results just came back. <*shuffling papers*> Apparently, the blood on the knife is yours. Where'd you cut yourself?

Geoffrey Hollon: Cut myself?

Officer Bedrin: Let me get someone to look at that. It seems pretty deep. It's okay, Geoffrey. Why didn't you tell me when I brought you in?

<*Loud bang, muffled voices, then the tape stopped.*>

Maggie played the tape over two more times just to be sure that she didn't miss anything. It was the same every time. Geoffrey's words were replaced by static until the haunting words at the end of the tape. This kid is good, she said to herself; I guess it will be a little trickier than I thought.

SIX

It was all over the papers the next day. Somehow a local reporter had gotten hold of the story and plastered it all over the front page of the Sheltham Gazette. They had left out the names, but that didn't matter in a town like this. Everyone knew them, everyone knew the families, everyone knew.

Marissa set the paper on the bar without reading the article. She knew what it would say: Local kid goes bad. Everyone had already convicted him, already given up on him. Marissa expected as much from Father Maria but not McMurray, not from the man who hadn't given up on her, who visited her in prison, counseled her. Geo had been her brother's friend since kindergarten. She knew he wasn't responsible for this; she just wished the town wouldn't convict the poor kid to have a scapegoat.

She had been lost in thought and didn't hear the bell as the door opened, ruffling the papers with the cool afternoon air. The bell rang again as the unnoticed door swung shut, startling Marissa from her thoughts. She sensed someone's presence before the stranger spoke. There was an odd familiarity to the voice that made her slightly uncomfortable as she looked up over the bar into the benevolent face of a ruddy-cheeked stranger.

"Sorry 'bout that," Marissa said, "didn't hear you come in."

"Ah, it's no problem," the stranger said, taking a seat at the bar directly in front of her. "You open?"

"Yeah, opened 'bout an hour ago," she motioned towards the empty room. "As you can see, it's a good thing too. The place is packed."

The stranger chuckled, "Well, it's good for me. Got any Bud?"

"Sure thing, twenty-two ounce?"

"Sounds good," he motioned to the paper, "mind?"

"Help yourself. There's nothing good in there anyway."

The stranger eyed the front page while Marissa poured him a beer. His head bobbed slightly, and he let out a thin whistle as he folded and set the paperback on the bar. "Tough break about those kids, eh?"

"I'd rather not."

"Sure, whatever," the stranger took a slug from his beer and looked around. "What happened here anyway? The place is a mess."

"A little bit of a bar fight last night, but don't worry, that stuff doesn't normally happen here."

"Well, I'll try to stay out of everyone's way," the stranger chuckled as he pointed around the room and took another drink.

Marissa looked down at the soapy water and grabbed one of the sticky glasses from last night, submerging it beneath the suds. Her thoughts wandered as she scrubbed the glasses, putting them on the rack to dry. Usually, she took care of this sort of thing the night before, and she'd spend the mornings at the pub working on her classwork from the old dell McMurray kept behind the bar just for her. Granted, the blasted thing moved like a snail because, like everything else, he bought the cheapest version, thrift, he'd say. It worked well enough to complete her online coursework for Cappella. Two years ago, at Father

THE LOST

McMurray's urging, Marissa had begun a bachelor's degree in business at Cappella Online University after he'd hired her. She used her quiet mornings at the bar to complete the coursework and then worked the evening shift most nights to keep an eye on Father McMurray. On his good days, the Father could hold some excellent conversation; on his bad days, he'd drink his profits from the bar, but there'd never been a night like last night.

"Is it always this quiet around here?" the man asked from behind the newspaper.

"Pretty much. Occasionally I'll get the odd passerby in, but most of the locals come by only after six or so. Even the hard-core drinkers wait until at least five."

"On of those hard-cores cause the problems last night?"

"Ya, the guys a regular," she thought about Father McMurray sitting at the end of the bar with that bottle of whiskey. His words echoing in her ears, *you can't see the big picture. You're too young.* Marissa had been hearing this for years, despite her refusal to agree. "He's a good guy," *you don't understand the depravity of man,* "just going through a rough spot. He used to know the kids everyone is talking about."

"Think he did it?"

"What? Father McMurray? Did what?"

"No, that kid. Think he offed his friends like that? The way the paper's talkin', easy money says he'll burn for what he did." The paper rustled as the man folded it on the bar.

"Want another," Marissa ignored the man's questions.

"Sure thing."

Marissa looked at the guy as she filled the beer. With the paper down, she could see the man was probably in his late forties or early fifties. Bald as a cue ball except for deep reddish-brown mustache grown out and waxed at the ends so it would curve up lightly into a carefully shaped handlebar. His small dark eyes seemed to almost meld into the shadows of their deep sockets, giving the impression that the shadows themselves were his eyes. Beneath the mustache, partially hidden by the hair, two bright red lips, drawn tight and then separated slightly to reveal teeth stained by years of tobacco use and coffee. He was in good shape for his age, with solid muscle definition in his jaw and broad shoulders. A button-down shirt, freshly pressed and unbuttoned on the top, was under a fresh dark grey blazer.

Marissa finished pouring the man's beer and walked over to grab a mop to clean up the beer she'd poured on the floor the night before. She had to get it cleaned up before the customers came into the place. They were used to having a clean place to come and drink. Things like that mattered to people. The man turned around to watch her work. She could feel it, the man's eye's boring a hole in her back, the silence in the room, stifling almost. Typically, this was her favorite time of the day, the sun coming through the slats on the window, the quiet she could feel. Today was different, though. It wasn't about last night, that wasn't abnormal, and the cleaning always felt good, like in juvie. She would mop the floor in the mess. Each time, each morning was . . . how had Father McMurray put it . . . cathartic, penance. Either way, Marissa knew it usually felt good. Today, though, cleaning felt menacing. It wasn't that the guy was particularly frightening. He was just sitting there watching as she spread the dirty water across the floor; the finished boards seemed to not want to give up the filth today.

Glancing up, Marissa tried to size up what it was about the guy. He was ordinary, as ordinary as a guy drinking alone at 10:30 in the morning can be. He had a pleasant smile, was quiet, polite, and even respectful of the silence that fell in the room between them like the dust that filtered through the beams of

THE LOST

sunlight escaping from the half-drawn blinds. He seemed to be sizing her up as well. Trying to judge through the silence.

"So what brings you in here so early?" it was an unusual question, but today's silence was the kind that needed to be broken.

"The light was on." He swilled down the beer and motioned to the tap.

"Yeah, no problem," Marissa made her way back over, leaving the mop soaking on the spot. Hell of a way to answer, but she couldn't blame the guy. It wasn't her business, after all. The bar was open. She took the glass off the bar and went over to the tap. "Bud, right?"

The man nodded and watched the pour. The open newspaper lying on the bar in front of him. "Says here it was a local boy that did it."

"What?"

"The murders. Paper says it was a local kid."

"Ya," Marissa knew what was coming next, she didn't want to hear it, but she knew the question. This conversation sucked, but she really couldn't get mad at this guy. He didn't know that her brother was one of those kids that were killed. She silently corrected herself, whose bodies were missing. She and Mikey hadn't always had the best relationship, but he was her brother, and family is family, even if they never visited you in jail.

"I knew a kid once," the guy started, "kind of a rough kid."

This was better than where she thought it was going. The questions the tourists always ask when there's a tragedy in the papers. *Did you know him?* Looking for some sort of connection, a face to connect with the pain of others so they could go back home and feel like they are a part of things, like they had a right to talk about it at work the next day. This was different, somehow more real. This guy seemed to want to relate. Maybe that was why he was watching Marissa clean, trying to figure out if he could share this.

"Broken home, fell in with the wrong crowd. Became something of a small town gang-banger. Did some petty theft, nothing major mind you, but if you knew her, you could tell she was working up to something big. She was good too. Well, good at it." He paused to take a sip of the beer that Marissa had set next to the paper.

This wasn't unusual, especially for the early drinkers. It was part of what she liked about the job here. The money was good, tips and all, but it was the conversations, the coster confessions as she'd called them when talking to her therapist in those first few months. Her P.O. had been concerned about Marissa working in a bar, thought it would lead her back down the wrong path. She agreed to go see a therapist if she could still work at the bar. It seemed to be working too. She'd finished the court-mandated therapy, and her P.O. had gotten off her case about the whole bar thing.

"It was one of those small jobs that tripped her up, though," the guy continued after wiping some drops of beer from his mustache with the back of his hand. "She was robbing some loser's house early one morning when the guy came home. The kid hadn't kept track of time; she was caught reading of all things. This guy was apparently some kind of writer. Wrote short inspirational speeches."

Marissa couldn't look at the guy. The story he was telling was all too familiar, but this guy couldn't know anything he was talking about. She remembered the feeling, that heat that ran up her neck when she saw the guy standing in the doorway almost a decade ago. She felt like she was caught with her pants around her ankles. The guy had been nice enough, considering. He'd

THE LOST

made her put everything back, then he told her that she could leave. Made her promise to straighten up. She tried, even finished high school, but a couple of years later, she was back at it, and this time the guy who caught her was not quite as kind. But this guy, sitting alone in a bar in the morning seven years later, shouldn't know this stuff.

"Kid went to jail over it. Well, less over breaking in and a bit more over breaking the guy's jaw and taking what turned out to be charity money. Ended up, the guy was a priest." The man started laughing, not a big laugh, a thin, humorless laugh, the kind that breaks uncomfortable silences at wakes.

Marissa didn't ask anything else. She hoped the guy would stop. All of that was behind her; this was a new life. She had to remind herself that what this guy was talking about was some other person's story. Not her's. She'd never met this guy before. Besides, when that happened, Father McMurray didn't press charges. Marissa's moment came later. She stole a Buick pickup from in front of the bowling alley and almost killed a kid riding his bike without any reflectors. Her first visitor, even before her mother came to bail her out, was Father McMurray.

"You still with me, kid?" The man was looking at Marissa with a knowing smile on his lips.

"I'm sorry, sir. It was a late night. I must have spaced out," her cheeks flushed.

"Don't worry about it. I'm running late for an appointment anyway. Do you know how to get to the hospital from here?"

"Oh man, yeah. I hope everything is alright."

"It's not for me. I need to see one of the patients. I'm a public defender of sorts. I'm hoping to take him in under retainer."

Eric Johnson

Marissa gave the man directions and wished him luck. She didn't ask who he was visiting but was pretty sure she could figure it out. At that moment, Marissa couldn't help but hate herself for being creeped out by the guy. She watched through the window as he drove off in a dark sedan, the dust from the over-dry parking lot clinging to the fenders and floating up as the car drove off. Marissa shook her head, returning to her almost forgotten mop. "Shouldn't judge people," she said aloud. "That's one of the good guys."

THE LOST

SEVEN

When Geoffrey opened his eyes, the world was still a blur. Shadows menaced the corners of his sight, and the room's white on white played tricks on his mind again. There was a throbbing in his right arm, and it was hard to move like he was running in the pool down at the Church's rec. center. He looked from left to right, the surroundings slowly coming into focus in the whitewash that passed as sight. Sounds danced at the edge of his consciousness, breaking through the silence. A door opened somewhere, letting in muffled conversations in short staccato accompanied by whirls and beeps.

"Where am I?" he asked aloud, but there was no answer except more beeps from machines that surrounded his bed.

Freeing his left arm from the swaddled covers, he froze, feeling naked. The book, he thought. I need to get that fucking book. Peeling the covers back from his bed, Geo let out a relieved breath as he noted the pale blue of a hospital gown and tried to remember how he got there. That's when he heard the voice, as cold and sterile as the room—another shadow at first, wisps of blackness in the white fog.

"I see you're feeling better," the darkness said as it moved to sit on something a few feet from where Geo lay, making him feel even more exposed. His vision cleared as the shadow moved closer, revealing a man in a pinstripe business suit. He opened a briefcase and began shuffling through what sounded like papers, his attention fixed there.

"Sure," Geo said without any conviction leaning on his left elbow and looking around himself, still fighting the images that seemed to move in the foggy white of his peripheral vision. "Better than what I'm not sure, but we'll go with better."

"I'm Lucius Tanis. You can call me Luc. I read about your situation in the papers and thought I could lend you some help."

"My situation?" Geo tried remembering without success. Based on the surroundings, he could tell he was in a hospital room. He had no idea where the damn book was, but he had a feeling that wasn't what this guy wanted to talk about. "You don't look like a doctor," he said after considering the man in his pinstriped suit and briefcase for a while.

"You don't look like you need a doctor."

"So what sort of help are you looking to offer?" he asked. Geo was about to add that he needed help finding the book, but he caught himself in time. It must have shown on his face because Luc smiled. It wasn't a comforting smile, though; it was the kind of smile you would imagine from a catfish seeing a salamander on a hook. Geo felt exposed again and whipped the covers back over himself, hiding the hospital gown and his bare feet.

"Don't look so incredulous," Luc said smoothly. "I'm a lawyer." He reached inside his coat and pulled out a business card, handing it to Geo. "I read about your arrest and injury. How is that arm, by the way?"

"Alright," Geo looked at his left arm, vaguely remembering something about that in the police station. There was a large bandage wound around it, and it seemed to throb now that he was looking at it.

"You do realize that you're in a lot of trouble here, right?"

THE LOST

"I'm a little foggy about the details of the past couple of days, to be honest." He thought back to the shack in the woods, the coals, the wolves, all that blood, and the book. The book most of all. The trouble was that he couldn't get to the book; those cops must have it locked away in their evidence room.

"Good," Luc said with that catfish grin. "Stick with that story, and we'll have a strong case for not guilty on the grounds of temporary insanity."

"Insanity? I'm not nuts." Geo shot upright in bed. Then his head sagged as his world began to spin slowly, his blood trying to catch up with him.

"Oh relax, everyone's a little bit nuts. Besides," Luc sat on the bed next to Geo's, "if you're not, why the hell did you kill your friends?"

Geo's arm throbbed, "Look, I don't know who you're getting your information from . . ." He put his head in his hands, letting his words trail off. He could feel the bright white creeping into the corners of the room again, the rushing sound of blood filling his ears. He buried his face deeper in his hands to stifle a cry. The throbbing in his arm spread up to his shoulder, causing him to sink back to the pillow.

"Well," Luc said, "it seems you are not there yet." His voice cut through the rushing sound in Geo's ears, causing searing red flashes in the ever brightening room. "I will be here when you're ready to work together." His body was now nothing but a shadow, blotting out the blinding white that filled Geo's vision. Those things were back in the corners of his sight, but whenever he turned to them, they would dissipate into a white fog, intensifying the light even more.

"I didn't kill . . ." Geo pushed the words into the light. They seemed to float in the air between them.

"So you've said," Luc's words seemed to come from far away. "The newspapers are saying something else. They're saying that you killed your friends. Brutally and mercilessly."

Geo seemed to hear the last three words in his mind, more in thought and feeling than actual words. The corners of the room seemed to be alive, squirming, moving closer to him. The sound of the blood in his ears was making it hard to concentrate. He brought his fists to his ears to try and muffle the sound, but it only intensified. Squeezing his eyes closed, images of that day flickered across his closed lids.

Mikey smiled from behind the wheel of the truck, bouncing along the dirt road. Jacki laughed at something Geoffrey said and kicked the back of his seat. Everything sounded like it was underwater, far away, and Geo opened his eyes. The shadow loomed out of a glaring white background, mechanical beeps drawing him back to the room. His arm throbbed, and he sunk back onto his bed. With each throb, the room swam with light. *The fire crackled in front of the cabin door. Jacki and Jeff bent over that book.* The book. He felt the longing for it, the word itself clawing at him. He tried to remember where he put it, the police had said something about there being books in the truck, but he couldn't remember seeing it after coming out of the cabin.

The blood in Geo's ears rose to a defining pitch, and he felt the urge, deep inside, to let it carry him away. The pressure bubbled in his chest, and he ground his teeth against it, trying to choke it down. His stomach churned, nausea gripping him by the base of his brain, drawing all his focus. Geo lurched once with enough force to pull the IV from his arm, and Luc reached forward, turning off the alarms. The tendons in Geo's neck pulled taught, his clenched teeth parting. The sound was hollow at first, like air in a wind tunnel, before the sound rolled over his lips, low

THE LOST

and guttural at first, but billowed into a fervent howl. Primal and cruel.

Luc watched it all with a detached catfish-grin until Geo quieted. "Better?" he asked. His voice felt soft to Geoffrey, comforting. As if he knew the pain Geoffrey was feeling and actually cared how he was.

"What the fuck are you doing?" Geoffrey spat through clenched teeth before another spasm of pain ripped through his body. The room faded in the corners of his vision, and the mist returned. *The fog swirled through a hole in the cabin door; the woods had gone eerily quiet. Geoffery could hear his breathing. As a matter of fact, that was all he could hear clearly. His friends, making noise, clearly talking, but they sounded far away as if they were underwater. He saw his own hand reaching around the side of the fire to where Jacki and Jeff had been sitting, they weren't there, but the book was.* That damn book. *The fog cleared around it, open to where they had been reading. Geoffrey picked up the book, and the cover seemed to give under his fingers as he did. It was somehow both softer and dryer than other books. He hefted it onto his lap and started reading the words aloud.*

Geoffrey's body spasmed, his right arm hitting the nurse call button on the side of the bed. Luc hit the button to cancel the call and looked to the door waiting for someone to enter, but instead, a voice came through the speaker.

"Is everything alright, sir?"

"Just fine," Luc replied, mimicking Geoffrey's voice. "I accidentally hit it when I was trying to adjust the bed."

"Alright, sir," the voice sounded tired on the other end. "We'll be by in a couple hours to give you your pills."

"Thank you."

Geoffrey's spasms were subsiding, and Luc turned his attention back to the boy in the bed. He looked tired but not weak enough yet. Luc could see the business card in the boy's hand. As long as he held that, Luc could get in for now. Eventually, he wouldn't need the physical link, but the clock was ticking. They only had a couple of hours. For now, he needed to focus.

"Geoffrey," Luc made his voice as gentle as possible, "are you alright?"

"What are you doing to me?" Geoffrey's vision was clearing a little as the pain subsided

"Nothing. We're just talking. You were telling me what you did after you picked up the book next to the fire."

"But I didn't—I don't know where the book is."

"Are you sure? Did you drop it somewhere?"

"No, I . . ." Geoffrey closed his eyes and shook his head. "It must be the pain killers. I can't . . . I'm not sure."

"It's okay," Luc grinned, "we have some time."

"I don't know what you're trying to do, but I don't want you here. Please leave."

"No, Geoffrey, that is not the way to talk to someone who is trying to help you."

"Help me? I didn't ask for your help," the pain subsided, and Geoffrey laid back on his pillows and closed his eyes. He fought the exhaustion that threatened to draw him back into the darkness. "You can leave now."

"I think I'll just wait a little longer. So after you picked up the book by the fire, you began to read it out loud, right?"

Geoffrey shifted in the bed. "I didn't get the book. I ran when it all started."

"Think Geoffrey, think," Luc whispered into his ear.

Geoffrey felt his breath on the side of his face. He didn't open his eyes because he didn't want to see the man. His breath was cold, and something didn't feel right. He began to feel the

THE LOST

blankets move slightly around his legs and his eyes snapped open, sitting up too quickly and paying the price in his swimming head.

"What the hell do you think you . . ." the words died in his throat as he saw the foot of his bed awash in a swarm of small red beetles.

EIGHT

Geoffrey felt the soothing warmth of the beetles crawling under his skin. His bruises and cuts began to tingle as the last of the bugs worked their way into his wounds. Then the convulsions started, Geoffrey's eyes opened wide, and a strangled gasp escaped him. He began to thrash his head back and forth against the bed, the pillow having fallen off some time ago, his sheets darkening with sweat and urine. Luc stood next to the monitor, blithely smiling down at Geoffrey's struggles.

"Just relax and let them do their work," his voice taking on the tone of a patient teacher to a stressed student. "Fighting it only makes things take longer."

Geoffrey's eyes ranged the room, looking for the shadows in the corners like last time, but he was utterly alone with Luc. The nurses outside seemed too concerned about their other patients to check in on him. He stared at the door, almost willing them to come in and stop this, or the machines to scream out his distress as he struggled to try and move his arms or legs. Even his jaw seemed locked closed. Strangled, guttural spurts of noise the only thing that escaped him.

"Look, Geo," Luc moved closer to the bed, placing his hand on Geoffrey's shoulder, "I can call you Geo, right?" When Geoffrey didn't answer, he continued. "I want something from you, well, a couple somethings, but let's start small, shall we. I need that fucking book. I know that you had it. I mean, you released our little friends from their captivity, right? So where is it?"

Geoffrey stared at him from the bed, more of the guttural noises escaping between his teeth. His muscles spasmed, jerking his right arm slightly. He could feel as the beetles crawled under his skin, spreading into his torso, burrowing deeper into his tissue. There was no pain; it felt more like pins and needles, a warm tingling that spread as the beetles pulsed.

"Right," Luc chuckled, patting his shoulder. "I almost forgot that you still need to talk. We'll fix that soon, but until then," he tapped Geoffrey's chin, and his jaw began to loosen up. "As I was saying, the book, the one you used in the woods. Where is it?"

Geoffrey licked his lips, lightly chewing on his tongue, relaxing the stiff muscles. "How do you know about the book?" His voice was rough, strangled slightly but audible.

"It's not your turn to ask questions at the moment," Luc said, shaking his head. "I'll let that one go, but if you keep this up, I'm going to have to get the information in some other way."

"I already told you, I don't know where it is. Didn't even read the damn thing."

"That's odd, normally you'd have to read it. But no matter. Doesn't really change the fact that you don't currently have it."

"Did you check the damn truck?"

"Now now," Luc shook his head. "Is that any way to talk to someone who is going to help you?"

"I didn't ask for your help, remember. You just walked in here and started asking . . ." Geo was cut short as the tingling reached his spine. The pain exploded through his whole body. Arching his back, he inhaled sharply, trying to catch his breath.

Luc came out and touched his chin again, his jaw locking back up immediately.

"I told you not to be ungrateful," Luc backed up to the monitors again. He rested on them, and the readouts went from showing the chaos of pain Geoffrey felt to the calm chart rhythms showing a patient at rest. Geoffrey's eyes widened, and his pupils dilating as he watched through the pain. "This little parlor trick is nothing, boy. I have such a world to open up for you if you just let my little friends do their work. You're fighting them. That's what you're feeling right now. I can take that pain away from you. I can give you wonderful things. All you have to do is ask."

Geoffrey closed his eyes, his back spastically arching as he thrashed in the bed. Luc walked over to the door and looked out of the window, his back to Geoffrey, and continued talking.

"You see, Geo, I want to help you. I want to help you become more than you are, more than that scared little kid who kowtowed to authority. More than that boy in the back of the fifth period thinking about your friend's sister, but too chickenshit to do anything more than dream. I'm starting to see things more clearly now. Not everything, but we're making progress."

Geoffrey tried to call out again, a guttural croak thing escaping his rebellious throat.

"Relax, Geo. Relax. You can have her if you want. You can have it all—respect, power, love. Oh yes, I can get you her love. That's the easiest emotion for your type, after all. Well, you call it love," Luc chuckled a humorless, hollow sound. "All you have to do is give me what I want. You don't even really want it yourself, do you? Think about all you could have. I can provide you with your wildest dreams.

THE LOST

"I've done it before, you know. I have made kings out of paupers, made the ugly beautiful, and given the ignored fame beyond their wildest dreams. I can do that for you too. I've seen your dreams. Oh, don't blush, you pansy; there's nothing wrong with those. You can have them too. Your dreams are so small-time, I could give you them right now, and it wouldn't even so much as make me yawn, except maybe from boredom. Oh, but I could teach you to dream," Luc turned back to the window. "If only we had the time."

Geoffrey thrashed in the bed as the tingling sensation spread through his limbs and over his skin. His spine ached. The back of his head hurt. He struggled to stay conscious, but the pain was beginning to cloud his senses. He couldn't move anything except his neck, so he turned away from Luc and looked toward the window. All he could see was a deep blue sky, a few white clouds lazily gliding across his window, and the leaves on the tree outside his window dancing in the breeze.

"Think about what I said," Luc's cold breath poured over Geoffrey's ear. "I will get what I want. It's really only a matter of whether or not you will."

Geoffrey shuddered as he was overcome by nausea. Already on his side, he threw up and passed out. Regaining consciousness with a cold paper towel on his head and a warm hand holding his, he jerked his hand out of the way and turned toward the room. Moving quickly brought another bout of nausea, but this time a bucket came up to his face, and the cool cloth was placed back on his forehead. Geoffrey relaxed, closed his eyes, and let his stomach settle before opening them again to see who was with him.

"Take your time Geo," McMurray's voice, tinged with the sweet smell of whiskey, smoothed out his raw nerves.

"Hey Padre," Geoffrey said, his voice weak and distant-sounding to his own ears. "Come to give me those last rights I've head about."

McMurray chuckled, a warm sound compared to what he'd heard from Luc, but it still made him shiver slightly. "No, I don't think you're all that bad off. The doctors say you're doing just fine. Marissa just asked me to come by and check in on you."

Geoffrey felt the familiar tingle up his spine at the mention of his dead friend's sister, but this time there was a slight scratching at the back of his neck. He reached back to scratch it, surprised at first that his arm responded so readily to his request. Geo thought of Luc's words, *I can get you her love.* He felt guilty for the thought and bit it back before he spoke, hoping that Father McMurray hadn't noticed him blush at Marissa's name.

"Really? Didn't think she'd care given what happened to her brother."

"Of course she cares. You were Mikey's best friend. You practically grew up at her house," he smiled down at Geoffrey, crooked teeth, grizzled beard, and reeking of whiskey, but his eyes were unmistakably the same priest he'd grown up with. The man he'd gone to when his father had died.

"Can I ask something?"

"Sure, bud, what is it?"

"Why'd you quit?" Geoffrey was desperate for the connection he'd had with McMurray before, "You were all I had, but you left us."

McMurray looked down at his feet, took his hand off of Geoffrey's, and sighed. "It's not that simple an answer, and I'm not sure this is the place for that discussion."

"I need to know," Geoffrey had never asked, never really cared before, but now it seemed to be the only thing that really mattered to him. He needed to know; somehow, it seemed to matter more than anything else.

"It's complicated," McMurray shook his head. "I'll tell you sometime, but right now, you need to focus on getting better. How are you handling everything? I know the doctors have said you're physically fine, but you've gone through a lot in the past few days."

"I need to know."

"Geo, I can't tell you right now. I'm here now, isn't that enough?"

"No."

"Why does it matter? That was years ago?" McMurray looked out the window at the gathering clouds and waited as Geoffrey let the question go unanswered. He glanced back at the door, pulled a flask from inside his coat, and took a sip before continuing. "Geo, I wanted to tell you that what happened wasn't your fault. I know the police have been around a lot, they've been asking people about you, and I can only assume they think you had something to do with that mess in the woods. Marissa wanted me to let you know that she doesn't believe a word of it. Frankly, neither do I." McMurray paused to take another sip before Geoffrey turned back to the window.

"There's this thing," he continued, "it's called survivor's guilt. I'm not sure if they teach you about it in school or not these days, but I want you to know. You might feel bad about surviving that attack in the woods, start thinking that it was your fault or that it's unfair that you survived. I want you to know that it has nothing to do with fair or unfair. You survived. That's a good thing. It may not feel it right now, but trust me, it is. You lost some good friends in there, and that's something that you're going to have to deal with, but you need to understand that it wasn't your fault. Got it? It wasn't your fault."

Eric Johnson

Geoffrey turned away and watched the rain begin to beat against the windowpane, making streaks of water obscuring the tree and the clouds into some grotesque version of themselves. After a few minutes, McMurray patted Geoffrey's arm. Geoffrey heard the chair slide against the floor, and a few moments later, the door clicked closed. He was left alone. Something kept nagging at the back of his mind, something he'd heard. He thought about what Father McMurray said about it not being his fault as he watched the rain sputter to a drizzle. *Oh, but I could teach you to dream.*

NINE

Maggie Dias stood at the nurses' station on the third floor of Prescott General and waited for the head nurse to bring the paperwork releasing Geoffrey Hollon into her custody. It was a little tricky, seeing as they couldn't locate his mother, but the state police tended to get a little better service than the locals.

"I'm sorry it's taking so long, Detective. The doctor is just in surgery at this moment, and we need to wait for his signature," the desk nurse looked pained at the holdup.

"It's alright, Nancy," Maggie said, reading the young woman's name tag. "I'm sure you're doing everything you can to expedite this."

Nancy sat up a little straighter and, smiling, picked up the phone to page the doctor for the fourth time. Maggie excelled at getting people to do what she wanted. It was a skill that served her well on the force. Whether a perp, a new widow, or a witness, she could turn the situation, so they felt that talking to her was their idea, and they actually wanted to help. That's why she needed to get this fucker into the interrogation room. The tape from the Sheltham PD had been a waste of time. The static shows simple incompetence at a level she had not seen in years.

"Here he is now," Nancy stood up and flagged down a man in a white coat who was hurrying past the station on his way someplace far more critical. "Doctor Stephan? Detective Dias has been waiting on your signature to release the Hollon boy."

"Is he cleared?"

"Just waiting on your signature," Nancy persisted.

Without even a nod in Maggie's direction, the doctor scrawled some illegible symbols across the bottom of the page, then continued on his way.

"Charming man," Maggie said, smiling at Nancy.

"Charming enough, when you know him," Nancy said, getting the rest of the discharge papers in order. "We've been a bit short-staffed this flu season."

Thanking Nancy, Maggie folded and placed the discharge papers in her coat pocket and went to Geoffrey's room. The little shit lay in the bed, his back to the door, and looked small, surrounded by the inert machines. He was dressed, shoes by the foot of the bed, but other than his slight restlessness, there was no indication that he was even awake, curled up fetal position on top of the covers. Maggie moved further into the room, watching Geoffrey like some animal held on a thin tether.

"Hey there, Geo," Maggie used his nickname intentionally, "How you feeling?" He seemed to stiffen at the sound of his own name. "We haven't met yet. I'm Detective Margarette Dias, but you can call me Maggie." She sat down, intentionally heavily, in a chair placed next to his bed, still talking to the back of his head. "Pfff, hell of a week, eh?"

Geoffrey's back seemed to relax a little bit, and Maggie pressed on.

"I have to ask a couple questions. I'm sure that Matt, eh Officer Bedrin might have covered some of this, but there was a problem with the recorder, and we couldn't get a solid transcript. Kind of a formality, you know, like homework.

THE LOST

"Anyway, doctors said you're being released. That's good, right?"

Geoffrey rolled over on his back. He seemed stiff but other than that, he didn't seem that bad off, especially compared to his friends. "I'm kinda tired, Detective. Can we do this another time?"

"That's the thing, Geo. We can, I suppose, but if you want to get home today, we kinda have to take care of this here and now. We have a bit of time anyway. The doctors are getting your discharge papers ready." She pulled the chair closer to the edge of the bed and took out her pad, pen, and recorder. "I know this is a pain in the ass, but we all have our bosses, after all, right?"

"Fine," Geo sighed, staring at the ceiling.

"Officer Bedrin filled me in on most of the night, but there were just a few things that I needed to clarify. First off, I want to offer my condolences about your friends." Maggie waited for a reaction. Often the most superficial show of courtesy would break some of these fucks, especially the young ones, but he didn't even change his breathing, smooth and even, his eyes distant but dry. It could be shock, but she was almost positive this kid was guilty and simply told the officer what he wanted to hear so he could get himself free and clear. "Anyway, pretty impressive story, really. You are the sole survivor of an animal attack. What was it that you said?"

"Wolves." Geoffrey sat up and rested his head in his hands.

"Right, wolves," Maggie leaned back and took a moment to exhale. "Tell me again, how'd you get out."

"I ran. Got in the truck and drove away."

"Just leaving your friends there, at the mercy of the animals?"

"Not much mercy."

"True, I guess not. But I want to know what was going through your mind, just leaving your friends there. If I remembered correctly, you even pushed one of them out of the way so you could get into the truck."

"He was dead."

"Right, ya, you said that too, didn't you. Funny thing though there."

"Funny?"

"Ya, I mean you were so specific on where you left them and how they were dead, even a little coldly graphic if you ask me, but I guess there's something to that video game generation thing. Anyway, despite all that, the bodies weren't there."

"Wolves."

"Ya, I know. I thought it too at first. It was more than that though, there was nothing. I mean, the cabin was there, the shack really, and the ashes from your fire. Funny thing is, that was it. No blood, no signs of a struggle, nothing."

"You have an odd sense of humor."

Maggie smiled. This fucker was good, calm, border-lined psychopathic really, disassociation maybe, but clever and likable. "Suppose I do. But the fact remains that there was no evidence of anything. I mean, sure, there were your footprints, the tire tracks from the truck, even the burnt-out coals of the fire, but really that's it."

"What are you trying to say?"

"Well, I guess I'm trying to say that I don't really believe that's what happened. I mean a freak wolf attack in a well-traveled area. There aren't really that many wolves in this area anyway. Now, if you'd gone with a bear, even a bobcat, that would've been more believable. But I'm not buying the wolf story." Maggie leaned back and watched waited as the message sank in. "So, how about we forget all that bullshit, and you tell me what really happened."

Geoffrey took a deep breath, his neck twitched, and he lay his head back on the pillow.

"Look, Geo," Maggie went on undeterred. "If you were attacked by a wolf, like you said, where's the scar. I know you were bleeding, or at least there was enough blood on you for it, but your arm looks like nothing happened. It's a little red, but that's it. No puncture scars, no bandages, just soft pink skin."

"I already told the story, and I'm not going to tell it again," sitting up, Geo pulled a black business card out of his pocket. "Besides, if you want to continue questioning me, you are probably going to have to talk to my lawyer."

"Your what?" Maggie flipped back through her notes, looking for any mention of a lawyer. "That's new."

"So is being called a liar," he looked her in the eyes. "I think that if we're going to continue this, I'm going to need to make a call."

"I was giving you a chance here, kid. You don't want it. That's on you." Maggie stood up and put her notebook back in her pocket. "I'll send Officer Bedrin to get you out of here and back to your mother. You might want to have that lawyer of yours on speed dial."

Geoffrey sat up and looked at Maggie for the first time. His eyes seemed bloodshot, and his head twitched. For a second, Maggie thought she saw something moving underneath his skin, but it was the look in his eyes that sent a chill through her. He was still staring directly at her, eyes narrowed and dangerous, almost predatory. There was no doubt in her mind that he was guilty.

"One more thing. I'll be taking the evidence back with me to Monterey."

Eric Johnson

"And I should care why?" Geo looked away, his eyes wandering the room.

"Right, I didn't think you'd really care, but Officer Bedrin mentioned that you were going crazy about some book." Maggie watched as he turned his eyes on her again. She squirmed a bit in her seat. "Turns out we had the book all along. Ends up it was in the truck bed. Got covered over by a tarp. Weird how that happens. Anyway, as you said, no need for you to care about it." Maggie could feel his eyes burning into her as she walked out the door.

Ten

When Officer Bedrin got there, about half an hour later, Geoffrey was waiting to head home. The nurses seemed surprised that he hadn't left already, but they had let him stay in the room until his ride arrived.

The sun was beginning to set when they walked out of the hospital and toward the waiting cruiser. Officer Bedrin walked to the driver's side and motioned for Geoffrey to climb into the passenger side. Bedrin seemed almost sorry for how they had treated him before bringing him to the hospital, but he didn't say anything.

Geoffrey squeezed into the passenger seat of the police cruiser, his knees almost hitting the dashboard, Officer Bedrin's shotgun digging into his left thigh. He looked at the gun, the dashboard computer, and the radio before he settled on watching out the passenger window.

"Detective Dias said you lawyered up?" Bedrin asked as they pulled onto the highway. "Honestly, I don't understand why. Makes you seem guilty, you know."

Geo watched the trees speed past and let his silence be his answer.

"Well anyway, Detective Dias thinks you did it," Bedrin continued. "She doesn't like that we can't find the bodies, says that you probably hid 'em elsewhere in the woods," Bedrin let the sound of the tires on the road fill the space. "Not real talkative eh?"

"I'm thinking."

"Really, 'bout what, if you don't mind me asking."

"What do you think I'm thinking about?"

"Oh, right, I supposed it'd be them friends of yours. Jacki, Jeff, and Mike. Ya, their folks are mighty beat up over their deaths. I guess you've got your own grieving to deal with too."

Geo watched the road in front of them. The traffic was light at this time of day, most people already home for dinner, but the few cars on the road seemed to avoid the cruiser. Geo knew he'd have to wait for the right time before he did anything.

"Good friends?"

"They were."

"Look, I know you've got yourself a lawyer, and I'm not trying to get any incriminating evidence on our drive here. I'm just looking for a bit of company on the ride. Don't want to talk about them, I understand, but let's have some conversation. We still have about twenty minutes before I get you home," Bedrin took his eyes from the road for a moment to look at Geoffrey. "Let's talk about something."

"Alright," Geo turned to look at Bedrin, who had one hand resting gently at the top of the wheel. "Let's talk about your future."

Bedrin chuckled, turning back to the road. "My future. Good one, Geo. What do you care about my future?"

"Are you happy being Officer Matthew Bedrin? A nobody officer in a nowhere town?" Geo didn't take his eyes off of Bedrin. "Chauffeuring people around and kowtowing to the staties every time they come rolling in? Didn't you want more out of life?"

"A little rude," Bedrin shrugged. "I like it enough. Job keeps me busy. I'm doing something that matters."

THE LOST

"But you have dreams, don't you. What is it you really want?"

Bedrin looked off in the distance as the last rays of the sun disappeared over the horizon. "Always hoped I'd make fed some time."

"Detective Matthew Bedrin, FBI."

"Nice ring, isn't it. But I got this job and never really tried for it. I just figured it wasn't for some backwater cop to do something like that. I grew up here, seems fitting to stay."

Geo took that moment to grab the wheel and crank it all the way to the right. Bedrin, not expecting it, overcorrected, and the cruiser tipped up on two wheels and seemed to hang there as Bedrin thew his weight toward the driver side, trying to crank the wheel and regain control. His clipboard and papers flittered toward Geo, who sat pensively in his seat waiting for the inevitable. For a moment, it seemed like the car would tip full over as Bedrin brought the wheel around and hit the gas. The cruiser slammed back down on all four tires and stalled out.

"What the hell was that," Bedrin screamed, his heart pounding in his ears. "You got a death wish, kid? You almost killed us."

"Not exactly," he watched cooly as Bedrin took a deep breath and tried to restart the cruiser, "but you may want to hurry."

Bedrin looked up at Geoffrey's cold stare and followed his gaze, turning to look out of the driver's side window in time to see the horns of a black Dodge Ram before he was thrown against his door by the force of the impact. The Ram's driver hadn't seen the cruiser in the failing light and hit full force on the driver side door going highway speeds. Not wearing his seatbelt, the driver flew through his own windshield and draped, half in and half out, over his hood.

Eric Johnson

Bedrin took the brunt of the hit on his left side, and flying glass from his window left several more minor cuts across his arms and face. He hit his head on the hood of the Ram and cut a large gash just over his left eye. In the seconds that followed the collision, the cruiser rolled onto its passenger side, rendering Bedrin's heroics only seconds earlier a moot point, and continued onto its roof and back around two more times, leaving the upside-down cruiser spinning on its lights. Bedrin shook out his haze from the head wound and tried to see Geoffrey through the settling smoke from what he assumed was the airbags deploying. Nausea and fading consciousness threatened to overtake him as he struggled to pull himself together and assess the situation.

"Geo," he said between coughs, "Geoffrey, you still with me?"

Geoffrey seemed to be hanging limply from his seatbelt in the settling chemical smoke, a small pool of blood forming on the roof below him dripping from his left arm. The smell of oil and fuel mingled with the acrid chemicals, and Bedrin coughed, putting his hand over his nose and mouth. His eyes and face felt like they were on fire from the airbag, and his head throbbed. He reached for his belt cutter, hanging just over his shoulder, and readied for a fall to the roof of the car.

"Geo, I'm going to cut myself free and come over to help you. Hang tight, kid."

Bedrin looked back over to the passenger side, hoping to see some movement from Geoffrey, some acknowledgment that he was still alive, but instead, he saw an empty seat. The blood was still pooled on the roof, but the kid wasn't there. The frayed ends of the seatbelt dangled where his arms were moments ago.

"Geo?" Bedrin called out.

"Don't worry, Officer," the voice came from above him, through his own shattered window. "I'm excellent." Geoffrey

THE LOST

crouched down to look through the window. "Never felt better, really."

"I don't understand how," Bedrin stammered, "but you are one lucky kid. Can you give me a hand?"

"I'm a little busy up here. There's the guy from the other car. He seems pretty banged up, you know. Worse off than you."

"Get me out of here, and I'll give him a hand. You really shouldn't be moving around. You might have some internal bleeding. This was a pretty nasty accident."

Geoffrey stood up, and Bedrin watched his feet turn and walk away from the cruiser. He reached over his shoulder and cut the belt, bracing himself with his right arm to keep from injuring himself further. After cutting the seatbelt, he realized that his legs were still pinned under the steering wheel, but he had shifted enough to be able to see Geoffrey standing next to the man dangling out of his windshield. Bedrin watched as Geo picked up the man's arm and let it fall back to the hood with a light thud. Then he grabbed a handful of the man's hair and did the same to his head. The man groaned, some blood gurgling from the side of his mouth.

"Geo," Bedrin called out as he grabbed the handle of his receiver. "That man needs a doctor. I'm calling dispatch. Leave him be."

Geoffrey looked back over his shoulder and bent down to pick up a piece of windshield glass, and ran it down the inside of his own arm. Blood dripped onto the fender of the Ram as Bedrin watched in disbelief, and the blood seemed to congeal and move up the hood toward the unconscious man. Geoffrey dropped the glass, let it fall to the ground, and returned to the cruiser, crouching down blocking Bedrin's window again.

"How you doing in there?" Geoffrey asked.

"What the hell," Bedrin sputtered. "Your arm. I watched you cut it."

"An unfortunate necessity."

"Necessity?"

"Oh, Officer, you have no idea."

Bedrin looked at the roof on the passenger side where he'd seen Geoffrey's blood dripping and watched as the small pool of blood began to bead up, seemingly on its own. The blood separated into five tiny drops, then one by one, the drops started to move toward him, making a slight clicking noise. As they reached his right shoulder, Bedrin tried to brush them off, but Geoffery grabbed his left arm with a strength unexpected in his slender frame.

"It's so much easier if you just let them do their job, Matt," Geo seemed to spit the last word at him.

Bedrin frantically tried to pull his arm away from Geo as the drops, now clearly five red beetles began to move toward the cut over his left eye. Bedrin heard a resounding scream of terror and pain from behind Geoffrey as the first beetle pushed its way into the wound over his eye. He screamed himself as the beetles burrowed through his injury and moved subcutaneously toward the back of his neck.

"Relax, Officer. This won't take long," Geoffrey said, letting go of Bedrin's arm, which immediately tried to claw at the small bumps moving under the skin on his face, only to reward him with another searing wave of pain.

As the last beetle burrowed into his right eye socket, bursting a couple blood vessels on the way through, Bedrin's muscles finally relaxed, and his breathing evened out.

"Don't you think it's time to call this accident in, Officer Bedrin?" Geoffrey asked as the driver of the Ram approached the police cruiser.

THE LOST

Bedrin felt the smooth skin over his left eye, the cut now healed entirely, and picked up the radio. "Dispatch," he said in a calm, even voice, "there has been an accident. I will need you to send two tow trucks to mile marker 47 on route 215."

"Are there any injuries, Officer?" The voice over the radio asked.

Bedrin looked over at Geoffrey; the driver of the Ram was standing next to him. Bedrin's neck twitched slightly. "No dispatch. No injuries."

Eleven

"Matt," the dispatch officer said as they walked into the station. "Milner wanted to see you in his office when you got in. Something about those three kids you've got in lockup."

Bedrin nodded and continued past with Geo being pushed ahead of him. Geo kept his eyes down, shoulders slumped forward, playing the part of the arrested youth, a picture of defeat. Bedrin pushed him into the station and moved to his desk. "Just let me book this kid, and I'll get to him."

"Book him? I thought he was going home. I just got off the phone with his mom," the dispatch officer checked her notes. "She was wondering where you two were. Said you were supposed to drop him off?"

"Well," Bedrin looked at her and smiled, "I guess she was misinformed."

"You alright?" she leaned toward Bedrin. "Your eyes look weird. Where you drinking last night?"

"I'm fine," Bedrin rubbed the back of his neck, "just a bit of a headache from the accident. Nothing to worry about."

"If you say so," she said, turning her attention back to the radio as a call came in.

Geoffrey sat in the chair next to Bedrin's desk, head in his hands. "Is she going to be a problem?"

THE LOST

"No," Bedrin said, sitting down and scratching something on a piece of paper. "I'll take care of her and the Sergeant."

"What about those three kids she was talking about?"

"Small-time. Smoking pot in the woods."

"They could be useful," Geoffrey looked at Bedrin; the man seemed to flinch and rub the back of his neck again.

"They're just kids," he said, "a couple of baseball players and their stoner friend. Their folks should be here shortly."

"Put me in with them," Geo put his hand on the papers Bedrin was looking through.

Bedrin looked at him for a second and shuddered, "No, they're going home soon. We have no need to keep them."

Geo moved his hand to Bedin's arm, and Bedrin's head twitched visibly. "I want to keep them," his voice smooth and emotionless. "Put me in there."

"Right," Bedrin shook his head. Speaking loud enough to be heard by the dispatch officer. "Let's get you into lockup so I can go see the Sergeant."

"I'm going to borrow this," Geoffrey said, taking a small letter opener off Bedrin's desk and slipping it into his pocket.

Bedrin pushed open the door to the holding area and led Geoffrey to the only occupied cell. The three boys, seniors by the looks of them, were sitting on the bench, not seeming too concerned about the fact that their parents were coming to get them out of jail. All three were sitting on a bench near the far wall talking loudly.

"You got company while you wait, boys," Bedrin said as he opened the cell door and pushed Geo inside for effect. "Play nice," Bedrin closed the door and left.

The scrawniest of the boys stood up and walked over, "Yo, Geo. What's good?" he asked, holding his fist out.

Eric Johnson

"Steve," Geo returned his fist bump and smiled, "figured you'd be in here."

"Come on, that's not fair, man. I've been good for like two months now."

"Ya," Geo laughed, "good at not getting caught."

Steve laughed, "Well, that's a form of good, i'nit?"

"Hollon, right?" one of the kids from the bench called over to them. "You're that kid from the papers."

"Dude, chill," Steve turned to them. "Not cool."

"I'm all outta chill Steve," the kid said. "Lost it when you got us caught. Right, Dev?"

"Zach," Devin said, "you were the high mother fucker that wanted to streak the fuckin' girl's cross country."

"Shut up," Zach shoved Devin lightly on the shoulder, then started giggling. "It was funny, though."

"Wow," Geo said, looking at Zach. "You're a fucking moron, aren't you?"

Steve looked back over his shoulder, "Geo, dude."

"No, Steve," Zack stood up, "let him talk. You got a problem, Hollon?"

"No, not at all. I'm impressed, actually. I'd figure with such a small dick, you'd be afraid they'd laugh."

"Geo, what's got into you?" Steve walked between the two of them. "Not cool, bro."

"I'll show you who's got a small dick," Zach pushed up his sleeves.

"Come on, man," Devin said, grabbing Zack's arm. "Aren't we in enough trouble?"

"Besides," Geo continued, "I don't have a microscope."

"Geo," Steve shook his head, "what the fuck."

THE LOST

"I'm sorry," he said, looking at Steve and then toward the door. "It's been a rough few weeks for me, I mean with that thing in the woods and the whole world thinking I did it."

"I get it, man," Steve put his hand on Geo's shoulder. "Tell ya what, when we get out of here, you and I hit the ledge and smoke a blunt. That'll help take the edge off."

"Okay," he nodded. "Oh, and Zack, tell your mom she needs a little more practice. I didn't get a chance before your dad came home if you know what I mean."

"You little shit," Zack yelled as he shook off Devin's arm and pushed past Steve, trying to tackle Geo, who stood smiling. Steve, knocked aside by Zach's charge, sat stunned on the floor as Zack fell on Geo, fists pounding into his face and chest. Geo didn't seem to react until Devin finally was able to pull Zach to his feet. Out of breath and straining against Devin's grip, he flailed his arms toward Geo as he slowly pushed himself up on his elbow.

Geo's lip was split, and his right eye was already beginning to swell and take on the deep purple of pooling blood. He rubbed his arm across his nose and winced slightly as the broken cartilage shifted. His arm came away with a large smear of blood on it. Geoffrey smiled, his gums and teeth covered with blood then turned and spit a large splatter of blood on the floor next to him.

"Well now," he said as a small bump moved across his cheek and over his broken nose. "Is that all you have? Somehow, I expected more."

"Dev, let me go," Zach sneered, "I'll show this little prick what more looks like."

"No need," Geoffrey said as he walked over to Zack. Devin let go of his friend and backed up, hitting his knees on the bench and falling hard into the seat. "I already know." Geo grabbed Zack's arm and lifted it level with his eyes. Zach grabbed at Geoffrey's arm with his free hand, trying to loosen his grip, but Geo started walking forward, pushing Zack back toward the wall.

"You fucking freak," Zach stammered when he saw two more bumps move to the spot under Geo's swollen eye. "What is that?"

Grinning as the blood on his teeth beginning to disappear, Geo didn't answer. Zach let out a hard breath as his back hit the stone wall at the back of the holding cell. Tightening his grip on Zach's arm, Geo's veins bulged in his hand. Zack let out a whimper and tried to pry his arm out, but Geo pulled his arm back and slammed Zach's hand into the wall. The snapping sound of the small bones in Zach's hand was lost in his scream. Letting go of Zack's arm, Geo watched as he slid down the wall cradling his broken and bloody hand, shock slowly setting into his eyes. Then Geo turned to see Devin and Steve on their feet behind him.

Catching Devin by surprise, Geo sucker-punched him in the stomach. Devin doubled over and fell to a knee, the force of the punch knocking the wind from him in one sharp wheeze. Taking advantage of this position, Geo brought up his knee into Devin's face, breaking his nose and sending a gout of blood across Devin's cheek. Immediately Devin's hands went to his face to ward off any other blows. His trembling gasps for Geo to stop sounded weak and garbled as blood flowed freely between his fingers.

"Fuck Geo," Steve called out. Then turning to the bars, "Help. Get the fuck in here. He's gone fucking Fight Club."

"What's the matter, Steve?" Geoffrey asked, his voice even and calm, not even winded from his exertion.

"Dude, what the actual fuck. I don't know what shit you're on, but I don't want any," he said, scrambling to put the

THE LOST

bench between them. "Just chill the fuck out and leave me alone. They'll be in here any minute now."

"Oh, Steve," Geoffrey shook his head, "you always were a little slow to catch on."

"Help," Steve called out, his voice trembling, "Like now. Get your slow asses in here."

Turning his back on Steve, Geo walked back to stand over Zach and pulled out the letter opener. The metal edge caught the overhead florescent lights and glared back menacingly.

"Look," Steve tried to get control of his voice, throwing furtive glances at the cell door, "I'm not sure why you picked that fight. I'm sure you have your reasons. I know these guys can be jackasses sometimes, but you don't need to kill them."

Geo looked back at Steve and cocked his head to the side. He looked for a moment like a puppy trying to figure out a new command. "What makes you think I want to kill them?" He pulled up his right sleeve and drew the letter opener against his arm cutting himself.

"Oh God," Steve said as he turned to the side and threw up.

"I wouldn't go that far," Geo said as his blood began to drip from the wound on his arm and coalesce into a group of small red beetles; some broke off and skittered across the floor to Devin, and some began to swarm Zach's hand. "That will never do," he said after a moment and took a swipe at Zach's face. Zach, still in the clutches of shock from his hand, didn't flinch until the first bugs began to crawl into the new cut along his left cheek. Then his screams and Devin's mingled in the echo chamber of the cell.

Steve, backed up to the cell bars, watched as the beetles burrowed into his two friends. They thrashed against the floor, violently slamming against the cement in sickening thuds. "You're killing them," he said, his hands going up to his ears as their screams turned into choked groans.

"Why would I do that?" Geo asked, his back still to Steve. "They're no use to me dead."

"No use to you? What the hell happened to you in those woods?"

He smiled as Zack began to relax, his limbs twitching slightly against the concrete. Glancing at Devin, he seemed to be fighting things more; Geo shook his head, "This will be harder for you if you fight it." He turned toward Steve, who pressed his back against the bars and renewed his calls for help. Turning to try and shake the holding cell's door. Geo didn't move, waiting for Steve to calm down. "Steve, man. It's alright," he said, "they're going to be fine. Better than fine, actually. Give them a minute. You'll see."

"How can you say that. You just beat the shit out of them."

"An unpleasant necessity, really."

"An unpleasant . . . Shit man, you're twisted."

"You'll see. Just give them a minute. You can ask them for yourself."

Steve turned back around in time to see Zach relax before twitching one more time, stretching as if he'd just been sleeping instead of violently attacked, then slowly get to his feet and walk toward Geoffrey. Steve held his breath, expecting for him to sucker-punch Geo, but instead, he stopped just a little behind him on his left side. Other than the blood on his clothes, there was no evidence that he had just been bleeding. Zack flexed his right-hand open and closed, not winching or menacing, just flexing sore fingers.

"Uh, hey Zack," Steven said, looking from Zack to Geo. "You alright? How's your hand Zack, it looked pretty rough."

THE LOST

"Sure thing, man," Zack answered. "The hand feels great." He flexed his fingers one at a time into a fist, then shook his hand out. "Matter of fact, I haven't felt this good in a long time. It's like the smoothest high I've felt in a long time. Not like that shit you get us to smoke."

"See Steve," Geo said, looking over his left shoulder. "Right as rain. As a matter of fact, I want to share this with you. You've always been so nice to me at school. We're friends."

"Ya, sure, man," Steve said, the bars of the cell digging into his back, "we're friends."

Geo smiled and held out his hand for Steven to shake. "Come over here so I can show you how they're feeling."

"Look, Geo, I'm not really sure that I want to try whatever it is that you guys are on. I mean, I appreciate the offer; it's just I think I'm going to take a break from drugs for a bit."

"That's the best part. You won't need to use any drugs anymore. This is a constant high that you never come down from. It feels amazing." Zack echoed Geoffrey's statement. "You really shouldn't turn down a gift, man. It's rude."

"Hey, I'm not at being rude here, Geo, seriously," Steve kept glancing at the door; he heard voices on the other side. Sounded like his dad was asking to see him, but before he could call out, he felt Zack drive him to the ground and clamp a hand over his mouth. Steve fought against him, but his scrawny frame would have struggled to get free even on his best day. Today his arms felt like iron shackles. He screamed through the hand on his mouth and bit down, tasting blood, but the hand didn't budge.

Geo pulled up Steve's shirt and drew the letter opener across the back of his shoulder, cutting deep into the soft tissue below Steve's shoulder blade. Standing over him as he struggled in Zack's grasp, Geo drew the red edge of the letter opener along his own wrist, letting a few drops of blood fall on Steve's exposed back. His struggles grew more ferocious the drops coalesced and began to move toward his freely bleeding shoulder blade. When the last beetle wriggled into the already closing gash, Steve began to convulse. Zack held him down until his body relaxed, twitching slightly.

The door to the holding area opened up and the conversation from the front filtered back to the boys in the cell.

"Sal, you're looking exhausted," Steve's dad's voice came closer to the door. "I keep trying to tell the selectmen that you guys need to hire another officer, but they say it's not in the budget."

"Well, Mr. Harris," Sal Milner said, ushering Mr. Harris into the holding area, "we really appreciate your voice at the town meetings."

"The safety of our citizens should be our utmost concern." He looked into the cell, noticing the blood on Zack and Devin's shirts. "What happened to them?"

"Oh, they were a little out of it when we caught them smoking with your son. Tripped over a log when they tried to run from Officer Bedrin. A couple of bloody noses."

"Serves them right," he looked at the three of them standing together in the middle of the cell. "I was just talking to your parents last week at parent-teacher conferences, boys. They are going to be very disappointed with this betrayal of their trust."

Geo sighed and said, "We're really sorry, Mr. Harris." Zack looked down at his feet. Mr. Harris nodded curtly at them, then glanced at Devin laying curled up on the ground. "What's up with him?"

"Dev?" Zack asked. "He's busted up about getting caught, says his scholarships might disappear."

THE LOST

"That is a possibility," Mr. Harris nodded. "Probably should have thought about that before you boys went off smoking." He turned his attention to his own son, "As for you, Steven," he used the voice usually reserved for his disruptive classes, "we're going to have a long talk once we get home. That is if your mother doesn't kill you first."

"Sorry, dad," Steve said. Then he turned to Geo, "I'll see you at the ledge tomorrow, alright."

"I'm afraid that's not going to be happening, Geo," Mr. Harris said, looking at Steve. "You are grounded for the foreseeable future. You will not be leaving our sight, and you can be damn sure that I'll be talking to your teachers so that when you're not in my sight, you're not out of theirs. Get over here and let me see your eyes," Steve walked to his father and looked his father in the eye. "Are you still stoned? Your eyes are all bloodshot. Get in the car," Mr. Harris turned to the other three boys. "I'll see you three in school on Monday if your parents don't kill you. And Zack, what about your scholarship? You better hope the recruiters don't get wind of this. I've seen college offers rescinded for less." Mr. Harris shook his head, ushering Steve, who was rubbing the back of his neck, out to the car and toward home.

Twelve

The lunch crowd, if you could call it that, was just finishing up their last round, and Marissa went into the backroom to restock the cherries. Turned out the bluehairs really like their microwave pizzas, overpriced shrimp, and highballs. She heard the bell from the door and called out to into the front room.

"I'll be right out. D'you know what you want?" Marissa asked grabbing the rest of the supplies to fill the well for the afternoon crowd.

"Information would be a good start," the voice was familiar, but Marissa couldn't place it from the stock room.

"Could always use Google for that," she said, smiling to herself. "But I'll do what I can." Marissa stopped short as she rounded the corner from the stock room, the old milk crate of well supplies in her arms. Standing in the middle of the mostly empty bar was Officer Michael Bedrin, badge blaring on his chest. "Oh Mike, it's– well, it's good to see you."

"No, it's not."

"Good enough," Marissa shrugged, getting her legs under her again, and headed behind the bar to fill the well. "To what then do I owe the visit? Our license is in good order."

"You mean McMurray's license, right? See, an ex-con like you can't really get a liquor license, can you?"

THE LOST

"Alright, we're in this game," Marissa put down the jar of cherries she was holding and looked Bedrin in the eyes. "Yes, Officer. Father McMurray's liquor license is in full order. He filed his renewal paperwork with the state last month, and we just passed the health inspection two weeks ago." Marissa smiled a toothy, humorless smile at Bedrin, then turning back to her work, "So unless you're here to order a drink, why don't you find some kid to harass and let me get back to my customers? Enough information for you?"

"Not why I'm here, though it does remind me to check in on *Father* McMurray to see if that old drunk actually remembers *he's* the owner here and not his little convict."

"What do you want?" Marissa asked, banging the jar of cherries she was using to refill the well onto the bar.

"Aren't we a little impatient today?" Bedrin smiled. "Feeling a little guilty?"

"Not sure what you're talking about, Matt? Maybe for once, you could actually say what you mean."

"Look, you little bitch," he leaned into the bar, his face inches from Marissa's, "you better watch your mouth. You are talking to an officer on the law, and you're in a good deal of trouble."

"Officer of the law, my ass, you were a bully in high school, and you're a bully now. You just have a fucking badge to hide behind."

"Aww, you're just sore because I'm the one that always catches your sorry ass."

"Are you drunk?" Marissa backed up a little, sensing that she had the upper hand for once. "Your eyes are a mess. You know, drunk on the job is not something that looks good on the sergeant's review. I suppose I could call him and let him know, or you could simply leave, and that will be the end of it."

Bedrin backed down a little. At least he stopped leaning as far across the bar. Instead, he stood straight up and crossed his arms over his chest. "Information."

"Question," Marissa retorted.

"Your brother got a spare key for his car?"

Marissa was caught off guard, "spare key?"

"You know, those things that normal people use to start their cars," Bedrin smiled, reminding Marissa, more of a snake than a man. "A hard concept for a con like you."

"Of course, he had a spare key," Marissa decided not to take Bedrin's bait. "Our folks probably have it at home. What happened, you idiots lock the keys in the truck while you were dusting for prints?"

"So, where is it?"

"The truck?" Marissa didn't like where this was going. "I'd assume it was in your impound lot."

"Familiar with the place," Bedrin raised an eyebrow, "aren't you?"

"I did my time for that."

"So, where is it?"

"Where is what?" Marissa started putting the well supplies away again. Clearly, he was fishing for something, and she just wanted to get rid of him at this point. "Besides, this is harassment. My brother is missing," she felt her eyes tear up when she said it aloud, "have some decency."

"Right," Bedrin scoffed, "grieving sister. I know you two never got along."

"That's not true," not entirely true at any rate. "You need to go now unless you want me to call your sergeant about all this," she motioned to him.

Bedrin smiled, "You won't need to call him. You can just tell him in person."

THE LOST

"Oh, is he out in the car? Did you want to ask about our specials today?" Marissa pushed her advantage. "Why didn't you just say so. Today from the grill we have–"

"Shut up," Bedrin cut her off, "and get the fuck over here. You're under arrest."

"What the hell are you gonna try to pin on me now? Harassing an officer?"

"Try theft, you klepto," Bedrin reached to his belt and took out his handcuffs.

"Wait, you're serious?" Marissa looked around at the three elderly couples who were still in the bar. "I'm in the middle of the breakfast rush."

Bedrin looked around the room, "Bar's closed, ladies and gentlemen. Your bills are on the house. Time to go."

The customers stood up and got their purses and jackets, then headed to the door, several eyeing Marissa or shaking their head as they passed.

"You can't do that," Marissa protested.

"Just did," Bedrin moved around the bar pinning Marissa in a corner. "Marissa Hail, you are under arrest. You have the right to remain silent."

"Fuck silent," Marissa said as Bedrin turned her around to put the cuffs on her. "What the hell is it I'm supposed to have done?"

"Anything you say can and will be used against you by a court of law. You have the right to an attorney," Bedrin continued as if she hadn't said anything.

"I have a right to know why I'm being arrested, don't I?"

"If you cannot afford an attorney, one will be appointed to you. Do you understand these rights as they have been read to you?"

"What did I do?"

Eric Johnson

Bedrin tightened the cuffs around her wrists a little more. "Do you understand your rights as I have read them to you?"

Marissa slumped her shoulders. "Yes."

"Good," Bedrin said. "Now, are you going to walk out to the car, or do I have to carry you like last time?"

"Do I get to know what I did this time?"

"I told you already. You're charged with theft."

"What did I steal? I've been with my damn family or here in the bar ever since Mikey went missing."

"Someone broke into the impound lot and took the evidence we collected from the truck."

"What evidence, you losers haven't even found his body."

"We'll talk about what evidence once we get down to the station," Bedrin jerked the cuffs. "Now, are you going to walk, or am I throwing you over my shoulder like the sack of shit you are?"

"I'll walk, you fucking bastard."

"Too bad," Bedrin said as he pushed her toward the door.

"Can I at least lock up?" Marissa asked, looking around the bar. "It's not exactly safe to leave a place like this unlocked. You never know what sort might just walk in and take what they want."

Bedrin grunted, "Takes a thief to know a thief."

"So, can I lock up?"

"Where are the keys?"

"Back in the office, in my jacket."

Bedrin pushed her toward the office, "Surprised you're still worried about this dump given the circumstances."

"What circumstances, false arrest, and harassment?" she spat back at him.

THE LOST

"No," he said, opening the office door, "the fact that after this, you're a three-time loser. You know what that means. It's off to the state pen for you."

Thirteen

Marissa rubbed her wrists where the cuffs had been removed and looked around the room. The empty metal table she was at, the chair she was in, and an identical opposite her were the only furnishings in the room. There were no windows to the outside, but there was a giant mirror in front of her. She wasn't sure if anyone was watching from the other side, but she put on a big smile and flicked them off just to be on the safe side. It wasn't until after she stood up to stretch that the door opened.

"I told you to stay seated," Bedrin said as he closed the door behind him.

"Well, you know us three-time losers," she said, standing behind the chair.

"I do know you," Bedrin said, sitting down across the table from her and opening up a manilla folder, "and despite your little show earlier, you're scared shitless."

"Oh good," Marissa smiled and motioned toward the envelope, "I was afraid that went to waste."

"Always were a piece of work, Marissa," Bedrin said. "Why don't you sit down so we can do this properly." He pulled out a small silver rectangle and pressed a button on the side. "Oh, we'll be recording this to play back at your sentencing hearing."

THE LOST

"Okay, Matt," she scraped the chair loudly along the floor, "let's 'do this properly.'" She made air quotes for emphasis.

"Do you want to just confess and get it over with? That'd make things a lot easier. You remember last time, right? That was a mess. You lying, me uncovering your lies one by one."

"The difference there, Matt, last time I actually did something. This time, well, I've been a bit busy with my brother missing and all."

"Funny you should mention that. I was going to work up to that a little slower, you know, out of compassion."

Marissa laughed, "Now that is something I've never heard you accused of."

"But let's just start right there. What do you know about your brother's death?"

"Excuse me?"

"I wanted to know what you can tell me about your brother's death. I thought the question was clear."

"I thought he was missing," Marissa knew all reports were calling them dead, but she needed to hold out hope.

"Well," Bedrin put his hands together under his chin, elbows resting on the table, "officially this is a missing person, but really, with the wolves and the blood. I mean, let's call a spade a spade."

"News says that it was animals, but you shits think my brother's best friend killed him. You can't find a body, but there was a lot of blood on the truck, so now you're saying dead. Other than that, he was in the woods with two other friends of his, and you had to get help from the state cops because you're incompetent. So fine," the tears threatened to push past her defenses, "he's dead then."

"If we can't find a body, how do you know he's dead?"

Eric Johnson

"Because Mike would have been home by now unless something happened to him. My folks are holding out hope, but there isn't a single thing in the world that would keep him away from home so long without at least calling mom," she couldn't stop the tears this time. She hated to show weakness in front of Bedrin, but she hadn't said it aloud before.

"That could be, or you could know because you were involved."

"Involved in killing my brother," Marissa leaned in, her hands on the table's edge. "Is that why you dragged me in here?"

"You have been seen yelling at him."

"Of course I have, you neanderthal. He's my little brother. Maybe if you ever had any friends, you would have known how siblings act."

"Why else would you have broken in and stolen the evidence from the impound lot?"

"Fuck," Marissa leaned back in her chair and rolled her eyes. "What else do you want to pin on me today? Did I kick your damn puppy too?"

"Alright, Marissa, you're getting a little combative. How about you cool your heels here, and we'll continue this after I get some coffee?" Bedrin turned off the recorder and stood. Instead of walking out of the room, he moved around the table and twisted her chair to face him. He put one hand on his service pistol and one hand on her shoulder, pressing her hard into the chair. "You really might want to rethink being helpful here," he sneered down at her, "there are worse things that could happen to you than going to jail over a robbery."

"What the hell?" Marissa pushed at his arm. "Let go of me."

THE LOST

Bedrin squeezed her shoulder, eliciting a small yelp. "Two strikes already, don't forget." Then he let go and walked out of the room, slamming the door behind him.

Marissa sat watching the door for a minute, messaging her aching shoulder before turning back toward the table and putting her head in her hands. She knew she was innocent, but Bedrin had been the arresting officer on her other three brushes with the law. He'd pressured Father McMurray to press charges, albeit unsuccessfully. She knew he hated her and wasn't sure if he was above planting evidence to put her behind bars permanently. Leaning back, she looked at the fluorescent lights burning down from the ceiling.

"Alright, Bedrin," she said after a while. "I know you're listening over there. I'm ready to cooperate. I don't have anything to confess, but let's go through why you really brought me in here so I can clear myself. Does that work?" Marissa sat in silence, waiting for an answer.

After several more minutes, Bedrin walked into the room with his recorder and a cup of coffee. "Glad you came to your senses."

"What did you actually bring me in for?" Marissa asked.

Bedrin hit record before he answered. "You were arrested due to the theft from our impound lot. Seems someone took something from your brother's car sometime after it was brought in."

"And you thought it was me because I broke into a couple of places before?"

"We figured it was you because you broke into our impound lot before."

"Fair enough. Don't you guys have cameras? Wouldn't you have seen me?"

"The camera feed went down. Electrical interference."

"Bummer," Marissa said, thinking of another way to clear herself. "What about witnesses?"

"Nope, no one saw who took the stuff."

"Alright, so why bring me in?"

"I already told you, you broke in there once for something you wanted, who's to say you wouldn't do it again? How'd you do it?"

"I didn't," Marissa shrugged.

"Alright, but how'd you do it last time? You've already served the time for that, not like you can be locked up again for it."

"I'm not gonna tell ya."

Bedrin closed the folder and looked over his shoulder at the mirror. "So much for being cooperative."

"I said I'd be cooperative, not stupid," Marissa shook her head. "I'm not about to tell you something that you and whoever else is watching can warp into how the thief did it this time so you can pin this on me."

Bedrin leaned back in his chair, rubbed the back of his neck, and nodded. "So, cooperative on your terms."

"When was I supposed to have broken in?" Marissa asked him after an uncomfortable silence. "Aren't you supposed to ask me where I was on some given day and time?"

"What?" Bedrin shook his head and shifted his weight in his seat.

"You know, like on Law and Order? Where were the night of October 8th?"

"I don't care where you say you were. I'm pretty sure you were here."

"Judge and jury?" Marissa shifted in her seat. "Do I want to know what comes next?"

"This what you call cooperative?" Bedrin stood up.

THE LOST

"I'm sorry," Marissa relented. "When did the break-in happen? I want to help as much as I can."

"Some time night before last or yesterday morning."

"That's a little vague, but it couldn't have been me," Marissa leaned back, hoping that this would be enough. "I was at the bar until midnight when I brought Father McMurray home, then went to my house. You can ask my parents if you don't believe me. Then back to the bar the next morning for opening at eight. It was dead, but I was there."

"Dead, eh?" Bedrin reopened the folder and made a note. "Anyone happen to come in? Anyone see you, or am I supposed to just take your word for it?"

Marissa shook her head, then her eyes lit up. "There was someone."

"I don't suppose he was a regular? Or that you remember his name, do you?"

"Wasn't a regular," Marissa looked up at the lights, trying to remember if he said his name. "Shit, I didn't get his name."

"Right," Bedrin closed the folder again, "so no alibi."

"Wait, wait," Marissa reached across the table to stop the closing folder. "I don't have his name, but he said he was a lawyer. The guy was going to the hospital to try to represent Geo. Didn't say his name, but he said he was defending that kid in the news. Could only be Geo."

"So you're telling me that the guy defending your brother's friend just happened into your bar when the evidence locker was being robbed?"

"I guess I am," Marissa smiled. "So, I have an alibi. Give him a call. I'm sure you have his number."

Bedrin looked at his watch and shrugged. "Too late to call him now," he smiled at Marissa as he turned off the recorder. "My shifts ending soon. We'll just get you processed, and I'll check with him in the morning when I come back on."

"You can't do that," Marissa stood up, her chair tipping over with a loud crash.

"Sure I can," Bedrin pointed to the chair, "I mean, you just tried to assault me."

"Like hell I did, the chair fell over."

"That's your story."

"There are cameras in here, you ass."

"Don't work. I told you, electrical interference," Bedrin shrugged as he reached for his cuffs. "So much for your cooperation."

Fourteen

"Fuck you, Matt," Marissa yelled as Bedrin closed the door to the holding area. "You can't just lock me up in here. I have an alibi. You haven't charged me." Marissa grabbed the bars of the holding cell and rested her head against them. "Fuck."

The cool metal felt unsettlingly familiar, the comforts of a past life. The difference was, the last time she was here, she belonged, not now. She thought of McMurray's disappointed voice back then, how she had promised herself that she wouldn't let him down again. Yet here she was, sitting in the holding cell, hoping he gets the message on his answering machine in time to bail her out, hoping he won't just give up on her.

A voice from behind her broke her thoughts, "Dev, it looks like we got company for the night."

Marissa turned around to see two boys about her brother's age sitting on the bench against the holding cell wall. Marissa didn't recognize them, and she hoped they didn't recognize her. She didn't know all of her brother's friends from school, but these two didn't really look like his typical friends, but knowing how high school was, she couldn't be sure. The kids were wiry, not thin per se, but like they played sports.

"Wow," Marissa said, "looks like Bedrin's been busy. What'd he pinch you guys for?"

"Being unlucky," said the one who had spoken before. "But now it looks like my luck has changed. Right, Dev." He turned to his friend, who was sitting on the bench, his head in his hands.

"Doesn't look like your friends doing so well," Marissa walked over to him. "You alright, kid?"

"He's fine," the first kid stood up, putting himself between Marissa and his friend. "Besides, we're having a conversation here."

"I can see that," Marissa stopped, putting her hands in front of her. "How about a name then, if we're having a conversation. I'm Marissa."

"Marissa," he hissed her name. "Pretty name for someone in here."

"Don't act like this is anything special. Just 'cause you're in the local holding cell doesn't make you a tough shit."

"Oh really?" his fists balled at his sides.

"Zack," his friend said, rubbing his temples. "Leave her be. 'Member what happened last time."

"I do, Dev," Zack turned to look at his friend on the bench and scoffed in disgust. "I've never felt better."

Devin looked up from the bench; he looked like he'd been crying. "Seriously, man, somethings not right."

"Zach, right? Your friend looks like he smoked some bad stuff."

"He'll be fine in a minute or two," Zack waved his hand dismissively at his friend. "He's just a bit more hard-headed than I am."

"He really doesn't look good," Marissa moved around Zack and knelt next to his friend. "Devin, right?"

"Ya," he said, looking down at his feet again, gritting his teeth together.

THE LOST

"You doing alright?"

"No," he said through gritted teeth. "Hollon. He did something."

"Did you know them?" she asked, thinking of her brother and his friends. "The kids from the woods. They were about your age, right?"

"Ya, but that's not it," he said, looking up at her, the red veins in his eyes glaring against the whites. "He's not human."

"Look," Marissa put her hand on his back. "I know it's gotta be tough, Mike was my brother, but Geo's a good kid. I believe what he said happened. I believe they were attacked. I've been hearing the howling in the woods for a couple of years now. It makes sense."

"No," Devin scrambled to his feet, backing away from her. "He's already gotten to you. He's a monster. Fight it. Fight." Devin's voice rose with each word until he was almost unintelligible.

Marissa turned to the other kid, who was leaning calmly against the wall, watching his friend lose his mind. "I think your buddy smoked some bad shit."

"So what?"

"So what? He's your friend, isn't he?" Marissa looked back and forth between the two of them. Zack was calm and relaxed. He looked like some of the long-timers from lockup, someone who had nothing to worry about. Devin was in a panic, eyes frenzied, hallucinating, and he'd clearly been crying for a while in here, the redness around his eyes a clear giveaway. She could still smell the earthy-sweet scent coming off him that could only be pot. "I don't know if you were both smoking a different batch, but he's having some sort of reaction."

"No," Zack moved away from the wall. "We both got the same stuff. Aren't you worried about me?"

"Not really," Marissa said, keeping her attention on Devin. "You just seems like an ass, and I know weed ain't gonna do that. We gotta calm him down."

"Give him a minute," Zack said. "He'll come around."

Marissa turned to face him, jumping slightly because he was standing right behind her. "Fuck you, you little shit. He's having a bad trip right now, hallucinating and shit. You're his friend; help him out. Calm him down."

"Oh, he'll just freak out more if I go near him," Zack grinned at Marissa and moved past her to Devin.

"No, no, no, no," Devin trembled. "Get away from me. Get back." Devin sank to the floor, pulled his knees to his chest, and began rocking.

"Buddy," Zack said flatly, "just relax, don't fight it, and it will pass."

"What the hell were you guys doing?"

"Just smoking a little," Zack replied, still standing over Devin. "Nothing bad."

"No, no, no," Devin moaned, rocking and trembling on the ground.

"He's not acting like it," Marissa shook her head. "That's more like shrooms or acid or some shit like that."

"An aficionado?" Zack turned around to face Marissa, and Devin's body seemed to relax.

"You were right," she said, "your buddy seems scared of you. What'd you do to him."

"Nothing."

"Then why was he freaking out so much when you came over?"

"He's fine now," Zack said, pointing at Devin, who lay on the floor, curled up like before, but not moaning or rocking anymore. He looked like he was sleeping, breathing calm and

THE LOST

evenly. "He'll sleep through the rest. He's a tough kid, bit hardheaded at times." He added that last part looking over his shoulder at his prone friend. "Though I'm a little more interested in you."

"Back off, kid," Marissa dismissed him. "I passed your league five years ago."

"Oh, come on. You like a badass. I can see it in your eyes."

"Even if I did," Marissa sat down on the bench, "being an ass and being a badass isn't the same thing. Besides, this isn't the first time I've been here, and your not as intimidating as you think you are. Now, if you don't mind, I'm waiting for someone to come get me, so just go hang out with your friend." Marissa lay down across the bench, hands resting on her stomach, and closed her eyes. She knew this type of kid, all talk and no action. She was safe. These two were high school potheads, and though Zack was acting tough, his bluster would be tamed easily with one shout to the cops in the station.

When a hand came down on her mouth, her eyes shot open. Inches from her face, Zack grinned back at her. His hand pressed her lips uncomfortably into her teeth. He reached with his other hand and pinned her arms to her stomach. She let out a scream of surprise, muffled by the pressure, and tried to turn her head. He was a lot stronger than he looked, and if his eyes were any indication, a bit crazier than he seemed at first. Marissa rolled her body toward him and slid off the other side of the bench, freeing herself from his grasp.

"Feisty, aren't we," Zack moved around the bench.

"Look, kid," Marissa moved to keep the bench between them, "I'm not looking to bind you up here or make things worse for you. I scream, and they're going to be in here in seconds. They're just on the other side of the door. As a matter of fact, if you look up there, that thing, that's a camera. If they happen to check the feed while you're doing this, you're fucked."

"I wouldn't worry too much for me," he lunged at Marissa, who darted back around the bench.

"I'm not really," she said, going another turn around the bench. "I was just trying to appeal to some sense of self-preservation. I'm a little more worried about myself getting in trouble for kicking your ass if you lay a hand on me again. Bedrin's got it out for me."

Zack laughed. "I'm not worried about Bedrin. We have," he stopped for a second and looked at the door to the station, "an understanding."

"Some understanding, you're in here like anyone else."

"Well, not exactly like anyone else."

"Like me then."

"Partially true," Zack faded to the left, and Marissa moved to avoid him, but he switched direction and caught her arm before she could react. His grip was like steel, and his fingers dug into her wrist, his thumb pressing on her palm bending her wrist back.

"I'd let go if I were you."

"Why's that?" Zack asked. "You think I'm afraid of you? There is more to me that you think, Marissa."

"I said I don't want to screw you with your buddy Bedrin, but that doesn't mean that I won't," Marissa tried to jerk her arm out of his grip and backed up toward the bars. "I warned you. Bedrin," Marissa yelled toward the door. "Get your ass in here, you sorry suck of a cop. Don't you know you shouldn't lock a lady up with hooligans?"

"Oh, that's effective," Zack laughed.

"He's going to come in any second," Marissa said, fending off Zack's other hand. "Bedrin, seriously, get your ass in here. The chief won't like it if someone gets hurt in the holding cell. Bad press and all." The door remained closed. "Bedrin. Fuck."

"How's that screwing me over with Bedrin thing going for you?" Zack asked, moving closer to her, pressing her body against the bars with his own. His breath hot in her face.

"Well, there are other ways of dealing with things," Marissa said as she brought her rights knee up into his balls.

Zack doubled over, letting go of her wrist to grab his own crotch. Marissa shoved him back, sidestepping around him. She surveyed the area; Devin was still sleeping off whatever they had smoked before getting caught, and Zack knelt in front of the cell door, groaning and holding his balls. Everything else in the cell was nailed down. She moved to put the bench between them if he got up and ran through her options. She could wake Devin, but who knew if the shit he'd done had worn off yet? Having him freaking out would be less than helpful, plus she had no clue if he'd side with his buddy if he was coherent. Bedrin and the other useless shits that passed as the police force in town weren't answering her, so that left her with only one option. Prison yard justice.

Having received that once or twice herself when she was an inmate, she'd vowed never to do that to anyone in her life. Being on this side of the bars already broke one of the vows she'd made to herself when she got out. She figured, what's one more. Taking a deep breath, she walked around the bench and stood over Zack. He'd managed to get up to his knees.

"You're going to want to stay down, kid," she said quietly.

"Fuck you," he spat.

"Don't say I didn't warn you," she said as she pulled her leg back and kicked him square across the face. His headshot to the left, and his hand went to his face. Marissa followed the first kick with a second, then a third, on his side and face again. Zack went down; this time, blood dripped to the floor, creating tiny beads by his head. Blood oozed from a cut under his right eye, and he looked like he'd cut his lip on his teeth. Marissa walked over to him and turned him over with her foot. "I told you to stay down."

Zack didn't respond, and Marissa walked over to the bars to wait for the inevitable. Any minute Bedrin would come in, and then she'd really be in for it. He'd finally have what he wanted on her. Assault charges could definitely count as strike three, despite being in here for nothing. She was thinking about how she'd be able to afford a lawyer, and the tape would show a clear self-defense case, but in the meantime, Bedrin would be unbearable.

When the door opened, and Bedrin walked in with Father McMurray, Marissa felt a huge weight lift from her shoulders. McMurray hadn't abandoned her; he hadn't given up on her after all. She watched for the glee in Bedrin's eyes as he surveyed the cell behind her. McMurray eyed the cell also, but Marissa didn't want to see the disappointment in his eyes, so she kept her attention on Bedrin, whose reaction she could handle; she expected it, really.

"Well then, Marissa," Bedrin began in his lazy drawl, "I see your company is as engaging as ever."

"Look here," she was ready to argue self-defense, "it's not my fault."

"Never is," he smiled. "Did you bore them with the tired stories of your crime sprees?"

"If you look at," Marissa stopped short of telling him to check the camera feed when his words registered. Marissa turned to see Devin laying on his back, sleeping peacefully, and Zack had curled up in the corner, his face hidden from view. She looked to where the blood had fallen to the floor, but there was nothing there.

THE LOST

"Please open the door and let her out, Mathew," Father McMurray said, watching Marissa's reaction to the scene behind her with curiosity. "I believe Miss Hail is free the leave."

"I'm sorry, Father," Bedrin said, opening the door. "Take care of this little lost sheep of yours. From what I hear, you don't have a lot left."

"Don't worry about her, Mathew," McMurray adopted the old tone he used to reserve for the confessional box, "you seem to have a couple of lost sheep of your own."

"Oh, those two," Bedrin motioned to the two boys in the cell. "They're basically good kids, just a little bad company. Unfortunately, we weren't able to get ahold of their parents, so they'll be our guests for the night."

"I don't want to appear ungrateful, Father McMurray," Marissa eyed the cell warily, "but do you think we could get out of here. I need to get that bar cleaned. Officer Bedrin interrupted my prep-work, and I'm sure all the limes are dried out by now."

"Sure thing Marissa," McMurray put his arm around her shoulders, she leaned her head into him like a child, and McMurray smiled down at her.

Fifteen

"I swear it was self-defense," Marissa repeated as she was putting the last glass away. "The kid was crazy."

"Well, if his friend was as bad off as you said, he was probably suffering from the same stuff differently," McMurray said as he sipped his whiskey.

"It was something other than that. I'm not sure what it was, but he was very aggressive, like more than you'd expect from a kid," Marissa took the knife out of the sink, wiped it, and began cutting new limes for the evening. "And another thing. No one came when I called for help."

"Maybe they just didn't hear you."

"I'd be shocked," Marissa laughed, "you know how loud I can be when I want."

"Don't remind me."

"You're in a good mood today Father," Marissa commented as she put the limes in the well and began cutting lemons.

"I'm sorry?" he raised his eyebrow.

"No, it's a good thing," Marissa stopped cutting and put the knife down. "It's just that you've been really down since, well, since I've been back really. I was beginning to think it had to do with dealing with me all the time, but it's nice to see you smile again."

THE LOST

"It's nice to feel needed again."

"No offense," she smiled and returned to cutting, "but I wish I hadn't needed you to bail me out tonight."

"Not that," McMurray said, "I wish you hadn't needed me for that either. It's a little worse than that, I'm afraid to say, but that you and your parents wanted me to handle your brother's, well," McMurray faltered.

"It's alright, Father, you can say it. His funeral," Marissa felt the familiar tightness in the back of her throat at that word. He was only a kid, graduating next year. She put the lemons away, dropped the knife in the sink, and grabbed the rag to wipe down the bar. "It sucks."

"Yup."

"He was the good one, the one my folks had hope for."

"Marissa, you sell yourself short," McMurray said, lifting up his glass so she could wipe up the condensation ring it left on the bar. She tossed a coaster down, and he replaced his glass. "You're a good kid too."

"I think I left good kid back in prison," she rubbed the rag vigorously at a spot on the bar. "They're taking it hard. Like really fucking hard."

"Watch your mouth."

"Sorry, Father," She moved to wipe down the tables. "I'm glad you'll do it. I don't even really know this new guy. He seems standoffish to me."

"I'm just surprised your parents agreed to it," McMurray took another sip of his whiskey and swirled the rest around his glass, watching it. "I thought they had believed the allegations, didn't think your dad approved of you working for me even."

"Well," Marissa shifted on her feet and wrung the towel in her hands, "about that."

"They haven't asked me to, have they?"

"Well, not exactly," she looked at his pleadingly, "but I really need you to do it. It's important to me. I'm sure it won't matter to them."

McMurray raised his eyebrows at her, tilting his head down to give her a look. Marissa hated it when he did that; it felt like she would get detention even though she hadn't been in school for five years. He moved his gaze back to his whiskey glass. "I'll have to get their permission."

Marissa sighed and felt some tension leave her shoulders. She smiled to herself as she continued to clean the bar in companionable silence. Getting permission first would have made sense, but her parents probably would disagree. She'd hoped that if he expected to speak, it would be easier to convince them.

"Your brother and his friends seemed to like Father Maria," McMurray turned around and leaned against the bar, breaking the silence. "He seems like a good kid. The diocese spoke very highly of him, and the town's responding well. I've even been to a sermon or two of his. He's a little more liberal than I was and a little less focused on sin than my last few years, but change is good."

"Well, dropping the doom and gloom is a plus, I'll admit."

"Thanks."

"What? No one likes to be told they're doing bad things," Marissa threw the rag over her shoulder and began straightening the chairs. "Trust me on that one, I've heard enough of that for today."

"That reminds me, we're a little off task here," McMurray raised his eyebrow at Marissa. "Weren't you going to tell me why you ended up incarcerated again?"

"Because Bedrin's a dick."

"Marissa," McMurray scolded.

THE LOST

"But he is. He barges in here and begins questioning me about missing evidence in my brother's investigation. Truly crass of him, to be honest, but he barged in here and kicked out all of your customers so he could drag me down to the station for no reason."

"No reason?"

"He said he had a reason, but he's full of shit," Marissa smiled meekly. "Sorry, full of crap."

"Marissa, what did he say you did?"

"You think I'm guilty too?" Marissa shot back, staring at McMurray, the rag clenched in her hand. "I'm not surprised. Everyone else has given up on me. My folks barely talk to me, and my friends stopped when I went upstate. Now Bedrin's got you on his side," McMurray put his glass down and walked over to Marissa. "I heard you back there, talking about how he had sheep to tend and all that other crap."

"Marissa," McMurray put his hand on her shoulder. "Calm down."

"Don't tell me to calm down," she threw the rag on the table, shrugged him aside, and walked over to the bar. "You don't have to pretend to care about this shit."

"Marissa Maire Hail, you stop this now," McMurray commanded.

Marissa turned to face McMurray, tears running down her cheeks. Her features relaxed, and her eyes were pleading with him even as she tried to say she didn't need his help.

"As I was saying," McMurray said, "Mathew has been a good cop. A little vigilant at times, definitely inflexible, but a good cop," he stopped her by putting a finger up before she responded. "I think, wait, I know he's wrong this time, but I can't help you if I don't know what he thinks you've taken."

"A book."

"A what?"

"Book. Apparently, there was this book that Geo had when they took him for the first time. It was on the seat of Mike's truck or something. They had it in the truck in the impound lot. Then they didn't. Who do we know who has a rap sheet for stealing? Voila."

"They think you broke into the police station to steal a book?"

"The impound yard."

"Why?"

"They didn't say, but I'd guess to slow down the investigation."

"To slow down the investigation into what happened to your brother and his friends?" Father McMurray laughed. "Well," he said when as the laughter passed, "at least your reading." Then he started laughing again, big rolling laughter that Marissa hadn't heard from him since her childhood.

Marissa stood and watched McMurray for a moment, then giving in to the infectiousness of his laugh and the absurdity of the whole situation, and for the first time since her brother's death, she laughed.

Sixteen

With the door finally unlocked for the morning, Marissa started folding the napkins for the afternoon's lunch special and prayed that things would go smoothly. After yesterday's impromptu trip to the police station, she was looking forward to dealing with the cranky old people who always came in for their morning eggs. She used to think it was weird for a bar to be open for breakfast, and this place, from the bottles on the walls to the pool table and dartboards, was definitely a bar, but Father McMurray had always told her that it wasn't the place that mattered, it was how you used it. Besides, he would add, everyone needs someplace to be. Marissa was never quite sure if that last part talked about their customers or about themselves, not that it mattered much.

The bell over the door jingled, and for a second, Marissa felt her shoulders tighten, imagining Matt's voice telling her he had more questions, but what that didn't come, she took a deep breath, lowered her shoulders, and turned around. Standing in the entranceway was some high school kid playing hooky; he was the picture of the awkward teen years, wearing worn jeans and a Nirvana teeshirt, scrawny arms sticking out, and a mop of brown hair just above his eyes. She couldn't really remember his name but was pretty sure that he was the local stoner.

Eric Johnson

"Sit anywhere you want," she put on her best smile, "I'll be over in a minute."

He nodded and moved to one of the high-backed booths, probably hiding so he wouldn't be caught by the cops and sent back to school for the day. Marissa smiled, knowing that she had been there a time or two when she was in school. Coming out from behind the bar, she walked over to the booth.

"Shouldn't you be in school?" she asked with a smile.

"Maybe," he didn't look up at her.

"Hey, no worries, kid," Marissa smiled down at him. A few years back, this would have been her. "By yourself today?"

"Nope, meeting some people here," he said, glancing up at her.

Marissa noticed the telltale red in his eyes, definitely the local stoner. She looked around as if someone had appeared from nowhere while she was talking to this kid. "Wanna order, or you just gonna sit here 'till they come?"

"Coke."

"Anything for your friends?"

"No."

"They seniors too?"

"They are," the kid didn't seem to be in a talkative mood, so Marissa went back to the bar to get his coke. When she brought it back, he asked her for an egg and toast. Marissa went into the back room and started cooking; the bell over the door rang again, but she figured that it was probably just this kid's friends, but when she brought the food to the table, it was empty. She was about to clear his soda when the bell rang again, and he came back in holding his cell phone.

"Sorry, shitty reception in here," Marissa said. He shrugged and sat down in the booth.

THE LOST

"Look who is it," a familiar voice came from behind her. Marissa instantly tensed as one of the kids from the cell walked up behind her. She turned to face him, ready to defend herself, but it was the kid who'd been curled up in the corner most of the time.

"Donny, Dell," Marissa tried to remember what his friend had called him, "what was your name again?"

"Devin," he said, sliding in across from the other kid. "And you are that Hail kid's big sister, aren't you?"

"Looks like you're feeling better at least," Marissa was still creeped out by the kid. Something about his eyes gave her the creeps when he looked at her. "Last time I saw you, you weren't doing so hot. I wouldn't buy from that dealer again if I were you." She glanced at the stoner, wondering if he was the dealer. "Still think Geo's a monster?"

"No," he said. His friend looked at him, furrowing his brow. "Geo's a good guy."

"Told ya so," Marissa said. "What'll it be?"

"Fried egg and a coffee."

"Comin' right up."

Marissa left the kids in the booth and went in back to make the food. When she came back out, they weren't talking. They sat there, silently looking at one and another. It's not like they seemed angry, just silent. Marissa brought over the eggs then headed back into the kitchen to wash the pans. She left the door open so she could listen to the bell. Cleaning hadn't always felt good, but since McMurray got this place and hired her, there was something about it that just made her feel better. The sound of the freezer door closing startled her. There shouldn't be anyone else back there. Turning quickly, pan still in her hand dripping water on the floor, Marissa moved back to the freezer door.

Eric Johnson

"Hello?" She called as she moved deeper into the kitchen. Typically, Father McMurray would be here to cook for the lunch rush when he wasn't drinking, but she always handled the light breakfast crew by herself. "Father McMurray? You back here?"

There was no answer. Marissa stopped to listen and could only hear forks clicking against the plates out in the bar and the water that she had left on in the sink. Her hand tightened around the handle of the pan, and she moved back toward the freezer, again calling to Father McMurray. It seemed like an eternity before she reached the freezer and, with shaking hands, set down the pan and opened the door. The automatic lights buzzed on and spilled from the small walk-in out into the dim morning light filtering through the back windows of the kitchen. She stood in the doorway of the empty freezer as it hummed away undisturbed.

Marissa chuckled nervously, shaking her head, as she closed the freezer and reached for the handle of the pan to go back and finish washing the dishes. After putting the last of the dishes in the drying rack, she went back out to check on her two customers. Kids don't typically tip well, but a no tip was far better than when they put a dime under an inverted water glass. If these two were anything like that Devin kid's friend, she wouldn't put it past them.

She busied herself around the bar, prepping for the drink orders that generally came in around lunch while the kids finished their breakfast. She was about to head back to their table and see if they needed anything when a crash from the kitchen made her jump. Devin and his friend looked over at her, and Marissa gave them a smile.

"Probably just something falling out of the drying rack," she said while walking back into the kitchen. "Be right back."

THE LOST

"While you're back there," the scrawny kid said, "could you get some extra napkins? I think we're going to need them." He smiled at Devin.

"Sure thing," she said, positive she was getting a dime under a glass of water. She figured she'd be lucky if they didn't dine and dash. She pushed the door open, leaving it open so she could hear the inevitable bell when they left the bar. She pulled the clean dishes out of the sink, made sure there weren't soap suds on them, and re-stacked them in the drying rack. As she headed back out, she caught a draft coming from the freezer, the light spilling into the kitchen from the open door. "Shit," she mumbled, hoping that she hadn't ruined the food by leaving it open all morning.

Closing the freezer, Marissa made sure it was latched this time and headed back to the bar area. She hadn't heard the bell over the door, so there was still a chance that she would be able to stop them before they flipped the water. She grabbed a handful of napkins and a fresh bar towel, just in case, and turned to see two figures framed in the light of the door to the bar—one scrawny with shaggy hair, the other an athletic build.

"Hey, guys," she said, hurrying toward them. "You can't come back here. I'm on my way out."

"Did you get the napkins?" the scrawny kid asked.

"Ya," Marissa held up the napkins so they could see them in the dim lighting. She didn't like the feeling she was getting by their stance. There had been enough traps in prison. She knew when someone was getting ready to ruin her day. She cursed herself for leaving her cell phone in her coat. "I just have to grab something from the office, then I'll be over to your table."

"That's alright," Devin said, "we'll come and get them."

"I already said you're not allowed back here," Marissa looked around for something to grab to help defend herself and saw a knife in the drying rack. A bit drastic for a couple of high schoolers, but she hoped it'd work as a deterrent, and if she was overreacting, she'd just go cut some more celery for the Bloody Mary's she'd be making in the afternoon. Marissa edged herself closer to it as Devin and his friend began walking into the room. She noticed that they left the door open behind them, a small favor that allowed her to escape if she could get around them. The only option right now was to draw them further into the kitchen, between the sink and the prep table, so she could go around the other side of the table and get into the main bar. Then she'd have more options.

"Aww, come on," the scrawny kid said, "no one else is here. Devin and I are just looking to help you out, right, Dev?"

"Sure thing Steve," Devin responded, slowly closing the distance between the door and Marissa, who had moved over by the sink to get closer to the dish strainer.

"Steve?" Marissa asked, "Steve Harris? I knew you looked familiar," Marissa kept moving toward the knife, trying to buy time as she drew them into the narrow space, hoping they would trip over each other when she went for the door. "You and Mikey used to play together as kids."

"Yup," Steve responded but didn't slow his advance.

"How're your folks?" Marissa tried to get him to stop whatever he was planning, hoping the connection would help, but his continued advance and the menacing look in his bloodshot eyes made her doubt it.

"Why don't you tell me when you see them?" he said, smiling a joyless smile.

"They coming in?" she asked hopefully.

Devin and Steve just laughed and lunged forward. Marissa was able to jump back just in time for their fingers to miss, and just as she had hoped, they tripped on each other in the small space and tumbled forward. She turned and started toward the other end of the table, hoping to go around it and get the fuck out. Instead, she ran directly into Zack and lost her footing, catching herself on the table before she fell to the ground.

"There you are," she said as if she'd expected him to be there.

"Miss me bitch?" Zack sneered.

"Now come on, you're not still mad about that little thing in the cell, are you?"

"Hardly," Zack grimaced, "didn't even feel it."

"Right," she glanced back at Steve and Devin getting up and then back at Zack. She was trapped between them. "Well, it's been real nice having this little reunion and all, but I need to get back to the front. So why don't you guys just get going, alright?" She caught sight of the knife in the strainer again and reached for it.

"Not so fast," Zack said. Before she could grab the knife, Steve grabbed the rack and threw it off the counter; it glanced off the table and then scattered across the floor, giving Marissa an idea. "You have something that we need."

"Excuse me," Marissa asked. "Didn't your mom's ever tell you this wasn't the way to ask for a favor?"

"We don't want a favor," Zack said, "and it doesn't really matter if you cooperate or not. Right, Steve?"

"That's what he said," Steve chimed in. "He gave me permission to do this how I wanted. He'd prefer if she didn't die, but the book is really what matters here. Do what you want, Zack."

"What book?" Marissa looked back at Steve, her back to the prep table so she could see all three of them, who, for the moment, we're staying a couple feet away.

"You know what book," Steve said. "You took it from the station."

"Holy shit, you fucks sound like Bedrin," Marissa said. "Wait a minute, did that fat fuck send you? Are you working as his thugs so he can mess with me without having to face me himself?"

"The book," Zack said, beginning to move forward again. "Or else."

"Or else what, you little shit?" Marissa spat at him. "I held back in the police station, but here you're attacking me where I work. No need to hold back now. Bring it."

Zack paused for a second, seeming to rethink what he was going.

"The book," Steve said, "now."

"How about I go get it for you?" Marissa asked, looking at the table in front of her. "It's in the office."

"She lying," said Devin.

"We could kill her and then go find out," Zack offered.

Marissa knew it was now or never; she threw the napkins she was still holding into Zack's face and, kicking her legs up, launched herself over the table, but by the time her feet landed on the other side, all three of them had moved around the edges of the table. She was still blocked from the door. She squared off, getting ready to fight the three of them even though she didn't like the odds.

The bell for the front door of the bar jingled, and she heard someone talking. The three attackers looked at the door, then back to Marissa. She could see the questioning look in their eyes; this was going to be the chance that she needed.

"Just in the back," she called up to the people who'd just entered, "I'll be right up." Marissa smiled at her attackers, almost daring them to continue now that there would be witnesses.

THE LOST

"Don't think this is over bitch," Steven said. "We'll get that book from you soon enough. Just wait." With that, he turned and walked to the back door of the bar, opened it, and called back to Zack and Devin. The three of them left, the door swinging closed behind them, plunging the room back into its semi-darkness. Marissa looked around at all the dishes that they'd scattered when Steve threw the drying rack, "Worst dine and dash ever," she said to the empty room.

Seventeen

A sense of nostalgia washed over McMurray as he walked into the parish office. The anteroom to Father Maria's office was just as McMurray had left it. The same bible verse hung on the wall, "Do not conform to the pattern of this world but be transformed by the renewing of your mind. Then you will be able to test and approve what God's will is—his good, pleasing and perfect will." Romans 12:2, he'd had this superimposed over an image of the World Trade Center standing out against a bright blue sky, much as it had that fateful day. So many people came to see him in the weeks after the towers fell. He knew it was a defining moment for his congregation. He had wanted to help them come to peace with the loss, and it was the best he could think of. Apparently, Father Maria agreed because it was still there. Of course, so were the couches that had been falling apart before he handed over the parish.

"Peter," Father Maria said, walking in from the hallway, his voice smooth with a slight hint of an accent that belied his Manhattan upbringing, "I didn't notice you coming in."

"Just got here," McMurray said, turning around.

Father Maria strode across the room, his vestments flowing behind him like a ceremonial magician leaving the scent of incense in his wake. He seemed at peace in them, comfortable in a way that McMurray struggled to remember feeling. He

THE LOST

remembered wearing them for the last time, the weight of the cloth pulling his shoulders down making him feel as if just wearing the trappings of his office was dragging him down to hell. Watching the youthful Father Maria cross the room, his slightly olive skin contrasting with the white of the vestments.

"I haven't seen you at Mass," Father Maria said as he opened the door to McMurray's old office and stood blocking the entrance. "What brings you here on such a nice Sunday afternoon?"

"I've been to a few of them," McMurray protested, "you seem to be taking care of the congregation."

Father Maria nodded his head a little and said, "God willing." He walked into the office inviting McMurray in, and moved behind his desk. "In truth, they have been keeping me busy. I haven't even had time to update the waiting room. It just seems so depressing in there."

"I hadn't noticed," McMurray mumbled as he looked over the office. Not much had changed; the small table with a glass decanter still sat along the wall by the door. He'd bought it for twice the sticker price from a tag sale that Johnathan Hutchinson, one of his parishioners, held to raise money for a surgery his daughter had needed. At the time, McMurray hoped to raise the family more money, but all of the troubles started and the accusations. Soon that decanter became a symbol of his own failure to lead his people, and he'd used it to drown out those failures. He'd hoped that in leaving it, he could be rid of it. Now it sat encompassed in a warm amber glow as the sun shone in from the window across the room.

Father Maria watched McMurray looking at the decanter, "I kept that because it sometimes helps those who come in here to feel more comfortable talking about what is really bothering them." He crossed over to it and began to pour out two glasses. "I know it's not exactly standard protocol, but I figure if it helps my people, then who am I to judge." He handed a glass to McMurray and took the other with him as he sat behind his oversized oak desk.

"The desk is new," McMurray observed, taking a seat across from Father Maria. The chair was old and worn, and McMurray could almost feel all of the people who had come looking for God's counsel. He felt terrible knowing that they had only found him.

"Oh, this thing?" Father Maria said, tapping the bottom of his glass on the wood. "The old one seemed a bit cheap, and I had this sitting in storage since my parents passed away. My father's old desk." He ran his hand along the decorative edge wistfully, "Don't make 'em like this anymore." He took a sip from his glass and licked his lips, "But I'm sure you didn't come to talk about the furniture. What's on your mind?"

McMurray shifted in the chair and cleared his throat, "I heard that the Hail family has asked you to do Mikey's funeral."

"They did," he leaned back in his high-back leather chair. "They're pretty broken up over the whole thing. He was their only son, and well, you of all people know how much of a lost cause Marissa is."

"Lost cause?"

"Well, they're not so sure of her rehabilitation. I mean she works as a bartender on the highway," he smiled warmly. "If it wasn't for the fact that you owned the place, I'd think it was a front for some drug dealer."

"You would?" McMurray didn't know how to respond. He stared into his cup, the smell of the whiskey enticing him to take a sip. If he did, that would be the end of the day. He thought about the bottle in his trunk and sighed.

THE LOST

"You hear about the heroin epidemic making its way into a small town like this one, and you just pray that our children are spared."

"God willing," he replied.

"So, what was it about the Hail funeral you wanted to know."

"Well," McMurray cleared his throat again, "Marissa asked me to deliver Mikey's eulogy, and I wanted to talk to you about how we could arrange that. I have been thinking . . ."

"Let me stop you there," Father Maria raised his hand slightly over his empty glass, looking for a moment like he would give a benediction to the last few amber drops clinging to the bottom of the glass.

"Excuse me?"

"It's just that," he smiled again and folded his hands on the desk in front of him. "Well, now, this is awkward. I'm not sure how to say this."

"Say what?"

Father Maria sighed and got up to fill his glass again. The sound of falling liquid and the oaky smell of the whiskey filled the room. McMurray rubbed the bridge of his nose, fighting the urge to take a sip from the glass in his hands.

"The family," Father Maria continued, still standing at the table with the decanter, forcing McMurray to turn in his chair to see him, "They have requested a closed service. Given the publicity of the event. They requested that only family be allowed to attend."

"Right, but his sister . . ."

"Is not in charge of the funeral," Father Maria interrupted.

McMurray sat there for a minute before he stood up to face Father Maria. He was taller than the young priest, but there was something about seeing a priest in his full vestments that always disarmed McMurray and had since he was a small child. Standing there in his old office, wearing jeans and a flannel shirt, the smell of whiskey and insolence intermingling, McMurray felt uncertain. Marissa had been adamant that McMurray deliver her brother's eulogy. Still, Father Maria had a point, the parents' wishes were always honored as long as they did not go against the Church's teachings.

"Besides," Father Maria placed a hand on McMurray's shoulder and pointed at the empty glass in his trembling hand, "I think we can agree that you are probably not in the best shape to be delivering any souls to the Maker. Unless, of course, it's Maker's Mark."

McMurray's head spun. He hadn't even noticed drinking the whiskey in his glass. He'd tried to fight the temptation, and losing was one thing, but to not remember losing, Father Maria's words started to make some sense. McMurray wondered if maybe he was right.

"Now," Father Maria continued guiding him from the office with a hand on his shoulder, "why don't you head back to the bar and let Marissa know that her parents have the final say in who sends their son on his final journey."

"But I didn't drink it," McMurray said, looking at the empty glass in his hand.

"I'm sorry, but you did," the young priest tried to take the empty glass from his hand. "I think it's time for you to leave. I have another appointment in a few minutes, and as you can see, I still haven't changed since Mass."

"But I . . ." McMurray started, then with a vehemence seeming from nowhere wrenched the empty glass away from Father Maria and, turning to put it on the table himself, tripped over the rug. He caught himself on the table, causing the

THE LOST

decanter to slide off. Both men watched as the stopper tumbled from the opening and the amber liquid arched toward the top. A rainbow cut across the wall as the sun caught the edge of the ornate glass tumbling through the air. The fall was silent, but the landing caused a deafening crash as the decanter shattered on the hardwood sending the amber liquid careening across the floor and soaking into the edge of the rug, darkening the red border as it absorbed the pooling liquid.

"Peter," Father Maria reached out for McMurray's arm, his voice harsh and a little forceful, "I think you need to go home now. Should I call someone? You're clearly in no shape to drive."

"I didn't drink it."

"Unless you poured it out onto my rug, which by the lack of spot under your chair, I'm rather sure that you didn't," he motioned. "I'm not sure what you think happened to it?"

McMurray looked at the shattered decanter on the floor and thought again about Jonathan and his daughter's surgery. Jonathan had sold his house and had to move back in with his family in the next town over. McMurray called him once after the move to check on him and his daughter, but the news hadn't been good more surgeries, unknown prognosis. He had hung up from that call, said a prayer, and drank heavily. Now, each shard reflected a failure to help one of his flock, each broken promise. He bent to start picking them up. His tears, falling from sunken eyes, flowed freely across his grey stubble.

"Don't, Peter," Father Maria said, trying to help lift him to his feet.

McMurray shrugged him off and continued collecting the shards. Looking at each one, picking up the pieces felt good. He was vaguely aware of a catharsis of sorts as if each piece he collected was one step closer to something meaningful. Father Maria tried to lift McMurray from under his arms, forcing him to his feet, but McMurray was stouter than the young priest and twisted from his grasp, slipping on the pool of whiskey. McMurray lost his footing and fell to his knee, putting his hand, still clasping the pieces of the decanter, down to stop his fall. He didn't even feel the smooth edge of the glass slice through his palm, but as he brought his hand up, the thick blood had already started dripping from the edge of his closed fist.

"Peter, you getting blood everywhere," Father Maria said. "Please, get up before you make more of a fool of yourself."

McMurray rose to his feet and dropped the bloody pieces of the decanter into the trash bin by the door, and looked at the blood pooling in his left palm as if it were someone else's. "I'm speaking at Mickey's funeral. It may not be the eulogy," he said with confidence long missing in his voice, "but I will speak." He pulled a handkerchief from his pocket and wrapped it around his hand, tying it off using his other hand and his teeth. He would not fail his flock again. He wouldn't fail Marissa.

"I'll see what I can do," Father Maria conceded. "But Peter, be careful what you say. The Church defended you when you were accused, but it was you who walked away. The bishops weren't unhappy with your resignation after the reports of drunken sermons and when more kids stepped forward. But they paid up and kept you out of prison and out of the papers. The fact that you stuck around here was surprising enough, but don't forget who left who here."

"And what's that supposed to mean?"

"These people stopped coming. They didn't want to be your flock," Father Maria spat the word out. "You were disgraced and killing this parish. Your resignation was more of a formality than anything else. You left the Church when that Hutchinson girl died. You stopped believing in any power higher than that," he motioned at the pool of whiskey on the floor. "Do you really

THE LOST

think another kid's death is the best place to make your appearance?"

McMurray didn't respond. Looking again at his hand, he curled his fingers over the handkerchief and reached for the door. As he did, a small red beetle dropped from the ceiling and landed on his closed fingers. The beetle seemed to move around the curves of his fist, looking for shelter. He looked up to see a group of beetles in the corner of the ceiling over by the door. McMurray turned to look at Father Maria, who was standing stock-still, watching him expectedly.

"I will speak for Mikey. With or without your blessing. I made a promise."

"I'll talk to his parents, but you might want to prepare that lost soul of yours that she might not get her wish."

McMurray looked back at the beetle on his hand as it started burrowing under the bandage. He pulled it off, looked at it for a second, then said, "I never liked the ones without spots," and flicked it into the pool of whiskey. The beetle struggled to right itself and, though McMurray was sure it was a trick of the light, seemed to shrink. He turned to Father Maria and, motioning to the beetle as it struggled in the edge of the pool of whiskey, said, "You're infested."

Father Maria flinched, and McMurray pointed to the ceiling, "Those damn ladybugs get in here every year." Father Maria seemed to relax a little.

"That they do."

"I will be speaking," McMurray said, then with one more glance at the shards of the decanter on the floor, he turned and left Father Maria to clean the rest up.

On his way out of the narthex, he saw Geo escorted by Officer Bedrin walking in. Geo looked at him and smiled. McMurray, still feeling the adrenalin rush of his argument with

Father Maria, nodded briskly and continued on his way. As he passed them, he saw Geo lean over to Officer Bedrin and say something he couldn't quite make out. McMurray walked to his car and opened the trunk with his keys. Leaving the keys in the lock, he pulled out his bottle of Jamison and twisted off the cap. The sweet smell washed over him. He brought the bottle to his lips, the fumes calling him like a siren of oblivion.

    Father Maria's words echoed in his head: Don't forget who left who here. He lowered the bottle and slowly put the cap back on. He would not let his weakness cause him to break his promise to Marissa. He said he'd speak for Mikey; he owed him that much. Mikey and his friends had urged him to reconsider leaving the priesthood; they were part of the reason he'd even stayed in town. Now they were dead, and he'd failed to help protect them, to guide them. The bottle felt heavy in his hand, and the taste of the whiskey he just drank lingered uncomfortably in his mouth. Looking at the bottle casting an amber glow on the ground where the sun pierced the glass, his stomach rolled. He took a deep breath and, clenching his jaw, silently promised himself that he would not drink again. He brought over his shoulder to throw it into the woods by the church parking lot, imagining it shattering against a tree, the tiny pieces of glass falling like ice at the edge of the forest. He smiled at the image in his mind until Destiny Hutchinson's face, laying in her coffin as it had so many nights, reflected in each of the imaginary shards. She was so young, so innocent, and God took her and destroyed her family. He lowered the bottle, feeling tears burning behind his eyes. McMurray closed them tightly, but her face floated there too, behind his eyelids as it had years ago. He tore off the cap from the bottle and cried as the liquid fire burned his throat.

THE LOST

EIGHTEEN

Marissa leaned back against the freezer door and slid to the ground, all the energy draining from her legs as the adrenalin from her confrontation with the four boys subsided. She put her head in her hand and shook. Memories of being cornered in the kitchen at the prison flooded back to her. That time had been worse, much worse, landed her in the hospital for a week. After that, she learned to fight, and she decided she was never going back there. Now here she was, seconds away from having to fight and run the risk of someone pressing charges, and she knew Bedrin would make sure she went away for that. She sighed, thankful to be saved by an unlocked door.

"Hello," called a voice from the front. "Everything alright back there?"

Marissa leaned her head back, feeling the coolness coming off the metal freezer door, and sighed. "Coming," she called and began to stretch her adrenaline sore muscles.

She walked from the backroom, careful not to kick any pans scattered through the kitchen; a single man was sitting in the middle of the bar, directly in front of the taps. He seemed too well dressed to be the standard customer, but there was still something familiar about him. His bald head and reddish grey mustache were what she first noticed, but it was his eyes that drew her in. They were small and dark and seemed to disappear into the shadows of their deep sockets. She could have sworn she'd seen him somewhere before but couldn't place him. Walking over to him, she grabbed a new bar towel and tossed it over her shoulder so she could wipe down the area in front of him. She cleaned it regularly but found people liked to see the area wiped down anyway.

"What can I get ya?" she asked, working hard to keep her voice steady.

"How about a Bloody Mary?" the man said.

She turned to start making it, her hands still shaking slightly, causing the vodka to slosh over the edge of the glass.

"You look upset," the man had clearly watched her pour.

"It's been a tough couple of days," Marissa said, trying to be noncommittal without dismissing him outright.

"You and me both," he said with a sigh and leaned forward on the bar and watching her work.

"Celery?" He nodded in agreement, and she continued, "I'll be right back. We keep 'em cold in the back."

"I'll be here."

Marissa still couldn't place where she'd seen him before. He was so familiar, but she couldn't figure it out. She grabbed a few sticks of celery from the cooler, just in case he wanted more than one, and went back up front to finish the drink. She found him right where she left him, leaning forward on the bar and watching the door. He looked down at his cell phone and scrolled through something when she entered, but she knew he'd watched her leave. It wasn't uncommon, and his athletic build wasn't unpleasant, but there was something about him that made her uncomfortable with it, something more than the fact that he had to be in his forties.

THE LOST

"So barkeep," he said with a lighthearted voice, "what's eatin' you?"

"What?"

"Somethings on your mind," he said, his hand brushing against hers as he took the drink from her. "Even a blind man could see that."

"It's nothing, just some kids I had to kick out."

"Really?" He asked; a disarming smile flashed across his face. "What were they up to?"

"They were roughhousing a bit," she was unsure why she didn't want to let him know what had happened. "Nothing I couldn't handle."

The man nodded and sipped his Bloody Mary. "So you handled that," he said, "what's eatin' you?"

"I told you," she turned to clean up the vodka she'd spilled.

"I'm sorry to pry, but my job has me dealing with people who aren't quite willing to tell me everything. I've gotten pretty good at telling when someone is not giving me the whole story."

"An interrogator then?"

"Oh, no," he said, putting his glass down, "nothing as blunt as that. You don't remember me do you?"

"Should I?" she said, then thinking better of it. "You do look familiar, but I can't place it."

"I was here about a week ago. On my way to see a client."

Marissa shook her head, a habit she had when trying to remember something, "Shit, that's right. Sorry, you're that public defender who was going to help Geo. How's that going?"

"Well, I'm not exactly a public defender, but I did take his case pro bono. Can't really talk about an ongoing case, confidentiality and all, but he is quite the special case."

"Well, I hope you win," Marissa said with a smile.

"Me too," he took another sip of his drink and leaned in toward her. "I have a confession, though."

"Well," Marissa was warming up to him, she remembered that she'd misjudged him last time and didn't want to make the same mistake, "that is the trade of the barkeep, isn't it?"

He chuckled, "That it is."

"So," she tossed the bar cloth over her shoulder, leaning on the bar in an almost comical way, "what's eatin' you?"

"No fair," he said, "that was my line?"

"Too bad," she smiled at him, "I'm stealing it."

"Funny you say that. You see, I was at the station the other day and overheard the local police talking about some red-headed barkeep that was in a bit of trouble with the law. I thought to myself that if it was that same barkeep that poured such a good pint of beer last time I was here, I needed to see if I could help her out."

"Oh, Bedrin. He's got a bit of a big mouth."

"Yes, Officer Bedrin does seem to like to hear himself talk. But, at least, in this case, that could be to your benefit."

"How do you figure?"

He leaned back and looked hurt. "Because it brought me back here." A broad smile crossed his face, and he pulled out a business card and placed it on the bar. "Lucius Tanis, Attorney at your service. But please, call me Luc."

"Well, Luc, I don't think I could afford your legal fees," she motioned around the bar. "The tips here don't exactly leave me with much expendable income."

"Consider it an investment."

"Doesn't matter what I consider it, I can't make money appear out of thin air."

"No," he chuckled again, "consider it an investment I'm making. You see, the world is horribly short barkeeps that can make a good pour and a good mixed drink. I mean, if you can pull off the right proportions for a long island iced tea, I think I might just fall in love with you."

Marissa didn't know how to respond, looked at his card, but didn't take it. Something inside her was screaming at her to refuse the offer. No one did something for nothing. She tried to figure out his angle but couldn't. "What's the catch?"

"No catch," he said. "I might be joking about the long island ice tea thing, not really sure myself there," he smiled, "but you need my help. Should be an easy case, from what I heard. You seem like a nice kid, and you don't want to go back to prison, right?"

"You'll help, just like that?"

"Just like that," he smiled warmly. "I'm one of the good guys."

Marissa thought about it. She'd been hoping that this whole thing would just blow over, that Bedrin would find the lost book, and they'd drop the charges, but that plan didn't seem to be working out. "Let me think about it?"

"Alright, but I just stopped in here on my way to an appointment, so I'm going to need an answer by the time I finish this spectacular concoction you made."

Marissa left him to his drink and went over to finish the prep she had started before the boys came in. She was cutting up her third lemon when she heard a loud slurping sound coming from the bar. She turned around to see Luc, a ridiculous grin on his face as he loudly finished his Bloody Mary. She walked over, slapped her hand down on his business card, and said, "You got yourself a deal."

"You won't regret this," he said. Then he paid for his drink and walked to the door. Before he left, he turned around and said,

"You know, Marissa, if I get you off, you're gonna owe me." Then he left.

Looking at the business card on the bar, Marissa wondered if she'd done the right thing accepting the offer. Something about the thought of owing him, something about the way he said it, didn't sit well with her. He's one of the good guys, she reminded herself, then sweeping the business card into her pocket, she finished the morning prep.

Nineteen

Marissa wondered if she was making the right choice driving to the funeral with Father McMurray. Her parents had wanted her to come with them to the limo. Still, after the blowout they'd had over her insistence that Father McMurray spoke, she wasn't sure that she wanted to deal with the overwhelming silence and the continuous looks of disappointment they gave her. Marissa knew they blamed her. She told Mikey about the cabin in the woods, and Bedrin's questioning her didn't help any. She hadn't told them about it, but they found out all the same. Small towns are notorious for their gossip. But here she was, in the passenger seat of McMurray's sedan, smelling the whiskey fumes that reached out from him. She knew there was a bottle in there somewhere, maybe more than one, but he'd insisted on driving.

There was something about knowing he was a functioning alcoholic that let her accept things like this. He is driving, he will speak at the funeral, and he is drunk. Marissa didn't like the last part, but she didn't have much power to change it, though it never stopped her from trying. She wanted him to speak. She needed it, and she was pretty sure that he did too. McMurray had baptized both her and her brother. They'd grown up in his church. He'd come to see her when she was at her lowest, and he had believed, more than she did even, in her ability to come back from there. By the time she got out, he was no longer the priest, Father Maria had taken over, and things were never the same. Looking over at him in the driver's seat, a grey shadow of the vibrant man he used to be, slouched as if the weight of the world rested on his shoulders, and he was crumbling beneath it.

"Thanks for doing this," she said, more to break the silence than anything else.

"What?" he asked, looking over at her. Then recognition hit him, "Of course, Mikey was always a good kid. Still I wish you had gotten your parent's permission before you asked me," he paused for a moment to let his comment sink in before adding, "but I'm happy they agreed to let me speak."

"Begrudgingly."

"Still tough between you?"

"To say the least. It's like they blame me for Mikey's death," she looked at the side of his face, with his stubble shaved, he looks more like his old self. She thought of herself, just a teenager, when he came into the police station after she was arrested that first time. "They reminded me this morning that I used to go drinking where he was killed. As if I forgot. I told him about the fuckin' place."

"And?"

"And what?"

"And do you feel like it was your fault?"

Marissa bristled at the question. He was using the inflection that only a priest or a shrink uses, that one where they already know the answer but are asking the question for your own benefit. If it were anyone else, Marissa would have gotten out, whether the car was moving or not, by McMurray knew that, and he also knew he could get away with asking the question.

"Of course not."

"Then why does it make you so angry?"

THE LOST

"You ever been accused of killing someone? No, I didn't think so."

"Neither were you."

"Same thing, and you know it. My folks think that if I didn't tell them to go there that night, then their golden child would still be alive." She could feel the tears on her cheeks but didn't wipe them away.

"What do you think?"

Marissa didn't answer. If she hadn't told them about the shack, told them to go catch a movie, or even told them to fuck off, they'd still be alive. She could complain about how Mikey gets a car, and she never got anything. She could watch how her parents looked at him with pride and hope as he graduated; she could hide in his shadow and let her own disappointment fade away in his success. She'd told them where it was. They were killed while they were there. She didn't physically kill them, but that doesn't mean it wasn't her fault.

McMurray left the question hanging in the air as he parked the car at the cemetery. Father Maria wouldn't agree to let McMurray speak at the church, but he decided to allow it at the graveside, only after Marissa's parents finally caved to her relentless badgering. She opened the door and was getting out when Father McMurray put his hand on her shoulder. She stopped and looked at him. His eyes were serene and friendly, so opposite to how her family saw her, but they screamed in their sunken sockets, tortured by some unspeakable demon.

"Marissa," he paused, "if you keep on this path, it will only lead to ruin and more loss."

"No offense Father," she pulled her hand away, "but there's not that much left to lose." Marissa closed the door and walked over to the small group of mourners her parents deemed worthy of attending Mickey's funeral. In a way, she was glad they had closed the service. The last thing she wanted was to be surrounded by a bunch of fake teenagers trying to use her brother's death to ramp up their angst or give themselves a martyr complex or, worse still, get a few extra hits on their social media accounts. She was a bit surprised they'd put her on the list. She saw Geo giving her mother a hug; it made sense that he'd be there. People like Bedrin might think he had something to do with Mikey's death, but he and Mikey had been friends since sixth grade, countless sleepovers, birthdays, dinners, they'd never doubted his innocence. He was like a surrogate son for them at this point, a replacement for the son she had robbed them of. She smiled bitterly at the thought and wiped the tears away from her cheeks.

Marissa took a deep breath and walked over to her parents. Her father put his hand on her shoulder. He used to be such a warm person, but since she'd come home from prison, the most he'd do is pat her back as if she was diseased. Her mother hugged her, not with the same emotion that she'd embraced Geo, but she at least wasn't afraid of catching something. They shook Father McMurray's hand with even less warmth.

"Geo," McMurray turned to him, "I'm glad to see you here. I was worried that Officer Bedrin wouldn't let you come."

"Ya, it was close. We met with Father Maria about it. Bedrin was afraid that since I had been a suspect in the," he paused, looked at my mother and back at McMurray, "well, you know, everything that happened, Bedrin was afraid I'd do more harm than good coming here."

"Had been?" Marissa asked.

"I was just telling your folks when you came over," he said with a smile, "they cleared me yesterday. I mean, they don't want me going anywhere for a while, but at least I'm not living in the police station anymore. So, there's that."

THE LOST

"Thank God," Father McMurray intoned, clapping his hands onto both Geo's shoulders at the same time. "I tried to tell Mathew he was barking up the wrong tree. The four of you were always such good friends. I couldn't believe that they were even looking at you for it.

"I was there," Geo shrugged, "I was covered," he paused again, looking at my parents, and didn't finish. "I had the truck and the book, though I've no clue where it is now. You know they say they lost it. I'd tried to get it to give back to Jackie's folks, but when I mentioned it to them, they didn't know what book I was talking about."

"Either way," Marissa said, "I'm glad you're cleared. Take it from me. Bedrin's a pain in the ass."

"Marissa," her father said, "have some respect."

"Anyway," she continued as if he hadn't spoken, "I know Mikey would have been happy you're here. Remember the time he broke his arm."

"He was so miserable," her mother said, her hand going to her chest.

"Ya, he was," Marissa smiled wistfully, "but then you called out of work and came over with that stupid video game. What was it?"

"Lego Batman?"

"That's the one. You two stayed up all night playing it, and that morning was the first time I'd seen him smile in a week. You looked out for each other. Thanks for that." Marissa's voice cracked. She bit her lip and took a deep breath. Her father reached out for her but let his hand hang in the air between them. "Excuse me," she said and then turned to go look at the casket. She knew his body wasn't in there; they never had found it. They weren't burying him; they were burying his jacket, boots, and a picture of him. Marissa looked back at her parents, now talking to the next-door neighbor. She felt like a traitor standing there at his graveside, fighting back the tears, as if it wasn't her right to grieve. She caused this, and everyone knew it.

McMurray put his hand on her shoulder and gave it a light squeeze. "They look happy in their grief."

Before she could ask what he meant by that, Father Maria asked everyone to be seated and began the service. Marissa moved to sit next to her mother but saw her mother usher Geo into the seat and moved to an empty seat on the other side. Someone offered their condolences, but Marissa just nodded and mumbled a thank you as Father Maria began his eulogy. It was nice, she still would have preferred McMurray to deliver the eulogy, but her father refused. He didn't believe that McMurray was innocent of the charges against him and didn't approve of Marissa working at his bar either. She'd worn them down to let him speak, but the eulogy was out of the question. She'd given in when her father mentioned that he was paying for the funeral, and he would honor his son the best way possible, and that didn't include having some drunk rambling about a God he betrayed when he fucked those kids. Marissa had almost hit him right then and there, she knew that the charges were bogus and told him as much, but he stopped listening to her years ago.

Marissa realized that she hadn't heard most of what Father Maria had said but focused as he invited Father McMurray up to speak a few words, Marissa thought it was funny that he'd called him Peter instead of Father, but it didn't surprise her. They crossed right in front of her, and Father Maria took McMurray's hand to shake it, put his other hand on McMurray's shoulder, and, smiling, leaned in saying just loud enough for Marissa to overhear, "Listen, you drunk screw-up, I can smell the whiskey on your breath. This family has been through enough. If you're too drunk,

THE LOST

I'll cover for you, say you're too upset to speak, but if you go up there and make a mockery of this funeral, it's your neck."

McMurray visibly tensed, squeezing Father Maria's hand hard enough that his knuckles went white, and said something that Marissa couldn't hear. Then let go of his hand and put both hands on Father Maria's shoulders, said, "God bless you, Father Maria," and walked past him up toward the podium. Father Maria went ashen as he shook his head and moved to stand at the foot of the casket. McMurray stopped at the head of the coffin and placed his hand on it, bowing his head for a few moments in silence while Father Maria glared across the casket at him. Marissa had always known some animosity between the two men, but she had never seen so stark a portrayal. McMurray, in a suit that was clearly made for a larger man, looked frail and small. If he hadn't shaven his ever-present stubble, even Marissa had to admit he would have looked more like a vagrant off the street than a priest. At the same time, Father Maria, in his freshly pressed vestments and collar accentuating his thin but fit form, stood like a man fully aware that he was in control of the situation, a stance that the anger in his eyes did not reflect. Seemingly unaware of the look from Father Maria, McMurray straightened up and walked to the podium.

"I wanted to thank Mr. and Mrs. Hail and Marissa for allowing me the opportunity to say a few words in honor of Michael. Having known the family," McMurray surveyed the crowd, "most of your families, for years, I feel a kinship with all of you in this community." Several people shifted in their seats behind Marissa as McMurray continued. "Michael Hail was a special young man, a man of promise and a man of praise. He was quick to offer his assistance to those who needed it, and he was also quick to forgive, a quality I know is shared by his sister Marissa and her parents."

Eric Johnson

A noise on the other side of the folding chairs caught Marissa's attention, and she looked over to see her father standing up, shedding her mother's arm, and stalking away from the funeral. Geo took Marissa's mother's hand and squeezed it as he whispered something into her ear and followed after her father. Marissa turned her attention to the several other noises that permeated the small gathering and watched as several other people stood to leave, taking the cue from her own father. She turned back around and made eye contact with Father McMurray, offering him an apologetic smile, hoping he would continue. The smile he returned to her didn't reach his eyes, but he drew in a deep breath and continued his remarks.

"As a child, Michael would come to services, and, on days when his parents permitted, he would stay after the service and ask me questions about religion and God. His curiosity and thirst for knowledge knew no bounds, nor did his drive to uncover the truth. That is probably the quality that I will miss most now that he has gone home to find all of his answers from the Source."

While Father McMurray continued to talk about Mickey, Marissa couldn't help but picture her brother standing in front of God, quizzing Him on all of the things that he'd found wrong with religion and life in general. All those questions that he'd never found satisfactory answers to. Despite herself, she smiled at the image, then returned her attention to Father McMurray. She felt the guilt that she had held like a security blanket melt away, and for the first time since her brother's death, she let herself cry.

TWENTY

The tears had dried on Marissa's cheeks by the time the crowd, smaller after Father McMurray's speech, filed past the coffin and the remnants of her family. McMurray watched her as she numbly shook hands with people and accepted condolences. His speech may have been about her brother, but it was made for her, and McMurray was glad that he'd finally broken through the shell that she'd erected since her brother's death. As much as he hated seeing her in pain, her tear-stained cheeks and red puffy eyes were what she needed, and he'd seen enough funerals to know it. He'd also been to enough funerals to know that he was not needed here. Filtering through the line like all of the bereaved, McMurray faded into the background and his own thoughts.

"That was nice," an unfamiliar voice spoke next to him as he stood watching, lost in his thoughts.

"I'm sorry?" McMurray turned to see a woman, probably mid-forties, in an official-looking suit.

"What you said about the kid," she said, "it was nice."

"Oh, thank you," McMurray tried to remember if he'd met the woman before but kept coming up blank. "It's a big loss for the community."

"Always is when it's a kid. All that potential squandered," she stood next to him quietly, watching the crowd like he was.

After a while, she continued, "What I don't understand is why everyone left when you started talking."

"You're not from around here then," McMurray retorted, unable to hide the bitter edge to his voice.

"Nope, I was just here for the investigation," she looked over at McMurray. "Not sure we've met, Magdalena Dias."

"Peter McMurray."

"You clearly knew the victim well," she said, turning back to the funeral. "I'm sorry for your loss."

"He was a good kid, but I've found that funerals are more often for the living than the dead. I'm really here for his sister. She was the one that needed to hear what I had to say," he scoffed, "clearly her father wasn't interested."

"That was odd," they stood in silence again. "What do you do around here, Peter, if you don't mind my asking."

"Nothing much anymore. I own a dive on the edge of town. Marissa basically runs the place for me."

"Really?"

"You don't approve?" McMurray looked at her; he was used to the disapproval by now; he'd come to expect it.

"No, I didn't think that at all. Just an odd person to have speak at a kids' funeral, that's all. You talked about him as if you'd known him his whole life. Didn't you mention something about him talking to you after Mass or something?"

"That was a lifetime ago."

"What do you mean?"

"I used to be the priest for this parish. Baptized him and his friends. But that was another life." McMurray shivered and took a small flask out of his jacket pocket, offering it to his companion.

"Why not," she said, accepting the flask and taking a quick sip. "You have a strange town here, Father," she said as

THE LOST

McMurray took a long pull from the flask. "This has been the weirdest investigation of my career. Deaths' all ruled accidental caused by an animal attack." She watched as Geo talked with Marissa and her mother. "Kid had a killer attorney. Got all of the charges dropped."

"You don't sound happy about it."

"Something doesn't sit right by me. But, without a murder weapon or bodies, it's tough to prove murder."

"He's a good kid."

"So everyone says."

"He was Mikey's best friend."

"No offense Father, but you had better things to say about the kid who died than his friend did. They may have been friends, but from my experience, people suck."

"You don't need to call me Father. No one does anymore," McMurray said, changing the subject. "I haven't been in the pulpit in years."

"It suits you."

"What does?"

"The pulpit, the title. Some people just fit," she looked at him, her eyes seeming to size him up on the spot. "You, you fit. This," she motioned at the funeral, "this doesn't."

McMurray didn't answer right away; he just watched as Marissa's mother invited Geo, who'd returned alone near the end of his speaking, to join them in receiving condolences. He stood a little taller than the two women, more similar to Mikey's height. He thought back to their catechism classes a few years before, his last year. Geo and Mikey were inseparable. "You're wrong," he said finally.

"I hope so," she replied. She nodded, then turned and walked away toward the parking lot, calling back over her shoulder as she went, "I haven't been wrong about a person yet."

Eric Johnson

Her words struck McMurray as a little overconfident, but there was a casualness about them that he couldn't ignore. He also realized that she wasn't just talking about Geo and the funeral. She'd said that being in a pulpit fit him. In a way, she was right; he'd once felt so comfortable up in front of a congregation, his people. He'd done everything he could to guide them well, but the accusations and the Church's response had so shaken his perception of the world, of his world. At the time, the Church had been so willing to shift him to a new parish and pay off his accusers. He knew they were false accusations, he'd loved his kids, but he would never have touched them, never even been tempted. He was here to pray for them, not on them.

When he left the Church, he'd left everything about it, the ceremony, the responsibility, the faith. One by one, his friends abandoned him, his people turned their backs on him, and in the end, only Marissa seemed to think him worthy of her time. But he'd helped her when no one else had; she could be doing it out of a feeling of obligation. Other than the strange woman he'd just talked to, Marissa is the only one who still called him Father. He didn't even think of himself that way. McMurray was no one's father, no one's guide. How could anyone have faith in him if he didn't have faith in himself? They couldn't, and yet Marissa did.

He watched her hug her mother and Geo as the group around the casket dispersed, presumably headed to the funeral reception. To break bread with the family, McMurray was not invited to. Marissa's father's response to his talking at the funeral was evidence enough of that. There was no room for him at their table, no matter how much Marissa said he should come. He'd come here to speak for her, to her, and now that was over, he'd go home and drown his thoughts in whiskey once more. McMurray took a drink from the flask he'd offered Officer Dias and put it in his jacket pocket. Some people just fit, he scoffed silently at the

THE LOST

words echoing through him. She didn't know who he'd become, who everyone else knew. He was no longer the town shepherd; he was the town drunk. For the first time in a long time, the thought did not give him any comfort, neither did the weight of the flask in his jacket pocket.

A just God didn't allow his faithful to be wrongly accused. A forgiving God didn't punish the innocent with unbearable burdens. No, McMurray thought bitterly, if God exists, he's a God of shreds and patches, a God of misery who gets his jollies off watching those who love him and work in his name be crushed by the world He created. Hope, joy, love had no place in His world. And McMurray didn't want to be a priest to that God, one that killed children alone in the woods and didn't let their bodies be interred appropriately, one that tore families apart.

He watched Marissa hug her mother and head over toward him, and he took a deep breath. That Magdalena woman had gotten him worked up, and he didn't want Marissa to end up worrying about him.

"Hey Padre," she said as she came up to him. "Thank you for what you said. It really was special."

"Your brother was a good guy," McMurray said as Geo came up behind Marissa. "He deserved more than a memorial."

"He did," she agreed. "Are you sure I can't convince you to come to the reception at my parent's house?"

McMurray smiled sadly, "I'm not sure I'd really be welcome. You saw your father's response to me getting up to speak."

"He's just —"

"He's just in line with half the town," McMurray interrupted. "Thank you for the invitation, but I'm going to pass."

"Don't worry," Geo said from behind her, "I'll make sure that she gets home safe."

Eric Johnson

"Thank you, Geo," McMurray said, shaking his hand, "and I'm sorry that you had to go through everything. Mikey was a good friend and being wrongly accused —" McMurray trailed off.

"Thanks again," Marissa said and threw her arms around McMurray, pulling him unexpectedly into a hug, which he returned cautiously, aware that there were people who might see this as inappropriate, one more sign of his guilt. "I'll see you at the Pub tomorrow. Bright and early. Breakfast isn't going to serve itself."

When Marissa and Geo turned to leave, Geo put his arm around her shoulders, and McMurray watched the two of them walk off toward the parking lot. They seemed right, happy, despite the situation. He knew that Geo had always had a thing for Marissa, Mikey'd never really noticed, but McMurray had. It would be good for her to spend some time with people closer to her age. He smiled at the thought of this tragedy finally bringing them together and wondered how Michael would have felt about it. He reached into his pocket and absently took out his flask, opened it, and brought it to his lips. Instead of tipping it back, he lowered it, looked at the abyss waiting inside, and screwed the lid back on.

THE LOST

TWENTY—ONE

"I told you, Henry," Father Maria's voice grated against McMurray's thoughts, "once a drunk, always a drunk."

McMurray thought about arguing that he hadn't actually drunk anything, but he knew the argument would be hollow and untrue. Instead, he nodded at Father Maria and Henry Hail and said, "Mr. Hail, thank you for letting me speak about Michael on behalf of Marissa today. Your son was a special young man."

"You have no right," Henry Hail started, his eyes puffy and red from crying, "to speak for anyone in my family. I agreed to let you speak because my wife wanted me to humor Marissa, no other reason. The mere fact that you went through with this blasphemy shows how little regard you have for my son and my family." He grabbed the lapel of McMurray's worn sports coat, flipping it open to reveal the inside pocket that McMurray had slipped his flask. "And drunk nonetheless. You waste of fucking space. If you ever come near my family again—"

Father Maria put his hand on Mr. Hail's arm, placing himself between the men. "Henry," he said in a soft, calm voice, "Is this what you want to remember about Mikey's funeral?"

"I'm sorry, Father, but this drunken piece of shit has no right," despite his words, McMurray could see some of the fire leaving Mr. Hail's eyes. "Just going up there, sounding like he cared, like he knew my son," tears filled his eyes. "He ruined

Mikey's funeral," he turned to McMurray, "as if burying my son wasn't bad enough to listen to your fake-ass shit. I just – it's just too much."

"I know Henry," Father Maria glared at McMurray, "let me speak to him for a moment. Go, be with your family. They need you right now."

The last of the fight left Mr. Hail, and his shoulders slumped, "You're right, Father. Let them know I'll be there soon. I just need to say goodbye to Mikey." Then turning to McMurray, "This isn't over between us, not by a long shot." Then he turned and walked back toward the grave.

"Well, that was ugly," Father Maria said as he watched Mr. Hail leave.

"Emotions have always run hot with the Hails," McMurray said, pulling out his keys. "Besides, Michael was close to his father, this is hard on the whole family, but I think Mr. Hail is taking it a bit harder."

"Of course, Mikey was his only son."

"If he needs to take some of that anger for his son's death out on me," McMurray continued as he and Father Maria moved toward the parking lot, "so be it. I've had worse said about me."

Father Maria stopped in his tracks, "I wasn't talking about Henry."

"I'm sorry?"

"You should be," Father Maria said. "What you did up there was ugly. I mean, going up there in the first place when we both know that flask is probably empty at this point. I just thank the Lord that Henry left before you began speaking. If he heard what you said, I'm not sure I would have been able to calm him down so easily just now. Then hugging his daughter in front of everyone, someone with your history should be more careful. I know she's of legal age but have some decency."

THE LOST

"What do you mean by that?" McMurray turned toward Father Maria, straitening up to look the younger priest in the eye.

"I think we both know what I mean," Father Maria stared back at him, the accusation burning in his eyes.

McMurray turned back to his car without saying anything opened the driver's door. Father Maria stepped aside and leaned against the hood of the vehicle.

"Do you mind?"

"You weren't planning on driving," Father Maria asked, raising his eyebrows in mock concern, "in your condition?"

"My condition is none of your business," McMurray could feel his adrenaline beginning to rise. He knew that Father Maria was goading him, and he knew it was working.

"Maybe not," Father Maria said as he stood up from the hood of McMurray's car and moved toward the approaching police cruiser, "but I'm sure Officer Bedrin might be interested in it."

The curser came to a stop just short of blocking McMurray's car from leaving, and Officer Michael Bedrin rolled down the passenger window. McMurray closed the driver's door, curious what Father Maria was going to do. He knew he hadn't drunk too much, but he did just have a pull when that Magdalena woman talked to him, so if Maria pushed the issue and forced Bedrin to administer a breathalyzer test, McMurray wasn't so sure he would pass it. He cursed under his breath and walked over to the cruiser to hear what the two men were saying.

"– understandably upset by the situation," Father Maria finished as McMurray came into earshot.

"Michael," McMurray greeted, "it was nice of you to come, given your history with the family."

Eric Johnson

"Mikey came in a few times to bail out his sister. He was a good kid," Bedrin said. "Besides, the boss wanted me to keep an eye on Geo."

"You guys still think he did something?" McMurray asked.

"We had to close the case, lack of evidence, but we're keeping an eye on him." Bedrin motioned to McMurray's car, "Going to the reception?"

"I am not," McMurray said.

"I'm not really sure that Peter is welcome given his current state," Father Maria added.

"Current state?"

"You heard him speak," Father Maria said as an answer.

Bedrin nodded but didn't say anything.

The men turned to look at McMurray, waiting to see what he would do. He could see their eyes drift from him to his car and back again. The moment expanded for McMurray as he considered his options. If he took his car, Maria would certainly send Bedrin after him, suggesting that he was too drunk to drive. Although a good man at heart, Bedrin would be obligated to pull him over and breathalyze him, or at the very least follow him until he did something that he could be pulled over for, and McMurray knew he was not the best driver. He'd be arrested, they'd search him and his car, find the flask and the bottle in the trunk, that'd be it. Arrest, court, more shame. If he left his car, he'd tacitly be admitting that Maria and Hail were right to accuse him of being drunk at the funeral. They'd tell Marissa, and she might believe them. She had seen him take a drink before they left the car. She'd probably forgive him even if he was drunk, but he didn't know who she'd believe.

"Well, gentlemen," McMurray said, nodding to them, "I won't keep you any longer." McMurray turned back to his car and locked the doors before beginning home.

THE LOST

"Aren't you going to take your car?" Father Maria asked.

He looked at the young priest, standing tall in his black, funereal vestments leaning against the cruiser, a smug smile of superiority painted across his face. "No, I think I want to get some fresh air. Clear my head."

"Probably best," Maria nodded.

"Do you want a ride home," Bedrin asked. "It's quite a hike."

"Thank you, Michael, but that won't be necessary."

"Have a safe walk," Maria said before turning his attention back into the curser.

As he walked away, McMurray could hear the two men continue their previous conversation. He couldn't hear the words, but they clearly were getting along well, which annoyed McMurray for some reason he couldn't place. There was no reason that Officer Bedrin shouldn't get along with the new priest. There was no betrayal in their camaraderie, nothing even out of place, but it bothered him all the same.

Occupied in thought, he walked the back roads toward his home on the other side of town. He decided to skirt the center, keeping to the side streets to avoid running into Mr. Hail as he left the cemetery to join the rest of his family. He was a good man, but good men going through hard times can do things they regret later. McMurray didn't want Marissa's father to have to deal with guilt on his behalf on top of everything else. Besides being one of the few remaining lovely days in the fall, McMurray enjoyed the birds that he knew were going south soon. McMurray had always liked to hike when he was younger. During his time as the youth minister, when he first began at the parish in this town, he'd take the kids on nature hikes. Thinking back, those hikes were the closest he'd ever felt to God. He explained the importance of God's creation and delivered a sermon to the tired youths at the peak of a local hill, one everyone from the area called the mountain.

He considered taking a detour up the mountain when a white BMW skidded to a stop on the shoulder in front of him, and almost before the car had come to a complete stop, the driver's door flew open. McMurray stopped dead in his tracks and watched the driver get out and stalked toward him, fists clenched at his side and malice in his red, puffy eyes.

"Mr. Hail," McMurray said, putting both hands out in front of him to ward off the man's advance, "what brings you out this way?"

"You piece of shit."

"I know you're upset," McMurray was wheeling backward, trying to keep his distance, "but let's talk about this."

"Talk? Talk!" he laughed a hollow laugh. "Why would I want to talk to a fucking pedophile who gets his jollies off of wrecking people's lives? Not even, you're not happy stopping there–"

"Mr. Hail, Henry, think about what you're doing."

Hail continued as if McMurray hadn't said anything. "You're not happy with wrecking people's lives. You have to fuck with their funerals too."

"I was only–"

"– doing what Marissa asked, ya, I heard that before. That good for nothing, she's not much better than you, and if it weren't for my wife, she'd have been out on her ear years ago. I knew I should have listened to Father Maria when he told me I shouldn't let your drunk ass talk, but my wife insisted."

"I'm sorry that I offended you," McMurray looked around for a way out. "I have nothing but respect for you and your family."

THE LOST

"Respect?" Hail spat on the ground. "What do you know about respect?"

"Look," spotting a path in the woods, McMurray stopped backing up, "you're upset. You have been through a lot lately. You don't want to do anything here you're going to regret."

"You're going to regret that you ever knew my family," Hail rushed at McMurray, ready to tackle him to the ground. He looked like he was in average shape, but McMurray knew from past experience that even a scrawny man can take someone down if they were angry enough, and Hail seemed angry enough.

Lunging to the side, McMurray tried to evade Hail, but he was moving faster than McMurray thought, and Hail caught him around the waist, causing both men to tumble to the ground, knocking the wind out of McMurray. Spots swam in front of his eyes as he gasped for breath that wasn't coming. Hail, kneeling over McMurray's chest, drew his right arm back, ready to drive his fist into McMurray's face. Seeing his inexperience in fighting, McMurray took advantage of his Southside Boston upbringing and rolled his weight to his left, overbalancing Hail and sending him to the ground. McMurray scrambled to his feet and looked at Hail. Pity filled McMurray, and he said a quiet prayer for the man's pain, something he hadn't done in a long time, then turned ran for the path with everything he had. He could win the fight, he was sure of that, but that wouldn't be the right thing to do.

He heard Hail yell after him, "Stay away from my family, you piece of shit." McMurray didn't turn to see if Hail was following him. He didn't say anything in return; he simply ran, not knowing where the path went, just that it lead away from where he was.

Twenty-Two

When Father McMurray finished his story of escaping from her father, Marissa sat silently. The towel she was using to clean the bar was held forgotten against the bar's worn finish. She remembered seeing her father walking out of the funeral and assumed that he had left to the reception after. She hadn't expected that he'd have sat in the parking lot, waiting for Father McMurray. Her father was a businessman, worked in an office cubical and pushed papers, and made phone calls every day. She remembered going to his work one bring-your-daughter-to-work-day. She was bored out of her skull, spend most of the day playing on his phone. Marissa struggled to imagine him following someone in his car, then attacking and threatening them.

"That explains why you haven't been here for a couple of days," Marissa abandoned the rag on the bar and crossed her arms. "I'm sorry, I didn't know."

"It was his grief, Marissa," McMurray said, noting the look on her face. "I know he's not that type of person. I'm not even sure he meant it."

"Oh, he meant it," Marissa said, "he said basically the same thing when he came to the reception. He walked up, in front of Geo and my cousin, and he said that if I don't stay away from that ped–priest, I should start sleeping in his bar."

THE LOST

"I doubt he referred to me as 'that priest,'" McMurray said with a knowing smile. "Your father hasn't referred to me as that P-word in many years."

"I'm sorry," Marissa started wiping the bar again, "he just—"

"You don't need to make excuses," McMurray rubbed the cut over his left eye, "he made his opinion of me quite clear."

"I guess he did," Marissa looked up as the bell on the door rung gently. "Just sit anywhere you'd like," she called to the woman who entered, "I'll be right with you."

The woman who entered the door walked to where Marissa and Father McMurray talked and sat on the stool next to McMurray. "You're Marissa Hail, correct," she asked, then turning to McMurray, "Good to see you again Father, what happened to you?"

"Had a bit of a disagreement with—" McMurray looked at Marissa, who shrugged, "with a tree."

"Well now," she chuckled, a relaxed, warm sound, "that sounds like a story."

"Maybe one for another day," he rubbed the back of his neck. "Marissa Hail, Officer Magdalena Dias, she's working your brother's case."

Marissa tensed up, she didn't like the cops in town, but she really didn't like the cops that she didn't know. That typically meant state cops. Magdalena put her hand across the bar toward Marissa, who tentatively took it. "Was working," she corrected.

"What do you mean?" Marissa asked, forgetting her trepidation.

"Town closed the case."

"Can they do that?"

"Said it was solved, animal attack," Magdalena put a plastic bag on the bar and shrugged. "Let that Geoffrey kid go, the one I saw you with at the funeral."

"Geo said they were leaning that way," Marissa eyed that bag on the counter.

"Just got the call from upstate, case closed, and I'm heading back in," Magdalena noticed Marissa eying the bag and continued. "I was bringing this stuff back to the station, but my captain told me to just bring it to the family. I'm very sorry for your loss."

"Right, but shouldn't that stuff go to my parents?"

"Tried," she said, "no one answered at your home, and your father's office said that he has been out on bereavement and wouldn't be back until the end of the week. I figured you work at a bar, so you must be above 18," she paused and looked back and forth at McMurray and Marissa. "You are above 18, right?"

"I'll be 24 in a couple of months," Marissa said, "don't worry."

"Good," Magdalena said, a smile hinting on her lips, "so if you had answered the door at your house, I would have given your brother's belongings to you there. No reason not to give them to you here," she paused for a moment seeing the uncertainty on Marissa's face. "That is if you don't mind. If so, I could put them in the mail to your parents. I just like to do these things in person whenever possible."

"No, it's fine," Marissa said, looking to Father McMurray, "I was just, I mean, are his clothes in there?"

"Nobody, no clothes," Magdalena motioned to the bag, "not much, actually. Just a couple of things from his truck, your parents opted to have the department sell the truck for a scholarship fund with the local high school."

THE LOST

Marissa nodded, "Thanks for that. Can I get you anything? On the house," she motioned at McMurray, who'd sat there silently messaging his sore neck during the interchange. "How do you know the Padre?"

"We met at the funeral," McMurray said.

"A coffee would be great," Magdalena nodded at McMurray, "He shared some of his flask to help me warm up."

"Really," Marissa asked, raising one eyebrow at McMurray, who shook his head. "Careful," she set the steaming coffee in front of Magdalena, "it's hot."

"No problem," Magdalena said, blowing some of the steam across the top of the coffee before taking a tentative sip.

"Well," Marissa turned to McMurray, "wild animals would explain not having a body, and the blood they said was at the scene."

"It would," he said, looking at the bag.

"I'm gonna bring this into the office. That way, I don't forget it when I go get my coat," Marissa grabbed the bag and headed for the back room. "Hold down the fort?"

Father McMurray looked around at the empty room, "I think I can manage."

She heard McMurray and Officer Dias talking as she went back toward the office. The cop had seemed nice enough, and McMurray seemed to enjoy talking to her, but he could talk to anyone on his good days. She walked to the office door and pushed on it. Nothing, the hinges were stuck again. She pitched her shoulder into it and grunted as the heavy door sat motionless on its hinges. Rolling her eyes, she changed the plan and headed to the back door instead.

Walking out of the back door, Marissa headed to her truck. Opening up the door, she put the bag behind her passenger seat, but she couldn't bring herself to look into it. She closed the door and leaned against her truck, thinking about how someone's life really comes down to a few things in a plastic bag. What if the situation was reversed? She thought, what would be in her bag? Some tools, a couple of sweaters stuffed behind the seat, the bible Father McMurray had given her when she got out of prison.

She opened the door again and looked at the bag. All that remained of her brother was in that bag. She reached out to open it, but the red evidence tape sealing it stopped her. She figured her parents might want to keep this sealed up, or they may want to open it, rediscover their lost golden child. Fucking Mikey. Marissa slammed her door closed, tears welling up in her eyes. Wild animals, fuck, this shit wasn't fair. Leaving the bag in her truck, she went back to the bar, into the safe and secure sanctuary, where she could just blend into the woodwork and clean, forgetting about the rest of the world and all the unfair crap it dished out.

"Still, Father," Magdalena was saying, her coffee cooling and untouched, "it doesn't feel right." Father McMurray had moved behind the bar and taken out a bowl of pretzel sticks they both munched on.

"What doesn't feel right?" Marissa asked as she whiped the last of the tears from her cheeks.

"Officer Dias was saying that she doesn't think the animal attack theory is accurate," McMurray said, pouring himself a cup of coffee.

"Please," Magdalena said, "call me Maggie. Officer Dias just feels too formal."

"What do you think it is?" Marissa asked.

"I wouldn't normally say anything, but Father McMurray has a way of making people spill it," she smiled and patted his hand. "There've been more than a few interrogations that I could have used him in."

THE LOST

"He does," Marissa chuckled.

"I was saying that it doesn't sit right with me. None of this," Maggie continued. "Four kids attacked; first off, that's strange for a few reasons. They were awake and didn't have food. What drew the animals to them? Typically wolves look for easier prey, and bears are mostly defensive killers, which doesn't fit with Geoffrey's accounting of sitting around the coals of a fire. Then there is the fact that none of the interrogation tapes recorded Geoffrey."

"The department has old equipment," McMurray said, "I'm sure those tapes have probably been recorded over hundreds of times, probably hard to work anything out of them."

"No, I could hear Officer Bedrin just fine," Maggie continued, "just the kid's words were static. Listened to it probably five times, the same thing. Every time the kid talked, after the initial few questions, just static. Then there's this book everyone was so interested in. They kept saying it was one of the things in your brother's stuff. Everyone seemed to want it, but it wasn't actually there; all he had was school books and a library book. They wanted some leather-bound thing that wasn't ever there. And everyone at the station has been acting odd. Your Chief's kept his door locked tight and sends everything through Officer Bedrin. I don't know if that's how things work around here, but it just feels wrong to me."

"Bedrin can do that to people," Marissa said, sitting down next to Maggie. Father McMurray took down a mug and poured some coffee, putting it down in front of Marissa, who nodded her thanks. "So why are you going if you don't think it was animals?"

"Have to," Maggie shrugged, taking another sip of her coffee. "My Chief calls the shots, and he's fine with the town's interpretation of events. Your parents have accepted it too. Just too easy to sit well with me. Too easy with too many holes."

"Sometimes that's just how things work," Father McMurray said, leaning back against the back of the bar.

Marissa couldn't remember the last time he'd seemed this clear; it was as if he was coming into focus for the first time. He was standing, surrounded by bottles of liquor, but he didn't even seem interested in them. The last time she'd seen him behind the bar was about a month ago; he'd been pouring himself a whiskey for breakfast, now he looked relaxed back there with his coffee in hand. The cut over his eye was a dark red, making his naturally pale skin look almost ghostly, but his eyes shone in a way she hadn't seen in years.

"And sometimes you don't know where the bodies are buried," Marissa said, wincing a little at her own choice of words.

"Either way," Maggie said, grabbing a pretzel and standing up from the bar, "I should be on my way. The Chief expects my report by the end of the day, and I have a long drive." She reached into her blazer pocket and pulled out a small metal case. "Here's my card. I'm not sure what I can do for you, but something doesn't sit right about all this. If you need me, if something turns up about all this, call me."

Marissa put the card in her pocket and thanked Maggie, watching her walk out of the bar before turning back to McMurray, who was washing the coffee cup. "We gotta investigate."

"What now?"

"You heard her, somethings not right about this," Marissa said, sitting back down and drinking her coffee. "Even she thinks Bedrin's up to something."

Father McMurray put the cup in the drying rack, took a drink from his own coffee, picked up a pretzel, and examined it before popping it into his mouth. "The woods around here are full of animals, especially at night."

THE LOST

"But they don't just attack groups of people," Marissa motioned to the door, "Maggie said so."

"So you trust Officer Dias, but not Officer Bedrin?"

"I know Bedrin."

McMurray smiled and picked up another pretzel, "So what do you suggest?"

"Let's go for a hike."

"Back to the beginning?"

"We'll just have a look around, see if there are animal tracks."

"And if there aren't, it's been two weeks, Marissa?"

"A week and a half, but if there aren't, well, there might be something else that the police have missed. Besides, it had just rained before they went, and it's been mostly dry lately."

"We had a big rainstorm not long after."

"Fine, but –"

"If there are tracks, will you drop this?"

"There might be–" Marissa started.

"If there are tracks, you'll drop this. Right?" Marissa nodded under Father McMurray's gaze. "I know it's hard, Marissa. Believe me, I know, but it's not healthy to keep holding on like this. The lack of body makes things more difficult, but you have to let Mikey go."

Marissa stared into her coffee. The muddy depths rippling as she moved the mug.

"We'll go," Father McMurray said into the silence. "Let me go home and get some clothes that are better for hiking," he nodded at Marissa smiling, "some of us don't wear jeans and a flannel every day."

Marissa looked up, eyes glistening with tears, her voice failing her, and mouthed thank you. Father McMurray washed his mug, moved back around the bar, giving her shoulder a light, reassuring squeeze. She watched him walk out of the door and let out the breath she hadn't realized she was holding. Marissa picked up her own half-finished coffee and went behind the bar to wash it. As she put away the three mugs, the bell above the door rang gently as the cool air from outside wafted in. Marissa turned to greet the customer, but the man at the door caused her words to catch in her throat.

THE LOST

Twenty-Three

Blue lights flashed outside, reflecting on the ceiling and the backs of the booths in front. Standing in the open door, Bedrin glared into the room and grunted when he saw it was empty except for Marissa. He let the door close behind him as he strode over to the bar, a grimace on his face. The small bell over the door rang gently as the door closed. Marissa watched Bedrin cross the floor, her heart dropping more with each step. She took a deep breath and forced a smile.

"So good to see you again," she wrung the towel in her hands under the counter. "Here for another nice chat like last time?"

"Where is she?"

"You're going to have to give me a little more to go on," Marissa loosened her grip on the towel and brought it up to wipe a nonexistent spot off the counter.

"Don't give me lip," Bedrin's snarled at her. "The state. Where is she?"

"Statie?"

"You're not that dumb, the state cop, don't you jailbirds instinctually know to avoid them?"

"Funny, jackass."

"I could take you back in for obstruction," Bedrin smiled, "kinda a wide definition offense."

Marissa smiled at him and stopped scrubbing the counter, "I told you before, I can't tell you what I don't know."

"Officer Dias," Bedrin seemed to cringe at the name, "took something from the station that we need for the investigation."

"I thought you cleared Geo, investigations over, isn't it?"

"So she was here. I knew it." Bedrin leaned over the counter, putting his face inches from Marissa's. His breath smelled like meat left in the walk-in for too long, "I'll give you one more chance. Where is she?"

"Said she was going upstate to her station. Stopped by for a coffee and to see if I knew where my folks were," Maggie's words echoed in Marissa's mind, making her opinion of Bedrin even less than usual.

"Is that all? She leave anything here."

"She had my brother's stuff—"

"And?"

"And I told her to mail it to my parents," Marissa narrowed her eyes. She was hoping Bedrin didn't push this. "You think my dad wants me to handling Mickey's stuff?"

"At least you listen to someone," he stepped back from the bar.

Marissa let his comment drop and turned to face the back wall, pretending to straighten the bottles while she watched Bedrin in the mirror. He stared down at his phone and punched at the screen with his finger. After a few moments, he poked at it a little more and then put the phone away.

"You know," he said to the back of her head, "I could bring you down to the station. I doubt your savior is going to be around to help you this time."

"What do you mean?"

THE LOST

Bedrin smiled, then turned and moved for the door. "Don't get any ideas of going anyplace," he said over his shoulder as he wrenched the door open and left the room.

Marissa turned around as the door closed. She watched through the window as he walked to his car and climbed into the driver's side. The sirens blared to life, and his tires kicked up dust, pulling onto the main road. She let out her breath and leaned against the back of the bar. She hated how he would do that shit. This time he went too far, though, that shit he said about Father McMurray, he had to be talking about him, her savior. She wasn't really sure that it was a threat, but it definitely was a line crossed. She dialed Father McMurray's home number, and not for the first time, she wished he had a cell phone. He said that he never got one before because he didn't want to be distracted from the people he was with, but now it was more just a habit of not having one. She hung up after leaving him a message to call her when he got a chance and went back to preparing for the lunch crowd. As she headed into the back room, she heard the bell above the door and her shoulders immediately tensed.

"What the fuck Bedri–" she stopped short as she turned to see that it wasn't Bedrin but the lawyer from out of town. She tried to remember his name as she felt her cheeks flush. "I'm sorry, I just–" she wasn't sure how to finish, so she just let the comment hang in the air, a half-finished apology.

"Don't worry about it," he ran his hand over his bald head, "I've met him." A smile spread across his lips.

Marissa chuckled, smiling back at him. He wasn't unattractive for an older man; he had a friendly smile. "Well, he and I have a particularly rough history."

"What brings the good officer in here during his duty hours?"

"Other than to harass me?"

Eric Johnson

"Has he been? Harassing you?" His smile widened a little as he spoke, "You know he's not allowed to do that, right?"

"Someone should tell him that," Marissa smiled again. "What can I getcha?"

"Nothing for me, thanks. But I have something for you."

"Really?"

"Yup," cocking his head to the side, he continued. "You don't remember me do you?"

Marissa thought for a bit but couldn't place the man's name. "I'm sorry," she said, "it's been a crazy couple of weeks around here. You're that lawyer. You were going to talk to Geo, right? Seems like you did good work there."

"There and here," he said as he pulled a folder out of the briefcase he set on the bar. "Last time I was here, I told you I would take a look at that arrest of yours, see if I could get Bedrin off your back."

"That's right," Marissa's shoulders dropped a little. "I'm sorry, but I can't remember your name."

"Not a problem," he handed her the folder, "Lucius Tanis, but please call me Luc."

"Right, Luc," Marissa opened the folder and stared at the papers in front of her. His handwriting, scrolling and beautiful, was challenging to read. "So, what am I looking at?"

"Turns out that Officer Bedrin didn't fill out the appropriate documentation for your arrest the other day," he pointed to a copy of a blank form dated with the day of her arrest and with her name on it. The rest was empty, including the signature line. "So, I could simply file one paper to get the whole thing erased."

"Like it never happened?"

"Clear as crystal," he said, taking another paper out of his briefcase. "Just one minor problem to solve."

THE LOST

"What's that?"

"I looked into this without officially being your council," he said, taking a fountain pen out of this coat pocket, "to file this properly, I will need you to sign this to make things official."

"How much?" Marissa leaned back against the cabinets behind the bar, crossing her arms over her chest.

"Nothing like that, I assure you," Lucius smiled reassuringly. "From what I understand, the legal system hasn't been the kindest to you. I simply want to do my part to right this wrong."

"So –" said Marissa, waiting for the catch.

"Pro-bono," Lucius said, holding out his pen. "Just sign on the line, and I'll take care of everything."

"Seems too good to be true," Marissa tentatively took the pen from his hands and flinched, dropping the pen, when something pricked her finger.

"I'm sorry," Lucius said, holding out a handkerchief for her, "it's clean, I promise. I forgot to warn you that the clip in that pen had a little barb. I caught it on my seatbelt the first time I came here and haven't had a chance to get a new one."

"It's alright," she put her finger to her lips, waving off the offered handkerchief. Carefully picking up the pen, Marissa signed her name on the line and pushed it back across the bar to Lucius. "There, it's a deal."

"Can't beat the price, right?" Lucius asked with a chuckle putting the paper and pen back into his briefcase.

"Sure can't. I owe you one."

"You certainly do," Lucius smiled at her as he latched his briefcase.

"Well, you know where to find me," Marissa said, gesturing at the bar around her.

"I do at that," Lucius patted his briefcase and, with a brief farewell, headed out of the door.

THE LOST

TWENTY-FOUR

Two hours after Lucius left, Marissa was in the backroom, getting ready to lock up early so she and Father McMurray could get to the shack in the woods before dark. The bell on the front door chimed, and she checked her watch then rolled her eyes. It was too soon for McMurray to have gotten to his house and back and still an hour too early for the usual dinner crowd, but she'd left the door unlocked in case she was back here when he came back, seeing as he still forgot his keys more often than he remembered them.

"Out in a minute," she called as she put the day's money in the safe. There was no answer from the bar, so she locked up the safe, tossed her jacket over the chair, and headed out of the office, figuring she could always come back for her coat if it was McMurray. She jogged out of the back room and behind the bar before looking at the person standing in the middle of the room. The kid was tall and thin and unmistakable. Marissa stopped dead in her tracks, hand on the bar to steady herself, "Steve. What are you doing here?"

"We didn't finish our conversation last time," Steve looked back at the door and smiled. "Got interrupted. Don't worry that won't happen again."

"Look, Steve, I didn't file any charges against you guys last time," Marissa watched as Steve walked over to the front door,

"I'm not sure why you've come back here, but skip out, and I'll keep it that way. Fuck with me again, and things aren't going to go well."

"I'm pretty sure that you were backed into a corner last time," Steve said as Marissa backed along behind the bar, heading toward the back door. "This little bell saved you," he tapped the bell above the door, then reached down and flipped the lock closed. "There."

"Steve," Marissa fought to control the shake she felt in her voice, "Father McMurray is on his way. He'll be here any minute. Just–" she stopped as she backed into something that didn't feel like the door jam. She tried to step forward, but four arms grabbed her roughly, and half shoved, half dragged her further into the room. "What the fuck– Let me go."

Marissa writhed and kicked as best she could, but the arms around her were strong, and she couldn't break through, she landed kicks on the shins of her captors, but that just got her a shake that threatened to dislocate her shoulder. She couldn't turn to see who had her, but their hands looked smooth, young. Not that she needed to see them to know who it was. "Zack, Devin, let me the fuck go," she growled through clenched teeth.

"Shut up, bitch," she felt Zack's breath against her right ear.

"I let you guys off light last time," she said, hoping to sound more confident than she felt, "this time, it's not going to be so easy."

They dragged her to the front of the bar, and Steve brought his arm back, punching her in the stomach. Marissa hadn't expected the hit, and her knees gave out as she coughed and gasped for breath. Zack and Devin pulled her back to her feet as she struggled to get her breath back. Steve slammed a couple more punches into her now screaming stomach. Tears streamed down Marissa's face as she felt her vision start to narrow. She was barely able to get her hands up in time to keep her face from hitting the floor when Devin and Zack dropped her before moving to either side so they could get their kicks in. Marissa curled into a ball, her hands wrapped around the back of her neck to protect the more sensitive areas, but the beating still hurt like hell. When they finally let up, she lay there in the fetal position, tears streaming, fighting the bile rising in the back of her throat and her waining consciousness.

"She dead?" Zack asked.

"No," Steve bent down to get a closer look, leaning on her arm to keep her from taking a swing at him, "she's breathing. Give her a minute to come to. He's sure that she's got it."

"Will she tell us where it is?"

"Us or him," Steve's voice sounded farther away this time, "but she'll tell." The sound of a chair scraping across the floor let her know that one of them sat at a table.

Their conversation continued, but Marissa stopped listening for anything other than location. She didn't want to let them know she hadn't lost consciousness. The beatings in prison had been worse than this, though not by much. Steve sounded like he'd taken a seat somewhere behind her, so she wouldn't be able to get out that way; he was a lot stronger than she thought he'd be as a scrawny stoner. From the sound of the rattling bottles, one of the other two sounded like he'd gone behind the bar, but she couldn't tell where the third one was. She chanced opening her eyes enough to try to make out the room. She was lying with her back to the front door, she assumed Steve was still sitting at one of the tables close by, and the bottles still jostled behind the bar. They left the entrance to the kitchen open and unguarded from what she could tell. She still couldn't see Devin or Zack, but she had to take the chance.

She took a slow but deep breath, testing her ribs. They were sore but didn't seem broken. She could feel deep bruises forming on her side and arms, but there didn't seem the tell-tale pain of a break, though she knew all too well that those could hide until you put pressure on them. She knew that she couldn't stay where she was, and the only hope for escape seemed to be the kitchen and the back door. With every bit of strength she had, Marissa pushed herself up and tried to run for the back door and freedom. At first, the dizziness threatened to topple her, but she was able to get her feet under her fairly quickly, her hand went down into something wet and sticky, but Marissa kept her eyes on the door. It didn't take long for the shouts to start behind her; first, it was Steve, then the thunder of feet coming after her. She dove for the kitchen door and slammed it shut behind her, pushing the flimsy handle lock as she leaned against it to catch her breath.

"Get it open," Steve's voice sounded hollow from the other side of the door. "He wants her here."

The door shook in its frame as they slammed their shoulders into it from the other side. Marissa's head throbbed and brushed sticky clumps of hair from her face as she gulped at the air. She looked toward the back of the room, knowing the door out was there in the shadows. The door behind her shook again, more violently, and the sound of splintering wood was the last motivation she needed. With a closed door between them, the adrenaline that let her escape seemed to be draining away, leaving her unsteady on her feet. Leaning on the counter for support, she abandoned the door to the bar and moved through the dark kitchen. She had a straight shot past through the galley-style prep area next to the sink. The prep island opened up into the rest of the storage area for the kitchen and the taps, then to the back door.

THE LOST

The door behind her rattled harder as she passed the end of the prep island and headed toward the back door. In the shadows by the door, movement told her why she hadn't seen the third attacker in the bar, and Marissa cursed under her breath. The shadow moved to block the door as the sound of a door slamming to the metal cabinet rang through the room. Marissa backed into the shadows herself, slinking toward the office where her cell phone sat in her jacket pocket over the back of the chair. Hearing one of the boys bang into the shelf of cooking pans and curse as they clattered to the floor, she took that moment to break the shadows and rush the office door. She grasped the doorknob, turned it, and threw her weight into the heavy door. The door opened, and Marissa lost her footing as she tumbled into the room. She reached for her jacket as two strong hands grabbed her legs and dragged her out of the room, the coat sliding off the chair just out of reach. They dragged her through the kitchen, face down, as she squirmed and struggled to get free. Her face banged heavily against the corner of the metal prep island, and she lost consciousness.

"She's waking up again," the voice sounded from somewhere, and Marissa couldn't make out whose it was. "Bitch is tough."

"He said she was," another voice said.

Marissa struggled to focus; one of her eyes seemed swollen and hurt like hell. She brought her hand up to her face to check the damage, only to have it wrenched back down.

"Not so fast," the voice was familiar, but Marissa still couldn't place it. She felt like she was waking up from a dream, though it was more like a nightmare from the way she felt. Bits and pieces started falling into place as she sat there on the floor. "Fool us once– you know."

"Got it, Steve," a third voice, softer than the other two, chimed in from the door to the kitchen area. At the sound of Steve's name, everything locked painfully into place, and Marissa shot her eyes open, the world coming into painful focus.

"Good," Steve said, "use it to tie her up." He smiled at her, "Tightly."

Devin and Zack knelt down on either side of her and pulled her arms painfully behind her back. She tried to wrench them free, but Zack just elbowed her in her swollen eye. Struggling not to throw up, her world swam in pain. The cord they used was digging into her wrists, but at least they didn't seem to be tying her feet, so when they were done, she figured she'd have a chance to run now that they were all in the bar. Her breath came in short bursts, the pain in her shoulders, and her ribs melted together.

"What do you want?" her voice sounded small and weak in her own ears.

"She lives," Steve used the toe of his sneaker to lift her chin. He let her head drop back down and laughed as she winced. "Nothing in particular. Just looking for some light reading."

"What the fuck," she exhaled, "all this shit for a book."

"Well, he wants it, and if he wants it, so do we," Steve motioned to Zack and Devin. "Right, boys?"

"You got it," Zack said. "Oh wait, I got an idea." Zack hopped over the bar, and Marissa heard him shuffling through the bottles again.

"Toasting to your success?" Marissa asked with all the sarcasm her swollen face could muster.

"Funny," he said, hopping back over the bar with a bottle of whiskey in his hand. "To your health," he said and then smashed the bottle against the bar. The sweet-smelling liquor splashed to the floor, leaving a sizeable caramel-colored puddle

THE LOST

next to her. The booze that splashed on her open wounds stung, and Marissa flinched again. He brandished the broken bottle like a knife and motioned to her leg. "Dev, grab that."

Marissa kicked at Devin as he bent down to grab her legs. She landed a lucky hit to his mouth, splitting his lip. He stood up, a look of surprise on his face, and licked his split lip. Smiling as he tasted his own blood. As Marissa watched, a small bump appeared on his chin, under his skin, and moved toward his lips. As she watched the bump move under his skin, the split lip seemed to heal in front of her eyes, and Devin stomped down hard on her left ankle. Marissa heard a pop as pain washed over her and spots spread in her vision. She felt his hands grab her right leg and lift it. More pain washed over her as Zack took the broken bottle and ran it along the back of her ankle, cutting into the tendon beneath. The entire world began to fade away as the pain dragged her once again into darkness.

"He wants her alive," the voices sounded hollow and far away as if they were in a tunnel somewhere.

"Don't worry, she'll live. Do we wait?"

"No, he said to leave the place locked up. He'll have a key."

"What about the truck?"

"It sure beats walking."

Then the world went silent.

Twenty—Five

Father McMurray pulled into the driveway of his small ranch and rested his forehead on the wheel. The past week was catching up to him, and he wanted nothing more than to grab a quick drink before he headed back to meet up with Marissa and traipse through the woods to that blasted shack. Instinctively, he reached into his jacket pocket for his flask that he'd kept there for the past four years, but his hand came back empty. During his flight from Mr. Hail, McMurray dropped his flask somewhere in the woods and decided to take that as a sign. He had a spare in a desk drawer in the house, but with everything that had been going on, he'd decided to leave it where it was. He turned off the car and looked toward his front door when something moving on his porch caught his eye. Getting out of the vehicle, McMurray looked over the roof to see Father Joseph Maria sitting on the porch swing, watching him.

"Father Maria," McMurray said, "to what do I owe this honor?"

"An apology," Father Maria held up a tall, thin paper bag, his hand grasped around the neck of a bottle within, and smiled sheepishly.

McMurray nodded and, locking his car door, walked around to meet Father Maria on the porch steps. "Apology?" he asked, walking up the steps selecting his house keys from his key ring.

Father Maria leaned against the post and watched McMurray walk past him and open the door to his house. "Come on, Peter, are you going to make me say it?"

"Well, Joseph," McMurray said, turning around in his doorway to look at the younger priest, "a true apology usually comes with the words, I'm sorry."

The two men looked at each other in silence before McMurray turned to go into the house, "Wait," Father Maria reached out to stop the door from closing, "a peace offering." he held the bottle out toward McMurray again.

Sighing, McMurray responded, "Come on in, I'll brew a pot of coffee."

Father Maria smiled as he walked through the door to McMurray's house. He looked around the sparse but tidy living room as he followed McMurray into a kitchen equally as sparse except for the dishes in the sink and a dirty pot on the stove. "Nice housekeeping," Father Maria said as he brushed some crumbs aside and took a seat at the kitchen island. He pulled a bottle of Knob Creek out of the paper bag setting it on the counter.

"Was there an apology coming, or am I brewing coffee for nothing?" McMurray said over his shoulder as he rubbed the stubble on his chin. His shoulder hunched as he filled the carafe with water to put in the coffee maker. Coffee sounded good to McMurray, apology or not, so he didn't wait for an answer.

"Alright, you're clearly going to make me say it," Father Maria took a deep breath before continuing. "I should not have told Mr. Hail that you were drunk."

"It set him off," McMurray said, scooping some grounds into the filter and searching the cabinet for two clean mugs.

Eric Johnson

"Well, can you blame him?" Father Maria twisted the cap from the bottle he brought. "It was his only son's funeral."

"No, Joseph," McMurray said as he turned and placed the mugs in front of Father Maria, "I don't blame him, I blame you."

Father Maria's smile faltered on his face for a brief moment before he slowly shook his head and chuckled. "Peter, I didn't expect you to be so petty," he said, pouring some of the whiskey into both mugs.

McMurray watched as the golden liquid sloshed into the mug. It was something he'd done himself a hundred times, easier to hide it when drinking on his front porch. The warm smell of caramel and smoke reached out to him, and before McMurray thought about it, the mug was in his hand, inches from his mouth. All the familiar images flashed before his eyes as he inhaled the smell wafting from the rich liquor in his mug. His congregation, Destiny's face, her father's tears, the accusations, the hate in people's eyes, and his last sermon all swirled through his mind in a matter of seconds. It was disorienting, the rush of emotions washing over him every time he picked up a glass. The welcome of oblivion swam inside that cup.

McMurray hadn't had a drink since sharing his flask with Officer Dias at Mikey's funeral two days ago. No great feat for most people, but it was the longest McMurray had been without a drink in four years. He looked into the depths of the golden fluid in his mug while Father Maria sat sipping from his mug, watching in silence. The warm smell seemed to reach up, pulling at his lips, at his thoughts, begging to drown the memories. McMurray jumped when the coffee machine beeped in the background, the mug, huddled in both hands, sloshed some over onto his hand. His reverie broken, McMurray set the mug down to get the coffee, drying his hand on the kitchen towel.

THE LOST

"I can see why you like this stuff," Father Maria said from behind him. "There's some comfort here when your mind is occupied."

"Something you want to get off your chest Joseph?"

Father Maria laughed dryly, "Like I said, I shouldn't have told Hail about your drinking."

"No, you shouldn't have," McMurray turned around with a clean mug and the coffee pot. He put the mug on the counter and poured the steaming coffee into it, then motioned to the mug in Father Maria's hand.

"Please," he handed the half-full mug to McMurray to added the hot coffee to the whiskey already there. The scents mixed into a heady, rich swirl that almost made McMurray dizzy before he handed it back to Father Maria. "Are you going to have any," Father Maria motioned to McMurray's whiskey abandoned on the counter, "it's quite good."

"I'm driving later," McMurray said, raising his eyebrows at the younger priest.

"I guess I owe an apology about that too, eh?" Father Maria said, raising his glass to McMurray.

"The walk was nice," McMurray thought back to the screech of Mr. Hail's tires on the road, and the smell of earth and blood mixed on his flight through the woods, "most of it." He picked up his coffee and took a sip, but his eyes didn't leave the cup of whiskey.

Father Maria nodded knowingly, "Henry told me about that," he seemed to weigh his words, "misunderstanding."

McMurray nodded and leaned back against the sink, putting some distance between himself and the siren call of the whiskey. "Ruined my good suit."

"That was your good suit?" Father Maria laughed. "Did you a favor by recking it then."

"You're bad at apologizing."

"Look, Peter," Father Maria put his mug down and leaned forward, his elbows on the island, "you have made a lot of enemies in this town. Why you didn't leave when the Church was going to pay your way, I'll never understand. What I know is, no matter what you may think of me, I came here to help you. Hell, I even brought your best friend," he motioned to the open bottle, "albeit a bit better quality than that swill you usually drink. But the fact remains, the world doesn't owe you anything, the Church doesn't owe you anything, this town doesn't owe you anything. They don't even like you here. Take this as a professional courtesy, or a priest protecting his parish, I don't care, but you need to leave this place. Close down that hole of a bar you keep on the edge of town and disappear. I've talked many parents down from doing to you what Henry tried to, a lot. You're a menace, and the town would be a lot calmer if you would just go."

McMurray watched as the blood rose to the young priest's face during his speech. He let out a low whistle and watched as Father Maria leaned back in his chair. After the silence stretched out between them, he looked at Father Maria. "Said your peace?"

The young man sat up and took a deep breath, the color returning to normal in his face as he regained his composure, "Please, Peter, you're not safe in this town."

"I appreciate your concern for my safety," McMurray set his mug down and moved around to stand next to the seated priest. They were close to the same height when the younger man was seated, but McMurray knew it was only an illusion. "I know the town doesn't owe me anything, or you, or even God for that matter. I'm not staying to get their forgiveness. True forgiveness is given by God to everyone who deserves it," McMurray felt his pulse quicken. Speaking the name of God again felt good; it felt right. "But there are people who are owed something. Marissa,

THE LOST

Geo, Mikey, they deserve better than they've gotten. And while I appreciate your apology, such as it was, and your heartfelt warning, I think I'll stick around and help where I can. Besides, I'm too old to be running off and starting someplace new anyway." McMurray stopped inches away from Father Maria, his eyes locked on the younger priest's.

"Don't say I didn't warn you," Father Maria said, standing up, looking down at the older man.

McMurray backed up so Father Maria could leave and glanced at the front door. Alarm shot through him as he saw the fading sun begin to set over the trees. He had promised Marissa that they would go to the shack before the sun went down. "I think it's time for you to leave," McMurray said. "I have a promise to keep."

The younger priest nodded and turned toward the door, leaving without another word. There seemed to be a finality in that gesture that was not lost on McMurray. He felt as if something had changed between the two of them with that bottle on the counter. After the young man closed the door behind him, McMurray turned to the bottle and replaced the lid. Then he took Father Maria's mug and dumped it into one of the less cluttered corners of the sink, followed by his own coffee. He paused for a moment with the mug of whiskey. The warm oaky scent comforted his nerves and slowed the heartbeat he hadn't realized quickened during the standoff with Father Maria. He brought the mug up to his lips, pausing briefly as the fumes burnt his nostrils. He closed his eyes and bathed in the aroma for a moment before he tilted his head back, and, in one swift motion, he dumped the untouched whiskey in the sink with the rest of the dishes.

Twenty—Six

Marissa lay on the floor, her torn pant leg soaking up the blood flowing freely from the gash on her leg. She could feel the numbness of shock setting in, dulling the pain from her severed tendon as she fought for consciousness. She thought back to the last thing she could remember. The last few hours were fuzzy, but she clearly remembered Father McMurray and Agent Dias were having coffee, and then they left. Dias for the state police station and McMurray was going to meet her back here for something. She couldn't remember much about their conversation, but she remembered they had talked about Mikey, about his case.

Shivering, she looked around, trying to clear her head. She was sitting on the floor in a pool of something sticky, blood and whiskey. The smells of iron and oak were unmistakable and churned her stomach. She pushed herself to try and stand, but her right leg refused to move, and even shifting made her left leg shoot sharp pins up her entire spine. Her vision swam in front of her, and she once again fought to stay awake. Crushing fatigue grabbed at her and tried to drag her back to unconsciousness.

"Help," she called out to the empty room around her.

Her throat ached, and she looked at her legs, being careful not to shift too much. Her left leg bent off at an odd angle just above the shin, and her right was oozing blood from near her

THE LOST

foot. Marissa caught her breath as she saw how large a pool she was sitting in. It looked too thin to be all blood, and the cloying scent of spilled liquor was more robust than usual, but she felt too tired.

"Don't sleep," she urged herself, "don't fucking sleep."

Marissa looked up at the bar looming over her, too high to grab the edge and pull herself up, but hanging over the edge was one of her bar towels. She took a deep breath, tried to prepare herself for the pain that was bound to come, and reached for the towel, screaming through clenched teeth. She knew if she could get the towel, she'd be able to tie it around her bleeding leg and possibly give herself a chance to get rescued. She felt her vision constricting around her, and she relaxed her reach, inches short of the towel. Marissa collapsed against the front of the bar, leaned her head back, closed her eyes, and focused on her breathing.

With her eyes closed, it became much harder to keep herself awake; sleep pulled at her constantly. She could feel pins and needles inching into her fingertips, and her eyelids felt like lead. She shivered, her whole body aching. In the back of her mind, she knew that she needed to stop the bleeding and stay awake until help arrived, but it was just so hard. Siting there, her back against the bar, eyes closed, Marissa thought about the day she and Mikey had gone for a hike in the woods, he couldn't have been more than five at the time.

"Hey 'Rissa," Mikey said as he climbed up onto a fallen tree, "watch this."

Marissa looked up from the wildflowers she had been gathering and smiled as the bark crumbled away, and her brother slipped into the mud. "Nice," she said with a smile, then went back to the flowers. She had dirt under her fingernails and a smudge on her left cheek. A small bundle of daisies from their backyard clutched tightly in her hand. Their mom had been having a bad day, and Marissa thought it would be good to bring her some flowers to cheer her up.

A couple of minutes later, Marissa heard her brother call out behind her again and turned to see him. He stood on the fallen tree, hands on his hips, his favorite bright red Mickey Mouse Clubhouse shirt smudged with mud and pieces of bark, his hands filthy, mud in his blond hair, and smiling ear to ear in triumph.

"Okay, nice work," Marissa looked at him and shook her head, always the daredevil, "now get down before you fall down. Mom's already having a bad enough day, and she'll kill me if you fall and break your arm. I don't want to be grounded again. Sarah's birthday party is tomorrow."

"I'll be fine," he said and started walking up the sloped log toward the thinner branches at the top. "Go back to your flowers. I'm not gonna fall."

A coughing fit dragged her back to reality; the air seemed so thick, like she was breathing in a liquid. She pried her eyelids open and looked over her head. The towel hung down a few feet away, teasing her. She took another deep breath, the air caught in her throat, and she coughed, her aching ribs and stomach throbbing with each cough. She focused on the pain; if she could feel pain, then she was still alive. That had to be good, she thought to herself as she reached out for the stool next to her, dragging herself closer to the towel and her only hope of stopping the blood. Her arms shook as she pulled herself inches across the floor, the red pool around her rippling slowly across the floor.

She had carried him out of the woods that day. He'd been right, kinda. He hadn't broken his arm, but he was definitely not fine. About four feet up the slippery trunk, his feet had gone out from under him as some of the rotting bark let loose. She looked up as he screamed, a sound she never wanted to hear again, just in time to see as his feet went backward and his face came in contact with the log. She got up, crushing the stems of the small white flowers in her hands, and ran toward him, careful of the rat's nest of branches surrounding the fallen tree. By the time she made it over to him, Mikey had rolled off the log and was screaming, high pitched and incoherently.

It wasn't until she had gotten up to him that she saw the bloody stick coming out of his stomach. She screamed and fell to her knees next to her brother as he writhed and grabbed at the stick. "Mikey, God, Mikey, are you okay?"

He just screamed as an answer, and Marissa wracked her brain for what to do. She remembered from Health class that she shouldn't move someone who was injured, and movies told her not to pull the stick out, but she had to get help and couldn't leave him here. "Help!" she called to the trees around her, "Help me!"

No one came, and eventually, her brother stopped screaming, tears welled up in her eyes, and she decided to carry him out of the woods to get help. She found that the stick was already broken and hadn't gone all the way through, so she carefully scooped him up and struggled her way out of the woods.

Evidently, people had heard her scream because she was met halfway down the path by her mother and their elderly neighbor. Both pale and out of breath. Her mother's face twisted in grief when she saw Mikey limp in Marissa's arms.

The wait for the ambulance felt like an eternity. Marissa's mother shaking Mikey, calling his name until her voice was only a croak. Marissa watched as the ambulance pull away, her bother and mother tucked in the back, and she was afraid that she'd never get to see him again. Their neighbor stood behind her, his hand resting on her shoulder as tears fell down her face. She looked down at the flowers in her hand, their delicate stems bent and broken, their white petals crumpled and turned pink with her brother's blood. She opened her hand and let the ruined flowers drop to the ground. A neighbor squeezed her shoulder and brought her into his house for some chocolate milk while they waited for her father *to get home. While they waited, they picked wildflowers in his backyard to give to her mother.*

The sweat dripped off of her forehead as she strained to move the last few inches that would put her in reach of the towel. Straining, she reached up, her fingers brushing the edge of the towel. Marissa's arm fell back to her side as her world closed in tighter around her. Part of her wanted to give up and go to sleep; part of her knew that would not end well. Marissa lunged for the towel with her last strength, and hooking the seam with a finger, pulled it down beside her. She wrapped it around her leg and tried to tie it. Her stiffening fingers fumbled with the towel. She knew that she'd have to pull it tight for this to work but didn't know if she had the strength left to do that.

"Heya 'Rissa," a familiar voice came from above her, "bit of a tight place you got yourself into again, eh?"

"Mikey?" She looked up to see her brother, sitting just out of her reach, "Mikey, help me," her voice sounded far away.

"What happened?" he was sitting there as if there was no hurry.

"Help me," she pleaded, "I can't do this."

"Sure you can 'Rissa," he smiled at her, "you can do anything."

"Fuck you, I can't do this," she spat at him.

"You got this far," Mikey motioned to the towel wrapped loosely around her leg.

"I'm too weak."

"This is something you have to do for yourself 'Rissa," there was something odd about him, but she couldn't place it.

Marissa fumbled with the ends of the towel again; they slipped from her hands, the pins and needles making it hard to move. Her limbs seemed to weigh ten pounds. "I can't," she cried, "help me. Why won't you help me!"

THE LOST

"I can't."

"You can just tie it," she leaned her head back against the bar and closed her eyes again.

"I can't help you."

"Why not?" she asked, "I'm so tired. I just want to sleep."

"Don't quit on me 'Rissa," his voice seemed to be coming from far away, "open your eyes."

"Help me."

"You know I can't do that."

"Why not? Just tell me why you can't help me."

"You know why," he said.

The doctors said he was lucky because the stick had missed all the vital organs. He was going to be okay. Marissa cried again when she heard that news; the tears streamed down her cheeks freely and openly. Her mother sobbed too, and her father, stoic as always, held her mother as she cried. Marissa walked over to them, the flowers hugged tightly to her chest, tears dripping on the delicate petals. "Mommy?"

"Go sit down, Marissa," her father's voice was sharp, like when she would get caught stealing cookies from the jar on the counter before dinner. "Can't you see your mother's upset already?"

"I just—"

"Sit down."

Marissa backed away, watching her father rub her mother's back as it heaved up and down with her sobs. Her tears ran silently down her face, and she looked at the flowers clutched in her hand and saw them for what they were, the pointless gesture of a child who gathered together weeds, hollow and unwanted. She dropped the flowers into the trash, walked out of the waiting room, and headed for the lobby.

"I don't know why," Marissa said bitterly, "you're here. You're the only one who can help me."

"You know that's not true."

"Look around Mikey," she glared at him, angry that he wouldn't help. "No one's here."

"Exactly."

Something clicked in the back of Marissa's brain. She put the last few weeks together, the police, the newspapers, the funeral. The funeral. "No, Mikey," she said, tears streaming down her face like when she was a child, "the doctors said you were fine."

"That was years ago 'Rissa."

"But the casket was empty," she choked back the sob threatening to drown her. "They haven't found you, but you're here now. We can set it straight; just help me tie this up."

"No 'Rissa," he looked at her, the sadness evident on his face.

"Mikey," she said, her voice breaking around his name.

"You need to do this yourself," Mikey leaned forward. "Do you understand?"

"No,"

"Then there is no hope left."

Marissa reached up to wipe away the tears and snot running down her face, leaving a smear of her own blood there, and looked at Mikey as the room closed in around her. She was still staring at him when the front door shook as someone tried the handle. Mikey turned to look silently at the door. Marissa tried to call out, but her voice caught, and the only sound that escaped was a weak moan. The person at the door knocked a few times, and tried the knob once more, then left. Marissa remembered they were usually still open, so the dinner crowd must be trying to get in. This was the only time she'd ever been thankful that people never read the closed sign when she puts it out. If someone tried, there was a chance that another customer might try, or even better, McMurray was on his way.

THE LOST

Those thoughts gave Marissa the strength she needed to try again. She grabbed the ends of the towel and, with a little more trouble than she thought she should have, managed a loose knot. She looked around and found a stool that must have broken during the fight. She didn't remember the fight, but there must have been one for her to end up like this. She winced as she shoved a broken leg from the stool under the knot and began to twist it around to make a tourniquet. Exhausted from the efforts, she looked up at the empty chair that Mikey had been sitting in a moment ago and let her chin drop to her chest.

Sitting in the silence as the dusk fell into night, the raspy sound of her own breathing the only company, Marissa wondered where McMurray was when a noise at the front door caught her attention. The key sliding into the lock and turning sounded like a cannon in the silence. When the door opened, headlights behind a shadow blinded her, and she brought her hand up to shield her eyes. Squinting into the lights, Marissa tried to see who it was.

"Marissa?" the shadow asked.

At the sound of his voice, Marissa felt the tension drain from her shoulders. She was saved. She leaned her head back against the bar, closed her eyes against the light, and sighed heavily. "Thank God it's you."

Eric Johnson

Twenty—Seven

There was never any traffic for McMurray to blame his tardiness on, but he knew that he'd never be able to convince himself to lie about it anyway. Besides, Marissa would be proud of him for not taking the drink. There was something strange about the new priest, he needed to make sure that he wasn't just upset about his taking the parish, and Marissa would be able to provide an excellent sounding board for what he had said before leaving.

"Don't say I didn't warn you," McMurray said Father Maria's parting words aloud as the sign for the bar came into view. He had never gotten along with the young priest, but the threat seemed out of character for him.

McMurray watched the sun setting on the horizon and, without intention, said a quick prayer to end the day, a neglected habit. He ended the prayer as he pulled into the front lot of the bar. Usually, he'd park around back like Marissa, but they were going to close early, so he wouldn't be taking a spot away from paying customers. Probably a futile effort seeing as there were no cars in the parking lot, but the old place had her moments. Besides, he thought back to when Marissa had come to see him after her parole. It has its purposes.

THE LOST

"I'm sorry, Marissa," a younger McMurray said. "Most of the town believed the accusations. I had to step down for the good of the parish."

"Bullshit," she snarled at him.

"It's not."

"Where am I supposed to go then?"

"Home?"

"You have met my parents, haven't you? You think my Dad's going to be there to welcome me home with open arms?" She leaned against his porch railing. He'd avoided asking her in so his neighbors wouldn't gossip, "Fuck, I mean, you think they'd have picked me up instead of making me take a cab."

McMurray had felt bad for her. Marissa was in jail because of him, because he'd called the cops to start with. She didn't deserve what they'd done. She was a kid that made a mistake, nothing more, not even a bad kid. He hadn't pressed charges that day, but he had put her on their radar, and small-town cops have big memories. He took a sip from his coffee cup, the oak and caramel scents mixing with the rich earthy coffee aroma. "There might be something I can do," he said, scratching the stubble on his chin.

Pulling up to the door, McMurray searched through his pockets for the key that would unlock the front door. The closed sign was hanging in the window, but he thought he saw Marissa moving around inside, knowing her, probably cleaning. He'd used his savings to buy the place, but Marissa was the one who ran it mostly. Without her, the bar would have been a failure.

"Damn keys," McMurray mumbled to himself as he climbed out of the car to head in back for the spare set. She'd convinced him to hide one behind the dumpster a couple of years ago because he was constantly losing his.

"Here," she said, moving aside a loose brick in the back wall, "if we slide one here, then you'll be able to get in if I'm too busy or not here."

Eric Johnson

"I don't need to hide a bloody key."

"Really?" she looked at him with one eyebrow raised, "Then where is your key?"

"I –" McMurray flushed. "I just left it at home."

"There we go," Marissa held the loose brick in her hand, a new key gleamed in the spot it belonged in. "This is happening, Father McMurray. This key lives here now."

"But it's not safe," McMurray protested.

"Who the hell wants to come at me?" Marissa laughed, "Besides, don't you think I learned how to defend myself by now?"

She never talked about her time in prison, but McMurray assumed it hadn't been good. Something had happened inside, and she was changed by it, fundamentally changed, but not broken. It almost seemed as if her time in jail had taught her something that she needed. He wasn't going to pry though, she'd tell him when she was ready.

"I don't need to hide a key," he insisted one last time, "I'm not some doddering fool."

"Doddering? No, not doddering," Marissa smiled easily, her eyes lighting as she teased him.

"Hey," McMurray protested, returning her smile, "I take offense."

"No, you don't," she said, sliding the brick back in place.

McMurray looked at the wall. If he hadn't watched her take the brink out in the first place, he'd have never known it was there. "Alright," he acquiesced, "but I doubt I'll ever use it."

He walked the familiar path to that brick in the wall. It was a little more obvious now if you were looking for it. Over the years, he'd accidentally left it out some times, and rain had eroded the mortar on the bottom. The brick had chipped and broken a few times as he dropped it, his fingers too drunk to function, but Marissa had always made sure there was a key there. More than once, he'd taken it home or left it in the bar. He'd go back the next day, and the key would be back in place, ready if he needed it.

He rounded the corner and heard Marissa's truck start, then the tires scramble across the loose gravel of the back parking lot. He ducked out from behind the dumpster to flag her down but just caught sight of the truck bed as it sped around the corner toward the street. He shook his head went to get the key. She wouldn't have left without leaving him a note in the bar, so before he chased off after her, he'd find her message and figure out what to do after that.

Clicking on one of the flashlights he brought for their hike, McMurray scanned the wall behind the dumpster for the tell-tale brick. He saw it lying in the gravel under the empty hole. He cursed under his breath and went back to the front to search through his car for the key one more time.

"What's this for," she asked, eyeing the little cake with a single candle in it.

"A celebration," he'd set the cake down on the bar in front of her.

"Okay," she looked from the cake to him and back to the cake. "Celebrating what?"

"It's been exactly one year since that conversation on my porch when you were paroled," he lit the candle and smiled over the tiny flame. "You're now free and clear to move on with your life."

"My life," Marissa said, staring at the candle, "right."

"Right," McMurray echoed, a smile spread across his face. "College, a real job. Your life."

"But I like it here," she looked around the bar they had built together. "Besides, who would hire me with my record?"

"Fine," they'd had this argument many times over the past month, and McMurray didn't want to ruin the mood. "You want to say here, that can work."

"It can," Marissa stood up straighter, a look of joy across her face, "You mean it?"

"Under one condition."

"I'm not going to like this, am I?"

"Probably not," he said, placing a brochure for online business classes on the bar next to the cake.

The second search of his car came up empty again, but he did manage to scrounge up an old envelope and a pen from the console. McMurray scrawled out a quick note in case Marissa came back. As McMurray tucked the envelope carefully between the glass and the frame in the door where Marissa was sure to see it, he thought it saw something move inside near the bar. He looked through the window, trying to see if there was really something there, but the light's from the street had come one, lighting only the first few feet into the room. He banged sharply on the door twice and called out to Marissa and watched through the window. The darkness inside was almost palpable. McMurray gave the door another tug, turning the handle. The door didn't budge.

Walking back to his car and climbing in, McMurray headed back to the street. He hadn't seen which way Marissa had driven off, but she had been adamant about going to the shack, so he didn't doubt that's where she was headed. He pulled out of the parking lot and headed out of town toward the dirt road that would lead him to the shack.

Twenty—Eight

Sitting in the silence as the dusk fell into night, listening to the raspy sound of her own breathing, Marissa wondered if McMurray was still planning to come when a noise at the front door caught her attention. The key sliding into the lock and turning sounded like a cannon in the silence. When the door opened, headlights behind a shadow blinded her, and she brought her hand up to shield her eyes. Squinting into the light, Marissa struggled to see who it was.

"Marissa?" the shadow asked.

At the sound of his voice, Marissa felt the tension drain from her shoulders. She was saved. She leaned her head back against the bar, closed her eyes against the light, and sighed heavily. "Thank God it's you. Help me," the exhaustion was evident in her voice. "I think I got most of the bleeding stopped, but I need to get to the hospital."

"What happened here?" he moved through the door, closing it behind him. "Marissa, you're bleeding."

"I was attacked," she pleaded. She thought he was moving so slowly. Either he didn't understand how badly she was hurt, or she was hallucinating again. She could feel the world begin to constrict on her vision again, "Help, please."

"That's why I'm here," Geo walked over to the table Marissa had seen her brother sitting at and set down a piece of paper.

"Geo, please," she began to doubt reality, wondering if this was like the vision of her brother. "They got me really badly. It was some kids from your school, Zack and Dylan and Steve, I think. They've lost it. Beat the shit out of me and took my truck. Please, help me, call an ambulance."

Geo pulled his phone from his pocket and dialed. "Can we get some help down at McMurray's Pub? – Ya, she's here. – Well, they did a number on her, that's for sure. – Alright, see you in 20."

"Twenty minutes," Marissa couldn't feel her left foot anymore, "Geo, I need help sooner. I'm not going to make twenty minutes without help."

"No," Geo said, sitting down in the chair she'd imagined her brother in not long before, "you probably won't."

"Then fucking help me," her eyes burnt with tears, and she struggled to keep them open. Tears of pain and frustration dripped from her chin unheeded.

"I told you I was here to help, didn't I?" Geo picked up the piece of paper on the table, "Found this on the door out front. Seems McMurray stopped by but forgot his key," Geo dangled a key in front of himself and tossed it on the table, "good thing I had already taken this from the hidey-hole out back then."

"What do you mean, good thing. I need help. He could help."

"Right, but that's not the kind of help you need," Geo dismissed her concern with a wave of his hand.

"What the hell?"

"As I was saying, it seems the good priest is headed out to the woods," he put the letter down next to the key, "interesting."

THE LOST

"The fuck Geo," Marissa pushed herself back against the bar so she was sitting up as much as she could. The blood from the gash on her leg had slowed to oozing, but it hadn't stopped.

"I'm going to help," Geo got up and moved closer. The relief that Marissa had felt when he came in drained from her body, leaving her to shiver against the bar, "I told you that." He stopped just at the edge of the too sizeable red pool that surrounded her and picked up a piece of the broken bottle. "Though I do think that Steve might have let things get a little out of hand."

"What do you mean?"

"Well, I asked them to make sure you didn't go anywhere."

"You – asked them."

"Ya, you've been so hard to get alone 'Rissa," Geo played with the piece of glass in his hand, turning it over and over. "I've wanted to help you all along. I tried to do it at your brother's memorial service, but there were just too many people, and I'm not ready for that yet. Not that scale."

"That scale?"

"Right, you get it, start small. That's how you did it, pushing your brother off that log, then running away from the hospital."

"That's not what happened," Marissa said through her clenched teeth.

"Doesn't matter. It's what people think. No one ever cares about what really happens. It's just the perception of things. Your buddy McMurray would agree, don't you think?"

"Leave him out of this."

"No offense meant," Geo said, putting his hands up in mock surrender. "It's just, the whole messy business with the molestation charges, doesn't matter if he did it or not, the town's already judged him."

"I'm not sure what you're getting at with any of this," Marissa could feel her consciousness stealing away. "Please, you said you'd help me—"

"And I will," Geo ran the piece of glass down his thumb, drawing a line of blood that began to drip down his hand. "That's all I want."

"Fuck," Marissa gasped as she watched his blood drip to the floor. "What are you doing?"

Geo didn't answer; he looked at Marissa with a greedy smile, then down past his thumb to the place where his blood left small red droplets on the floor. There wasn't much blood because his thumb had already healed from the small wound the glass had made. He put his thumb in his mouth to clean off the red smudge left on his finger, watching as the blood droplets began to coalesce into four red beetles.

"Beautiful aren't they?" he asked, switching his gaze to Marissa.

"What the—"

"Oh, I suppose you must be a little surprised. I was at first too," Geo crouched down, so he was eye level with Marissa and continued. "They look almost like ladybugs, delicate in a way that most of us forget to notice."

"What are – How did? Fuck."

"I see you're eloquent as always," he stood and moved back to the table by the note. "I'll take that as your appreciation for the gift I'm giving you. They'll heal you, Marissa. They'll take away your pain, fix your body."

The beetles moved to the edge of the red pool Marissa was sitting in and skirted along the border. They seemed to be looking for something. One of them charged toward the gash on

THE LOST

Marissa's right leg, but as soon as it hit the pool she was sitting in, the thing vanished, melted into the red pool of whiskey and blood. The other three backed up.

"Interesting," Geo said, leaning back in his chair.

"What just—how—what are they?"

"Nothing much to worry about," Geo dismissed her question. "Look 'Rissa, I'm trying to help you here. Without these, you will die. It's only a matter of time, even with your tourniquet. Clearly, McMurray isn't coming," Geo waved the note in the air. "He'll find you here eventually if he finds his keys, but by tomorrow— well."

Another one of the beetles made a tentative move to get to Marissa's left hand, but again it disappeared into the pool of blood and whiskey. Geo shook his head and looked at Marissa. "You should join us, you know. I can save you."

"From bleeding out?" Marissa looked at the door to the kitchen, her jacket, the office phone all back there out of reach. "You could also call an ambulance."

"I can save you from so much more than just death 'Rissa."

"Geo, what is going on here," Marissa looked from the door to Geo and back again. "You're scaring me."

"I'm helping you," he insisted, "you'll see. Just reach out and let the beetles help."

"I'm not letting those creepy things crawl on me."

Geo smiled gently. "Not on you," his voice sounded like he was talking to a child, "in you."

Marissa's eyes went wide, and she let out a gasp. The third beetle had found its way onto her left hand and was crawling up her arm, finding a path around the pool she was seated in. Marissa swung at it with her other hand, wincing as her movement shifted her broken leg, and the pain shot out, shattering her thoughts.

Gasping for breath around the pain, she looked for the beetle; it lay on its back next to the puddle with its little shiny legs frantically wiggling to right itself. Marissa tried to scoot it further away but ended up splashing it instead. The beetle wiggles its legs more frantically as it slowly dissolved into a small puddle swirled with red.

"Now now," Geo said, "is that any way to treat something that only wants to help?"

"You mean like you *helped* those kids in the police station, Dylan. He was saying something about you being a monster."

"That's harsh," Geo pouted, "I just want to help."

"What did he mean about you being a monster?"

"I don't know. I only helped Dylan the same way I want to help you."

"You healed him?" Marissa looked at the one remaining beetle, keeping its distance from the puddle but circling to find a way past it. "With those?"

"Yup. He was grateful in the end," Geo leaned forward, his elbows on his knees, "you'll see."

The beetle scurried away down the bar, and Marissa gave a sigh of relief.

"There is so much pain and hurt," Geo looked at Marissa, staring at her face unfalteringly. She met his gaze defiantly, setting her jaw. "You've been through so much, so much hurt, so much pain. It's not fair. Your brother, your parents."

"What did you do to my parents?"

"Nothing, nothing. Your father and I had a chance to talk at the funeral, but he's felt much better since then. I helped him."

"Helped him?"

"There are so many ways that people hurt, so many ways that they struggle. I want to relieve that— I can relieve that. Like I said, though, start small. Bedrin, some random guy in the right

THE LOST

place at the right time, then Steve and his two cellmates. They used drugs to get rid of the pain. I just gave them something lasting, more permanent."

"What did you do to them? They're cold. I remember Steve as a nice kid."

"I gave them what I'm trying to give you, a way to get rid of the pain. People change 'Rissa. Look at me; I used to be so timid and shy. I was never able to tell you how I felt about you before," Geo leaned back and looked at the ceiling. "I used to annoy Mikey, telling him how beautiful I thought you were. He'd get so pissed." Geo smiled at the ceiling.

"You don't get to talk about him. You're delusional. Call a fucking ambulance."

"Won't need to if you just let those beetles do their work," he shrugged and looked back down at Marissa. "Dylan fought it too. He's a bit scarred from the ordeal. Zack, he was easy."

"Are you– you're controlling them? You made them attack me?"

"I wouldn't have had to if you weren't so hard to get alone."

"You'd have done it yourself?"

"Probably, but they enjoyed it so much. Besides, it's not like it's going to matter in an hour or so. Either you'll be one of us, or you'll be dead," Geo leaned forward again. "You can't stop this 'Rissa, so you might at well join it. We're going to help everyone. Your pain is not unique; it's not what makes you special. I want you to be there with me as we help this town. Start small, you know. Then we can branch out from there. Everyone has some pain to get rid of."

"What about Mikey or Jeff or Jackie? Didn't they have pain you could help with?

"They did," Geo looked down at his feet, "but I wasn't what I am now." When he looked back up, his eyes seemed lost for a moment. "They never did find their bodies."

"What the fuck is that supposed to mean?" Marissa spit the words at him, "Are you bragging?"

"No," he shook his head and looked dazed for a minute before returning his eyes to hers, an inner fire burning behind them. "Never mind that, it's for someone else."

"You're not making any sense. Look, Geo, I need you to call the cops, Bedrin even, I don't give a shit, I just need help."

"We don't need him," Geo waved a hand dismissively at her, "Your choice is pretty simple after all. Let the beetle do its work and join me or bleed to death. Would you really rather die than help me rid the world of its pain? Steve, Zack, Dylan, Bedrin, the rest of them, your dad, they're free now. They can live their life. They can move on without the pain of what has happened. They feel joy; they're happy."

"They're psychotic. Bedrin always was, but those other three beat the shit out of me, and my dad attacked Father McMurray," Marissa's understanding caught up with her words. "My dad. I'll kill you if you hurt him."

"Hurt him? I've helped him. He was in so much pain at your brother's funeral. After McMurray spoke, I just gave him his freedom. What he did with it was up to him."

"Freedom from what?"

"Pain. From having to follow society's rules about what is right and proper. I released what he really wanted and gave him the permission he needed to break the rules, to make his own choices, free of consequences."

"At Father McMurray's expense."

"Someone always has to pay the price of freedom."

"How can you be so casual about it?"

THE LOST

"McMurray wasn't hurt," Geo said, "he's well enough to go for a hike. Interesting place to choose, though. I may have to send someone to meet up with him."

"Geo, this isn't you," Marissa pleaded.

"Sure it is. Who else would it be?" His eyes shifted above her, "You'll see."

"What?" Marissa looked saw the red beetle perched on the edge of the bar above her. It leaped onto her face and scurrying toward the cut above her eye. Instinctively she put her hands up, trying to wipe the thing off her face, but there was nothing there. Suddenly an intense pain shot through her eye as if something was burrowing under her eye socket. She heard a hollow laugh and looked at Geo, pupils wide and frantically searching for help.

You'll live. Geo's voice spoke into her mind. He stood up, looking at her with unsympathetic eyes. His lips didn't move, but she heard his voice just a clearly as if they did. *I'm helping you.*

"Fuck you," she tried to spit at him, but it just dribbled down her chin, "I'm not going to join you."

Fight all you want. It won't matter. Geo turned and walked toward the door. *All I really need is one.*

Marissa heard the lock click shut seconds before pain ripped through her head, and she writhed on the floor, screaming and toppling the stools around her.

Eric Johnson

Twenty—Nine

"Think you're hot shit, don't you?" was the first nice thing anyone had said to her since she'd gone through processing. Even that wasn't saying much, but at least the tone was friendly. Still, Marissa didn't answer. After the first few times, she'd learned that it was best to just let them say what they wanted to say. People tended to hit less when that happened, and she was already bruised enough. "Don't worry, I ain't gonna do you like that. How old'r you anyway, twelve?"

"Twenty," Marissa looked up to see a matronly woman with long raven black hair pulled up in a bun.

"What do they call you, twenty?"

"Marissa," she said, her voice barely a whisper.

"Too damn long," the woman said. "Callin' you Ri," she said with a curt nod of her head. "Name's Toni. Stick with me, kid. I'll get you through."

Marissa's skin burned as the beetle burrowed under it. Her vision blurred, and her breath caught. She could feel her broken leg, stomped on by Dylan to keep her from moving, grind back into place. She screamed as the smaller shards of the broken bone slipped through her muscle and soft tissue to find their original location. She almost blacked out again when the bone began heating up, making it feel like she was being cooked from the inside, her muscles spasming, causing her to kick out against the stools of the bar. Her arms flew reflexively to her head as she tried to keep the toppling stools off of her.

She pushed the stools off of her, letting them clatter to the ground. She could see the small lump moving toward her lower leg, and instinctively, her hands went to it. She tried to claw at it, her fingers tearing at her jeans, making the small fashionable rips larger so she could get at her leg. She watched as the beetle burrowed over the bruise where her leg had been broken. A flash of white-hot pain lanced through her. Screaming, she grabbed for her leg again, trying to scrape at her swollen and bluish skin to get to the beetle. Each time she winced against the pain, but she didn't stop. She clawed red lines in her skin, the blood beginning to seep out under the raking nails. Another lance of pain threw her head back, and she grabbed at her temples.

It wasn't the first time they had approached her in the yard, but they weren't taking no for an answer this time. "Bitch, why you be hangin' with that spick motherfucker? We stick with our own in here."

"I'm not looking for any trouble," Marissa said, walking away from the group and toward the tables where Toni held court.

"Aww, kept bitch looking for mommy," one of the other girls said as she walked around, blocking Marissa's way.

"Might not be lookin' for it," said the first to talk, "but bitch, trouble looking for you."

Marissa turned slowly in a circle, looking for a way out that wouldn't get her beat up or punished by the guards. She'd had enough of both. Subtlety was needed here, she knew that, but subtlety had never been her thing. Marissa looked pleadingly to Toni, who simply nodded and stood up, her court following her.

Marissa caught her breath and looked back at her leg. The scratches she'd put in her leg were gone. The bruising was lightening up, it looked a day old instead of the hour, or so it should have been. She felt the beetle moving back up her leg and across her stomach before the burning started again as it moved down her left leg. She knew that she had to get this thing out of her. She grabbed the brass rail of the bar, dragging herself across the floor, working herself toward the back of the bar and the door to the kitchen.

The world swam before her eyes, stools complaining as her shoulders pushed them out of the way, some clattering to the floor when she shoved them out of her way. It was slow, pulling hand over hand along the floor, but she was glad that she always kept the place clean at least she wasn't dragging herself through somebody else's filth. She chuckled to herself when that thought sunk in as if she wasn't enough of a mess. At the end of the rail, she reached out, cupping her hands around the corner of the wooden bar, then pulled with all her might, propelling herself halfway across the walkway between the bar and the back wall. She couldn't reach the door yet, but back there, in the drying rack, was her salvation.

She began to use her elbows to crawl toward the door. It was hard dragging her useless burning legs behind her. She could hear Geo's voice in the back of her head, *"I'm only trying to help."* She cursed to herself, some help. How could he, her brother's best friend? She knew something more was going on here, those high school kids, Geo, even Bedrin, as much of an ass as he was anyway; this was not normal.

"Some fucking help, asshole," she said to the empty room. Another shearing pain coursed through her, this time radiating from the gash on her left leg. The tourniquet had slowed the beetle down for a little bit, but it had gotten caught on one of the stools and loosened just enough; the blood had started to pick up too. This time the pain felt like someone had put a thousand lit cigarettes against her leg. She screamed out, arching her back as the loss of blood and the pain began to narrow her field of vision.

THE LOST

At the edges of her vision, the shadows pulsed and writhed but were still every time she turned to look at them.

She was army crawling under the counter in the laundry room. They'd managed to corner her when she'd let her guard down. She looked around furiously for the guard's boots, but they weren't there. She must have stepped out for a minute; they did that when the room got too hot for them, a luxury she was never afforded. Toni had just been reassigned, and the other girls were not her friends.

Marissa felt their hands on her legs, pulling her back. She was trapped, cornered, and she knew that it was now or never. Screw the guards, screw the punishment, she needed to end this, and the only thing that these girls listened to was violence. She heard their jeers as they pulled her to her feet. The usual names and taunts flew past her, rendered meaningless by overuse.

"Let me go," she halfheartedly said. There were three of them, but Toni had been training her, and she was a quick study when her life depended on it. McMurray will be disappointed, but he doesn't know what it's like here.

"Let me go," one of the other girls mocked her. "Mommy's not here to protect you this time." She brought her arm back and rammed it into Marissa's stomach. She'd been ready for it, though, her tensed her abs absorbing the hit with little effort. Looked up through her hair and grimaced at her attackers.

"You had your chance," Marissa said as she grabbed a handful of detergent that had spilled on the table behind her and threw it in their faces, then she let loose. They landed in the infirmary, and she landed in solitary for a day. McMurray was disappointed, Toni was proud, and Marissa wasn't sure how she should feel about either.

Her vision began to clear, but the burning was still just as intense. She'd managed to drag herself to the door, and the kitchen loomed in front of her. There were plenty of handholds through the back, shelves rattled, and dishes threatened to crash down on her, but she managed to make it to the sink. She dragged her weight up the leg of the metal counter, her hands wet with blood and sweat, slipping as often as not. She got her fingers to the edge of the counter, their tips just touching the drying rack where she'd put one of the knives last night.

Marissa let out a cry that sounded half-feral to her own ears. She strained to pull herself up, bending her waist over the edge of the counter, hoping to avoid pulling the dish rack off the counter and dropping the knife on her head or cutting herself worse than she already was planning on. Geo's voice was in her head again, *"Without these, you will die,"* he was so sure. She had her left hand on the handle of the knife when her right hand slipped off the counter. Her chin slammed into the counter, violently throwing her head back and landing her on the floor, the knife clattering harmlessly next to her.

Sitting across from McMurray, the glass separating them, she heard herself tell him to fuck off. He didn't understand what it was like.

"You're right," McMurray said into the phone, his eyes never leaving hers, "I don't know what it's like. But I do know what you're like."

"Ya, a thief, don't you remember?"

"The two men on the cross next to Jesus were thieves."

"So?"

"So if he could forgive them, why can't you forgive yourself?"

He was right, she hadn't forgiven herself for screwing her life up so badly, and that pissed her off. "You think you're so smart? Why are you here talking to me on a Sunday and not in the fucking pulpit Father?"

He didn't answer her. He just looked down at his hand, leaning his head on the phone, and closed his eyes.

"I'm sorry," Marissa said after a minute. "That wasn't fair."

"No," McMurray said after a long sigh, "it wasn't." Then he smiled at her, a smile that lit up his entire face. It was a warm face, his

THE LOST

nose a little redder than the last time. "But it wasn't undeserved. It seems that we both have some forgiveness to look for."

"I didn't mean—" Marissa started, but McMurray held up his hand to stop her.

"Tell you what," his eyes glistened with unshed tears as he spoke, "let's start with forgiving each other and doing what we can to survive, then, once you're out, we can work on forgiving ourselves."

Marissa smiled sadly at the old man who sat across from her, his button-down open at the collar to reveal a neck devoid of the crucifix he'd always worn when she was younger, his jacket, threadbare and stained. Red-nosed with shadows under his eyes, eyes that still shone with compassion and hope that belied the rest of his appearance. "Deal," she said as the guard came over, ending their conversation.

Marissa rolled over and sat on the rubber mat McMurray placed in front of the sink to keep the floor from getting too slippery if water sloshed out while she was doing the dishes. She pulled her knees up to her chest, the knife sitting on the floor within arm's reach. The pain had begun to lessen, there was some slight burning, but her vision was coming back. She felt the beetle moving beneath the skin in her shoulder, a bump raised out as it crossed over a bone before moving on to her left arm. Without taking her eyes from the bump moving inside her arm toward a cut in her forearm, she reached with her right and grabbed the knife. She put the blade to her arm, and a shiver ran down her back as the cool metal touched her burning skin. This was crazy, she told herself. Her hand shook, and she could feel the knife's edge scratch against the soft flesh on the inside of her arm. Geo's voice sounded in her head again, *"It's only a matter of time."* What was he up to, she wondered. He'd talked about saving people, about the town and moving beyond that, about sacrifice. She knew he was talking about her bleeding out, but there seemed to be something behind his words, something else she didn't quite understand.

The beetle moved around to her wrist and seemed to sit there, nestled in against the arteries. She pushed the knife to her wrist, pausing before she put the blade to her skin. Her right hand shook as she readied to slice through her skin. She took a deep breath and drew the knife across her wrist. The sharp blade cut deep into the soft flesh, and she let out a whimper as her stomach did somersaults at the sight of the fresh thick blood pouring out of her newly opened wrist. She could see the beetle, blood-red carapace with six black legs and small black mandibles, just inside the wound. Letting the knife slip from her hand and fall to the mat by her side, she reached her fingers into the bleeding wound and pulled the beetle out. It squirmed between her fingers as she began to apply pressure, readying to crush it between her fingers.

She heard Geo's voice again, faint and fading, *"you will die,"* followed by McMurray's, *"do what you can to survive."* Tears streaked through the drying blood on her face. This was wrong; she knew in her heart that whatever Geo was trying to do was not good. She didn't want this thing in her, this beetle of his, this thing that came from his blood, but she was not ready to die.

The blood from her arm was warm and thick; Marissa realized that she cut too deep. The edges of her vision blurred as she sat pinned the beetle between her fingers. Her breath coming in fits through the pain. She struggled to slow her breathing and make a plan, but all she could focus on was the blood. She'd lost too much before Geo arrived and was shivering uncontrollably. The beetle helped, but now, with the new cut, things were getting worse. She struggled to remain conscious, to stop shivering. This had been a mistake; slitting her own wrist had been stupid.

THE LOST

"I'm sorry," she said to the empty room, the still silent darkness closing in around her once more. Her stomach rolled as she put the beetle back on her arm and watched as it skittered toward her open wrist. The searing white pain closed around her, and the shadows writhed once more. She could feel tears pressing at the back of her eyes, "I'm so sorry."

THIRTY

Marissa watched the last few tendrils of skin reach across the gash she had put in her wrist. Watching the beetle work on her wrist was fascinating when she finally got over the intense burning and the fact that this beetle couldn't possibly be ordinary. It spun skin like a spider spins its silk, skittering across the open wound and using its legs to attach the new skin to the old. The cut was mainly closed by this point, where the skin was new and healed. There wasn't a scar, not even that fresh raw skin that comes with a healing scab. The beetle healed the cut like it never happened, no evidence. Without seeing it with her own eyes, she'd never have believed it.

When the cut had fully healed, the beetle no longer visible under her skin, Marissa made a fist and relaxed it three times before she shook her hand. No pain, no numbness or soreness. She ran her hands down her legs, the bruise she'd had only hours ago was gone, and her legs didn't hurt. No cuts, scrapes, she pulled up her shirt to look at the scar she had from getting her appendix out as a kid, nothing—smooth, clean skin.

Marissa leaned her head back against the metal counter and cried. She didn't hold back, didn't suppress her feelings as she always had. She cried for her brother, her parents, her broken past; cried for the things that she had done, the people she'd hurt. Everything came crashing down on her. Her whole life, every mistake, every cruelty, every theft. Each tear that fell lightened her burden. When she was done, the tears drying in the dirt and blood on her cheeks, her pain was gone. She was free of all the burdens she'd carried with her since that fateful day picking wildflowers for her mother.

She still felt the beetle under her skin, but it didn't bother her as much now. It simply felt like a part of her, something that belonged there, that'd always been there. It was somewhere near the small of her back at the moment, along the side of her spine. She pulled her knees up to her chest and tried to put a little pressure on them. No pain, no weakness. She pressed harder, using her hand to help herself stand up. Once standing, Marissa tested her legs, bending her knees, a little hop. Healthy. Heading into the bathroom, she searched her face for black eyes, the cut from the shattered glass. Smooth, healthy skin stared back at her under a layer of filth. Turning on the skink, she splashed her face with some water, loosening the gore that covered it. Her eyes were still a little puffy and red from crying, but otherwise, there was no sign of the fight with the boys.

"Shit," she breathed at her reflection, "what have I done?"

You let me help; Geo's voice was quiet in the back of her mind, like a whisper on the other side of a closed door.

Marissa rushed from the bathroom, trying to find Geo, ask him what he did to her; what the beetle was all about, but he wasn't there. She saw the blood, her blood, dragged across the floor. The fight, the crawl for the knife, Marissa remembered it all, but something about the memory didn't seem real. It was hazy in her mind, like something that happened to someone else or years ago, not something she just experienced.

She felt compelled to clean the bar, get rid of her blood on the floor. She grabbed a mop and a bottle of bleach from the back room and dumped the bleach on the pools. She mopped it around, soaking some of it up and staining the mop red. When she was done, she looked around with detached interest; she didn't feel the typical happiness that cleaning gave her. Taking the mop outback, she threw the head into the dumpster and grabbed a new one from storage. Then she went into the office and stood looking at the safe, one hand on her jacket, and thought about the money that was behind the door. A few twists of the dial, and it would be hers.

Yes, came Geo's voice in the back of her head.

Marissa was startled at the sound that wasn't a sound. She had heard it, but not with her ears. His voice was different somehow, somewhere between a thought and a sound. She shook her head, a new tear gathering in the corner of her eye. She closed them and took a trembling breath before her hand closed on her jacket, and she turned to storm out of the bar leaving McMurray's note on the table.

Her truck was gone, she knew that, but not who had it or how they'd gotten it. She started walking toward the edge of town. It was time to go, that much she knew. Everything here was too close, too much the past. Suddenly, she felt the need to get away, far away.

You'll come back to me. Geo's voice was disturbingly close. A shiver ran up her spine in the hot night air. *Don't you like to feel free?*

"Fuck," she said into the night air, "fuck, fuck, fuck. Get out of my head," she could feel the pressure of his words, his suggestion to return. She needed to put some distance between herself and this town. She turned back and looked at the shadow of the bar. McMurray had tried so hard to help her forgive herself; she'd tried, but it wasn't going to happen, and she knew it. You can't build on a foundation made of sand; that's what he tried to do with her. She was nothing but a shiftless mass, useless for

THE LOST

anything except sucking the life out of everything around her. The further from the shadow of that place she went, the heavier her memories weighed down on her.

Headlights in the distance briefly lit the front of the bar, passing her only to pull over a few feet away, spitting dust-up around her. The passenger side window rolled down, and Marissa strode over to the car, bent down, and let out a startled gasp when staring back at her from the driver's side was the lawyer from the bar. He leaned over, his eyes catching the light of the streetlamp, and unlocked the passenger door. Marissa's stomach rolled.

"Get in," he said with no more preamble.

"What?" Marissa held the door open and bent down to look in at him.

"I said, get in," Lucius leaned back against his seat, looking out over the steering wheel.

His words were echoed by Geo's own words in the back of her mind. She felt herself wanting to get into the car, but she remained standing next to the open door.

"I think I'll walk," she said but couldn't seem to get herself to close the car door. Lucius simply sat behind the wheel, looking down the road, "Thanks anyway, though."

"We need to talk," he looked toward her, "there's something you don't know about a mutual friend of ours."

"Mutual friend?" She knew who he was talking about, on some level, but she couldn't seem to bring a name to mind, so she let the question hang in between them.

"Don't play the idiot. I've heard better," Lucius patted the passenger seat.

In the back of Marissa's mind, she could almost feel Geo's words, *Get in the car 'Rissa*. She hesitated for another beat but then gave in to the urge she felt. It was as if she had wanted nothing more than to be in the seat of this car right now. On some level, she still knew that made no sense, but that level didn't matter. What mattered was the pressure of the words in the back of her mind. Closing the door behind her, Marissa reached for her seatbelt as Lucius put the car into drive, locking the doors automatically, and drove off in silence.

"Talk," Marissa said as the sign of the bar came back into view. "If you're bringing me back into town, you're going the wrong way."

"I'm not," Lucius responded, eyes still on the road.

"What about our mutual friend? You're either talking about Bedrin or Geo," she said, looking across the console. "Spill it."

"As you know, the first time I saw you, I was headed down to see Geo in the hospital. I was going to represent him," Marissa saw sweat beading on his forehead, the vein at his temple pulsed.

"You seem to have been successful."

"Didn't need to be," He leered across the car at her, "Geo had everything well in hand by the time he got out of the hospital. Well in hand."

"Meaning?"

"Meaning he'd already come to accept his new calling."

"His calling?" Marissa raised an eyebrow toward Lucius, "What are you, some religious nut?"

Lucius laughed humorlessly before he continued. "I wouldn't say I was religious. I make a point not to believe in anything I haven't seen. But, let's stick with calling for now."

"He told me a little about that not too long ago," Marissa looked at the door handle, "why I was headed out of town, in fact."

"Change of plans," Lucius looked far off like Steven had a couple of times when he and his boys had attacked her. He looked calmer, though, the sweat no longer beading. "I have a job for you. You need to retrieve something for me."

"I'm not your errand girl," she crossed her arms over her chest.

"You need to find something," Lucius began as if she hadn't said anything, "A book. Leather bound, gold leaf edging. Get it."

"Again, not your errand girl."

Do it. The voice pushed at her mind. Marissa rubbed the back of her neck and grimaced and thought, *I need that fucking book.* The voice was stronger than her own thoughts. McMurray would love this, hearing voices now. Her head began to ache, and she rubbed her hand against her forehead.

"Really," Lucius said, his voice unhurried, confident, "it's much easier if you just do as we ask."

"Who is this fucking we?"

He turned to look at her, head cocked to the side, and smiled. "I know you hear him. He knows too. Do you think that little headache is the worst he can do to you if you refuse?" He looked back at the road and continued. "If he wanted to, he could boil your brains turn them into so much mush that they will simply drain out of your ears and nostrils. He could turn your blood to poison and keep you alive until it dissolved the last nerve cell capable of feeling pain. He could make you fucking eat your own arm and laugh as you bleed to death. You live right now because you are useful. If you want to keep living, you'll do what I say. If I say kick a puppy, you kick the puppy; if I say shoot some old lady, pull the damn trigger; and if I say get a book, you get the fucking book," spit flew across the steering wheel as he finished his speech. He was breathing heavily, trembling slightly, knuckles white across the steering wheel.

Eric Johnson

"Look," Marissa put her hand on the handle of the door and wondered how badly she'd get hurt if she tumbled out of the moving car, a trick she had pulled once in high school on a dare, "I know you helped Geo out, and me for that matter, with the legal stuff, and I'm grateful. Really I am. But this calling shit, this burn you from the inside shit, I'm not on the same page as you. Fuck, I'm not on the same planet as you, so if you could just stop the car, let me out, I'll just head out of town and disappear."

"No."

No. Lucius's words were echoed in her head, and she squeezed her eyes shut against the force. Taking a deep breath, she could feel the pain receding, and her hand released the seatbelt as she pulled on the door handle. The air roared into the car, pushing the door closed against her, trying to trap her inside. *Calm down 'Rissa, calm down. Just listen.* She could feel the words dragging her back into her seat, letting the door close.

"See," Lucius said next to her, "so much easier just to give in."

The pain had left Marissa's head as she settled back into her seat. "What's so important about this book?"

"I knew you'd come around," Lucius's shoulders seemed to relax as he steered the car over to the shoulder of the road, next to the forest. He turned in his seat and looked at her.

"Didn't say I'd do it."

"You will," his confidence pissed her off, "Leather-bound, gold-trimmed. The thing is, it might look dried out by now, don't worry about that. Just get it and bring it back to the police station. Geo'll meet you there and take it. No need to open it; the thing's done its job. He just wants it as a—*keepsake*—right, so get it and then back to the station."

Something deep in Marissa's gut screamed at her to refuse, said this was the wrong move. It was that part of her that

THE LOST

had kept her from getting too hurt in prison, too damaged. She wanted to listen to it, she knew it was right, but she heard herself agree with Lucius. Then, like a dream, she began to get out of the car and head toward the forest's edge. She felt pushed, like she was confined in her own body. She didn't like the feeling. *It's easier to listen, easier to do what you're told.* Marissa hated that voice. Her stomach twisted in knots when she heard it when she felt herself agreeing with it. She planted her foot halfway between the forest and the edge of the road and turned.

"I'm out," she said. She could feel the pressure building behind her eyes like someone was trying to push them out of her skill with their thumbs. "I'm not doing it."

"Not wise," Lucius said through the still open passenger door.

"Fuck it," she spat back, "and fuck you, both of you can go to–" the word dissolved into a scream as the pain in her skull crescendoed, crashing through her consciousness. She felt a pop behind her eyes, and her hands flew to her face as she fell to her knees. She brought her hands away to see if there was any blood, but all she saw was darkness, soul-sucking darkness that even Lucius's headlights didn't penetrate. She heard the door to the car open and then close, the engine of the car idled where it had been this whole time. Footsteps crunched on the gravel, moving toward her. "I can't–" she turned her head left and right, trying to catch a shadow or the lights from a passing car, but all she saw was darkness.

"I told you it wasn't wise," Lucius was standing over her, and she started at his voice. "There's an easy fix here, just do what we ask, and you can have your sight back."

She could feel his breath on the back of her neck and shivered. He was almost touching her, but she couldn't feel any warmth from his body like she expected. Instead, he seemed to leech the heat from her. She shivered even as sweat from the humid night air caused her shirt to cling to her back. Her shoulders heaved as she tried to catch her breath between tears. Survive now, she told herself, forgive yourself later. *It's only a book, a keepsake. It was your brother's.* Part of her, deep inside, screamed that there would be no later if Geo got this book. She opened her eyes to the darkness, warm tears flooding down her face as she shivered against the cold behind her.

"Alright," the word sounded more like an exhale than any effort to speak. She heard the car door open, then close again before the engine revved up, and the tires crunched across the gravel. She saw a blur of tail lights pulling away, barely more than a light spot against the inky dark that had taken her. *Good girl.* She dropped her forehead down to the dirt at the roadside, shoulders hitching up and down in the moonlight. *Good girl.*

Thirty—One

There should have been police tape or something, McMurray thought to himself, some evidence that there had been a bunch of cops on the scene looking for the bodies of those kids, but it wasn't there. Come to think of it, McMurray couldn't even remember a search party being called for the bodies. The police had just accepted that they wouldn't find anything. He looked around again; things were quiet, empty. Nothing but the muddy dirt road he'd driven down, the old shack with a scattering of coals from a fire in front of the door, and discarded beer bottles from the kids that came here to drink and do God only knew what else. He closed the car door and wandered into the clearing. He knew that Marissa hadn't come here yet if she was still coming tonight, but since he was here, he started looking around.

There was no evidence of an attack, wolves the article had said when the story of Geo's acquittal made the local paper. No paw prints, no disturbed pine needles from last winter, nothing. He walked over to the fire, putting his hand over the coals; the grayish dust felt no different than the air around him. The door hanging over the fire was open slightly, but the moonlight didn't penetrate inside. He walked around the shack, the windows were too dirty to see inside, but he doubted he would find anything in there. Still, something urged him to see for sure.

Eric Johnson

Walking back to his car, a sound off to his right caught his attention, and he paused for a moment, trying to decide if he should break for the car or wait to see what was out there. The shadows of the trees seemed to grow more menacing as he weighed his options. He had a flashlight in the trunk of his car, two as a matter of fact, but the doors were unlocked, and if whatever made the noise in the woods wanted to hurt him, McMurray figured a flashlight wouldn't be much help, especially not the old, orange plastic ones he had in his trunk. Being inside the car, on the other hand, would let him escape, but he'd never know what was out there in the trees or what was in that shack, and he felt he needed to know that more than he needed to breathe.

Another noise from the trees broke his reverie, and McMurray slowly made his way to the trunk of his car, unsuccessfully avoiding stepping on any sticks in the moonlight. Opening the trunk, he fished around inside for one of the flashlights. His hand brushed up against the whiskey bottle he kept back there, and he thought about taking a sip to calm his nerves, but one taste always leads to another until the bottom of the bottle matched the hole he felt in the pit of his stomach. He rested his hand on the bottle, fantasizing about pulling it out and embracing the oblivion offered in the warm embrace of the whiskey. All of the craziness of the past few weeks could wash away for a few hours, leaving the numbness he'd grown accustomed to. Closing his eyes, McMurray picked up the bottle, the amber liquid sloshed around inside. He wanted to open it and smell the woody earthiness inside, and he tried to convince himself that it would end there. He knew better, but he could almost convince himself that smelling it would be enough, that he could let himself face down his demon and not lose. The sound of something moving in the brush at the edge of the clearing drew him back. Putting the bottle back into the trunk, he pulled out a flashlight and shone it around the clearing. Marissa walked toward McMurray's car at the far side, bathed in the moonlight and squinting away from the flashlight.

"Marissa," McMurray said, lowering the beam of the flashlight, so it was no longer blinding her, "glad it's you."

"Father McMurray," her voice sounded hollow to him, "I didn't expect you to be here still."

"Are you alright?"

"Fine, fine," she insisted. "Just hard to be here right now."

"I bet," he said as she got closer. McMurray noticed that her eyes were red and puffy like she'd been crying. He imagined her walking those familiar paths alone, thinking of her brother and everything she'd lost. Thinking about the easier time when they would walk the path during catechism season, a walk he did with her brother a couple of years ago. "Where's your truck?"

She paused for a moment and got a faraway look in her eyes. "I wanted to walk in," she said, "take a few minutes of privacy."

"Are you sure that's safe? The paper said that once animals attack people, they need to be put down because it increases the likelihood they'll do it again."

"You're here by yourself."

"But I have light," McMurray raised the flashlight sidewise, then smiling, he tossed the one in his hands to her and went back into the trunk to get the other one. When he looked up again, Marissa had a faraway look still, only this time she was grimacing, and sweat beaded on her forehead. "Marissa, you look like – well, not good."

She shook her head and smiled toward him, "I'm alright, I promise." She walked up and put a hand on his forearm.

"If you're sure," McMurray wasn't convinced, but he knew Marissa well enough to know that pressing the matter wouldn't do any good. "I was just about to go into the shack and have a look around, coming?"

"No," her voice came out harsh, and McMurray looked at her with an eyebrow raised. Concern was written across his face. "No," she repeated a little more softly, "that place creeps me out."

"Come on," McMurray smiled at her, "you used to drink here, and don't try to tell me you didn't."

"Outside the shack," she shivered despite the warmth, "never inside."

"Okay," McMurray stepped over the coals of the fire, careful not to disturb them any more than they already were, and pushed the door open. The old hinges complained at being put to task again after such a long exposure to the elements.

Inside, the building was dark despite his flashlight. The cloying air seemed to absorb the light without giving anything away. It was a small shack, big enough for a twin bed frame, the mattress having long ago rotted away or been removed for other reasons, a small table and one chair. A broken hurricane lamp sat on the table along with a thick layer of dust. The whole room was covered in dust and dirt, and cobwebs. He shone the flashlight around the small space, the light reflected back at him from the window panes, but other than that and darkness, the shack didn't seem to have anything of interest.

Outside, McMurray could hear Marissa talking to someone on her phone. She sounded angry. He couldn't make out what she was saying or who she was talking to, but based on the tone she was using, he figured it was probably her father, those two hadn't gotten along in a while, and things seemed to be getting worse between them. He stood in the dusty air to give her a moment of privacy and relaxed his hand by his side, the flashlight shining on the floor.

Everything in this shack was covered with a layer of dirt and dust, except for one section of the floor, one board about a foot long, seemed just a little cleaner than the others, like some of the looser dirt had recently been knocked off. McMurray bent down and touched the board, found it loose, and began to look for something to pry it up with. Settling on a piece of the broken glass from the hurricane lamp, McMurray dug at the seam in the floor, cutting his finger as the board gave way, causing the glass to slip in his hands. He got his fingers under it and pulled the floorboard up, shining his light into the space below. The darkness seemed thicker there, almost palpable, but he could see something sitting on the ground beneath the floor, leaning against one of the rotting supports for the shack. McMurray reached through the opening and pulled out a rather large book. It was bound with some sort of leather that he couldn't make out below the cracks and dirt caked on it, but there was a dim sheen to the edges of the paper. He tried wiping the dirt off the cover to read the title but instead smeared blood across the dirt from his finger.

McMurray stood up, put his finger in his mouth to clean off the cut, and then walked out of the cabin. Marissa was standing by his car, her back to him as he stepped through the door. Her shoulders were slumped, and her head was leaning against the roof of his car. She looked exhausted, more exhausted than when she first stepped from the trees. He watched her in the moonlight for a moment and felt a pang in his chest. She looked like a child still; in many ways, she was a child, forced to grow up quicker than she should have, but still a child, and he wanted to protect her and keep her safe from the cruel world. He felt like he'd already failed at that. It was his fault she had gone to prison. He knew that in his soul, and he'd been doing everything he could to make up for it ever since.

"Marissa," he called out to her. She jumped a bit at his voice, shoulder tensing like an animal about to strike. He held the book over his head and called out, "Look what I found."

Thirty-Two

Marissa stepped through the clearing and saw his car immediately. Her eyes had long ago adjusted to the dappled light of the full moon, and she had marveled at how much better her night vision was now that she wasn't fighting. He was here too, just as he should be, rummaging in the back of his trunk, she could see his shadow from the trunk light. *Get the book, bring it to the police station.* Her instructions were clear, simple. What harm could there be in bringing some old book to them? She knew it was them, Lucius was working with Geo, plus if they wanted her to get it to the station, then the cops must be part too. Things were too big for her to fight. She could do nothing to stop this from happening; she knew that even without the voice telling her.

McMurray stepped out from behind the car and raised the light to scan the edge of the trees. The light stopped on Marissa, and she brought her hand up to block the blinding glair. It burnt her eyes. Pain lanced at her retina as they strained to adjust quickly enough. It was a dull pain compared to what she had experienced at the side of the road, a normal pain. This one she could handle. Now, she said to herself, to find the book.

"Marissa," McMurray said, lowering the beam of his flashlight, "glad it's you."

"Father McMurray, I didn't expect you to be here still."

"Are you alright?"

"Fine, fine. Just hard to be here right now," it was true, for the most part. She had her instructions—the book. Everything was for the book. She felt it deep in her mind, gnawing at her.

"I bet," he said. "Where's your truck?"

She wasn't sure what to tell him. It was stolen, not precisely a lie, but then he'd want to take her to the police to file a report, and she didn't have time for that. *Don't leave without the book.* She ground her teeth at Geo's voice; she didn't like him being in her head like that. "I wanted to walk in, take a few minutes of privacy."

"Are you sure that's safe? The paper said that once animals attack people, they need to be put down because it increases the likelihood they'll do it again."

"You're here by yourself."

"But I have light," McMurray smiled. It was a good smile. It came from his eyes and crossed his face like a wave of good cheer; something was different about him lately. He smiled more, more genuinely than he had in a long time. *Doesn't matter; stay focused.* She caught the flashlight that he tossed her way without even thinking about it. *He's dangerous.* She didn't know if Geo could hear her thoughts, if she could somehow communicate to him but based on what happened back a the road, she was almost positive he could listen to what she said out loud. She tried thinking that Father McMurray was a good man, helpful, but she didn't get any response from the voice in her head.

"Marissa, you look like – well, not good," the concern in his voice was unmistakable.

She shook her head and smiled toward him, "I'm alright, I promise." She wanted to tell him everything, but she didn't know where to start. In the end, she had done this to herself. It was her punishment for a life lived like shit. She would have to bear it alone like she did for her time in prison.

"If you're sure," McMurray said.

She could tell he didn't believe her, and she wanted him to push her on it; she wanted it so badly. She'd tell him everything if he just asked. He didn't ask. Instead, the voice in her head piped in. *Kill him. He's going to get in the way.* She couldn't believe that she was considering the best way to do what she was told. McMurray said something, pointing at the shack, but Marissa looked around for a good-sized branch on the ground. Something in the back of her mind, some part deep down, was screaming at her to wake up. *Kill him now.*

"No," she growled at Geo's voice. McMurray looked at her with his eyebrow raised. "No," she repeated a little more softly, "that place creeps me out."

"Come on," McMurray smiled at her, again, "you used to drink here, and don't try to tell me you didn't."

Kill him now. This time the voice was accompanied by intense pain in the back of her neck. She fought back against the suggestion. Something was working its way into her mind. Each time the fight was more brutal to commit to. Each time, the little voice in the back of her mind was weaker. *Follow him inside and kill him.*

"Outside the shack," she shivered despite the warmth, "never inside."

"Okay," McMurray said and walked to the door. She watched him step over the coals and pushed the door open, then she turned her back on the cabin. It felt like she was moving through water instead of the summer night; each movement contradicting the suggestion felt like she was walking up a river against the current. It would be so easy to follow him in there, to grab something hard and knock him over the head, but every fiber of her being screamed at her not to do it.

Putting her hands on the roof of his car to stop them from trembling, Marissa took a deep breath. The pain was starting to build behind her eyes again, but she refused to turn around. *I said to follow him in there.*

"No," she said to the roof of McMurray's car. White pain seared across her vision, and she let out a short gasp. She kept her voice quiet so that McMurray wouldn't hear her.

You can't stop this—any of it. The voice was calm, cold. Marissa could feel the dispassionate way he said it. The words were more of a thought, but she knew it was Geo.

"I might not be able to stop this, but I'm not going to kill him."

Then you'll die. The beetle scurried, under the skin, to the back of Marissa's neck, down the spinal column. Her muscles twitched involuntarily. Her headache intensified, and she brought her hands to her temples and squeezed her eyes shut against the suddenly blaring moonlight. *Turn around.* Like in a dream, she felt her legs move on their own. She tried to stop them, but she was a passenger in her own body. *You're getting weaker 'Rissa.*

"I'm not going to let you do this," she ground through clenched teeth, digging in her feet and refusing to move any further. Her mind raced, trying to find a way to stop this. The suggestions were getting harder to resist. Soon she wouldn't be able to do anything about them, and she knew that as deeply as she knew she was fucked.

It's not really up to you anymore, is it? Even in her thought's his voice sounded smug.

Marissa turned back to McMurray's car, dragging her feet against the dirt, struggling against the current of her own will.

THE LOST

She worked back to it like a drowning child clings to a too-small log to keep her floating.

Kill him. Kill him. Turn your fucking ass around and kill him. The insisting voice screamed through Marissa's body as she fought to hold onto the tiny voice telling her to resist. Each step that brought her away from the shack drove needles of pain into her feet and legs.

"No," she said, her hands pressed to the roof of the car. Her body shook with the effort, tears stained her cheeks, and her stomach felt like it wanted to escape through her throat. "No, wait. He could help." She could feel the grip on the suggestion slip just a little bit, "Let's be smart about this.

How can that drunk help us? The question felt less genuine than the other suggestions, more like the voice was laughing.

Pain lanced through her gut as her body tried to pivot; he kept her hands pressed against the car roof, standing like she was waiting to be frisked. "People won't suspect him. They'll trust him." Another pain as she wrenched her rebellious body back to the car, shoulders hunched. "He'll do anything for me. He cares about me."

Use his weakness. The pain subsided, and Marissa dropped her head to the roof of the car and focused on breathing. She didn't know how much more fight was in her. Her own willpower, that voice deep in the back of her brain, screamed like a child being pulled down by the undertow. She knew it was inevitable, that voice would be smothered, snuffed out by the weight of Geo's suggestions, but she would cling to it as long as she could while the current pushed her deeper over her head.

"Marissa," McMurray's voice made her jump. *Kill him.* The suggestion came as a whisper, and she felt her muscles try to comply. Barely able to stop herself from rushing at him, she

Eric Johnson

turned around and saw him walking hold a book over his head, and called out, "Look what I found."

I need that book.

THIRTY-THREE

The book sat on the hood of McMurray's car as they flipped through the pages. The voice in Marissa's head was stuck on repeat. The pleading had taken on a sinister commanding presence in the back of her mind. Geo's voice clawed at her consciousness, chipping away her resolve, back and forth relentlessly between *Kill him* and *Get the book* until those two thoughts, neither of which Marissa was ready to give into, were the only thing that had meaning.

". . . I'm almost positive," McMurray continued a thought that Marissa couldn't follow. The voice was becoming all she could focus on; the insistence was like a thick blanket pulled over her head, muting the rest of the world.

"What?" Marissa asked, gritting her teeth. *Kill him.*

"I was saying that I'm almost positive the language is Latin," he pointed to a phrase in the middle of a page. "See this, I'm a little rusty, but I think it says: *anima mia* which I think means my soul. This here, *transcendentem* means surmounting or possibly transcension, I can't remember. Been a while."

"So why is it here?"

"Your brother and his friends?"

Marissa winced noticeably. *Get the book. Kill him and get the book. The book.* A shiver ran its way down her spine. She closed her eyes and took a deep breath, focusing on the whisper in the back of her mind that screamed out against the commands. "No clue, never seen it before."

"Should we bring this to Bedrin?"

Yes. "No," Marissa said as her head throbbed, "not yet." She hated lying to Father McMurray, but she needed to be away from the book to think for a while without bringing it to the station. She felt like the whisper in the back of her mind was right. "Let's wait and see if we can figure out what it is all about," Marissa continued. *Bring me that book.* The voice was screaming. She felt the anger as her adrenaline spiked. "They've closed the case. They wouldn't need it. If we can't figure anything out, we can bring it to them. I mean, it's not like Bedrin aced Latin in high school."

"Alright," McMurray said slowly and closed the book. "Let's head back to my place, and I'll get my old Latin dictionary from seminary. We can have some coffee and go over it there. Figure this thing out."

Yes, at his house. Kill him there, and we can have the book. Marissa went to the passenger door of the car without a thought. She opened the door and stopped herself from getting in. *Kill him.* She stood there with one hand on the top of the door, the other on the roof, physically prying herself out of the car. *Get in. Get the book.* McMurray walked to the driver's door and got in, watching Marissa strain against her own arms. She lunged out of the open car door and slammed it behind her.

"I- 'll walk," she said. "My truck is still by the road, so I don't want to leave it there. I'll meet you back at the bar." In a public place, she added to herself. "It would suck if my truck got stolen."

"Hop in," McMurray said through the open window, "I'll drop you off."

THE LOST

"No," Marissa said, her chest heaving with the pressure of resisting the voice. "I need the— the fresh air."

"Suit yourself," McMurray said as he turned the key and tossed the book on the passenger seat. "Sure you're alright?"

"Ya," Marissa said, grinding her teeth together, "I'm great."

She watched McMurray turn his car around and drive down the dusty road. The voice in her head was giving her hell over refusing his commands, but she breathed easier the further the book got from her. She had some measure of privacy in her own head as long as she didn't say anything, that much she'd figured out. McMurray had the book. It would be safe; he would be safe. She just needed to get away from him and the book and this Godforsaken town. That'd be a big fuck-you to Geo, just leave, and he won't be able to do shit about it. *What are you thinking 'Rissa?* He clearly couldn't read her mind; she knew that now, or else he would be boiling her down like that lawyer said. *I want that book, and you will bring it to me.* Marissa turned around and walked back to the edge of the road where Lucius had dropped her off, knowing that she had a long walk ahead of her. She wasn't in pain, she wasn't fighting against the voice, but she knew it would be back as soon as she met up with McMurray.

A large semi rumbled down the road behind her, headed east, and she threw her thumb out as he got closer. Hitchhiking was stupid, she knew the risks, but at the moment, she considered that being kidnapped or murdered might actually be helpful. She wouldn't be able to help Geo and Bedrin in whatever they were planning. The truck slowed down a little ahead of her, and Marissa quickened her pace to catch up. When she got to the cab, the passenger door was open. Without a second thought, she grabbed the rail and hoisted herself up into the passenger side of the cab.

Eric Johnson

It was grimy, and she had to push aside a few empty McDonalds bags before she could settle into the seat. There was a faint odor of fast food, motor oil, and sweat. She closed the heavy door behind herself, resigned to whatever fate had placed on the road.

"Where to?" asked the man behind the diver's seat. He was a big man with a long, greying, grizzled beard. He looked her in the eye with a more grandfatherly look than lecher, and for a moment, Marissa was disappointed.

"East," she said, laying her head back against the seat.

"East I can do," he said, shifting the truck back into gear and starting off the shoulder of the road. "Headed to the coast myself. Away or toward?"

"What?"

The driver's smile seemed effortless, "You running away from something or toward it?"

"What makes you think it's either of those?"

"East is a big direction, and you don't seem too particular. Way I see it, ain't got nothing with you, side of the road, ain't shit around but woods, you're probably running away. I mean, you look like you can't be more than nineteen or so. But there's those who look a lot younger than they are, so there's that too. If you're older, livin' on yo' own and all that, you could be heading for greener pastures, as they say. Running toward a boy or a new future. Maybe a job out on the coast? I hear Wellfleet is nice this time of year."

Marissa found herself smiling at the man's easy chatter. She felt her shoulders relax for the first time since her brother hadn't come home from the woods. "Does it matter?"

"Nope. Both the same in some ways, I suppose. You were here, now you're going to be there. No difference in that either from what I can tell."

THE LOST

"What do you mean?"

"You know the old story, grass always greener. Picked up this one kid once, probably what, some five years back, he wanted out of the small burg he lives in, right? Doesn't care where to, just elsewhere. Like you," he nodded his head at her, his grey hair bouncing slightly. "Well, he was the son of someone or other, wanted him to follow in their footsteps. Farmer or something. But the kid, he dreamed of the big time, wanted to design skyscrapers or some shit like that. Dropped him off in the city. He said I'd see him one day, big corner office in a building he designed."

"Ya," Marissa said, enjoying the silence in her own head.

"Sure enough. Like you. Head East, don't care where. Far enough East you'll hit the water, then what? Roots or you goin' sailing?"

Marissa smiled and sighed deeply, "Following the wind sounds good to me."

"Problem with the wind is sometimes there's too much."

Marissa let the comment float between them in the silence and watched the road laying out in front of them through the windshield. East would be good. She'd never been to the ocean and didn't mind the thought of sunrises and seagulls. She'd miss McMurray but figured they could send letters or something, keep in touch. He'd be able to hire some other deadbeat to help out at the bar. The town was full of them. Marissa imagined starting a new life out on the coast, working in a book store or cafe, not a bar this time, someplace clean with good light.

The sign for McMurray's Pub came into view, and Marissa looked out the other window. Since leaving prison, so much of her life was there, so much wrapped up with that bar and McMurray. He'd been there when even her father had turned away. He'd understand if she didn't say goodbye. She could explain it all in a letter, hope he didn't think she was crazy for hearing voices. He'd survive without her.

"Stopped in there once," the man said, "that place over there."

Marissa kept looking out of the window on the other side of the truck and didn't respond.

"Met some mad fucker," he chuckled. "He was wrecked. Tried to start a fight with me over some newspaper article. Guy near knocked himself out tryin' too. Bartender stopped him. Good thing she was there, or the old guy'd probably get himself killed picking a fight with the wrong person. Seemed like a nice enough guy though, 'spite all that." He let out a light whistle. "That guy in the black car over there must be really hard up for a drink if he's sitting on his trunk waiting for the place to open," he chuckled again. "Would've missed him too if it weren't for the headlights off his bald head. Wonder if he waxes that?"

"Shit," Marissa breathed at her window.

"What's that?" the driver shot a sidewise glance at her under his bushy eyebrows.

"Stop the truck," she sighed and felt the tension immediately return to her shoulders.

"Change your mind?"

"I forgot something."

"Want me to check for you next time I'm through here? Got this run for the next month or so."

"Maybe," Marissa said, the image of seagulls and sand fading from her imagination, "but I have something to take care of first."

"Suit yourself," he said as he pulled the truck over to the shoulder and brought it to a slow stop.

THE LOST

"Thanks," Marissa said as she opened the door and began to climb out. She stopped halfway out of the seat and turned back to the man. She felt an urge to ask, "Ever see him again?"

"Who?"

"That kid you picked up," Marissa asked, "did he ever get that corner office?"

The driver chuckled, "I did see him on a corner about two years later. He was headed back, a little worse for wear, you ask me. Said he missed the simpler life, the ground beneath his feet. Sometimes roots are good."

Marissa smiled at him and lowered herself to the ground, closing the door behind her. She watched him drive off to points East, then turned her back to the rising sun and started off toward the bar.

Thirty—Four

"If it isn't the prodigal child," Lucius's voice grated in Marissa's ears. It had the quality of an over-sweetened drink, the kind you knew was unhealthy for you, but always saw kids drinking anyway. "Decided to come to your senses?"

"What the fuck," Marissa said somewhere between an answer and a question. She stopped in front of Lucius, hands on her hips, giving him her best stare-down. He cocked his head to the side and leered at her. She felt immediately self-conscious in a way she hadn't felt in years but continued anyway. "You're here. What do you want?"

"Can't I stop by to say hello to an old friend?"

"Sure," she said, not taking her eyes off of his face, "when are they showing up?"

Lucius grinned and slid down from the trunk. Marissa's shoulders clenched as he crossed the dusty parking lot to stand directly in front of her. She wanted to run, wanted to give in to the little voice in her head that cried out for self-preservation above all else, but a bigger part of her didn't want to let him win, especially not on her own turf. He circled her slowly, like a wolf sizing up its competition, and stopped with her back to his car before stepping forward, so their toes were almost touching. He was a foot taller than her, so she had to look up to avoid staring at his throat. The smell of cheap aftershave and sweat hung on him

THE LOST

like the high school boys she'd known before she'd left. He reached up with his left hand and cupped her cheek gently. Marissa reached up and smacked his hand away.

"I like a bit of fire," he said before taking half a step back. "I have a message for you from our mutual friend."

"Why doesn't he just deliver it himself?"

"That, my dear prodigal child, is a good question," Lucius tapped her nose like she was a child, then walked around her back to lean against his car, forcing Marissa to turn to keep her eye on him. "Seems our good friend had been having a little trouble reaching you, and he asked for some help."

Marissa crossed her arms and smiled, relaxing her stance a little bit, "Poor boy."

"Well, I suppose so," Lucius said, putting a hand into his pocket and pulling out a zippo lighter. He reached inside his coat pocket and pulled out a pack of clove cigarettes, examined one, then lit it and inhaled deeply. The smoke wreathed around his head before the light breeze picked it up, dispersing it. This was not a wolf sizing up a competitor, Marissa thought. This was a cat playing with his dinner. She became acutely aware of the beads of sweat dripping down between her shoulder blades with that realization. Focusing on her breathing, she watched as he took another drag of the black cigarette.

"And?"

He cocked his head to the side again before realization flashed across his face, "Right, the message," he took another lazy drag before continuing. "Well, that book is coming to the station today, and quite frankly, no one really cares how it gets there. Geo asked me to stop by and see who shows up. It seems he lost touch with you after you got into that truck. I just figured the trucker killed you, but I guess not," Lucius paused again to contemplate his cigarette. "Anyway, McMurray has the book, and we're not too sure where he is. Had the boys stop by to pay him a visit at his house, though."

Marissa felt her shoulder blades unclench slightly. If Lucius was still here, there was a chance that they didn't get him. "So why are you still here?"

"To see you, of course," there was no warmth in the smile that accompanied his words.

Spreading her arms out to the sides, Marissa said, "You see me."

"So I do," he nodded, taking another pull of his cigarette. "What I don't see is the book."

"Don't have it," she shrugged.

"Right, the priest," his words dripped with venom. "Geo said he was going to meet you here. I figured I could join your little powwow."

Let him in. Geo's voice echoed in her head again. She cursed silently and imagined she was putting the voice in a box and closing the lid. *Let him join you. You have failed me. He won't.* The box thing didn't work, and she felt a pang of regret having failed to get the book. She shook her head, knowing it wouldn't do any good. "No," she said in answer to both of them.

"Now, be realistic," Lucius said, "do you think you're really up for this?" Pushing off the car, he dropped his cigarette and crushed it under one of his loafers. "There's a job to do. That book, no excuses. McMurray probably won't want to hand it over, so we take care of the issue here, quick and easy."

"You're going to kill him?" Marissa asked, feeling a weight in the pit of her stomach. *You had your chance.* Marissa winced at the coldness that washed over her with Geo's words. Part of her wanted to just do it and have it over with. Fighting the suggestions was making her headache worse again. *Kill him.* "No," she answered aloud to the voice in her head. Either Lucius didn't notice or didn't care. He simply watched as she brought her hands to her temples. *Or Luc will.* Marissa's eyes shot up the man who was flipping his Zippo lighter open and closed. He just shrugged at her.

"I'll tell you what," Lucius put his hand on her shoulder, "I'll make it quick. He won't feel anything for long."

Marissa could feel her will to resist begin to slip away; giving in would stop the headaches again. It would end the fight, take away the pain of her own father's rejection. The voice, her own voice, shouted at her from a darkening corner of her mind to keep fighting, not to let them kill the man who had helped her when she had nothing. "I'll take care of it this time," she whispered. *You'll kill him.* Her inner voice screamed out against the suggestion. "I'll get the book," she looked at Lucius, "I'll–" *Kill him.* "I'll get it for you."

"There is no failure this time," he urged. "There are no more chances. You understand that, don't you?"

"I'll do it," she said to the dirt under her feet and thought about the number of times she'd swept that dirt from the entryway of the bar, cleaned it off the windows, off her own truck. She looked over at the bar's front door, her sanctuary since getting out of jail, and thought about the first time McMurray had brought her into the building. The dirt had been everywhere, a coating on the bar, the tables, grinding beneath the chairs when they slid across the floor. Cleaning it was the penance for a life lived in the dirt. *Say it.* She wondered what the penance was for this. *Say it.* It was almost a palpable feeling, a pressure that built until it felt like it would pop. *Say it now.* She felt tears fall unbidden down her cheeks, a warm line drawn from the corner of her eye to her jawline. "I'll do it."

Eric Johnson

"I'm going to need to hear you say what 'it is,'" Lucius's voice sounded stiff and sad at the same time. It was empty of the slime and venom she'd come to expect from him.

Marissa took a deep breath before she spoke. "I'll kill Father McMurray." There was no pain, no hurt, no sadness in the words she said. No thunder crashed through the sky; the ground didn't shake. She had expected something more. She'd always thought that the breaking of someone's will should be accompanied by something palpable, but it never is.

"Good girl," Lucius turned to get in his car but stopped with his hand on the handle, cocked his head, and looked off into space for a moment. He turned to look at her with a vicious smile and a sparkle in his red-tinged eyes, "Just remember, no second chances. If you don't get this done, I will. This time, I will not be gentle," he walked over to Marissa and placed his hand on her cheek again, then he pulled it back and smacked her hard across the face. Marissa let out a whimper as every nerve ending in her cheek screamed out, but she didn't move. "To either of you." With that, Lucius turned and stalked back to his car, got behind the wheel, and drove off, leaving Marissa in a cloud of dust kicked up by his wheels.

Thirty—Five

The bar was just how she'd left it, note on the table, bleach stain on the floor where she'd cleaned up the blood. She looked dispassionately around the room and wondered what she had ever seen in this dark, dirt-pit of a bar. Walking around the room, replacing tables and chairs overturned in the struggles, Marissa walked through the plan that felt as much hers as if she'd come up with it herself. *When the priest arrives, first get him to show the book, then when you know he has it, take the knife you'll be cutting with and jam it into his throat. As he bleeds out, take the book, then burn the place to the ground.* It seemed a little extra violent to her, but the plan felt right. McMurray lied to her over the years, convinced her she could overcome her past, but now she knew there was no escape from past mistakes. They follow you, cling to you like a tick to a dog.

Sweeping up the glass felt foolish, given she was going to finally torch the place, but he couldn't know that when he walked in. Some part of Marissa twinged when she thought of the bar burning down, but it felt more like an echo of a thought, nothing like the clear focus on the plan. It was a good plan, simple, not over, though. Wound him so he can't talk, then if the bleeding doesn't do him in, the smoke or fire will. Marissa looked at the knife she had to work with, a small utility knife, not more than two inches or so, *hardly* practical. She knew there were several knives in the back they used to prepare some of the food, a chef's knife *would work*.

When she came out of the back, chef's knife in hand, the bar was still empty. She moved behind the bar top and began to sort through the fruits, absently looking for something to cut. She selected a large lemon and began to slice it, enjoying how the knife made a sliding sound as it bisected the skin. *Imagine what his skin will sound like.* She watched the juice form a small pool on the cutting board, and another twinge echoed below her consciousness. There was a discomfort in the echo that she didn't like. *Make sure the knife is sharp.* A dull knife wouldn't do.

Marissa looked at the flesh where her left thumb met her palm, soft, fleshy. She put the blade of the knife, still wet with lemon juice, to her skin and drew it down her palm. The knife slid smoothly through the flesh, the lemon juice burning the fresh wound as blood welled up and dripped down her wrist. *Sharp.* She watched dispassionately as a small lump moved over her wrist and to the new cut. The small red beetle spun skin across the wound like a spider spins a web. She vaguely remembered that she hadn't always had the beetle inside of her, but she couldn't pinpoint where it had come from. The warmth that it generated under her skin as it moved through the connective tissue comforted her.

The slam of the front door pulled Marissa's attention from the soothing warmth, and she looked up to see Father McMurray walking toward the bar, battered leather messenger bag over one shoulder. The blood was still on her wrist and had dripped onto the lemon she'd been slicing, turning the small pool of juice a delicate pink color. Whiping her hand off on a towel discarded nearby, she swept the cutting board and lemon slices into the sink, throwing the towel over it for good measure.

"Marissa," McMurray said as he crossed the room, "thank God you're alright."

THE LOST

"Why wouldn't I be?"

"I saw your truck," McMurray let the statement stand between them.

"My truck?" Marissa tried to remember where she had parked it, but she kept coming up blank.

"It was outside my house when I got there," McMurray placed the messenger bag on the bar. Marissa could feel the pull, *it's in there,* and she wanted it. He continued after a brief pause, "There were some boys from the high school class, I think your brother's classmates, in the bed, and it didn't look like you behind the wheel. It looked like some scrawny boy."

Marissa didn't know how to respond, so she just sat there pretending to think. She couldn't remember where she'd last seen her truck, but something about the description of the three boys was familiar. McMurray watched her expectantly, *the truck doesn't matter,* but she needed to respond to him. "Oh, that's right. When I got back here, three of Mikey's friends were here and needed to bring some stuff over to the school for my folks. They borrowed it and must have gotten lost."

"Or they just decided to take it for a joy ride," McMurray shook his head.

"That's what I'd have done."

That seemed to do the trick because he chuckled and leaned against the bar.

What's in the bag? The question weighed on Marissa. She wanted to snatch it off of the bar, but she wasn't positive it was the book. Instead, she responded with a noncommittal grunt and stared at the bag. She felt the saliva build in the back of her mouth. She wanted *that book* more than anything else right now.

"Are you feeling alright?" McMurray asked, "Your eyes look red."

"Allergies," Marissa responded, not really sure if she had allergies, "something in the woods got to me." Which wasn't exactly a lie.

"I didn't know you had allergies," McMurray placed his hand on the bag.

"They come and go," Marissa was flailing, and she wondered how she could not know if she had allergies or not. "What's in the bag? It is the book?"

"And some clothes. Those kids made me nervous, so I didn't stop. I went to the Goodwill and picked up something to change into. Something seemed off like they were waiting or watching for me. Sounds paranoid now that I say it out loud, though."

Marissa remembered Lucius sitting on the trunk of his car when she came by the parking lot. Geo must have sent the boys down to McMurray's place *as insurance*. Smart move, she thought to herself. "Can I see it?"

"See?"

"The book," Marissa could feel fluttering in the pit of her stomach. It felt like Christmas and being released from prison all at once.

"Of course," McMurray unlatched the messenger bag and pulled the book out from in between folded clothes. He shrugged sheepishly as Marissa looked into the bag, "They had some great deals."

The clothes held no interest for her; on her face was a smile echoed across town at the station. *Do it. Do it. Do it. I need that book.* She reached out toward the book and caressed its cover. The smooth leather seemed to purr beneath her fingers. It called to her to open it and read. She wanted to immerse herself between the covers, *bring it to me unopened,* but she knew she wouldn't look between its velveteen cover.

THE LOST

"That's odd," McMurray broke her concentration, "I must be losing it. Could have sworn that thing flinched when I touched it. Let me see it for a second."

Marissa hadn't been listening to what he said, but something inside told her not to let him touch the book. Now that it was in her hands, she knew that it needed to stay there. She looked at the knife sitting between them and moved the book to her left hand, placing her right on the handle of the knife. I'm *doing McMurray a favor by killing him*; Lucius would do worse. That echoing tinge rippled in her stomach again, and she could tell something was wrong with this. *I need that book.* But Marissa couldn't figure out what was bothering her.

McMurray looked down at the chef's knife on the counter and started to back up. "Was the pairing knife dirty?"

"What?" she could hardly think over the din of Geo calling for the book.

"What's the knife for Marissa?" McMurray put his hands up in the childish gesture of surrender.

Marissa picked up the knife and held it, pointing toward the ceiling, "This?"

"Yes," McMurray's voice trembled. "Kinda big to cut fruit, don't you think?"

"It's not for fruit," the calmness in Marissa's voice surprised her. *Kill him now.*

"What's if for then?" he looked behind him as he backed into one of the tables, losing his footing for a moment.

Marissa smiled as she set the book on the bar and hoisted herself over the top of it directly toward the stunned McMurray, the blade flashing in the sun as she landed a foot in front of him.

Eric Johnson

Thirty—Six

The clothes in the bag weren't the best he'd ever owned. He hadn't even owned them two hours ago, but they'd caught his eye, and he really didn't have a good feeling about the boys in Marissa's truck outside his house. McMurray figured he'd sleep in the bar for the next few days, be on the safe side. He wasn't going to tell Marissa this; she'd just accuse him of being paranoid, which even he admitted, was probably true. He lifted the clothes off the book, careful not to touch it. Something about the leather on the cover sent shivers down his spine. He watched as Marissa cocked her head to the side as if she were listening to something, then she reached her hand out to the book, a strange look in her red-rimmed eyes. McMurray's heart went out to her. This was possibly the last thing her brother touched before he was killed. The kid had been through so much in her life, jail, abandonment, and now her brother, and if he was honest with himself, McMurray hadn't been the type of help he'd intended. He tried to fool himself into believing that he'd saved her, but deep down, he knew the absolute truth was she'd saved herself.

Marissa cradled the book like it was a small child, one hand reaching to the cover, hovering for a moment, then, with a

THE LOST

faraway look in her eyes, she rested her left hand on the cover, lightly stroking the smooth leather beneath her fingers.

"That's odd. I must be losing it," McMurray shook his head and chuckled. "Could have sworn that thing flinched when I touched it. Let me see it for a second."

Still, Marissa shifted the book the hold it under her left arm with the faraway look in her eyes. McMurray watched her hand drop to the counter behind the bar. Her eyes narrowed on him as if sizing him up, and his shoulders tensed. He took a deep breath; this was Marissa, his friend. She wasn't the enemy. Those boys in the truck must have really spooked him because now he saw enemies, even in his friends.

It took McMurray a moment to realize that her hand had fallen onto the chef's knife on the cutting board, not typically the blade for cutting fruit. "Was the pairing kind dirty?"

"What?" Marissa looked through him, and McMurray didn't like the shiver it sent through him. He could feel the adrenaline begin pumping into his system. His flight reflex was clawing at him, but this was Marissa; he didn't need to run from her.

"What's the knife for Marissa?" McMurray put his hands up in front of himself, like he'd seen in the cop shows, palms toward Marissa.

"This?" she held the knife up with a smile on her face.

"Yes," he tried unsuccessfully to keep his voice even. "Kinda big to cut fruit, don't you think?" Something was wrong here, and McMurray's brain raced to try and figure out what Marissa was doing.

"It's not for fruit," her voice was calm, but there was something dangerous in the hollowness behind her eyes. It looked like she was watching him through a television screen.

Eric Johnson

Father McMurray began backing up slowly. Something was definitely wrong here. "What's it for then?" A table caught him in the small of his back, and he glanced behind him to get a hand on it to steady himself. Catching his balance, McMurray looked back at Marissa, who was perched on the bar, knife in her hand. Her eyes were what concerned him most though, they were sad. There was no hate, no malice, only a tragic resignation. As if attacking him with a knife was an unfortunate necessity in life. It was the way he'd always imagined his devout farmers looked as they lead a cow to the slaughter truck.

Marissa propelled herself from the top of the bar, landing about a foot in front of him, the knife still poised in her hand. He leaned back to avoid any attack she might have planned, but he overbalanced and, tipping the table, crashed to the floor, taking three chairs with him. He pushed himself back, putting as much distance between Marissa's knifepoint and his skin until his back hit flat against the upturned tabletop.

"Marissa," he pleaded, "put the knife down."

"Sorry, Father," her voice was sad when she spoke, "I'm afraid I can't do that."

"Sure you can," his mind raced through all of the possibilities. None of them looked good. "Nothing bad's happened; you've been through a lot. I understand." McMurray hated lying to her, but he didn't know what else to say.

Marissa shook her head and pouted, "That's not really how this is going to work, but if it makes you feel any better, I'm not going to enjoy this." She crouched down, so they were eye level. "I mean, sure, you're probably going to enjoy it less, but I promise to make it quick."

There could be no mistaking her intent at this point, McMurray couldn't imagine what had brought her to this point over a book that she already had, but he knew if he didn't act,

THE LOST

then he wouldn't be around to figure it out, and Marissa would have to live the rest of her life with his blood on her hands. Despite the impassive look in her eyes right now, McMurray knew that it would eat her up. He couldn't let that happen to her. He'd failed to save her before, making her do it herself while he drank himself into worthlessness; he wouldn't fail her this time.

"You're probably right about that," he said as he spun his right leg toward her, knocking one of the overturned chairs into her as hard as he could. She didn't fall, but the few moments of distractions were enough for him to get up and take a break for the back room. There was an exit door back there, but that wasn't his plan. If he ran now, he'd have no place to go. Those boys could still be at his house; besides, she'd just find him there soon enough, and he'd have to run again. Marissa needed help. Something was very wrong with her.

Rounding the corner into the dark of the back room, McMurray heard a chair slide across the room out front. He knew that she would be close on his heels, so he had to move quickly. Racing to the office door, he hoped to get the damn thing open. From there, he could call the police; Bedrin should be able to subdue her without too much danger. He turned the handle and pulled. The door stuck and groaned as he yanked. Sparing a glance over his shoulder, he saw Marissa framed in the light of the doorway to the bar, the shadow shape of the knife hanging carelessly by her side. Her head cocked to the side for a moment before she moved through the door. McMurray held his breath. If she figured out where he was, she would be on him well before he got the door open.

He felt the sweat trickle down between his shoulder blades as he fought to keep his breathing quiet. His back hurt from falling on the table, and he was sure that his leg was going to have a massive bruise on his shin where he'd kicked the chair. Of course, none of that would matter if she heard his breathing and came right to the office door. He'd felt it budge a little on his last tug, but he wanted her to be deeper into the kitchen before he yanked on it again. He was pretty sure that one more good pull would open the door, but if Marissa had a clear run from where she was when he did it, he'd never make it inside to close and lock the door before she'd catch up to him.

He watched as her shadow moved deeper into the kitchen, knife still held carelessly by her side. She was halfway through the galley of the prep area. The light from the bar was fading on her back as she moved deeper into the shadows. McMurray took a breath, trying to be as quiet as he could, and gave the door one last big tug. A loud creaking sound of the swollen door grinding against the jam echoed through the back room. The door moved, but not enough. He could get his hand in there, but nothing else. He knew even without looking that she'd started toward the office. His heart felt like it was being crammed in a vice and his vision narrowed, and for a moment, he wondered if he was having a heart attack. He pulled with everything he had, his hands wrapped around the side of the door for better leverage, and with a loud complaint, it opened enough so he could squeeze through.

He began to pull at the handle on the other side of the door, the door inching closed with each tug. Marissa slammed into the door like she was shot out of a catapult. McMurray said a brief prayer of thanks and flipped the lock on the door. Behind him, the old rotary phone he'd brought from home when he'd bought the place sat on the desk, and Marissa's coat hung half on, half off the chair.

Marissa's hand banged on the window. Her voice shouting something about it being her last chance, muffled by the wood and glass of the door.

THE LOST

"I'm calling the cops," McMurray shouted through the glass on the door, unsure if she could hear him any better than he could her.

"No, wait," Marissa held the knife up to the window, then lowered it, disappearing from view, only to pop back up a moment later, both hands visible and empty. "Let's talk first."

"Alright," McMurray crossed his arms, as much to keep himself from shaking as it was to show his disapproval for what she was doing. "Let's talk."

"I'm trying to help you out here," she smiled through the glass, her hands still visible.

"With a chef's knife?" McMurray was incredulous. "No thanks."

"Really," she insisted, "I am. You call Bedrin, and I might not be able to help you anymore."

"What are you talking about?"

"Bedrin, he– Well, Lucius said he was going to kill you."

"Who's Lucius? Who's– Wait, kill me?"

"He was that lawyer I told you about," she said, "the one who helped me out with the legal issues a few days ago. Ya, he said he'd kill you slowly and painfully, then kill me if I didn't get this book to him and Geo."

"What does that have to do with Bedrin?"

"Just don't call him."

"I know you and Mathew have—a troubled history, but the police are who you go to in a situation like this. You don't go after your friends with a knife. I'm calling."

Marissa didn't say anything else; she simply balled up her fist and began punching the window. McMurray stepped back, eyes wide. He knew he needed to call, but he was transfixed on her rhythmic pounding on the glass. Blooms of blood began to show on the window after the third hit. Soon the window looked like an impressionist painting of a poppy field in springtime. Then, with the sixth or seventh hit, the window began to crack. Spider webs of fissures channeled the blood until the thin red lines spanned the window. McMurray reached behind him to the phone, glancing quickly at the number for the police station written down on the pad he'd always kept on the desk for emergencies. McMurray dialed the phone without looking and brought it to his ear without taking his eyes off the fast-failing window.

"Sheriff's department," the voice on the other end stated. Small pieces of glass began to fall to the floor in the office.

"Hello, this is Peter McMurray, over at McMurray's Pub. I need to talk to Officer Mathew Bedrin."

"Well, Mr. McMurray," the voice intoned, "Officer Bedrin is busy at the moment. May I take a message?"

A small section of glass fell through onto the frayed carpet in the office. "No," McMurray insisted, "you may not take a message. I need to speak to Officer Bedrin immediately. It's a matter of life and death." McMurray guessed that he sounded melodramatic, but the person on the other side of that door did not want to come in here and have tea. He had to stop thinking of her as Marissa, or he'd go crazy.

"Hold, please."

The last piece of glass fell to the floor as Bedrin got on the phone. "Hello Peter, how can I help you."

"It's Marissa," McMurray hoped he was doing the right thing, "something's wrong. She's got me locked in the office, and she has a knife on the other side of the door." McMurray made eye contact with Marissa through the spot where the glass had been as he mentioned the knife.

"I told you not to trust her, you old fool."

THE LOST

"Please, Mathew," McMurray watched Marissa watch him, "name-calling will not help anything here. I'm calling you because I know you can do this without hurting her. Something is wrong. She is not herself. Please," he breathed out his plea, "please come help."

"I told you not to call him," Marissa said through the window. The sadness still framing her voice. "You don't want his kind of help."

Without waiting for an answer from Bedrin, McMurray set the phone down on the desk, still connected, and took half a step across the small office, "Marissa, you're not yourself. I know you don't want to hurt me. This isn't you."

"I don't," Marissa said, looking down toward her feet. "That is why I need to kill you myself. They want to hurt you."

"This doesn't have to happen," McMurray took another tentative half-step forward. Now he stood in the middle of the office, just barely out of reach of the door. "Just drop the knife through the window, and we can both meet Mathew out front, talk this out."

"There is no more talk," Marissa's eyes were distant as she spoke, "no more second chances. I am who I am, Father. It's like you told me back in prison, we do what we can to survive now and worry about forgiveness later."

"I'll give you forgiveness now," McMurray wanted to go to her, to comfort her. The pain in her voice was killing him, "for all of this, for everything. Just drop the knife through the window."

Marissa choked a laugh and shivered. Then she reached her arm through the door, bending down to try to get to the lock on the doorknob. McMurray saw blood dripping down her fingers from her cut knuckles, and some movement on the back of her hand caught his attention. A small bump moved over each of the bones in her hand, pausing at the knuckles. Each time the bump approached a knuckle, the bleeding would stop, then it would move on.

"Too bad you didn't listen to me," Marissa said, pulling her arm back through the window after failing to reach the lock. "I would have made it quick."

"I'll take my chances," McMurray said, watching Marissa cock her head to the side and then, almost mechanically, bending down to pick up the knife. "Come on, Marissa, drop the knife through. We can talk. You can tell me about what's going on with your knuckles. They should be all cut up, but they're almost already healed. What is that bump moving around in there?"

"A gift," she said as she stood back up looking at McMurray again, "from Geo."

"Gift?" McMurray wasn't sure he wanted to know the answer to his next question, but it was the only thing that made sense. "Did Geo come by and tell you to kill me? Was he with this Lucius guy?"

"Not exactly," Marissa said, tapping her right temple with the tip of the knife, "but I know what he's thinking. He's keeping an eye on us, wants to help us overcome our baser natures." Marissa's stared straight ahead; her eyes were far away as she spoke.

"Can I be saved?" McMurray asked.

Marissa cocked her head to the side again, eyes still looking through him, "I'm sorry," she said after a moment, "he's saving us from people like you." With that, Marissa lowered the blade from view and turned to walk back to the front room. "I'll be in the bar," she called over her shoulder, "see you when Bedrin gets here."

McMurray watched her walk out of view and let out a breath he didn't realize he'd been holding. His shoulder slumped, and he felt every one of the fifty-three years he'd lived. Sitting

THE LOST

down in the chair, he watched the jagged darkness through the door. Something was going on more than he knew, that much he was sure of. He wasn't sure what was wrong with Marissa, but people shouldn't have things moving around under their skin. McMurray sat alone in his small office, elbow on his knees, head in his hands, and, not for the first time today, wished he'd picked some other time to give up drinking.

He thought back to the meeting in his old office with Father Maria, the broken decanter. Maria had insisted that he'd drunk the whiskey, but McMurray didn't remember it. He was almost positive he hadn't, but what he did remember was the ladybug. He'd flicked it into the spilled whiskey; he was sure of it. Remember the little legs crawling on his skin. McMurray raised his head and looked at the door. He didn't like the thoughts circling around in his head, but he couldn't think of any other possibility.

"Occam's razor," he said to the empty room. "When you eliminate all of the other options, what is left, no matter how improbably, has to be it." McMurray put his head back into his palms, mumbled a quick prayer, then, looking up again, said to the empty air, "God give me strength." Placing his hands on the worn arms of the chair, McMurray pushed himself to a standing position. The muscles in his back twisting in revolt from his fall into the table, ignoring the pain, McMurray reached for the handle of the door and unlocked it.

Thirty—Seven

He could see Marissa sitting at one of the tables, leaning back in the chair, legs stretched out, and the book lying closed in front of her. She was flipping the cover of the book up a little and letting it fall back down as if she was debating whether or not to open it. Her back was to McMurray as he peeked around the corner of the door from the back room. He kept low, trying to make as little noise as he could. He'd thought the noise of the office door opening was loud enough the wake the dead, but either she didn't care if he got out or she hadn't heard it. Either way, McMurray smiled at the thought of how easy his plan would come to fruition.

Ducking back through the door, he looked around the storage in the back room, hoping to find something he could use to knock her out without hurting her too much. He could always use her knife for phase two. There were several pots and pans around, but he didn't think he could get one without making too much noise, noise she was sure to hear. He couldn't believe that this was happening, never had he, in all his years, resorted to violence to solve his problems. Honestly, he wasn't even sure that it would work, that he'd be able to hit someone over the head hard enough to knock them out, let alone use a knife on them afterward.

THE LOST

Everything by the door was either too soft or too big for the element of surprise, and McMurray knew that he'd have no chance if he lost that. Moving deeper into the back room, still careful not to make too much noise, McMurray found the boxes with spare bottles. He'd hoped to see the empties, but recycling had just been picked up, and with the way Marissa kept this place, those would be long gone. Grabbing a bottle of Jamison by the neck, McMurray pulled it out, cringing at every clink it made from the bottles stored next to it. Coming back to the doorway, he crouched down and spied around the corner one more time. "This could be trouble," he mumbled to himself. The chair that Marissa had been sitting in was empty.

The book was still sitting on the table, and for a moment, he thought about running for the book and taking it out of here to destroy it. It could end things if he found a way to make it go away forever. It could end this whole problem. The thought of touching the book's binding made his stomach lurch for his throat. He felt a powerful revulsion to it every time he even looked at the thing; that's why he'd gotten the bag in the first place. Besides, he thought to himself, he couldn't abandon Marissa like that. She needed help. Bedrin was coming, though she seemed more annoyed by that fact than concerned, which, given her current state, worried McMurray.

Making a break for it was out of the question. He needed to be here to help Marissa, even if he didn't know what type of help that was. He was sure the bump under her skin was the key, something about what had happened at his old office in the church— He was sure they were connected— but he didn't know how. *I need to get that thing out of her and get rid of it.* He took a deep breath and checked the room one more time. Empty. He didn't know where she was, but he did know where she wasn't. He moved into the room and slunk along the back wall toward the booths. If he could get himself into one of the back booths, he'd have a better view of the room, and he'd be able to hide in the shadows that hung to the back wall of the bar.

Focusing on his goal, McMurray moved slowly along the back wall, careful not to make too much noise, hoping to get there before Marissa came back. He watched the front door, sure that she would walk through any moment, hoping that this whole episode had simply been a misunderstanding. McMurray imagined the conversation about how everything had been a misunderstanding as he was tackled from the side. In his focus on the front door, he'd forgotten to check the short hall that led to the bathrooms. McMurray found himself sprawled out across the floor, the bottle thrown from his hand, spinning a few feet away.

Cursing his luck at the loss of surprise, he scrambled across the floor on all fours trying to get to the bottle so he could at least defend himself. Marissa's hand grabbed McMurray's left ankle and tugged. He lost his balance, and his chin came down on the floor hard enough to rattle his teeth. Shaking his head, he rolled onto his back, kicking out with his right leg, trying to free himself. Marissa crouched next to him, knife held out to the side, ready to slash his leg. McMurray managed to squirm and kick free of her clasp as the blade dug harmlessly into the wood floor where his leg had just been.

"I thought you'd come to your senses," Marissa said. "Come to peace with the way things are."

"What way is that?"

"That you're dying today," Marissa's tone was emotionless, "either quickly or slowly, but it is happening. I thought you'd come out to make things quick."

"I've done no such thing," McMurray assured her, scurrying like a crab toward the bottle. "You don't need to do this Marissa, you're not the person you were before."

THE LOST

She laughed at him, but there was no humor in her eyes, just sadness. "We can't escape our pasts, Father." She gestured to the room as she continued, "If it were possible, don't you think we'd be having this conversation in a church, not this bar?"

"Better yet, not having this conversation at all," McMurray reached behind him, hoping that the bottle was in range, but his hand found nothing but air.

"I take no pleasure in being the one to do it, of course," Marissa stood up and walked between McMurray and the chair she had been at earlier. "It's a mercy, really."

"A mercy? Killing me?"

"Fast or slow, quick or painful–"

"Either way, I'm dead."

"You're a priest," she said, watching him grope for the bottle, "you shouldn't fear God."

"I don't fear him," McMurray's hand hit something that spun away from his grasp, "but that doesn't mean I want to meet him just yet."

Marissa shrugged, "Don't see that you have much choice."

"There's always a choice," McMurray grabbed the neck of the bottle and threw it at Marissa.

Marissa, caught off guard by the sudden movement and the accuracy of McMurray's throw, was clipped in the shoulder by the bottle before it crashed next to the table behind her. McMurray used those seconds to get to his feet and sprint toward the bar, hoping that something back there would be able to stop her. He heard her curse behind him moments before she grabbed him by his shoulders, throwing him back onto the floor. He landed hard on his side and gasped as the breath was knocked out of him. Without thinking, he lashed his left arm out to grab at a chair and throw it at her, but a sharp sting caused him to recoil.

Eric Johnson

The sharp knife slid effortlessly through his skin, drawing a red line over the back of his left forearm. "What happened to painless?"

"Don't resist."

"Not happening," McMurray said, using his good arm to help him stand up. Marissa circled him slowly, like a shark waiting for a swimmer to tire before it drags him under. "Why don't you put the knife down, and we can talk this out."

Marissa looked at the knife, "Not an option."

"So we dance," McMurray said as he got into his best approximation of a fighter's stance.

Taking the cue, Marissa lunged toward him, leading with the knife. McMurray stepped out of the way, leaving the chair behind him for Marissa to crash into. The snapping of wood marked her tumble, but she was up and turned back toward him in seconds, seemingly oblivious to what must have been a painful fall. She lunged again, this time feinting to the right forcing McMurray to jump back to avoid the slashing blade. Breathing heavily, McMurray cradled his bleeding arm. Avoiding another lunge, he backed up, bumping into a table. His foot slipped on the glass from the bottle he'd thrown. The blade came across again at the level of his stomach, again McMurray backed up.

He knew this couldn't last much longer. His side ached from when she'd knocked him over then thrown him to the ground. His breath was coming in quick gasps, each more painful than the last. Spots swam in front of his eyes. He'd gotten himself out of the glass and watched Marissa as she advanced on him. He knew the timing needed to be perfect for this to work. Marissa's feet crunched on the glass, and McMurray stepped forward, hands out in front of him as if he were going to push her back.

Seeing her opening, Marissa lunged once again at her friend. McMurray had anticipated this and stepped back and to

THE LOST

the left. The glass below Marissa's foot shifted, making her lose her footing. As she tried to steady her already overbalanced position, McMurray grabbed the chair to his right and swung like he was trying to hit a line drive on the diamond behind the church. He cringed as the chair came apart across the back of Marissa's skull. Between her momentum and the added push from the chair, Marissa sprawled forward, the knife coming loose from her hand for the first time, and she was still.

McMurray leaned against the table and caught his breath. He was worried that she might be faking it, he was also concerned that she might be dead, but either way, he needed to breathe before doing anything else. After his ragged breathing evened out, McMurray walked to the side of Marissa, putting himself between her and the knife. He rolled her over and bent down, watching her chest rise and fall regularly. He put his fingers along the side of her neck and felt the steady beat of a strong, young heart. Comforted that she was still alive, McMurray took a moment to wrap one of the spare bar towels around his arm before he picked up the knife.

Standing over Marissa, Father McMurray said a brief prayer before he bent down and drew the blade of the knife across her chest, making a two-inch cut just under her collar bone. His stomach clenched as he watched the blood start to well up. Taking a deep breath to keep from throwing up, he watched as the little bump under her skin moved from the back of her head where the chair had come down to the new cut in her chest. When it got close to the wound, McMurray slammed his hand down, trapping it in the area left between his thumb and pointer finger. Marissa groaned under his assault, but she didn't wake up.

McMurray slowly closed up the space between his hand and the bump beneath her skin, causing more blood to come out of the cut. She was bleeding a lot, and he worried she was losing too much blood, but he didn't know how much was too much. He did know he needed to get this thing out of her. As his fingers started coming across the cut, Marissa stirred beneath his hand.

"I'm sorry, Marissa," he said, shaking his head, "this is gonna hurt when you wake up."

McMurray plunged the fingers of his right hand into the wound and grabbed onto the little bump slick with Marissa's blood. Marissa's body convulsed, and she let out a sharp scream of pain before she fell back to the floor, once again silent, her breathing a little less even. It squirmed in his fingers and tried to get away, but he pulled it out with a sickening slurping sound. In his fingers, Father McMurray looked at the small red beetle. It reminded him of a ladybug without any spots and writhed with a ferocity belying its size.

Standing up, McMurray headed toward the bar, planning to put the thing under a glass so they could figure out what to do with it after Marissa was taken care of. On the way, McMurray stumbled over the leg of a broken chair, losing his grip on the slippery beetle. Freed from the confines of the priest's fingers, the beetle scurried up his arm and toward the blood-soaked towel. McMurray swatted at it, but he could feel the little legs digging into his skin, making his skin feel like pins and needles as it crawled up his arm. It burrowed under the towel, and McMurray ripped it off, trying to get the beetle off of him. As the beetle neared the slice on the priest's arm, it veered into the still dripping blood. McMurray felt his skin begin to sweat. He watched, helplessly transfixed, as the beetle reached the line of blood still oozing from where Marissa had cut him with the knife.

The moment the beetle touched the blood on the priest's arm, a small flame flashed up and consumed the beetle. McMurray flinched away from the flame on his arm, covering it quickly with his right hand. The pain subsided in seconds, and

THE LOST

McMurray wiped away the blood on his arm, flinching as the rough cloth slid over the spot. A slight burn was visible, about the size of a cigarette burn, where the beetle had been moments before. Confused but relieved, McMurray hurried behind the bar to get the first aid kit Marissa had insisted they keep on hand. She'd always claimed he was clumsy with a knife, but once again, he found himself beyond thankful for the girl. Taking out the gauze, he bound his own arm before heading over to Marissa to do the same.

# Thirty-Eight

It was a few minutes before she could take in her surroundings. Something was off. She knew she was still at the bar but didn't remember falling asleep. She remembered the boys coming in, beating her up; she figured that she must have blacked out at that point. Now she was finally coming to, but the light seemed wrong. She reached down to her left leg, remembering the pain from the cut that Zack had given her. Her hand came back dry. Reaching back to rub her neck and alleviate the dull ache that was on the edge of a full-bore migraine, Marissa winced as pain shot through her right shoulder. She winced again and looked down at her shoulder, noticing the pinkish color of the gauze taped just below her collar bone.

She knew that she hadn't bandaged herself up, and with that realization came the sound of water running over behind the bar. Marissa tensed up; knowing someone else was in the bar, even if they had bandaged her up, was not comforting. She'd had a killer nightmare while she was knocked out, vaguely remembered something about voices in her head and actually wanting to kill McMurray.

"You're awake," McMurray's voice just made the memories of the nightmare more vivid. "I'm sorry about that bruise on the back of your neck. It couldn't be helped."

THE LOST

Marissa's blood went cold. Images of fighting Father McMurray flashed through her head, making her thoughts spin. "I'm sorry?"

"No need Marissa."

She heard his footsteps come around the bar and searched everywhere for something to defend herself with. Her hand landed on a broken chair leg, and she curved her fingers around it. She didn't want to think that it was McMurray that had knocked her out, but flashes of the fight were still coming through her head when she heard his voice. Given the day she'd had, Marissa was not ready to take that chance. Carefully getting to her feet, holding the chair leg in her left hand, she turned to face McMurray.

Father McMurray stopped mid-step, both hands up in front of himself. "I'm glad you're up and moving," he said, taking half a step backward. "How about we talk about things first this time?"

"Why did you hit me over the head?"

"To stop you from killing me," his hands were still up, and his voice so matter of fact that Marissa lowered the chair leg slightly.

"Killing you? Why would I kill you?"

McMurray lowered his hands and took a tentative step forward. Marissa raised the chair leg again, holding it straight out at him this time. He stopped and looked at her, his bushy eyebrows were raised, and his sad smile reflected in his eyes. "Marissa, what do you remember?"

"I remember Steven, Zack, and Dylan coming in and attacking me, but–" Marissa paused for a moment, trying to separate her dream from her memories.

"Go on," Father McMurray sat down in a chair.

Eric Johnson

"They broke my leg, but it's not broken, so that must have been the dream. I remember hearing Geo's voice trying to convince me of things, but he isn't here. The only thing that makes sense is that you attacked me. I remember fighting you, I remember wanting to kill you, and it felt– felt right." Marissa lowered the chair leg, tears began to well up in her eyes, "But that can't be right. I wouldn't–"

"I don't think it was your fault," McMurray nodded over at a large leather-bound book on the table next to the one he was at. "Seems when you saw this book, nothing else mattered."

Marissa walked over to the book. It was large and leather-bound, with gold-tinted letters on the cover that she couldn't understand. The air around it seemed to have a chill that was not unlike some of the food she took from the freezer to make the dinner menu. The cover was soft to the touch and felt extra smooth. Opening the book didn't clarify anything for her. She flipped through pages covered with symbols and diagrams that she didn't know, and it was written in a language that Marissa couldn't figure out.

"So," McMurray asked expectantly, "what's it all about?"

"This book?"

"Yes, the book," McMurray walked over to stand beside Marissa. "I couldn't even open the thing."

"What do you mean?" Marissa looked up from the book, leaving it open to a random page with the symbol of a triangle above another triangle with a cross below it. Next to those was an inverted triangle inside a regular triangle missing the bottom, all inside a circle. She stared at the image, feeling like she should know what it means.

"Exactly what it sounds like, the book would not physically open," McMurray pointed at the page, "I know those symbols."

THE LOST

"You do?"

"Ya, they're in one of the books that my grandfather had," McMurray looked around the room. Marissa watched the morning sunshine on his face. He looked like he'd been through a lot in the past week. His eyes were sunken, the lines on his face more pronounced than she could ever remember them being. He had gauze wrapped around his upper arm and something that looked like it was going to become an epic shiner. "This place is a mess," he continued, "let's lock this book up in the safe, then after we clean the place up, if it's safe, we'll swing by my house and see if I still have that book."

"Why wouldn't your house be safe?" Marissa asked as McMurray wrapped the book in what looked like a used button-down shirt.

"I told you about the boys waiting outside my place," McMurray slipped the book into a worn leather bag. "They have your truck."

"My truck?" Marissa's jaw dropped, "they stole my truck?"

McMurray shrugged, "You said you let them use it." Tucking the book under his arm, he looked at her, the concern clearly showing in his eyes. "Do you even remember meeting me in the woods, at that shack?"

Marissa shook her head no, but her mind reeled back to the dream she'd had. Something about being at the shack, something about Geo and the other three. She put her hands down on the table to steady herself.

"I'll be right back," McMurray helped Marissa into a seat before going into the backroom to lock the book in the safe.

After securing the book, he told her how he found the book, the boys in her truck outside his house, and finally, their fight. Marissa didn't move while he spoke. She sat in the chair, watching as McMurray cleaned the floor and the counter. At one point, he stopped and took down two whiskey glasses, but instead of filling them with whiskey, he filled both with tap water, and placing one in front of Marissa, he drank the other in a large gulp, then returned to cleaning. Things were lining up too neatly with her dream, and at each point, her stomach dropped until there was an uncomfortable hollow deep in her belly. Although she didn't want to admit it, the dream was beginning to look more and more like a memory.

After breaking out of her stupor, Marissa needed to do something. Gathering up the broken chairs, she stacked them in her arms, brought them out back, and put them behind the dumpster. She pointed to the gauze taped just under her color bone when she came back into the bar. "You never mentioned how I got this?"

Not looking at her, McMurray simply sighed and rubbed harder at a spot on the bar. "That was me," he told the cloth.

"Why?" Marissa could hear the pain in his voice. He'd teared up when he'd told her about smashing one of the chairs across her back, but he'd been able to look at her for that.

"I'm not sure I can explain," he put the rag down and looked at her. "And if I can, I'm not sure you'd believe me."

"Try me."

"You had a bug," he winced at how it sounded, "under your skin. It would crawl around, and I think–" he shook his head. "I think it was controlling you. Making you attack me, making you want to take that book to the police station."

"The police station?" Marissa laughed.

"I know it's–" McMurray stopped mid-sentence and looked toward the back room. "Do you smell that?" Leaving the towel on the bar, McMurray walked toward the back room, moments before the light began to shift. There was a glow

THE LOST

coming from the doorway that hadn't been there when Marissa brought the broken chairs back there.

Marissa rushed to the door beside McMurray and stared into the flames licking the ceiling of the back room. Her heart sank, but she sprung into action, pushing past McMurray, who mumbled some protest or other. Marissa began to fill the largest pot she could find with water. The smoke was filling the room, and McMurray tugged at her sleeve, pulling her away from the sink. He said something and pointed to the back of the room; Marissa couldn't hear him over the crackling flames and the pounding of her own heart in her ears. He gestured again and pulled Marissa toward the door to the front room.

When she saw what he was pointing at, her heart sank. The flames had begun to ignite the boxes where they stored the spare bottles. Once the bottles broke, the fire would spread quicker, fed by the alcohol fumes. She pulled her arm out of McMurray's grasp and, dropping below the smoke, crawled to the office, hoping to get the book out of the safe before it was destroyed. She didn't know what it was all about, but if McMurray was right about her attacking him, then this book was the key to figuring out what happened, and given that Geo was involved, it might be the only way to figure out what happened to her brother. She wrestled the door to the office open and had her hands on the safe when a loud whoosh from behind the paper-thin office wall let her know that the bottles were beginning to go.

When McMurray crawled into the office, holding a wet towel over his nose and mouth, the drywall was beginning to blacken. McMurray's strong hand grabbed her shoulder and, this time, refused to let go. He pulled her back out of the office, dragging her coat behind them. She took the offered towel, and the two crawled through the darkness breathing through the wet towels, acrid smoke burning their eyes, and found their way through the front room and out the door.

As the door swung open, pulling fresh oxygen into the building and speeding up the flames, Marissa saw a dark sedan speed out of the parking lot. She vaguely remembered it from the dream that she was beginning to doubt was a dream. Marissa grabbed her coat from McMurray and fished out her cell phone in the parking lot, pounding out the emergency numbers. The first call went through, and the operator asked for the emergency. As Marissa was telling her about the fire, the line went dead.

Sitting on the hood of McMurray's car, Marissa tried to call the fire department, but no one answered. She tried 911 again, but again she was disconnected before she could give the operator her location. Marissa and Father McMurray sat on the hood of his car and watched as the flames consumed their bar with nothing left to do. Flames danced in the morning sky, and smoke darkened the sun. It took three hours for the fire to completely destroy the building, and for three hours, they sat there as the ashes fell on them like snow.

THE LOST

THIRTY—NINE

"At least it was a good show," McMurray was the first to speak into the silence of the falling ash. "For I eat ashes like bread and mingle tears with my drink."

"What's that?" Marissa looked at McMurray expectantly.

"Psalms," McMurray still wasn't looking at her. "Too bad it's not Wednesday."

Again the silence settled on the pair sitting in the falling ash. Marissa couldn't understand how Father McMurray could take this so well. His life savings were tied up in that place, and sure, logically, there was insurance money, but there's more to a building than the structure. She brushed the ash from her hair and rested her head in her hands.

"We can't escape it," she said, "can we?"

"Escape what?"

Marissa looked up, tears drawing lines in the ash on her face, "The past."

"Never could," McMurray put his hand on her shoulder. "That's the thing about the past, good or bad, there's no getting away from it. Sure, you can hide out every now and then, put it out of your mind for a while, but there is no hiding from it. It's part of who you are, part of the fabric of our lives."

"But it sucks."

"Sometimes," he smiled at her sadly, "sometimes it really does. Mostly though, it only sucks because that's what we focus on. Take this bar."

Marissa gestured at the smoldering remains "What bar?"

McMurray chuckled. "We could focus on the loss, the destruction, or we could focus on what it really was."

"A dingy place where people came to get drunk?"

"Where people came to hide from their past. Not everyone who came here got drunk," McMurray patted her on the back. "You didn't."

"No, I came here to work."

"Sure," McMurray smiled and hopped down from the hood, "keep telling yourself that. It doesn't matter why people come to a place, it's what they do there, it's who they're with, that's what makes the place worthwhile or not. Here," he turned his back to the pile of debris, "here is where you never gave up on trying to save me. And if you could scrub your past out of those planks, well, you'd have done it a few times by now."

Warmth crept up Marissa's face as she watched him in the pale morning light. The remains of the bar smoldered behind him, ashes still filtering through the air, but despite the destruction that surrounded him, McMurray stood taller than she'd seen him stand in a while.

"I'm more worried about what's coming," McMurray said as he stood there, watching Marissa.

"What do you mean?"

"This wasn't a coincidence," he walked back toward the car, "the kids at my house, the barn burning. I'm not naive enough to ignore what's in front of my face."

"We should get out of here then," Marissa hopped down and started for the passenger side of the car. "Just get in the car and head to the coast or something, someplace far away."

THE LOST

McMurray walked over to the car and looked at her over the roof. "If only it was that easy. You can't run from the future any more than you can run from the past. There is a special providence in the fall of a sparrow."

"Psalms again?"

"Nope," McMurray smiled at her, "Shakespeare. You know, you really should read more."

Her retort was cut off by the screaming of an engine as it tore down the highway past the parking lot. Marissa watched as her truck drove by, barely a blur of color against the wooded backdrop. There was no doubt in her mind who would be behind the wheel. McMurray turned his head toward the noise.

"I didn't know that thing could go that fast," he said as the taillights faded into the distance.

"Neither did I," Marissa responded, "and it's my truck. Do you think they saw us?"

"No idea, but I do know that if that was your truck, then those boys aren't still at my house. Let's go see if we can find that book we needed."

"Why bother? That fire would have destroyed the book anyway."

"I'm not so sure of that. Besides," McMurray grinned at her over the roof, "it's a fireproof safe." Then he lowered himself into the driver's seat, ending the conversation until she got into the car.

Sitting down in the passenger seat, she remembered the last time she'd gotten into McMurray's car. Mikey's funeral had just been a few days ago, but it felt like months. "Why don't we go get it?" Marissa asked.

"Safe might be fireproof, but it's still going to be hot. Better wait until things cool down before we try to go back for it. For now, let's get back to the house and regroup."

Eric Johnson

"You're talking like we're going into battle or something," Marissa said, the hint of a laugh in her voice.

McMurray didn't answer her. He simply put the car into drive and pulled out onto the highway going in the opposite direction of Marissa's truck. Marissa let the silence hang on her last comment; she needed to sort through her dream. Many details she'd heard from McMurray about the shack and the fight in the bar were eerily similar to what she could remember. Still, she refused to believe that it was anything other than a dream because that brought implications she wasn't ready for.

If what she remembered was real, then that thing McMurray said he'd cut out of her had been put there by Geo, Mikey's friend. If he could do that to her, who else could he have done it to? Where Steve and his crew working with Geo, were they slaves like she was in her dream? The questions whirled through her head, but no matter how many ways she looked at it, there was no good solution, no simple explanation. By the time they pulled into McMurray's empty driveway, Marissa still hadn't made sense of the last few days. It seemed everything since her brother's funeral was some sort of sick joke designed to make her question everything.

"It's times like these that make me wish I'd cleaned out my garage so I could hide the car in there," McMurray said as he parked the car in his driveway.

"This happen often to you?"

"Good point," he put the keys in his pocket and started for the door. "Why don't you start a pot of coffee? I'll see if I can find the book."

"Sure thing," Marissa was thankful for something to distract her from the questions swirling in her brain. "Caffeine'll do me good. Want me to pour you a whiskey?"

THE LOST

"No," McMurray said, "coffee will be fine." He opened the door slowly as if he were expecting someone to jump out, then stopping with the door half-open, he turned to her, "Don't mind the mess. I don't really get company that often, until recently, it appears."

After his disclaimer, Marissa expected to see piles of bookstand boxes all over the place, but the living room was clean, sparsely decorated but tidy. When she went into the kitchen, she realized what he was referring to. Piled in the sink was at least a week's worth of dirty dishes. "I see what you mean," she chided him, "do I need to wash a couple of mugs?"

"There are clean ones in the cabinet, thank you," he scowled at her as he headed for the basement stairs.

Marissa smiled as she scooped the grounds from the bag McMurray kept in his cabinet and ran hot water into the carafe. It wasn't often that he turned down a drink, but she hoped this would be a new trend. It had been hard watching him descend into the darkness. In the beginning, she'd try to convince him that he didn't need to drink or that he was drinking away his profits, but when he didn't drink at the bar, he drank at home. At least at the bar, she'd been able to keep an eye on him.

"Got it," he held the book in the air as he walked back into the room, the same way he'd held the other book in her dream. "The old man had some crazy stuff, and when my father passed away, I boxed all of his stuff and put it in the basement." He put the book on the counter and took the offered mug of black coffee.

The book had a red burlap-style cloth binding with gold lettering and some symbols on the cover. The edges of the pages were covered with swirls of brown and tan, giving it a marbled look. Marissa picked it up, turned the spine so she could read the title. "The History of Alchemy and Alchemical Symbols by

Sherman Astershains?" She couldn't help the smile that was growing on her face and laughed, "You sure you were a priest and not some witch doctor."

"It belonged to my grandfather," McMurray shrugged. "I never said he was sane."

"Alright," Marissa said, flipping through the pages, "so where are these symbols?"

A loud knock on the front door caused both of them to freeze. Marissa's eyes went wide, and she brought her hand over her mouth to stifle a gasp. McMurray put a finger to his lips and raised both his eyebrows.

"Were you expecting someone?" Marissa asked as she shifted her gaze to the door.

"I told you I don't often have company," he motioned to the dishes with a smile, "guess I'm going to have to get better at the whole dishes thing if this keeps up." He looked back at the front door, "Stay here, okay?" He started for the front door. Marissa watched as he walked through the living room. The hollow knock sounded again, and McMurray flinched. Marissa held her breath and watched him reach the door and stop in front of it, hand poised over the knob. He looked back over his shoulder at Marissa and shrugged. From the kitchen, behind the island, Marissa watched as Father McMurray opened the door just slightly, and his shoulders relaxed. Marissa set down the coffee mug that she hadn't realized she'd been white-knuckling and shook her head, smiling at her own skittishness.

She could hear McMurray talking to the person outside, but she couldn't make out what they were saying or hear the other person's voice. Eventually, McMurray opened the door further, and stepping aside, invited the person into his house. Marissa turned around to get another mug, assuming McMurray had offered some coffee to his visitor. When she turned back

THE LOST

around, she forgot about the mug in her hand until it shattered on the ground at her feet.

"Something wrong 'Rissa?" the visitor asked.

Eric Johnson

Forty

As the mug she'd just taken from McMurray's cabinet shattered at her feet, Marissa gasped and shrank back against the counter. Luckily she had the island in between her and Geo as he stood in the kitchen's entryway. Her mind flashed back to the flashes of memory she had after Officer Dias had left the bar, McMurray had left, and she'd waited. The memory of her wounds flooded back, the pain and disorientation that had come with the blood loss. Then the memory of Geo walking through the door of the bar. Relief had flooded her then, not like now as her pulse raced and sweat began to collect between her shoulder blades. She wouldn't take her eyes off him, not now, not after what he'd done.

"Something wrong 'Rissa?" she'd gotten used to hearing the smile in Geo's voice, but now, matched with the smug look on his face, a look like he'd already won, Marissa's stomach twisted in knots. Geo cocked his head to the side slightly, and his red-tinged eyes went far away.

"What are you doing here, Geo?" Marissa asked, her hand strafing the counter behind her, looking for anything she could use as a weapon.

His eyes narrowed at her from across the kitchen, "Just checking up on you," he glanced back over his shoulder at McMurray, who was coming back into the kitchen. "Last time I saw you, you said you were going to come by with something you had of mine."

Marissa swore under her breath, the importance of Geo's words hitting the last of the pieces together like a sledgehammer. Marissa's realization came with heavy implications that she didn't have time to deal with just now. She was faced with Geo, her brother's friend since elementary school, the kid that had a crush on her since middle school, and the scariest motherfucker she'd ever set eyes on.

"So," Geo continued when she didn't reply, "about that book."

"Which book was that book?" Marissa asked, closing the book that she'd been thumbing through, meeting Geo's gaze with a straight face, "There are a lot of books around." She hoped her nonchalance masked the panicked scream that was echoing through her head.

Marissa saw McMurray stop about halfway across the living room, listening to the tense exchange. She knew that she had to tell him Geo wasn't what he thought, that Geo was the lynchpin of all the shit that was happening but at the same time not let Geo know what she was doing.

"'Rissa," she could feel the venom in his voice, "you know what book." Geo began to move around the island; Marissa tried to match his pace, always keeping it between them. "I want the fucking book you and the old pedophile got in the woods. I saw it."

"Excuse me," McMurray took Geo's place in the doorway, leaning against the frame like he hadn't a care in the world. "Don't you come into my house and accuse me of such– such filth. You above all people should know that it's not true."

Geo flashed his gaze at Father McMurray, hatred boiling over in his eyes, "You know that the truth is as irrelevant at this point as you are, *Father*." He drew out the last word letting it drip from his tongue like some forgotten slur.

"Leave him alone, you piece of shit," Marissa screamed, startling both Geo and Father McMurray as she grabbed the handle of McMurray's steaming coffee mug and threw it in Geo's face, mug and all. The porcelain of the mug broke on impact, washing Geo's face in scalding coffee and cutting him just below his left eye. Geo didn't even flinch at. First, he stood there, coffee dripping from his face onto his clothes. A small line of blood started from the cut, but before it could even reach his jawline, the drop began to coalesce into a small red beetle, which seemed to shudder slightly before turning and crawling back up to the cut and beginning its weaving process. Marissa's stomach turned, and she shuddered at the memory of the same thing happening to her own wounds.

Geo fixed his eyes on her. The narrow slits seemed to burn with an inner fire that she hadn't seen in him in all the years she'd known him. "You fucking bitch," his words were barely a whisper, then he let out a scream of rage and charged at her, "I will kill you for that."

Marissa tried to back up, seeing him coming, but her feet got tangled up in the stools around the island, and she went down in a crash of legs and stools. Kicking the stools off of her, putting them between the advancing thing that looked like Mikey's friend, Marissa pushed herself backward as fast as possible while trying to get to her feet and away from him. Geo lunged forward, kicking the chairs out from in front of him with a clatter, and then fell face-first on the floor. Marissa looked up from the floor, her back against the refrigerator, breath coming in ragged gasps.

Standing above Geo's prone body, Father McMurray held an old rotary phone with a bit of blood on the corner and smiled.

THE LOST

"I'd like to see you try and do that with one of those blasted cell phones you kept trying to make me get."

Marissa looked up in shock at the absurd man smiling down at her holding an old plastic rotary phone that she'd picked on him about daily at the bar and was slowly overtaken with laughter. "You're crazy," she said when her laughter subsided.

Father McMurray shrugged and held his hand out to help her up, "You wouldn't be the first person to call me that." Then when she'd gotten to her feet and around Geo, "Now help me tie him up with this," he held up the telephone cord.

"Is that going to work?"

"How would I know? I'm a priest, not an ex-convict," he smiled at her mischievously. "But I did see it in a movie once, back in the eighties."

"What kind of movies do you watch?"

"It was the eighties; what do you expect."

"Got me," Marissa smirked at him over the knots they were tying in the telephone cord, "I wasn't even born in the eighties."

"Are you calling me old?"

Marissa just shrugged and let the absurdity of the last few hours set in. She'd been possessed by and saved from some flesh weaving blood beetle, seen the only place she'd ever felt welcome since getting out of prison burn down, been attacked by her brother's best friend, and been saved by an old priest with a rotary phone. "What's next?" she asked herself.

"We save him."

"Save him?" Marissa hadn't meant to ask that aloud, but her shock pushed the question out before she could stop it.

"Of course," McMurray said, picking the phone off the floor where he'd set it and putting it on the counter. "It's not his fault that he was possessed by those things. I'm sure he didn't know what he was doing at the time."

"They brought the book out there, figured out the symbols, they knew what they were doing."

"Are you positive of that?" McMurray looked up at her from the floor, where he crouched next to Geo's body.

"Fairly," Marissa said, the uncertainty in her voice clear even in her own ears.

"Well, if we decide to pass judgment on this boy for what he's done, if we inflict punishment for his crimes, you had better be a bit more than fairly certain he wanted to be possessed," McMurray paused, holding Marissa's gaze. "What if that was the choice I made when you attacked me?"

Marissa bit her bottom lip and swore again. She knew he was right, but everything in her wanted revenge against Geo for what he did. Seeing that beetle crawl up his face drove home the truth of her dream. The fact that those things she'd thought were a dream, her attack, Geo, the woods, the trucker, Lucius, attacking Father McMurray, it was real. She refused to face the meaning of that she pushed back, but it couldn't erase the feeling that Geo had violated her somehow. Broken some unspoken bond of decency between people who grew up around each other.

"Get me a knife," McMurray motioned at the knife block on his counter, "I think I see it." He had his hand on Geo's back, just below his shoulder blade. Trapped in a triangle formed between his thumb, pointer fingers, and Geo's shoulder blade was a small bump under his shirt and probably under his skin. It moved around in the small space as if looking for a way out. "Hurry up before I lose it."

She pulled a carving knife from the mostly empty block and handed it to McMurray. "Smallest thing in there," she shrugged, "maybe you should do your dishes."

THE LOST

"This will have to do," McMurray said, "I'll worry about the dishes when this is done."

She watched as McMurray put the knife to Geo's shirt and say something under his breath. He pushed the blade against Geo, his teeshirt gave way easily, and the blade sank into his back. Marissa turned away, not wanting to see the beetle again and the odd webbing. The brief glimpse she'd gotten from the beetle on Geo's face made her realize whatever that beetle was weaving was inside of him; it had done inside of her too. She was sure there were implications to that, but now wasn't the time to worry about it.

"There," McMurray said, standing up and looking at the beetle squirming in his hands, "That should do it."

"How do you know?"

"Worked with you," he looked at the beetle. "What do I do with it now?"

"What did you do last time?"

"Honestly, I'm not really sure," McMurray examined the beetle, "it got out in my hand it—"

"Shit," Marissa started backing away from McMurray.

"Oh, don't worry," McMurray shook his head at her, "I promise I won't drop it again."

"No— Not— Behind— It's— Fuck." Marissa couldn't get her mouth and brain to effectively communicate what she was seeing. On the floor, behind McMurray, Geo lay in an expanding pool of dark red, but it wasn't blood that was pouring out of the cut McMurray had put in his back. The mass of dark red beetles crawled out of Geo and began to spread through the kitchen. "It's—" finally she settled for pointing behind McMurray, mouth slightly agape.

"What is it?" McMurray asked, turning around. He stiffened when he saw the beetles begin crawling the walls and spreading over his ceiling, "God help us." He dropped the beetle in his hands, and it disappeared in the advancing swarm. In the middle of it all stood Geo. He'd managed to get out of their crude knots, but he wasn't attacking.

"God left this place a long time ago, old man," Geo intoned, his voice sounded hollow over the skittering of thousands of red beetles. He was covered with them too, and more seemed to be coming out from the cut on his back. "If he was ever with you, to begin with."

"Marissa," McMurray's voice was quiet compared to the Geo's, "I think you need to leave."

"I'm not going anywhere without you," Marissa grabbed McMurray's coat and began dragging him toward the back door. "I don't think you can fix this one with your rotary phone. I've seen what these little beetles can do, and I'm not letting that happen to you."

"It won't," McMurray shrugged his shoulder out of Marissa's grasp.

"Damn right it won't," she said, getting a better hold on his arm and pulling him again to the back of the house.

Geo stood at the epicenter of the swarm laughing as the two backed from the room toward the door. The beetles scurried across the ceiling in all directions, spreading out evenly over everything. Anything moveable seems to be pushed out of their way, and she could hear dishes shattering on the floor. Crashed from other rooms in the house let her know that the same thing was probably happening everywhere.

"Let's go," she pushed McMurray past her, putting herself between him and the beetles.

"Don't forget the book," he said, giving in to her insistence, "we need it if we're going to figure this out."

THE LOST

The book lay on the island's counter, the beetles beginning to climb the spine, covering the golden letters. "Too late," Marissa said, still pushing McMurray out of the room and away from the danger, "we'll have to find another way." In the kitchen, Geo stood alone, surrounded by the chittering of thousands of red beetles, and laughed as Marissa let the screen door slam behind them.

After climbing over the chainlink fence that surrounded McMurray's back yard, a feat that Marissa was surprised McMurray could do, they opted to leave the car, neither really willing to risk getting close to the house as the beetles began to cover the windows from the inside. They trudged through the woods, neither saying a word until they had put several hours hike between themselves and McMurray's house.

Leaning against a tree, McMurray fought to slow his breathing, "I need to rest. I'm not as young as I used to be, you know."

"What do we do now?" Marissa asked, sitting on a fallen tree and massaging her calf muscles, silently thankful for the break herself.

McMurray frowned and looked up at the canopy above them, "I have an idea, but we need to talk to someone first."

Forty—One

"No," Marissa couldn't believe where they were, "we are not going in there. That guy's a total douche."

"I'm not going to argue that," McMurray looked up at the steeple that once marked his church, "but we can't do this by ourselves. Whether we like it or not, Father Maria is probably our best chance at beating whatever it is that has Geo."

"Is Geo still even in there?" Marissa asked McMurray's feet, unable to look him in the eye. She shuttered at the memory of his commands in her head.

"I have to believe he is," sadness tinged the old priest's voice. "He was a good kid, and goodness in people can't be that fragile."

"Fine," Marissa looked at the church, "I'll play nice, but I don't have to like it."

"Neither of us do."

The door into the parish house where Father Joseph Maria had his office was an aged wooden door; the paint had peeled back years ago. At the same time, McMurray was the head priest, but painting it never seemed a priority, particularly in the latter years of McMurray's time behind the pulpit. Father Maria hadn't seemed to feel the need either. The anteroom was another story altogether. A fresh coat of institutional grey paint covered the once bright walls, now devoid of any artwork. The door to the

THE LOST

priest's office was slightly ajar, and Maria could be heard on the phone talking to someone, but Marissa couldn't make out what he was saying.

McMurray knocked on the door, and Father Maria stopped talking abruptly, then appeared in the doorway, opening it the rest of the way.

"Peter," Father Maria's voice showed his surprised yet evident displeasure about his visitor. "I didn't expect to see you here."

"I know our last parting was not–" McMurray paused presumably to find the right word, "on the best of terms."

"Could say that," he turned to Marissa offering his hand. "Always a pleasure, though I haven't seen you at service for a while."

Marissa clenched her fists to her side and smiled. McMurray was sure they needed his help, so she'd be nice. Nice didn't amount to touching the man, even a handshake.

"Well," Father Maria continued, dropping his hand, "your parents are regulars. Hopefully, we will see you next Sunday?"

Marissa shrugged, but on a look from McMurray, she gave in and answered Father Maria, "I'm not sure, but we'll see."

"You don't still hold the whole thing about not letting Peter run your brother's service, do you?" He smiled at her as he continued, not waiting for an answer, "It was, after all, your parents' decision."

"She's always been notorious for missing services," McMurray said, patting Marissa on the back. The last time she'd been to church had been before she went to prison. Her parents once forced her to church every Sunday, but since the legal troubles and parole, Marissa assumed her parents preferred the anonymity of her not being around. Father McMurray continued despite the look she shot him, rescuing her from actually having to talk to the young priest. "That's not why we're here, Joseph. We have a problem."

Father Maria looked at Marissa with a raised eyebrow, "How far?"

"How what?" Marissa asked before the implication hit her, and she screwed up her face in disgust. "Fuck you, you sick bastard. I'm not pregnant."

"I'm sorry," Father Maria shrugged, "given the source—" he motioned at McMurray. "What is the problem, Peter?"

His voice held no sign that her words had offended him or that she had any right to be offended by his accusation. McMurray, for his part, ignored the statement. "It's Geo."

"Oh, he is a troubled one," Father Maria shook his head sadly.

"Possibly more than you know." McMurray said, then motioning to Father Maria's desk, "Let's sit down, and I'll explain."

For the next half hour, McMurray recounted everything that had happened since the funeral. Marissa added the occasional detail, such as hearing Geo's voice in her head and the beating she'd taken from the three boys whose names she left out. At first, Father Maria leaned forward and nodded through most of the story about Mr. Hail's assault of McMurray and the conversations with Officer Dias. Still, when Marissa explained hearing Geo's voice in her head and the beetle she'd had in her, he sat back and put his hands behind his head. By the time they got to Geo standing in McMurray's kitchen surrounded by the swarm of beetles, Father Maria was frowning and shaking his head.

At the end of the tale, Father Maria leaned forward and rubbed the bridge of his nose. The three of them sat quietly, the tension in the room thick with expectation until Father Maria broke the silence, "That is a lot to take in, Peter."

THE LOST

"I know," McMurray said, leaning forward, hands resting on his thighs, "as God is my witness, I swear it's true."

"Be careful what you say," Father Maria got up and walked to the table where he'd placed a new decanter, "blasphemy is a sin."

"I stand by it," McMurray said as he watched the younger man pour a glass of the amber liquid from the decanter into the class and hold it out to him. "No, thank you, I'm quitting."

Marissa looked at Father McMurray and smiled. She'd noticed that he hadn't been drinking, but to hear him say he was quitting made her feel light inside. She had seen the old light coming back into his eyes in the past few days, and she marveled at his strength.

"In case you change your mind," Father Maria said, setting the glass in front of McMurray. "Though that would explain the hallucinations and the mood swings."

"He didn't hallucinate anything," Marissa stood up from her seat, pushing it back loudly along the floor. "I saw it too."

"You have to understand–" Father Maria motioned at her seat, "please sit. You have to understand how this looks from the outside. Here you have a disgraced priest who abandoned his flock." Marissa was about to protest again, but McMurray put a hand on her arm and stopped her. Father Maria, noticing the exchange pressed his advantage, "You have to admit, Marissa, that is one way of looking at things."

"I've heard people say that," McMurray answered.

"But it's–" Marissa started.

"An interpretation," Father Maria finished.

"A misinterpretation," Marissa corrected.

"Be that as it may, it's an interpretation," he held up his hand to quiet Marissa, "mis or otherwise. And then there's you," he smiled sadly. Still, even the empathy in his smile didn't make it to his dull grey eyes, "an ex-convict who is one mistake away from going back to jail for quite some time."

"I told you it was a mistake to come here," Marissa stood up and headed for the door. "This prick is not going to help us."

"Miss Hail," Father Maria's voice dripped with impatience, "have a seat and let me finish. I hardly think name-calling is going to help this situation. You came to me for help, remember?"

She stopped with her hand on the door and looked back at the two men sitting on either side of the old wooden desk. Father Maria seemed to loom over McMurray, the latter sitting with his hands folded on his lap, looking pleadingly over his shoulder at Marissa. Letting her shoulders droop, she sighed and returned to her seat next to McMurray without saying anything more.

"Much better," Father Maria nodded, "that temper of yours is bound to lead you to more trouble, young lady." Marissa sat, hands clenched on the armrests of her chair. "Now that we're more amicable let me finish what I was getting at.

"I just want both of you to understand what you're asking me to do. You want me to stake my reputation in this community on the word of two of the least respected members. These two people have marginalized themselves through their own actions while simultaneously blaming everyone else for what has happened to them. Now you come here, to a man who both of you have turned away many times. A man you have insulted and called names, even while asking for my help and belief in a ridiculous story.

"If you were attacked as you both claim, if your bar was burnt to the ground, your truck stolen, and your home invaded, the police and fire departments are the ones you should seek, not a priest," Marissa tried to interrupt, but Father Maria held up his

THE LOST

hand and continued. "One more outburst or insult, you can both leave." Marissa closed her mouth and looked down at his desk.

"But, if as you claim the police are implicated and the fire department unreachable, two claims I doubt as much as I have faith in God, then as a good shepherd," he paused and smiled at McMurray, "I will take the wayward lambs into my fold and care for you the best I can. And so I will help you."

Marissa couldn't believe her ears; after all of his self-righteous bullshit, he was going to help them. She still wasn't sure what he could do. Short of a howitzer missile, Marissa wasn't sure anything could stop Geo. She shuttered at the thought of the bugs crawling over him, out of him, and through McMurray's kitchen.

"Don't look so happy, Miss Hail," Father Maria said.

"It wasn't—" he held up his hand to stop her again, and she could feel the hairs on the back of her neck stand on end with the effort to keep from snapping his condescending arm.

"I will help you, under one condition," Father Maria looked at McMurray, and Marissa felt her stomach tie into knots. "Peter, you have been no end of trouble for this community and its— its more impressionable youths," he looked pointedly at Marissa. "So, if you want my help, you will need to do something for me once I've helped figure out what is going on with young Geo. If, as you have suggested, he is possessed, or if you have simply crafted this elaborate story about possessions and books and becoming this young lady's savior. Once I figure all of this out for you and solve the problem at hand, you need to promise me that you will leave this town and never come back."

Marissa could feel the heat of her anger rise up, and she knew that she could no longer listen to this. Her ears hummed, and she felt like she was going to throw up. Before she could even open her mouth to protest, McMurray stuck out his hand to

Father Maria, and with a firm handshake, simply stated, "Agreed." Marissa's heart dropped to her feet, and she stared at the old priest, mouth slightly open in preparation to protest with words that would not come out.

"While I appreciate the ready acceptance, forgive me if I don't take you at your word," Father Maria did not take the proffered hand. Instead, he opened the upper left-hand drawer of his desk, and with a careless gesture, tossed a tattered bible onto the desk. "I assume this still means something to you even after abandoning it here too."

"That was my father's bible," McMurray looked at it in sad surprise, "I couldn't find it when I–" McMurray's voice broke with emotion as he fingered the frayed cover, "when you took over."

"It was in the back, under a bottle of cheap whiskey," Father Maria eyed McMurray as he stared at the old bible. "Swear on that. Swear that once this is over, I will never see you around here again."

McMurray stood up, reverently moving the bible closer to him, placed his right hand on it, and said, "I swear on my father's bible that I, Peter McMurray, will leave town and never return after you help us save Geo from the evil that has hold of him."

Marissa felt cold listening to McMurray's promise to leave. She didn't know what would happen or why he agreed to this, but she knew that she was powerless to stop it. Once the old man had set his mind, he would keep it. She watched the scene speechlessly and shivered at McMurray's pronunciation and Father Maria's sneer of victory.

"Good," Father Maria said after McMurray finished. "Come back later this evening. I need to get some things together and look into what you've claimed. I'm still not certain I believe any of it, but if enough of the pieces fit, I'll see what I can do.

THE LOST

You two stay out of sight until you come back, say around eight o'clock? I'll get together what I need by then," he stood up and began to usher them out.

"We don't have a car," McMurray said as he stood up, "we left my house on foot."

Father Maria rolled his eyes, then went back to his desk and rifled through the top drawer. Motioning at the still full glass of whiskey, "Since you're not drinking, borrow mine." He tossed the keys over the desk to McMurray, who caught off guard, fumbled the catch, and had to stoop to the floor to pick them up. Father Maria looked on with a half-smile, then pausing, motioned at the corner of his desk. "Peter, if you want that old thing, it's yours," he looked at the bible laying on his desk, "I have better ones."

Without saying anything else, McMurray picked up his father's bible, cradling it to his chest, and followed Marissa out of the parish house into the afternoon sun.

Forty-Two

"How could you agree to that?" Marissa paced behind Father Maria's car, the steeple casting a lengthening shadow over the parking lot. "He can't make you do it, you know that, right? He's just a priest; he's not God or anything."

"Doesn't matter," McMurray seemed calm, at peace with his decision. That calm demeanor was making Marissa's pacing quicken with each step.

"Of course, it matters. It matters because when this is over, life can just go back to normal."

"Normal?"

"Yes, normal. You and I running the bar. Back to how things were. How they should be."

"Those aren't the same things, how things were and how they should be. Besides, is normal even good? I'm here in a town full of people who hate me, surrounded by reminders of my biggest failures in life, running a dive bar that barely breaks even," McMurray leaned against the trunk. "Don't even give me that look. You know it's a dive, a clean dive, but a dive nonetheless. It's time to move on," he paused for a moment, "for both of us."

"It's not fair."

"Fair doesn't enter into it."

THE LOST

Marissa kicked a loose piece of pavement, watched as it skipped across the parking lot, then went over to lean against the trunk next to McMurray. They watched the lengthening shadows of the trees in silence. Marissa stewed in her anger that Father Maria would make such a demand to help them. "If he truly cared–" she started, but neither finished the sentence. To her thinking, neither needed to.

"What now?" she asked as the sun began to dance in the treetops.

"What now," McMurray mused. "I suppose we should get the book. It could help us convince Father Maria of what we're saying."

"We don't even know what it says."

"Most of it is Latin. Given time, I could translate it," McMurray crossed his arms and frowned. "I think. As for the symbols, there are other books on Alchemical symbols," he motioned at her phone, which she'd taken out of her pocket and was playing with, "or I'm sure the internet."

"Alright then," Marissa pushed off from the trunk and headed to the passenger door, "but why don't we swing by your house first? It's on the way."

"What for?"

"See if we can get that book your grandfather had, get rid of this condescending prick's car?"

"Be a good place to lay low for a while too," he ignored her insult of Father Maria, his hand on the driver's door handle, "if–" his worries dying on his lips.

"Only one way to find out."

On the drive to McMurray's house, Marissa searched the internet for alchemical symbols. She found that few sites agreed on their meanings, but she could cobble together some that looked familiar from what she remembered seeing in the book.

She wasn't sure which sites could be trusted and hoped that her efforts weren't futile.

The car slowed on the road in front of McMurray's driveway. Both of them sat, afraid to get out but unable to see what was going on in the house. Marissa looked from the curtained front windows over to McMurray, his face completely unreadable. She knew that if it were her house, she'd be terrified that it would be unlivable. On a good day, bugs gave her the creeps, but these bugs, what they did to you, a shudder went through her as she remembered the voice, Geo's voice in her head. This was nowhere near a good day.

"I'll go," she said, not taking her eyes off of the house as if it might crawl away itself if not watched, and given what was inside, she wasn't sure that it wouldn't. "My fault that we left the book anyway."

"It's my house," McMurray said, sounding more like he was stating a fact as opposed to arguing the point.

"Keep the car running," Marissa said. "Never know if we might need to, you know, make a quick getaway."

"Who's going to stop us," he sounded unsure of his own statement, "Geo's long gone by now."

"He's not what I'm worried about," she said, getting out of the car.

"Leave the door open," McMurray said, smiling sheepishly, "you know, just in case."

Marissa nodded and began the walk to McMurray's front door. She watched the windows while crossing the lawn to the front door, pausing a couple of times, sure the curtain moved, and she was about to be inundated by those beetles. The one beetle was hard enough to fight, and in the end, if it wasn't for McMurray, it would have won. With the number of them that had been in the house, there would be no fight, no moments of clarity

THE LOST

where she knew she was being manipulated. Peering through the sidelight, Marissa tentatively touched the doorknob as if she were testing the room to see if it was on fire. Her hand came away clean and dry. Looking back over her shoulder, McMurray had gotten out of the car and was standing in the driver's door, watching over the roof. She gave him a thumbs-up, then felt foolish about the childish gesture.

The front door was unlocked, and the handle turned smoothly. Pushing the door open slowly, she looked into the darkened room. She knew where the light switch was without even looking, but she didn't want to risk putting her hand in there if there was a chance that Geo might still be inside. Instead, Marissa pushed the door in, hearing it pushing pieces of broken glass, probably from the stained glass lamp McMurray had kept by the door. She didn't see any beetles, but the smell of sulfur choked her, and she had to put her arm over her mouth to breathe. Starting as a trickle down the open door frame, the beetles soon became a steady stream down the frame to the stoop, and toward her feet, the movement caught her eyes, and she jumped back, nearly tumbling into the grass at the bottom of the stoop.

Barely keeping her balance enough to jump back from the top step onto the grass, Marissa watched in horror as the dying light of the sun shone through the door into the teeming mass that was once McMurray's living room. Every surface was moving, seething over one and other in a steady flow toward the open door and her. As the beetles reached the edge of the grass, they paused for a moment, seemingly unsure if they should approach her, but in unison seemed to decide their pray was near and surged forward. Marissa's heartbeat in her throat, watching transfixed as they broke the edge of the lawn and began maneuvering their way through the grass to her sneakers. She backed a few steps as panic threatened to undermine her better judgment. Then, as if a switch was flipped, she turned toward the car and ran, yelling for McMurray to get in.

Once in the car, heading down the road away from the swarm, Marissa frantically searched her pant legs and shoes to make sure she didn't have a stray bug. Satisfied, she turned to look out of the back window and watched McMurray's house fade into the distance. Only when she could no longer see the roof over the hill did she settle back into her seat and let out a breath, running her fingers through her hair.

"So," McMurray broke the silence, "that could have been worse."

"Could have been better too."

As they neared the bar, McMurray broke the silence again, "Is that—"

"Lucius' car," Marissa finished his thought. "He was the one who said that if I didn't kill you, then he would."

"Books out of the question then," McMurray didn't slow the car down, hoping that the black sedan in the parking lot wouldn't pull out to follow them. "At least he was parked where we could see him."

"Where's he going to hide," Marissa pointed out, looking at the wreckage from her window.

"Where to now?"

"I guess we could go to my folk's place?"

"I'm not sure that your dad's going to like us showing up together," McMurray raised an eyebrow at Marissa, who simply shrugged.

"Got a better idea."

"No, I suppose I don't."

They took the back roads to Marissa's house, hoping to avoid both the swarm released from McMurray's house and

THE LOST

driving by Lucius' parked car again. The drive was quiet, the woods on each side gathering shadows as if the whole world was taking a collective breath, waiting for the moment that it was submerged once again into the night. This had always been Marissa's favorite time of the day, the tree-frogs starting to sing, and the buzz of the insects was the only thing to break the peace that settled into everything. Today, that peaceful feeling didn't come; with each noise, each chirp or buzz, Marissa felt the tension ripple through her shoulders. She imagined the swarm of red beetles marching down the road after them, devouring the world until there was nothing left except desiccated trees and dried grass. The gathering night felt more like a threat and the quiet of the forest, a dire warning of darkness that dawn would not break.

McMurray turned onto Marissa's street and stopped the car. Letting it idle five houses away from their destination. "What's up?" Marissa asked.

"Look," he motioned down the road toward Marissa's house. Half-hidden by her mother's Ford Escape, sitting in her driveway was Bedrin's police cruiser. "You don't think—"

Marissa took in a sharp breath, her voice catching at the back of her throat. "Please, no."

"You said that Geo wanted you to bring to book to the police station," McMurray's voice was gentle as if he were trying to soften the only conclusion that she could draw. "Were they ever alone with Geo?"

"Does it matter?"

"It might not be Bedrin."

"When you went up to speak," Marissa thought back to Mikey's funeral, burying the empty casket had hurt enough to her, but her father walking out on McMurray's portion, that had been a knife in her heart. "Dad left, Geo did too, but Geo came back. You don't think?"

"That was before he attacked me," he put his hand on Marissa's shoulder and gave it a squeeze. "We'll fix this. I promise."

"How can you be so sure?"

He pointed to the worn Bible on his dashboard, "We're the good guys." Then quieter, he continued, "We have to."

They watched Marissa's house in silence, her mind reeling. Mikey, Geo, her parents, the bar, everything was gone. She wanted to run, tell McMurray to just drive to the coast and forget everything about this little town, but she knew that he wouldn't do it. "What's left?" she asked.

"We head back to the Church," McMurray said, putting the car into reverse and slowly pulling away. "We'll be early, but I wouldn't mind sitting in the chapel. Maybe light a candle or two for everything that's happened."

"A candle or two," Marissa leaned back and closed her eyes, fighting the hopelessness that she felt growing inside of her.

"Candle or twenty sound better?" she could hear the smile in his voice but didn't understand how he could smile given everything that had happened.

"Yeah," Marissa said, "twenty sounds more like it."

Forty-Three

The chapel had an empty feeling when Marissa and Father McMurray walked in from the bright sun. Nobody was using it, so the candles had been extinguished, and the lights were off. McMurray tried the switch by the door, but nothing happened. Marissa watched as he walked down the central aisle toward the hanging crucifix. He stopped before the alter, shoulders slumped, arms loosely by his side, and looked up at the hanging figure on the cross. She didn't want to disturb whatever he was doing, so she walked over to the prayer candles and lit one, watching the match burn toward her fingers and how insignificant the light looked in the darkened Church, then she thought of her brother.

The door opened, flooding the dim chapel with the failing daylight. Marissa glanced at the door, seeing the entering shadow, and her pulse quickened. She shook the match, dropping it to the floor, and turned to face the door memories of Geo's shadow in the door of the bar bombarded her, and for a moment, she was sure that he stood there ready once again to control her. Soon the shadow stretched out, becoming a little taller and filling out a little bit. Shaking her head, she dropped her weight into her right foot and felt the muscles in her back and arms tighten in preparation for a fight.

"I'm sorry," the smooth voice came from the shadow in the doorway, "I didn't expect anyone would be in here yet." After speaking, the shadow let the door close behind it and disappeared into the darkness of the narthex. Then a few moments later, lights came to life throughout the chapel. "I would have thrown the breakers if I knew you were coming so soon. We're trying to save where we can. Where's my car, Peter?"

"Left it around the corner, so we didn't draw suspicion," Marissa jumped as Father McMurray spoke from behind her left ear. He put a hand on her shoulder, and she felt the pent-up tension release. "There weren't many places left for us to go, so we came here," he motioned at the pews surrounding them.

"Your house is," Father Maria stood before them in the entryway of the chapel "—well, still infested?"

"Afraid so," McMurray said, watching Father Maria's reaction. "You still don't believe us, do you?"

"That doesn't matter really," Father Maria said, "I said I will help, and I will. I've received permission from the bishops to perform an exorcism if I deem it necessary, though I greatly doubt it will be." He looked pointedly at McMurray, "After all, Peter, you know there are some spirits that can't be exorcised."

"If you're trying to say something," Marissa shot forward in an attempt to protect Father McMurray from the accusation, "just come out and say it."

Father Maria held his ground as Marissa raised up on her toes to look directly into his face, but she still needed to look up at him. "Alright," Father Maria said, "I think Peter is a drunk who hallucinated after drinking one too many whiskeys. And you, Miss Hail," his voice was quiet but clearly condescending, "are too much of a sycophant that you will believe anything this disgrace tells you." He bowed to Marissa, "But as a member of my flock, and in honor of all your parents have done for this community, I will humor the two of you just long enough for you to realize how wrong you are."

"Do you want to come to Father McMurray's house and see for yourself?"

"As charming as that sounds, my last visit was not so well received. Besides, I have preparations to make," he pushed past Marissa and walked down the center aisle, past the altar, and through a door in the chancel. Marissa watched him go, wanting to punch him in the face but unable to make herself follow him. After a few moments, he emerged from the door and motioned both Marissa and Father McMurray to join him at the altar. "Do either of you have a plan on how to get Geo to come here? I tried his house, but there was no answer."

"His cell phone?" Marissa asked, "I don't have the number, but I'm sure he has one."

"Without the number, that knowledge won't do us much good," Father Maria looked at her, cocking his head to the side slightly, "now will it?"

"Excuse me," Marissa shot back, "I don't see you coming up with a better plan."

"I am trying to help the two of you," Father Maria leaned over the alter toward Marissa, "if you're going to be ungrateful, then you can just –"

"You can both relax," McMurray cut in, "nothing is going to be solved by arguing."

Marissa could feel her nostrils flaring as she loosened her grip on the edge of the altar between her and Father Maria. She glared at the man across from her, imagining plunging her fist into the smug smile etched on his face. How McMurray was able to keep his cool with this guy was beyond her comprehension, but she focused on her breathing, letting the adrenaline drain from her system.

Eric Johnson

"Marissa," McMurray said, as much to get her attention as a warning not to go too far, "we saw Bedrin's cruiser at your parent's house. You said Bedrin and the police are involved. Perhaps he knows where Geo is or could get a message to him."

"Good idea," she pulled out her cell phone, called up her parents' number, and listened to the ringing. She looked at Father McMurray and shrugged, "Maybe we should figure out what to say before–" the sound of the phone being picked up silenced the ringing in her ear. "Hello? Mom, Dad?" Silence on the other side of the line greeted her. "Hello?" she persisted, "I know someone is there."

"Marissa," Officer Bedrin's voice sounded echoey through the phone, "you're on speakerphone with everyone. Where are you? Your parents are worried that you did not come home last night. They went to the bar, but–"

"Yeah," Marissa cut him off, "the bar's gone. Someone lit the place while we were in it."

"We?"

"You know damn well who we are numb-nuts."

"Marissa," her mother's voice was curt.

"You always said to call a spade a spade," Marissa said. McMurray gave her a questioning look, and she realized that he could only hear half of the conversation. "Hold on, I'm putting you on speaker. Still there?"

"Where are you, sweetie?" her father's voice asked.

"Ya," Marissa raised her eyebrow at the comment; he hadn't called her sweetie in years, "thanks for caring. Look, Bedrin, as much as I want to know what the hell you're doing with my family, I need to get ahold of Geo, and I'm pretty sure that you know how to do that."

"Why would I know," Bedrin's voice sounded cheerful. "He's a free man."

THE LOST

"Tell him to meet me at the church," Marissa ignored his comment. "Tell him that he and I need to talk."

"Talk about what?"

"Just tell him," Marissa was about to end the call but hesitated. "Tell him I have the damn book." She ended the call before Bedrin could respond. She turned to McMurray and Maria, "That went well."

"How do you know he can get ahold of Geo?" Father Maria asked, looking at the phone that Marissa had set on the alter, "Do you mind?"

Marissa picked up the phone, putting it in her pocket. "He knows," Marissa shivered, "if he doesn't know where Geo is, he'll be able to talk to him."

"Still, I don't think that I condone lying to the man," Father Maria scolded, "between Officer Bedrin being law enforcement and you standing at the altar of Christ, telling even a small lie is– well," he shrugged.

"I didn't lie," Marissa looked at the crucifix hanging above her. They always creeped her out, "not really."

"But the book was in the bar," Father Maria leaned forward, "wouldn't it have been destroyed in the fire?"

"Probably," Marissa grinned, "but it was in the safe, so the fire never got to it."

"Fireproof safe for all those important documents," McMurray shrugged.

The noise of the door opening drew the attention of all three down the center aisle as two men walked in and called a greeting up to the group. Marissa looked between Father Maria and Father McMurray questioningly.

"Don't ask me. Joseph?"

"I called in a few of the deacons. If what you say is true, we're going to need a lot of help," Father Maria walked to the stairs descending from the alter and looked back at them, "and if it's not, as I suspect it isn't, we'll all pray for your souls." Then without another word, Father Maria descended the stairs to greet the newcomers.

Over the next half an hour, more people came in and milled around in small groups, calmly chatting like a social hour after services. Marissa watched them with distracted curiosity. She and McMurray had planned out how they would confront Geo if he came, what they would say, run through a dozen scenarios, all ending with the successful exorcism. As more people gathered, she knew that this was the moment that things started to go her way. They had a virtual army of deacons and parishioners that came to Father Maria's call. She wondered if she had misjudged the man. Maybe her loyalty to Father McMurray had blinded her to the possibility that change is good.

The buzzing of her phone broke through her thoughts, and she pulled it out to check the screen. Her heart dropped as she stood up from the steps leading to the alter without taking her eyes off of her screen. "They're outside," she called over the din of the crowd.

"Whose outside?" asked McMurray, looking up at her from his seat on the steps.

She looked at him and then at the door, putting her phone back in her pocket. "All of them."

THE LOST

FORTY-FOUR

The chapel's doors stood closed, but Marissa did not want to go outside into the night. The night wasn't unbearably hot, but she could feel the sweat gathering between her shoulder blades. She wiped her palms dry on her jeans, and with a glance behind and a deep breath, she pushed the oversized doors and stepped into the night. She wasn't surprised by what she saw in front of her, backlit by the headlights of her own truck and Bedrin's cruiser, where eight people, their faces hidden in shadow. She heard murmurs behind her as the people filed out of the Church, forming a loose semi-circle behind her. The sound was comforting. Knowing that she and McMurray were no longer alone in this fight was comforting. Despite her dislike for Father Maria, he had come through for them when it mattered.

"Looks like the whole town's come out for our little party," Geo said, spreading his arms out in front of him as if to embrace the group.

"We want to help you, Geo," Marissa tried unsuccessfully to hide the shaking in her voice. "Father Maria–"

"– can go save his lambs," Geo finished her sentence. "The only help I need right now is you handing over the book. You do have it, right?"

"Not here."

"Then we wasted our time," Bedrin said as he started to turn. Geo reached out his right hand, placing it on Bedrin's arm. Bedrin's head cocked to the side, and then he nodded and relaxed.

"The book is mine 'Rissa," Geo's voice was calm despite being so outnumbered. She shivered at the memory of his voice in her head.

"Come on, honey," her mother stepped out from behind Lucius to Geo's left, "why are you acting like this?"

"It's the influence of that damn priest," Marissa's father stepped up next to Bedrin.

"Mom," Marissa felt the tears threatening in her eyes, "you can fight it. I know you can."

Marissa's mother blinked a couple of times, but then her head cocked to the side, and her shoulders relaxed, "Fight what? We don't need to fight here. Just give Geo back his book."

"Once a thief, always a thief," her father said.

She felt Father McMurray's hand on her shoulder; it was good to know that he still stood with her. She even saw Father Maria step up on her left and stand calmly in his vestments.

"Where is the book?"

"I'm not giving it to you."

"The book," Marissa felt a slight tremor as Geo's voice almost palpably went through her.

"Mom, Dad, fight this," Marissa clenched her fist, "please, I can't— not after Mikey."

"You don't get to—" Geo motioned her father quiet.

"You think they can fight it?" The smile was evident in Geo's voice despite the shadows covering his face, "I think I can remember a time when you were trying to kill faithful old Peter."

Marissa heard a murmur run through the crowd behind her again, and Father McMurray moved closer. The shuffle of feet told her that their plan was in motion. Father Maria must have

THE LOST

made up his mind and told the deacons to surround the two groups. She didn't bother to look behind her because she knew she'd see the people who had been behind her had filed away onto the sides and behind Geo's group as they'd discussed.

McMurray leaned into Marissa's ear, "I don't like this."

She turned her head slightly, maintaining eye contact with Geo's group. "Father Maria seems to think it will work," Marissa glanced over at the man who was reaching into his vestments, presumably for the Bible and holy water he stowed there earlier. "You said we needed to trust him."

"I know I did," McMurray sighed and looked around, "I just—"

"You have something of mine," Geo interrupted, "and I want it back."

"Geo," Marissa turned her attention back to the group in front of her, "let them go."

"No one is here against their will 'Rissa," he motioned at her mother, "I tried to get your parents to stay behind, but they refused."

"We want to help you, honey," Marissa's mother cut in. "Geo is not the enemy. He's helped us. Given us comfort, now he just wants what is rightfully his."

"Rightfully his? Comfort?" Marissa searched for some way to make sense of everything. "Mom, you don't know what you're talking about."

A squeeze on her shoulder brought her attention back to McMurray, "We need to get out of here."

"No," Marissa shot him a withering look. She couldn't believe that he wanted to run now when their plan was working. She was distracting Geo and could see the crowd had started to close ranks around behind his little group. "I'm not going to leave until we free my parents."

"You want them to fight this," Geo cut in again, "to fight me. You tried, don't you remember. You tried to fight me in the woods, in the bar, in McMurray's, how did you do? You're so tough," the three boys that had beaten her so severely in the bar stepped to the sides of the group, now standing next to each other. "The great Marissa Hail, avenging her brother. You've lost it like this old man," he motioned at McMurray, "conspiracies everywhere. You want to talk about Mikey, about the pain of his loss. He was my best friend, and I was accused of his death," he looked around at the gathered crowd. "Your poor parents, the ones you abandoned, in favor of that disgrace. How do they feel having lost not only their son but their daughter too?

"You want them to fight? What is there to fight for? I have given them peace, happiness. You attacked my friends, Steve, Zack, Dylan, they came into the bar for food, and you attacked them." Geo stepped forward from the middle of his group, his arms spread in front of him, palms up, "Honestly, it's you who needs the help. It's you who live under these imagined wrongs. But we want to forgive you. Everyone here wants to forgive you and forget all of your past wrongs. You came here looking for a fight, but that doesn't matter. Hand over what is rightfully mine, then go home with your family. We can make all of this right without anyone ever having to get hurt."

"Without anyone getting hurt?" Marissa clenched her fists, "My brother is dead, and you attacked me twice. We're way beyond no-one getting hurt."

"If that was true," Geo motioned back to Bedrin, standing a few feet behind him now, "Officer Bedrin would never have released me. Think about it? Officer Bedrin is not the type to let bad people walk free." Marissa could hear agreement in the crowd behind her; McMurray's hand tightened on her shoulder. "If I'd attacked you, I'd be in jail. If Steve had attacked you, he'd be in

THE LOST

jail. What you think you've seen, what you think has happened, doesn't make sense. You think you were attacked? Where are your wounds?"

"You know what happened," Marissa said, but she knew that things weren't going well, she hadn't told everyone about the bug, and as she started the sentence, she knew that it sounded ridiculous. McMurray pulled her shoulder, trying to move her back from Geo, to get out of the crowd that seemed to be buying into what Geo said.

"Right," Geo nodded, "there was a bug, right?" He looked around at the gathered people, now in a circle surrounding both groups. "That's what you and Peter said as you pinned me to his floor when I came to check up on you for your parents. That's why he did this," Geo turned around and lifted his shirt showing a bloodied gauze pad just under his shoulder blade. "He cut me with a kitchen knife claiming that he had seen a bug crawling under my skin." The conversations in the crowd were getting louder, and Marissa started feeling nervous that Geo would be able to turn them against her. "It's alright," he continued, "I'm not going to press charges. It's obvious that you both just need some help. You have both had rough lives."

"Marissa," McMurray whispered into her ear, "we need to leave now."

Inside she knew that McMurray was probably right, but she couldn't abandon her parents to the control she remembered Geo forcing into her mind, as if they were her own, though. "Father Maria," she said, her eyes on Geo, "I think we need to start this." The whole group stirred as Marissa's request was met with silence. She looked to her left to see nobody there, she searched the crowd, trying to see Father Maria anywhere, but all she saw were faces of her neighbors, looking at her with pity. She pivoted around where she stood; the people surrounding her and

McMurray did not watch Geo. They were watching her. Her eyes landed on Father Maria standing at the door of the Church. "Father Maria, you said—"

"I said I would help," Father Maria said, bowing slightly to Marissa, "and that is what I am doing. I agree with Geo, as do the rest of us. You are clearly grieving for your brother and have invented this conspiracy and these beetles. You have managed to convince my predecessor, infirmed as he is, as we all know, with whiskey. Let us help you."

She turned back to Geo and watched as the people who had stood behind him stepped backward into the crowd until it was just the three of them, McMurray, Marissa, and Geo, surrounded by an unbroken wall of pitying faces.

"Give me back what is rightfully mine, and we'll let you leave with your parents. You can go home, and they will help you," Geo said, his voice soothing as if he were talking to a wounded animal.

Marissa's mind reeled at what had happened. She was confident everyone here had come to help put an end to this evil that had taken hold of one of their own, but had they always thought that this was some sort of intervention, some rescuing of her from herself. She wasn't the one that needed rescuing. It was Geo, her parents, they needed it. She stood, penned in by a community that abandoned her once and again left her to face this evil alone. She felt the world pressing down on her. She turned to McMurray, who watched the scene with fear in his eyes. He, too, had been the center of the town's ire before, and he hadn't come out unscathed. Something about the look on his face told her that this time, things were going to get worse.

Forty-Five

"I think you might be right," she moved closer to McMurray, so their shoulders were touching. The crowd had closed up the circle around the three of them. Marissa looked around at the unfriendly faces, faces that went from pity to anger while Geo talked. She found her parents in the crowd now behind Geo. "I don't think Maria believes us. They're all here because they think we're going crazy."

"I don't think that's it either," McMurray's gaze darted around the crowd. Before Geo spoke, people who were smiling and relaxed suddenly dropped their stance and balled their fists.

"What do you mean?" Marissa felt the pit already forming in her stomach grow heavier as McMurray just shook his head in response.

"We might be too late for that anyway," McMurray's voice sounded lost in thought, distant as he looked around the crowd.

"Too late for what?" Marissa didn't like the implication he was making. The pit in her stomach exploded into full-blown panic as the crowd, almost in unison, began to move closer together, shrinking the circle around the three left in the middle.

"Give me the book 'Rissa," Geo pulled her attention back to him. He'd moved closer to her and McMurray. "You know you can't win here." He motioned to the group, "You're outnumbered and surrounded. Only a fool would fight everyone, and we both know that you are a lot of things, but you're no fool. Him, on the other hand," he nodded his head at Father McMurray, "he just might be."

"Marissa," McMurray's voice was taught, as if fighting back the same panic that she felt overwhelming all of her sensed, "Marissa." He grabbed her arm, pulling her out of Geo's reach toward the hood of one of the cars parked in the Church's lot.

Pulling her arm out of McMurray's grasp, Marissa said, "We can still do this," she looked between McMurray's pleading face and her parents behind Geo. They looked peaceful, happy. As if they were not in the process of cornering their own daughter. Marissa thought about all those moments that her father had called her a disappointment, a disgrace. He'd said that she was selfish, but here she was, planning to face the whole town to save them. Her mother stumbled forward, tripping over the flip flops she typically wore, and for a moment, she paused, a concerned look coming over her face, then as if a drain was pulled, the concern washed off her face, and she resumed slow encircling of her one remaining child. "We can save them," she couldn't hold back the tears forming in her eyes, "we have to save them."

The desire to help her parents, to make them realize that she was trying to do everything she could for them, paralyzed her. She knew they were still in there, fighting like she did. They needed her, and she couldn't leave them. Father McMurray was standing by the hood of a parked car, reaching out for the arm she'd pulled away from him, a look of barely restrained panic on his face. She knew that he wouldn't leave her there, at the mercy of this sudden hostility. Tears of frustration ran down her cheeks. She owed them both so much.

"Marissa," McMurray insisted, waving her over, "it's the only way."

THE LOST

With one last look at her parents, their faces now blank of the disappointment and love they'd so often shown, she stepped backward toward McMurray, letting him guide her up the hood of the car. Her face coming level to one of the deacons she'd seen enter the Church earlier that night, his bloodshot eyes fixated on her as he grasped for her arm or ankle, folding himself over the hood of the car as she scrambled up the windshield and onto the roof.

"Are they—" she stammered.

"Yes," McMurray responded to her unspoken fear as he shook off a hand on his shoulder and struggled up into the roof next to her. At the sight of their quarry scaling the car, the orderly group, one by one, paused and looked up briefly before beginning to mob toward the car. Any semblance of order or helpfulness was lost in the animalistic response to the call inside their heads. Marissa knew their pain, she knew the voice echoing behind those vacant pained eyes, and she pitied them for it. "Down the trunk," McMurray continued, "run, and I'll slow them down. You have to get out of here."

"No," Marissa could feel the shock through her system at his words, "I am not going to leave you here to this mob. They're not in control of their actions. Geo will have them kill you, or worse." She shuddered at the thought of McMurray under Geo's control, the humiliation that he'd wrought on the only person who never gave up on her. "I'm not going to leave without you."

"Fine," McMurray pushed her back toward the trunk, forcing her to either climb down or fall, "I'll be right behind you. Don't look back."

"Promise me."

"Just go. We don't have time for this," McMurray kicked at someone who had begun to climb up after them. "They're going to surround the car any moment."

She could see he was right, the mob had all tried to get to the front of the car at first, mindlessly charging at them, heedless of each other, but now some of them were beginning to circle around the car toward the trunk. "Promise that you're behind me, and I will go," she looked down and the herd of bloodshot eyes surrounding her, "otherwise we're both screwed."

"I promise," McMurray said, giving Marissa a firmer push toward the trunk, the exhaustion coloring his voice, "now go. We'll take different routes and meet up at Father Maria's car."

Marissa looked back at Father McMurray, standing on the roof of the car as the gentle priest she knew kicked someone in the head and followed her down the trunk. As her feet hit the ground, she put everything she had into running. At first, the sound of the footfalls was close, and she could feel the pull of fingers on her clothes. Her sweater, thankfully unzipped, was violently torn off of her causing her to stumble briefly. Someone jumped on her back, trying to pin her to the ground, and she threw her elbow back. Hearing a loud crack and the weight lessening, Marissa regained her feet and tore across the parking lot. She prayed that Father McMurray was having better luck.

She hit the edge of the pavement and took a sharp left into the woods that bordered the road, hoping that whoever was chasing her wasn't as spry on their feet. She leaped from root to root, vaulting over fallen logs and crashing through pricker bushes, ignoring the prickers as they tore at her now exposed arms. She'd been in that crowd once, and there was going to be no way she was going to let them put her back in there. After what felt like an hour but was probably closer to a minute or two, Marissa slowed her pace and risked a glance backward. The woods behind her were dark but silent, and she let herself slow the pace but didn't go directly to Father Maria's car in case anyone was still following her.

THE LOST

After some time wandering in the woods, she found herself at the side of a road. The darkness of the night had made the landmarks foreign and unfriendly, so she had to walk to the corner to get her bearings. She stayed close to the edge of the forest, hiding in the shadows behind the scrub-brush along the road. She moved toward the sign on the corner, careful to keep the road in sight, so she didn't get any more lost. Eventually, she reached the corner, the trees unable to give her any more cover. Marissa paused and caught her breath, trying to calm the heartbeat she heard in her ears.

The sign on the corner read Denwitch and CR 325, meaning she was about a block and a half away from where they left the car. Unfortunately, it was a block of residential houses backed onto the Church's parking lot. There weren't any street lights in this part of town, which wasn't the first time Marissa was thankful for that. She shook her head as memories of slinking through this neighborhood checking for cars that people had left unlocked, hoping to score some easy change or possibly a phone she could sell. Back then, her biggest fear was that her parents might find out. She chuckled as she realized that was still her biggest fear. Just the consequences would be a lot more severe if they found her now.

She was sure that she could keep out of sight of the parking lot of the Church, but what worried her were the two houses that had installed motion sensor lights. If she tripped one of those, then she would be seen for sure. If that happened, Geo would lose his dogs on her, and she wasn't sure how much was left in the tank to escape. With a quick prayer, an act that surprised her as much as it would have surprised McMurray, she stepped from the cover of the woods and broke for the first hedge she saw, repeating this step, stealing glances between the houses hoping to see what was happening in the parking lot.

Eric Johnson

After the third house, about halfway down the block, Marissa finally caught sight of the crowd in the parking lot. She dove for the cover of a low bush and lay there, face down and panting. Marissa braced herself for the clamor or people rushing after her, but when the sound didn't come, dug her trembling hands into the mulch to calm herself. Being sure to stay low, she squirmed around so she could peek down the side of the house for a better look. Half expecting to see a pair of shoes when sticking her head out of cover, Marissa took a deep breath and looked down the empty side yard to the parking lot beyond. The group that she had seen hadn't moved, but they seemed to surge and undulate with a strange rhythm.

She watched, entranced for a moment, before the mob stopped and backed away, letting Geo approach what or who was in the center. Realization hit Marissa like a stone.

THE LOST

FORTY—SIX

"Marissa, it's the only way," McMurray could feel his heart beating against his ribs as he watched her look back and forth between him and her parents, the indecision clearly etched across her face. He felt sorry for her; she had lost so much in the past few weeks, and now with her parents clearly against her, clearly siding with Geo, he was impressed she was able to hold it together as long as she had. "Come on," he whispered urgently as she began to back up. He grabbed her arm and hauled her up the hood of the car.

"Are they—" Marissa's voice broke off halfway between a plea and a sob as he pushed her up toward the roof in front of him.

McMurray wanted to tell her no, that this was a dream or a mistake. He wanted so desperately to protect her from all of this, but he wasn't the type to lie, especially when necessary. "Yes," He felt a tug at the back of his shirt, someone trying to get a purchase on his shoulder. Pulling himself sharply forward, like a fish trying to throw a hook, he felt the grip of his attacker slip from his shirt and silently urged Marissa to move quicker. For a moment after that, there was a silence, like the whole world took a breath at once. McMurray stole a glance over his shoulder saw the entire mob standing still, looking up at the sky. For a moment, he looked up, trying to see what they were looking at, but as he did, he caught sight of movement out of the corner of his eye. Father Maria was standing at the top of the steps into the Church, eyes closed with his hands moving as if talking, but McMurray didn't hear anything. Then the mob of people broke as if suddenly set free of any human convention, and with a primal scream, they broke on the car like a wave. Glass shattered, and he heard them begin to clamor up behind him.

"Down the trunk," McMurray knew that if she didn't go now, neither of them would make it, "run, and I'll slow them down. You have to get out of here." He felt the arms beginning to gab at his legs as he kicked backward, indiscriminately hitting faces and arms.

"No, I am not going to leave you here to this mob. They're not in control of their actions. Geo will have them kill you, or worse. I'm not going to leave without you."

He knew how stubborn she could be, but this wasn't the time. With a move far rougher than he had intended, he pushed her toward the trunk. "Fine," he said, "I'll be right behind you. Don't look back."

"Promise me."

He swore silently to himself. He'd said he would never break a promise and knew this was one he couldn't keep. "Just go. We don't have time for this," another arm came up and grabbed at his left ankle, forcing McMurray to kick out and push Marissa harder yet again just to keep his balance. "They're going to surround the car any moment."

"Promise that you're behind me, and I will go. Otherwise, we're both screwed."

"I promise," even saying the words he knew were not true caused him more pain than the fingernails now digging into his right calf muscle. "now go. We'll take different routes and meet

THE LOST

up at Father Maria's car." He knew that he'd never outrun them; if he tried, they'd both end up getting caught.

When she looked back at him, panic in her eyes, McMurray knew that he needed to at least make a show of his escape, or she wouldn't believe him. He kicked out at the person who had his calf, planting his foot in the bridge of the woman's nose. In that second, before the blood bloomed from her nose. Emily Brightwood; he'd baptized her son about 12 years ago. A mousy woman who was so pious and kind that she brought a pie to his house when he left the Church. He'd kicked her in the face like some street brawler. He crossed himself, asking briefly for forgiveness, although he knew even now that if he hadn't kicked her, she'd have pulled him off the car and beaten him until he couldn't stand.

The last shove had pushed Marissa off the roof onto the trunk, where she now dismounted and began sprinting for the woods. He watched her for a moment, standing on top of the car that was now surrounded. He knew there was no escape for him. There never had been. As much as he wanted to help Marissa, he needed to help his flock, the people who now clawed at him like animals. He'd run from them once, but he wouldn't do it again. He could see where the strings were being pulled now. He had been wrong; Marissa had been wrong.

He saw Marissa go down, buried under some skinny guy, probably Wade Herbman, a local farmer, from the look of his clothes. He shifted his attention to Miranda Pelham as she climbed up the trunk, and with a silent apology, he kicked her in the side of the head, just hard enough to knock her off the trunk. She fell to the ground with a grunt before clawing at the side of the car again. A quick glance showed Marissa disappearing into the woods by the side of the parking lot. McMurray looked for a way to get off the car to his target with a sigh of relief. He rubbed the burn he'd gotten on his arm and prayed that God gave him a chance to save them before they could tear him apart.

Hands grabbed his legs from behind, and before he had a chance to wrench free, his feet were pulled out from under him. His face came down hard on the car's roof, his red blood leaving an imprint of the side of his nose on the grey roof. The arms pulled him back almost as soon as his face hit, and before he could get his hands up to protect himself, he was dragged down the windshield of the car. The driver's side wiper blade leaving a gash just under his left eye. The arms kept pulling him down the hood of the car onto rough assault of the parking lot.

Getting his hands up just moments before his head hit the pavement, McMurray curled into a ball to try and avoid the blows coming indiscriminately from work boots, sneakers, and pumps. Disoriented, he saw an opening in the crowd and tried to drag himself away. He'd been ready to sacrifice himself for these people, knowing they were going to do this, but he was losing heart with each blow delivered. As he crawled across the parking lot, bloodied and battered by legs and arms, McMurray wondered if he'd made a mistake not trying to follow Marissa. His plan mainly had worked, but a few people had followed her into the woods, he wanted to believe that she escaped, but in his heart, his faith was beginning to fail him.

Someone landed a hard kick to his ribs, breaking a rib by the intense amount of pain it sent through the old priest's body. Shuddering, McMurray collapsed on the ground and once again rolled into a ball on his side. The throbbing from the blows he'd taken was all he could feel. The current assaults, though they were happening, felt like they came at him from a distance. He caught flashes of their faces, ghosts from his past. Samantha Tibbits, a spinster who tithed every Sunday, Aiden Camden, a regular at the pub, Felicity Noble, a local kindergarten teacher, the faces were distorted by animalistic hate, but he knew their true selves. Finally, the sounds, moments ago a defining roar of primal anger and rage, took on a softer hum, the kind you hear bees making in a summer field. Hands grabbed him under his arms and hauled him up, facing the woods behind the parking lot, and the crowd in front of him parted.

Father Peter McMurray hung there between the arms of Jason Pinderman and Hailey Smith, two people he'd baptized as children, but he didn't feel betrayed by them. He felt sorry for them. His head hung limp on his neck, barely having enough strength to keep himself conscious. If it weren't for their arms under his, he was sure that he'd never be able to hold himself up. The beating he'd taken had fractured at least one bone in his leg and definitely broken a rib or two. He struggled to get in a breath and could feel the liquid rising to fill his lungs, robbing him of the air he needed. A pair of sneakers stepped into view, and McMurray felt his head wrenched up by the hair on the back, probably Jason's hand intertwined in his own thinning hair. Seeing Geo standing in front of him was not a surprise, but it was a disappointment.

"Peter, Peter, Peter," Geo spoke slowly, clearly not in a rush to act. "I'm disappointed that it had to be you, but at least all these nice people were willing to help out." He smiled, gesturing at the mob of people who stood docile despite moments ago having delivered him a savage beating.

"Let them go," McMurray said through gritted teeth.

"They're free to leave whenever they want," Geo shrugged and turned to the crowd. "Thank you for the help, but I think we're okay. You can go home." When nobody moved, Geo shrugged and turned back to McMurray, "It's not my fault they want to see what happens to you. You are the one who betrayed them."

Eric Johnson

"I did not—" Jason and Hailey gave him a rough shake, and he changed the topic. "What do you want?"

"The book," Geo looked at the woods where three of the people from town, including Wade, were walking out empty-handed. "I had wanted 'Rissa too, but it seems that she has gotten away, for now, no matter. I will just use you to get her," he smiled as he pulled out a chef's knife. McMurray wondered absently if it was from his own kitchen before the reality of what was going to happen sunk in. "She has such a bleeding heart for you," he patted his free hand on McMurray's cheek. "I'll just have you get her for me." With that, Geo ran the knife across the old priest's chest, cutting deeply across his broken and bruised ribcage.

The pain shot through McMurray's system, flooding it with the bit of adrenaline that was left. He closed his eyes, screaming against the pain of the knife sliding across his chest. As he drew in his breath, pain shooting through his system, McMurray prayed to God for the strength he needed.

"I may not even need her to get the book after I have you," Geo smiled as he held the knife over his own arm. "We'll be blood brothers," he said with a joyless smile. Then waving his arms at the crowd, "we'll all be blood brothers." He drew the knife down his arm, letting out a torrent of red beetles.

"You will never get that book," McMurray said, the image of the beetle he'd cut from Marissa catching fire when it touched his blood. Using what little strength the new shot of adrenaline had given him, he looked up at the sky and said, "God forgive me." Then, pulling suddenly out of the grasp of his former parishioners, he lunged for Geo, grabbed his arm, and pulled it against his bleeding chest.

The sensation was one of coldness at first as the beetles weeded their way into his body. Geo laughed, helping to hold his arm, so the two wounds touched. At first, the old priest thought

THE LOST

he had made a mistake, that his interpretation of what happened in the bar was a mistake or a fluke, but then he felt it. The pain was excruciating as the beetles inside him bust into flames. Pinpricks of pain lanced through his system until, in one sudden warm, comforting burst of light, it was over.

Forty—Seven

Watching the crowd haul McMurray to his feet, Marissa swore under her breath. His head bobbed and rolled as they jostled him, but he looked alive, which she wasn't sure was a good thing given what Geo would probably do to him. She thought back to the bar and to Father McMurray's house when Geo had come for them. He needed them alive, at least one of them because he wanted that book, and for now, that was back in the safe surrounded by the smoldering ashes of the bar.

Balling her fist, she punched the dirt under the bush she was hiding beside. She knew he was going to do that, that's why she'd insisted on the promise, but he broke it. Wiping a tear from her cheek, she left a dirt smudge across her cheek. She needed him if they were going to interpret the book. He knew Latin and whatever those symbols were. She cursed again and moved forward, keeping low to avoid being seen.

There was no doubt in her mind that he'd done this to make sure she got away, but she couldn't leave him there to be taken by Geo. The thought of one of those things crawling around inside of him made her heartache and her stomach turn. He'd saved her; she knew that none of that had been a dream now. The eyes of those people had made sure she knew that. She couldn't leave him there, though that's what he'd want her to do.

THE LOST

She couldn't do anything for him if Geo got ahold of him, but maybe if she could hotwire one of those cars in the lot, she could at least get them both out of there.

Having made up her mind to go back, Marissa scanned the lot for a suitable candidate. Her own truck was there, but it was too close to the group, and Steve probably had her keys anyway. Most of the cars in the lot were newer, the kind that had the chipped keys, harder to get going without the chip, but parked near the back, angled in the spot, was a 1994 Jeep Wrangler, it wouldn't provide much protection, but she was pretty sure she could get it started and then pull McMurray in as she drove through the crowd. Some of the others might grab on, but she was pretty sure she'd be able to shake them. Besides, none of that would matter if she didn't rescue McMurray. Given what those bugs did for her own injuries, she wasn't too worried about hurting anyone in the process. They'd get back up, at least that's what she'd told herself.

Getting to the Wrangler wasn't a problem; neither was getting inside because the doors were off, but it had been a long time since she'd tried to hotwire a car. She pulled the wires out from under the steering column and traced the one connected to the ignition and the one that went back toward the engine. She didn't have any tools with her, but a strong tug pulled both wires out of the key housing. She tapped the two exposed ends together and flinched back as the connection sparked.

She glanced over her shoulder before she tried it again to make sure the noise she'd made so far hadn't caught anyone's attention. She knew that the starting engine was likely to draw their attention, but that would just help to thin the crowd around McMurray down a bit, so she was counting on that, but it wouldn't help her if they caught her before she'd gotten the damn thing started. Movement over by the woods she'd run into caught her eye before she had the wires in her hands again and dropped down next to the wheel, her breath coming in quick gulps as she prayed that she wasn't seen.

Geo's voice wasn't overly loud, but the unnatural quiet of everyone around him made his voice carry over the trunks and hoods of the cars. "I had wanted 'Rissa too, but it seems that she has gotten away, for now, no matter. I will just use you to get her. She has such a bleeding heart for you. I'll just have you get her for me." The ice in his voice made her shiver despite the heat in the parking lot.

She chanced a look through the footwell but didn't see the guys who'd emerged from the woods before Geo started talking. She took up the wires again and rubbed them together, a spark shot out, and the engine rumbled to life. She knew it was a matter of moments now before the people in the back of the group turned to see her, but as she prepared to hoist herself into the driver's seat, a scream, both piteous and savage, cut through the quiet night air. Marissa turned to see Geo drawing back what could only be a knife, the place near the hilt glinting in the lights from the church parking lot, but the rest of the blade disappeared into the shadows. She took one look at Father McMurray and knew why.

"I may not even need her to get the book after I have you. We'll be blood brothers. We'll all be blood brothers." Marissa watched in horror as he plunged the knife down toward his own arm, the already darkened blade disappearing from view. She forgot about the Jeep purring peacefully beside her and ran for the group. These were the people that Father McMurray had seen through so much, he'd baptized them, buried their dead, and now they stood silent as the thing that used to be Geo blatantly attacked him.

THE LOST

"You will never get that book," McMurray's voice was harsh and came out in pants, but to Marissa, it at least meant that he was still alive. She watched as he looked up at the sky and said something that she couldn't hear over her own pulse slamming in her ears. Then, like in slow motion, McMurray grabbed hold of Geo's arm and pulled it to his chest. The crowd around him cheered and closed in on the two figures now entwined.

"No!" The word ripped from Marissa's throat as she watched the scene unfold. A couple people outside the group turned around and watched her, almost shocked to see her running for them. One or two broke away from the group and drifted toward her, like friends coming to check on someone they missed.

As she neared the first of those who'd broken away, a slightly overweight woman who worked at the local hardware store, she dropped her shoulder and plowed into her, knocking the woman off balance and over the hood of one of the newer cars in the lot. The second person, a bank teller from the local People's Bank where she'd often dropped off the day's receipts from the bar, stopped to get a better footing, clearly hoping to catch her in a bear hug. Marissa kept the same approach dropping her left shoulder and leaning in to use momentum to her advantage, but this time she readied her fist to sucker punch him in his unprotected jaw before he could get a grip on her. Before she could manage this, the whole scene in front of her burned with a bright light. The shockwave emanating from the center of the light threw the bank teller forward and off-balance. Marissa felt the heat but was able to keep her feet. Her forward momentum slowed down, allowing her the precious seconds needed to jump over the teller's back as opposed to tripping over him.

Eric Johnson

As Marissa landed on the other side, she skidded to a stop. In front of her, the scene had changed entirely. By the time the light had faded, she couldn't see Father McMurray or Geo. Everyone else, including her parents on the far side of the group, had been thrown to the ground and were in various stages of standing up. Father Maria had been thrown back against the door on the Church's steps but was basically still on his feet. Marissa ignored him and scurried around the people to get to the center, where McMurray had been standing with Geo, but they were gone. She looked around for a sign of where they had gone, but the haphazard bodies all pushed back from where she stood made it impossible to get her bearings.

She turned in a slow circle, realizing for the first time the predicament she'd put herself in, and dropped into a fighting stance as the first of the people closest to her got to their feet. There, standing two feet in front of her, Zack looked at her in her crouched position, dirt and ash covering her face and arms, and took a step back.

"Whoa," he said, putting his hands up in front of himself, "what the fuck?"

"You're right to back up," Marissa felt the surge of adrenaline pump through her system. She was not going to let this kid take her down again. She was ready to put him down hard this time.

"I'm not—" he stammered, "I'm not looking for trouble here."

"You should have thought about that before you picked sides."

"Picked—" the confusion was so evident on his face that it gave Marissa pause, "Picked what with who?"

Marissa looked around at the people gathered in the parking lot in front of the Church. Most were on their feet now, but only the ones close by were paying her any attention. Most were milling around or stood in small groups, the same confused looks on their faces as on Zack's. She softened her fighting stance and shifted her gaze back to Zack, who flinched as she looked at him and looked back toward Devin, who'd come up behind him.

"What's going on, Zack?" Devin asked, rubbing a welt that was forming above his right eye.

"Dude," he shot a quick glance over his shoulder, presumably not wanting to take his eyes off of Marissa, who still had her fists balled, though her stance was far less threatening than before, "I got nothing. Last I remembered, Bedrin nabbed us at the ledge."

"Hey, isn't she– Aren't you Mikey's sister?" Devin asked, apparently unconcerned about her balled fists, "Sorry about your brother, I just– I mean, I couldn't imagine."

Marissa didn't answer, but she did drop the last of her defensive stance. She could feel the change in the air. There was a buzz of energy that wasn't there before, like some significant shift had happened. Someone behind her cleared his throat, and Marissa turned to see Father Maria's lean form standing not far from her. His face looked genuinely concerned.

"Is everything alright here?" he asked.

"Fine, Father," Devin and Zack said almost in unison.

"Marissa," he cocked his head to the side and looked down into her face, "you look troubled." He took a step back and looked her up and down, "And filthy." Then he looked around at the people in the parking lot, almost all of them on their feet and looking at him as he scanned the crowd, nodding at several faces. "Any idea why everyone's here?"

Marissa narrowed her eyes at the young priest. He looked friendly enough. All of the condescending demeanor that she'd always seen in him melted away. "You really don't remember?"

Eric Johnson

He shook his head and looked toward her feet as if noticing something for the first time. "What are you standing in?"

Marissa looked down at her feet. There in the center of the crowd, where moments ago stood the only person in the entire town that had never abandoned her, was a single neat pile of ashes. Off to one side, partly obscured by the ashes, was a slight glint of silver. Marissa crouched down and picked it up, blowing some of the ashes off. As the ashes fell away, raining down around her feet, Marissa closed her hand on the silver figure nailed to a small wooden cross and pulled it to her chest. She felt the hot tears falling down her face and gave into the sobs that wracked her body.

Forty—Eight

"No, Gerald," Father Maria patted an older man in a business suit stained with blood on the shoulder, "I'm sure you didn't hurt anyone."

"But then–" the man protested, gesturing at his ruined suit.

"Go in, have some coffee," he ushered the man toward the door. "I'll be along in a moment," he looked back over his shoulder at Marissa sitting on the steps absently watching the interchange, "and we'll figure all of this out. Everyone seems a little uneasy about what's happened."

The man looked at Marissa, and she looked away to study the dirt at the bottom of the step, turning Father McMurray's crucifix over in her hands. Her parents were in there, they'd tried to comfort her about losing Father McMurray, but she didn't want to talk to them, so eventually, they gave up and went inside with the rest of the people who had gathered. The door behind her closed, and she heard a sigh from Father Maria, who had spent the last twenty minutes trying to comfort a group and confused and worried people. He sat down on the steps next to her and leaned back, looking up at the sky.

"Well, that was–" Father Maria started, then shook his head and looked at Marissa. "What was that?"

"What part?"

"What part? Any of it," he said. "I have a parish filled with confused and bloodied people who have no idea how or why they are here or what happened. I found myself leaning against the door to the Church, and you looked like you were about to fight some poor high school kid."

"How is he?" Marissa kept staring at the dirt by her feet. It was easier to look there than anyplace else. Further down in the parking lot was a small pile of ashes she'd taken the crucifix from. Next to her was a man who had betrayed her, and all around were memories of Father McMurray.

"Zachary?" Father Maria looked back at the door. "As good as any of them, I suppose. He's scared. We all are, I guess," he shifted, so he was facing her. "What happened here?"

"I'm not sure," Marissa shook her head, trying to make sense of it all. She never liked Father Maria, but she couldn't leave him to put all this back together by himself. She would not set foot in his Church, but she knew better than anyone what the people inside had been through. The hours she was enthralled were like some crazy nightmare. She could almost explain everything away if it weren't for the evidence. She stopped twirling the crucifix and stared at it for a moment before she continued. "This was his, Father McMurray's. Some old lady gave it to him, and he said it reminded him of the importance of faith. Faith," the word had a sour taste in her mouth.

"I've never seen it before," Father Maria looked at the crucifix in Marissa's hands but didn't seem to want anything to do with it.

"You wouldn't have," she smiled, "he hadn't worn it in several years. Ever since–" how could she put into words the betrayal that Father McMurray had endured, the trials, the shunning, being driven from his Church by the people he'd worked tirelessly to help. Were there words to explain the inner

THE LOST

battle he'd fought against his own disgust and self-loathing despite his innocence? She didn't think there were, so she went with the obvious answer, "Ever since you came here. But it was his."

"Was?"

Marissa pointed at the ashes in the middle of the parking lot. "He and Geo."

"The boy from the papers?" Father Maria seemed unsure.

"Ya, I guess all this starts with him," Marissa filled Father Maria in on everything she knew. Being attacked by Zack and Steve in the jail, then twice more in the bar, her father chasing down McMurray after the funeral, Geo and the bugs. For his part, Father Maria sat intently listening. She couldn't tell if he believed or even understood what she was saying, and if she was honest with herself, she didn't care. She unloaded everything about the last few weeks, right up until she came to ask him for help.

"You came here?"

"Yup," she nodded slowly. "Everyone is here because you called them or did your whole phone tree thing. Everyone except Bedrin, Steve, Zack, Devin, and my folks. They all came with Geo."

"Why were they here? What did they want?" he leaned in closer, eyes expectant, mouth slightly agape.

Something about his demeanor made her angry, and she decided not to tell him any more than he needed to know. "I'm not sure," she said, eyeing the priest, "to infect us – he'd probably say to save us – however you want to put it."

"Strange," he shook his head again and rubbed his eyes. "Beetles?"

"That's how he did it," Marissa rubbed her shoulder, the bandage had fallen off a while ago, and it oozed a little blood staining her now ruined tank top. "He'd injure someone, make them bleed, or he'd have his cronies do it. Then he'd cut himself, and these things would come out. They weren't big, just like ladybugs, but without the spots," Marissa shivered, remembering the thing weaving her skin back together. "They'd crawl into you, through the open wound, then you'd hear him."

"The beetle?"

"No, Geo. At least I did. His voice was in my head, convincing me to do what he wanted. He didn't force anything, at least I don't think it was forced, it just felt—"

"Felt like the right thing to do—"

"Exactly," Marissa looked up at him for the first time. His face was pale, but his cheeks were a rosy pink. He had wrinkles around the corners of his eyes and by his mouth, like someone who was usually smiling and laughing, but his eyes were sad. He looked every bit the empathetic pastor talking to an errant parishioner. "It was like he made me want the same things that he wanted."

"No temptation has overtaken you except what is common to mankind. And God is faithful; he will not let you be tempted beyond what you can bear," Father Maria said.

"Bible?"

His laugh came easily despite the situation, "Bible," he said. "1 Corinthians."

"You know," she smiled at him, "you two are actually a lot alike. I was always surprised you didn't get along better."

He looked at the pile of ashes in the parking lot, "There but for the grace of God."

"Bible again?"

"Nope, but close enough. He was a troubled man. Brought his ghosts with him, my grandfather would have said. But I believe he was a good man underneath all of the pain."

THE LOST

"There are no good people, just some a little less terrible than others."

"I don't know about that," he said, putting a hand on her shoulder. "You did come back to face a mob of people to try and save him. That sounds pretty good to me."

Marissa watched as a breeze came up and nudged some of the ashes into a little dust devil. "I should collect those," she said, suddenly standing up, Father Maria's hand falling down her back. "I'll spread them, but not here," she looked around, "too much—bad. Not here."

"I have an idea. Hold on," Father Maria stood up and went into the Church. A moment later, he emerged with two Unicef boxes and a dustpan. "It's not fancy," he smiled sheepishly, "but I wasn't expecting to need to—well." He held them out to Marissa, who took the boxes but refused the dustpan.

"I'll take care of it," she said. "Go in, give them what comfort you can."

"What about you?"

"I'll be alright," Marissa walked over to the ashes and began sweeping them into the cardboard boxes with her hands. It was an unceremonious end for a good man, but she didn't have anything else. She was not going to put him into a dustbin. She heard the door closing and relaxed her shoulders, letting out a tension she hadn't known she was carrying.

It pissed her off that Geo's ashes were getting mixed into Father Maria's, but there was no way to know whose were whose, and even if she could, she wouldn't have been able to separate them as the light breeze carried some across the parking lot. It wasn't fair that Geo would be honored with the man who had been like the father her's had refused to be. All of this was his fault. If it weren't for Geo, none of this would have happened.

Her brother would be graduating in a month, McMurray would be drinking at his stool on the bar, and she would be serving.

If it weren't for Geo and his fucking book. Marissa paused, scooping the ashes into the little cardboard offering boxes. She wasn't sure why she hadn't told Father Maria about the book, but he'd been so interested in what Geo had wanted, and he had been so cruel to Father McMurray that she wanted to deny him that knowledge. He didn't deserve it; none of them did. They didn't deserve Father McMurray either. She passed judgment on them and glared at the steeple of the Church as the sun rose behind it. Maybe they should be forgiven because they were under the control of those bugs. A shudder ran through her at the memory of the bugs pouring over Father McMurray's kitchen. Those things had made her attack him too; she fought it as best she could, but eventually, she lost. But with them, she thought of the crowd closing in on them. They abandoned him years ago because some kids thought it would be fun to play an evil prank on a good man. It was that more than anything which ruined him, not the accusations which were proven false within a month, but the fact that his people, his children, had done it.

Marissa swept the ashes in the flimsy cardboard box, the bright colors on the sides making a harsh contrast to the new contents. In the end, she had given up on separating the two ashes, there was no telling where one began, and the other ended, and it wasn't all Geo's fault after all. If one of those beetles messed her up, Marissa didn't even want to think about what they did to Geo. After all, Father McMurray had always talked about saving Geo; he would have wanted him to have a proper burial, even if she didn't.

"Are you going to be joining us, Marissa?" Father Maria's shadow loomed across the ashes.

THE LOST

"I don't know," she looked at the ashes inside the pitiful cardboard donation boxes, "I think I want to be alone for a while."

"But your parents were hoping to talk to you about a few things," Father Maria bent down to look her in the face. "They do care about you, you know?"

"The fact that you need to say that should tell you a lot," she retorted as she closed the second box. Most of the ashes that she could get off the parking lot were tucked neatly into the small cardboard boxes. It struck Marissa, what gets left behind; a couple of boxes of ashes were all that remained of the man who had done so much good. In the end, he died to help his people, the same people who abandoned him when he needed them the most, and her parents were among them. She wasn't sure if she would ever be able to forgive them for it.

"Every family has their issues," Father Maria tried to put his hand on her shoulder, but Marissa stood up, effectively knocking it to the side. He continued undaunted, looking up at Marissa as she stood above him, "Family is about forgiving people even if you don't think they deserve forgiveness. Your parents aren't perfect, but they are trying to do their best for you."

"If their best is not visiting me because they are too worried about what other people think of their daughter the criminal, or blaming me for every bad thing that happens at their house, they can shove it," she felt the heat as her face flushed. "I know quite well how imperfect my parents are, and they've made it quite clear what they think of me over the past five years."

Father Maria stood up slowly and looked past her to the truck parked haphazardly over three spots. "Stephen asked me to give these to you once he realized they were yours," he held out her keys and smiled, "He was worried you might press charges."

She grabbed the keys from him and shoved them into her back pocket, then gestured over to the cruiser similarly parked by her truck. "I've had enough of the law in this town."

"Where are you going to go?"

"I'm not sure," she looked back at the steeple. The sun rose to light the cross atop it from behind, casting the shadow over the two of them. "Just not here."

"What should I tell your parents?"

"You could tell them to go to hell."

"Marissa," his voice made it clear he disapproved of her choice.

"Tell them I'll call them when I'm ready," and with that, she turned and walked over to her truck, started it, and drove out of the church parking lot.

*   *   *   *

Father Maria stood in the shadow of his steeple and watched as she drove away. Once she was out of sight, a bald man in a cheap business suit walked up to his right side. Looking in the same direction.

"She knows where it is," the bald man said.

"Yes," Father Maria replied, "I'm sure she does."

The bald man looked up and to the right for a moment as if listening to something only he could hear. "You know they still want it."

"Then go get it," Father Maria said as he turned around and walked back into the Church.

The bald man watched the empty road Marissa had left on for a moment, then simply walked over to his dark sedan and drove out of the parking lot through the same exit Marissa had taken.

THE LOST

FORTY—NINE

Deciding to go to the bar was the easy choice. Most of the best memories she had since she was released from prison were at that bar. The fact that the building no longer existed was going to be difficult for her, she knew that, but after everything that had just happened, she needed to be someplace that held some good memories. Pulling into the parking lot was harder than she'd imagined it would be.

The smoke had stopped rising some time ago, but the place still looked more like a scene out of some post-apocalyptic movie than the bar she'd spend most of the last three years cleaning. She could see the twisted metal of the dumpster behind a charred half-wall next to where the back door once was. Some remnants of the bar remained and a part of the office wall, but everything else looked like a campfire after a long night. She knew when she had decided to come here that there wouldn't be much left. They had stayed on the trunk of his car and watched as it burned, but seeing the grey ash covering everything Father McMurray had built was demoralizing.

Next to her, on the passenger seat, were the cardboard boxes of ash she'd taken from the church parking lot. It was appropriate to spread them here, she told herself, this was his place, his life savings had financed it, and he had taken a chance on her. There was no doubt that he belonged here. She climbed out of the truck and began to pick her way through the ashes and broken beams until she reached the spot. There wasn't much left, just the bottom corner of the bar that stubbornly refused to burn, but she would have known where it was even if there had been nothing. He sat here, years of wasted opportunity and self-destructive behaviors. Years of refusing to promise he would quit because he wouldn't lie to her. She opened the boxes over where his stool would have been, then stopped before she emptied the ashes.

"You were always the one who knew what to say," she said to the empty lot, "the one with all the quotes and phrases. I'm not much for speeches, but I feel like I have to– have to say something. So, here it goes.

"You looked out for me. All the way to the end, and you didn't deserve this, any of this, and you definitely didn't deserve to die," her voice hitched softly as she spoke. "I know why you did it, or I think I do anyway. Lie to me– in the end, you know. I forgive you for it, you know, lying to me," she closed her eyes and tilted her head to the sky. "God, this is stupid. You can't hear me. You're fucking dead. You lied to me, and you died, and now I'm here to put your ashes someplace meaningful, and I'm mad at you. I forgive you, but I'm mad at you because there had to be another way. A way that you didn't have to die.

"But, it doesn't really matter anymore if there was because the choice was made," she tipped the boxes slowly, letting the ashes spill onto the ashes of the bar. "Ashes to ashes, I think that's like one of those things you'd say. There's more to the quote, I'm sure of it, but I don't know it. You would, but now you can't tell me, so I'm here, making a mess as usual." She sighed as the last of the ashes fell to the ground and then let the boxes fall from her hands. Standing, surrounded by the remnants of her past, Marissa felt hollow, like the past few weeks took everything inside her and

THE LOST

emptied it into the ashes at her feet. For a while, she just stood there staring at the road beyond the parking lot. The tears had stopped because there was nothing left worth crying about.

The black sedan caught her attention because it was the only thing she had seen on the road since she left the church parking lot. She recognized it at once, and when the brake lights lit up, she groaned softly before heading over to the safe and mindlessly entering the combination. Inside the safe, tucked away where McMurray had put it, was that ragged messenger bag he'd bought at the thrift store before she'd— before he met her at the bar. Marissa grabbed the bag and started to close the safe. Thinking better of it, she reached back in and shoved some of the money they'd put in for deposit into the bag, then closed and locked the safe. When she turned around, Lucius's car was parked blocking her truck, and he was leaning against his hood.

"I'm surprised to see you here," he called out to her from where he stood. Marissa didn't respond; she simply threw the bag's strap across her body and began the careful climb back to her truck. He tried again when she was closer, "I said, I'm surprised to see you here."

"I heard you the first time," she shot back.

Lucius put his hands up as if to ward her off, "I figured that you didn't hear me because you never responded."

"I figured it was a statement, so I didn't need to respond." The two of them stood looking at each other, neither face giving away what was going on behind their eyes. "I want to be alone if you don't mind."

"Not at all," he said as he moved to his driver's door. He put his hand on the door handle but didn't open the door. Instead, he looked up as if he'd just realized something and said, "There is that little matter of our contract."

"Contract?"

"Yeah, I hate to bring it up, but as it looks like you're about to leave," he shrugged, "we really should settle up."

"Contract?"

"When I got you out of that little three strikes jam you had yourself in with the local law enforcement, Officer Bedrin. You remember that, don't you? We both agreed that you owed me; you even signed on the dotted line, if you remember. Well, now I'd like to collect on our little arrangement. It seems that you have something that I would like."

Marissa didn't like the way this was going. The only thing she had was the bag from the safe and some money. She needed the money to start fresh wherever she went, and she was not about to give this guy the book that Father McMurray had died to keep from Geo. As much as parting with the money would hurt, she sighed and asked, "How much?"

"Money?" his smile didn't reach his eyes. "I'm not looking for money from you. I have plenty of that. What I want is the book you have in that bag over your shoulder. I believe you know the one I'm talking about."

"No."

"You don't know which one I'm talking about, or are you trying to get out of paying your debt?"

"You are not getting this book," she clutched the bag closer to her and slowly started moving toward her truck. "Why do you want it anyway? Geo's dead. He can't control you anymore."

Lucius laughed, "Oh, you're funny. Did you actually think that weakling controlled me?" He moved around the back of his car to try and cut her off from reaching the truck. "You're either naive or stupid, not that it matters. Either way, you will give me that book, or I will take it from you, your choice."

THE LOST

Her mind raced to try and process what Lucius said. If Geo didn't control him, then Father McMurray had died for nothing. If Lucius got the book, he would continue with whatever his plans were, simply replacing Geo with someone else, if he hadn't already. She needed to get out of here and far away. Looking between Lucius and the door to her truck, Marissa broke into a sprint for the door handle. Lucius was on it before she got it open, and he shoved it closed again, barely missing her finger in the process.

Marissa threw her elbow into his chest, avoiding his nose the keep him from bleeding and releasing any of those beetles he had in him. Making the best of the couple of inches that gave her, she swept her right leg behind his and shoved him with her hands catching him off guard. Lucius's face banged against the truck, and Marissa cursed under her breath as the blood from his nose began to coalesce into a small red beetle. He swiped for her feet, his fingertips brushing against her pant leg as he backed up to open the door of the truck.

Leaping over him into the driver's seat, Marissa reached into her back pocket to get the keys as she closed the door, but they weren't there. She felt around the ignition and checked the visor but again came up empty. Marissa saw Lucius standing up with a big grin on his face, dangling her keychain from his fingertips through the driver's side window.

"Drop something?" Lucius yelled through the window. "Why don't you roll down your window, and I'll let you have them."

Marissa smiled at him and ducked under the dashboard. She'd never thought she'd have to hotwire her own truck, and looking at the smooth plastic under the dashboard, she realized that this would not be as easy as the Jeep was earlier. Sitting back up, she opened the glove box to get the knife she'd kept in there.

Eric Johnson

The Bible McMurray had given her when she'd gotten out of prison took up most of the space. Throwing it onto the passenger seat, she dug her knife out of the bottom of the glovebox and was about to duck back under the dashboard when a loud thud shook the car.

She looked over at the driver's window and saw a light smear of red in line with her eyes. Lucius's fist bashed into the window again, leaving more blood and shaking the car again. The breath caught in her throat as his fist came down a third time on the window. This time small cracks began to form, the blood dripping down the window even as it began to bead up and grow legs. With renewed urgency, Marissa ducked under her dashboard with the knife and pried at the plastic underneath. Her breath was coming quickly now, and she could feel the sweat beading on her nose. The sound of the beetles scurrying around outside her car combined with the cracking sound from her window made her hands shake as she pulled the wires from the ignition and twisted them together.

The engine start was met with the sound of shattering glass and a hand reaching through, trying to grab her. Lucius grabbed at her shirt, his fingers clawing for purchase on the strap of her tank top. Instead, they caught the edge of the bandage that she'd put back on her shoulder before collecting the ashes at the Church. The quickness of the tape tearing off seemed to catch Lucius off guard and gave Marissa the opportunity she needed. Jamming the car into reverse, she sped from the parking lot onto the street, dust billowing up in plumes before she put it in drive and floored it down the road, hoping to put as much distance between her and the town as she could.

THE LOST

Fifty

The wind tore through the open window as Marissa held the pedal to the floorboards of the truck. She never had cared much about the speed limit, but she had never tested the truck like this before. If she weren't running for her life, it might have actually been exhilarating. Instead, the hair blowing in her eyes and sticking to the sweat on her cheeks was pissing her off. Still, she figured that was better than whatever would have happened if Lucius had gotten ahold of her. She spared a quick glance down at her chest. The cut from McMurray was beginning to close up. It seemed too closed up, but who knew what residual effect those bugs had. Not that it mattered; without the bandage, she doubted it would stay that way.

The road ahead, like the sky, was clear, which was good because at the speeds she was pushing her truck, the last thing she needed was someone pulling out in front of her. Her breath, which came in gasps by the time she reached the road, began to even out, and for the first time that day, Marissa tried to make sense of everything. If Lucius was still like Geo, did that mean that the rest of the town was? Had Father McMurray been wrong? No, she decided quickly; they were clearly different, confused like she had been after he'd saved her. He had saved them. She knew he had. What did that make Lucius? He still had those things, those beetles in his blood.

Eric Johnson

The sun glinted off the broken glass, casting rainbows on the truck's roof, and for a second, she marveled at how there was no blood on any of the glass. The clear blue sky and the breeze coming through the window made her feel almost normal like this was just an average drive back home after a day of work. Glancing at the speedometer for the first time, the needle pinned to the right, she eased up on the gas, no sense in losing control of the pickup. The rearview mirror showed her storm clouds gathering in the east, and that meant a break in the humidity, a welcome respite from the oppressive heat. If it weren't for the seeping cut on her collar bone and the bag sitting beside her on the seat, she could almost convince herself that none of this happened.

Something moved across the dashboard toward the steering wheel, and Marissa felt every fiber of her muscles tighten at once. There wasn't any blood on the broken glass. She tried to think back to those hectic moments as she hot-wired her own car, Lucius banging on the window. His knuckles had split; there was a film on blood on the window then, she was sure of it. If the blood had been there, her thoughts grabbed at the implications she knew were there, but she couldn't quite put together what that meant. If Lucius was like Geo, like the town, he should have been back to normal. But he'd laughed. She looked in the rearview mirror again as Lucius's sedan crested the hill about half a mile behind her. She looked at the speedometer that now read a safe fifty-five and swore under her breath.

She turned back to the road in front of her and pushed the petal closer to the floor. She knew her truck couldn't outrun Lucius's car. Her only chance had been the initial lead and hope he wouldn't have found her, but she'd blown that by getting distracted by the weather. Her mind raced for a way to lose him, and she thought about any one of the dirt roads that wove their way through the woods. She'd used them as shortcuts many times,

THE LOST

and some of them were pretty rough. The truck could handle most of them, she'd have to slow her speed, but Lucius's car would probably be too low for the less used ones. She scanned the edge of the woods through the passenger window, looking for any indication of a path or dirt road, but the trees moved in an unbroken line, and Lucius's car was quickly closing the distance.

Her heart beat in her ears as Lucius pulled even with her and slowed down, driving on the wrong side of the empty road. Something moved on her hand, and at first, Marissa dismissed it for her hair in the wind, but when a flash of red in the sun caught her eye, her reaction was so quick, she almost lost control of the truck. She whipped her hand from the steering wheel and slammed it into the driver's door, trying desperately to get rid of the damned thing. The beetle dug its legs into her skin and wouldn't be dislodged, so she slammed her hand into the door again, this time crushing the beetle between her hand and the door with a satisfying popping noise. Then she saw the rest of them, probably ten at first glance, on the ceiling, the dashboard, climbing on the passenger seat, and some even braving the wind to climb in through the shattered window.

The truck shuttered and skidded to the right as Lucius swerved into the driver's side door. One of the beetles that had been hanging onto the roof above her dropped onto her shoulder. Wrenching the wheels back on the road, Marissa shuttered as she felt the little legs scurry across her shoulder toward the trickle of blood coming from the collar bone. With the wheels back on the road, she let go with her right hand to brush the beetle off, sending it out of the window into the wind. Marissa saw what she was looking for about two miles up, a break in the woods with clear tire tracks running from the road to the woods. She crushed another beetle against the dashboard and sped up.

Lucius matched her speed and swerved into her sideboard again. The wheel from the truck pulled from Marissa's hands as she bounced along the shoulder, sending two more beetles raining down on her. Trying to control the car and ignore the crawling sensations on her neck and arm, Marissa pulled the wheel to the left, effectively driving her bumper into Lucius's front left quarter panel, causing him to veer back onto the left side of the road. The truck hit a large ditch in the shoulder of the road, sending Marissa bouncing nearly out of her seat; the beetles scurried over her flesh, ever persistently toward the now bleeding line on her collarbone. She cranked the wheel to the left again, and her tires chirped as they gained purchase on the pavement. With the road clear for a moment, Marissa reached behind her neck and crushed the beetle between her fingers, then brushed at the beetle that had crawled up her arm onto her left shoulder. It clung to the strap of her tank top and wouldn't be dislodged like the last one.

Lucius recovered control of his car and sped down the left lane level with the bed of her truck. The break in the trees was just up ahead, and Marissa made her move, trying to ignore the beetle as it made its way down the strap of her tank top. With a quick edging of her truck to the left, hoping to make Lucius swerve or be knocked off the road again, she cut the wheel to the right, aiming for the break in the trees and hoping that the truck didn't roll in the process. The green canopy blocked out the gathering clouds, and Marissa bounced down the uneven dirt road. She'd hoped for a rougher path, but beggars can't be choosers. A check-in the rearview showed her Lucius's car blowing by the dirt road. She took advantage of the brief respite to put more distance between her and Lucius before he inevitably turned around to follow her.

She held no more illusions about the doggedness of her pursuer. Lucius wouldn't stop until he either caught her or destroyed his car, and she was banking on the second one, as long as she could keep her's on the road. The dirt road, more an unimproved road than a path, was going to be far easier on his car than she'd hoped, but it should slow him down some. She knew the beetle was about even with the cut on her collarbone, but she couldn't risk pulling a hand from the wheel just yet. The road might be smoother than she wanted, but it still took her both hands on the wheel if she was going to keep control of the truck at fifty miles an hour. Two more beetles crawled her neck, rounded her shoulder, and followed the one now perched on the seatbelt close to the promise of her blood.

When the muscles in her shoulder being to relax, she knew she couldn't wait any longer. The beetle, which had reached the edge of the cut, was beginning to crawl inside, relaxing her with whatever tricky thing they secreted, trying to lull her into a sense of security and safety. She'd fallen for it last time, but now, she pulled her right hand from the wheel, keeping the other one white-knuckled at twelve o'clock, and jammed her fingers into the wound, crying out in pain as she grabbed the slippery, squirming beetle and threw it out the window. The other two on her shoulder began to move faster to the newly opened wound, now bleeding freely. The wheel jerked violently in her hand, and she brought her bloody fingers to steady it before trying to dislodge or crush the other two. Still more scurried over the steering column, more than the original ten she'd seen.

Glancing behind her, she could see Lucius's headlights in the gloom under the trees. His car bounced left and right, but he managed to stay more or less centered on the road. Turning her attention back to the beetles now threatening to overwhelm her, Marissa's mind raced to find a way out. On the seat next to her, she saw several beetles moving across the bag, but they gave the Bible she'd tossed out of the glovebox a wide berth. Wracking her brain, she couldn't figure out how that could help her, but she was vaguely glad that it kept them away from hiding in the bag if she ever got out of here. The beetles neared the tender skin around the collar, and she felt that similar relaxation begin to come over her again. She slammed her already bloody hand into the collar bone, hoping to crush the beetles, and screamed as pain shot through her arm, forcing her to lose grip on the wheel, which bounced wildly, sending the truck toward the trees looming on either side of the road. Hoping that the pain indicated she'd succeeded, she slammed at the breaks and grasped the wheel. The blood on her hands made it slippery, but she managed to wrestle the truck into a quasi-controlled skid and finally to a stop.

Looming in the windshield, inches in front of the bumper, a tree was sitting dead center in the direction the runaway truck had taken. Marissa took a deep breath and went to work, trying to crush the beetles with anything she could get her hands on. Eventually, she held the Bible that McMurray had given her against the steering wheel, effectively blocking the largest contingent of beetles advancing on her. She fumbled for the handle of the driver's door and rolled out onto the ground feeling the dry leaves and dirt under her shoulders and clinging to her hair. She breathed in the heady scent of the forest that surrounded her, trying to calm her racing thoughts as she got to her feet and backed away from the truck. At least a dozen of the beetles scurried on the steering wheel, drawn by her blood, and began to look for a way through what they thought was her flesh.

The headlights were the only thing she saw before the sound of rending metal and shattering glass caused her to leap backward, covering her ears and screaming into the already deafening noise. Lucius had slammed his car into the bed of Marissa's truck, effectively pinning it between the twisted metal wreck that used to be Lucius's sedan and the tree that she'd

THE LOST

narrowly missed hitting herself. She cursed loudly as she realized that she'd lost her one chance to get out of here. For a moment, everything was still, the echo of the crash died down, and the animals in the forest, silenced by the noise, waited.

In that silence, Marissa was able to take in her surroundings. The truck sat at the edge of a clearing. On the far side of the clearing sat a little hunter's shack, the door slightly ajar, ashes scattered around the stone stoop. She sighed; at least she knew where she was and how to get out. Before she did, she knew that she would need to make sure that Lucius wouldn't follow her. Absently, she clutched the Bible to her chest and let her feet move her toward the driver's side window of Lucius's now immobile wreck.

Looking in, the first thing she saw was his face. He'd slumped on the right-hand side of the steering wheel and now lay there head seemingly resting on his right arm. His shoulders moved slow and rhythmically, which gave her the impression that he was sleeping, but the blood dripping from his nose and chin onto the floorboards told a different story. Satisfied that she would be able to put enough distance between them before he'd get out, Marissa turned to strike out into the woods. Before she'd gotten two feet from the tangle of metal, she remembered what he was after in the first place. She knew that Father McMurray had killed himself; no, he had died to keep Geo from getting the book. She couldn't dishonor his sacrifice by letting Lucius get it.

Picking her way around the back of Lucius's car, the popped trunk lid blocking her view of the unconscious man inside, Marissa made her way around the wreck to the passenger door. Holding the Bible like a shield, she carefully opened to door, ready to jump back as the beetles, sensing her throbbing shoulder, renewed their stalled pursuit. When the door opened, there was no scurrying, no movement, just a light red stain on the seat around the bag. Marissa stole a glance at Lucius' windshield, but the spiderweb of cracks made it impossible to see anything inside the car. She looked at the bag, the same sense of dread filled her that had when she'd first seen the thing after McMurray had saved her, and even though there was no other choice, she hesitated to take it from he seat.

The sound of grinding metal gave away the movement before she saw Lucius' bald head rise slowly from the wreckage of his car. The red stain on the seat began to shrink, and she could see small bumps moving around beneath the fabric of her seat. When the first beetle found the seam in the fabrics and broke through, Marissa threw the Bible at it and slammed the door to put a metal barrier between them and her. From the other side of Lucius' car, she heard his cold laugh.

"You might have been able to use that," he said, "but I guess we won't know, will we."

She looked through the cracked window as the first of the beetles began to climb the glass toward the less solid windshield. "Why are you doing this?"

"I want the book."

"But Geo's dead," she knew they'd had this conversation before, but she needed a moment to figure out what to do. " He was the one who needed it."

"He was simply a pawn in something much larger," he was moving up the driver's side of her truck toward the hood. Marissa backed up toward Lucius's car, reaching his passenger door as he rounded the passenger side of her truck. "You," he shrugged, "you're simply an annoyance."

"You're lying," she stammered. "Everyone, the town, they were being controlled by Geo, not you."

"Okay," he shrugged again, "I'm lying. Wouldn't be the first time." He moved closer to her. His wounds were just

THE LOST

wounds; no horde of beetles poured out of him like they had with Geo. "Doesn't really matter anyway."

"Doesn't?"

Lucius cocked his head to the side for a moment, then said with a smile that set the hairs on Marissa's neck on edge. "You're not leaving these woods." Before the words could register, he launched himself at her.

Already on edge, Marissa was able to take a quick step back, evading his grasping arms. He fought clumsily, not like Steve and Zack had fought in the bar. She turned and moved around to his open trunk; everyone she knew kept a ton of random stuff in their trunks, and she was sure she'd find something to use against him, but one look in the space made it clear he was not like the people she knew, the trunk was completely empty, not even a tire iron.

"While I have enjoyed our game of cat and mouse," Lucius said, not bothering to walk into view, "I believe it is time to end our little dance."

Marissa backed away from the trunk, trying to judge if she would be able to outrun him. She'd noticed that Steve and Zack had been fast, so was Geo, but this guy seemed clumsier and didn't seem to have as many of those things as Geo did. She hadn't even finished the thought before she knew it was futile. The chittering sound of hundreds of beetles came from behind her. Turning around, Marissa saw a sea of dark, read beetles making a tight semicircle around her. It wasn't that he didn't have as many as Geo; he just had better control of them. They didn't just pour out of him; they obeyed him. Outside of that semicircle, darker shadows sulked in the artificial dusk brought on by the trees and the gathering storm.

Her options limited, Marissa bent down, grabbed a stick that had been dislodged from the tree when the cars collided, and readied to fight the man who walked around the trunk of his car. Thunder rumbled off to the west, and the air seemed to thicken around her. Marissa held the stick out between Lucius and her; her arms trembled with the effort. She knew her left arm wouldn't be able to provide much power, and one arm wouldn't be enough, but for now, it kept the distance. If he used the beetles, they would overwhelm her in moments, so Marissa tried to keep him focused on her and occupied. She thrust the stick at his chest with as much force as she could.

Lucius took the brunt of the stick in the chest but didn't budge. Instead, he smiled, and grabbing the stick with his left hand, he twisted it and wrenched it from her hands, dropping it next to himself. "You have the option of joining us,' he said, "though, of course, I'd prefer if you don't, it'll be more fun that way."

"Far be it from me to let you down," Marissa said. That explained why he hadn't simply used the beetles. Unlike Geo, he didn't want her to be enthralled to him; he just wanted her gone.

"Just the answer I wanted," Lucius smiled and once again lunged toward Marissa, who sidestepped his advance and, pivoting on her foot, swung her fist, catching his back with a glancing blow.

His recovery was quicker than she had expected. Without any of the awkwardness he'd exhibited earlier, Lucius feinted left and grabbed Marissa as she tried to move to her left to avoid him. He wrapped his arms around her. She could feel his breath on her neck and the heat of his skin on her arms. "You're done, you little bitch. You've caused enough trouble."

Throwing her head back, she felt a crack as his nose broke, sending a stream of warm blood down her back. She hadn't wanted to draw blood, but there was no other way to get away from him. Getting away was the first concern. Stopping the beetles that she let loose would have to wait. He didn't let go of her. Instead, he pushed her out, so he had his hands on, pinning her arms to her side and turned her around to face him. She could see the beetles moving under his skin, moving the cartilage and rebuilding his nose from her attack.

"You know they protect me," he smiled, showing the blood between his teeth, "you had them once too. Why do you think you can beat me?" He pulled her closer to him, digging his thumb into the already angry gash on her shoulder, drawing a fresh scream from her that seemed to make him shiver. He brought her face close to his and licked her cheek, then pushed her back to arm's length to look at her. "I might be persuaded to give you some more. That drunk old man can't mess things up this time."

The look in his eyes told her everything she needed to know about what he wanted. His finger dug into her collar again, and her peripheral vision began to blur. She knew she needed to do something, or it would be over. She let her head sag down as if she was in too much pain, an act that was far less put on than Marissa would have liked, and she mumbled a response.

"What was that?" Lucius pulled her closer, "Just ask, and I will spare your useless little life. I will give you meaning."

Marissa mumbled again in response, lifting her head slightly before letting it flop back down.

Lucius pulled her in close, "Ask me so I can hear you," his smile hovered inches from her face, "whisper it in my ear." He drew her close to him and held her head to his ear.

"Fuck you," she said, and grabbing his shirt with both hands, she pulled him closer and brought her knee up between his legs.

Lucius screamed and backed away, throwing her roughly against the bumper of the car. Marissa reached back, steadying herself against the edge of the trunk. He didn't curl up like the boys who'd gotten too handsy with her in high school; in fact, she wasn't even sure that her knee had made contact. Instead, Lucius was grabbing his chest and snarling at her. He took his hand away, clenching and unclenching his fist, his eyes still filled with lust, but not a carnal lust this time. He wanted blood. "You," was all he said, a faint outline of a crossfading where his hand had been.

Marissa looked down at the crucifix she'd taken from Father McMurray's ashes. It hung around her neck but must have fallen outside of her shirt at some point. She looked up at Lucius and saw his rage building. His fists clenching and unclenching, his jaw set, eyes burning with pure rage and hate. Marissa smiled at him, her finger resting on one arm of the crucifix. "What's the matter," she baited him, "afraid of some useless little girl?"

The taunt had the effect she wanted. With a primal growl, Lucius dropped his right shoulder like a linebacker and ran full speed at her with all the finesse of a freight train, chewing up the soft ground behind him. Marissa waited until the last moment, then dove to the left, leaving him with nothing but the trunk to stop him. She rolled into the dive and came up inches from the chittering horde that obediently watched, waiting for their turn. Without waiting for a second, she pivoted on her right foot and grabbed Lucius's flailing legs, shoving them into the empty trunk.

Struggling to get out, Lucius turned over and snarled at her. "You fucking bi–"

As soon as his mouth opened, Marissa pulled on the crucifix, breaking the chain, and shoved the whole thing down his throat until it stopped. Then with renewed vigor, she pushed further, feeling the pressure give way as the long end of the crucifix punctured his soft pallet. Unable to speak, Lucius's eyes went wide, and his hands began to scrounge for purchase on the offending item, but each touch brought the sound of cooking

THE LOST

meat. Marissa slammed the trunk lid down on him and turned around to see the horde of beetles begin to thin out, melting into the dirt and leaving a dark red stain where it once stood. Exhaustion and pain washed over her as the thunder once again tore through the sky. Marissa sunk to the ground behind Lucius's now silent trunk put her face in her hands, and the first drops of rain found their way through the canopy above and fell sizzling on the lid of the trunk.

Eric Johnson

Fifty—One

The rain had been falling in steady sheets for the past twenty minutes, and Marissa, her wet clothing clinging to her battered body, trudged down the muddy shoulder. She had Father McMurray's tattered messenger bag slung over her right shoulder, cradling her throbbing left arm. Everything ached now that the adrenaline had worn off, but her shoulder, where the beetle had to be dug out with her fingers, was by far the worst. She watched the rain shatter the puddles along the road, not paying attention to where she was going. At this point, she wasn't really sure it mattered. Her truck was a loss, wedged as it was between the tree and Lucius's car, and his car, even if it had been drivable, had whatever was left of him in the trunk. She didn't like leaving McMurray's crucifix in there, but she was not about to open up that trunk, so there it would stay.

The road had been empty most of the morning, people didn't tend to come out this far unless they were headed out of town or to the lake, and with this rain, it seemed no one really wanted to be driving unless they had to. That and most of the town had been at the church not that long ago, Father Maria was probably still delivering a sermon or had called an impromptu barbecue to calm everyone down. Whatever the reason, Marissa was glad for the undisturbed peace. After everything that

THE LOST

happened, she wasn't sure that she wanted to be around anyone anyway.

The squeal of airbrakes in the rain forced her to stop contemplating the puddles and drew her eyes up. A semi pulled over on the shoulder several feet down the road from her, and the driver waved. The rain made it hard to see the driver in the mirror, but there was something oddly familiar about his smile. Marissa walked up to the cab's passenger side and hoisted herself up with the rail, opening the passenger door. The seat was covered with fast food containers, and the cab smelled a little like stale oil and body odor, but it was dry. She brushed the bags off the seat and got in, closing the door behind her.

From behind the steering wheel grinned a big man with a long, greying, grizzled beard. His bright blue eyes shone from under impossibly bushy eyebrows, and with a warm, deep chuckle, he said, "Picked a hellofa day to go walkin'."

Marissa smiled at the man, his blue mechanic's work shirt, red and white name patch, the beard falling onto the ample belly; everything fit the man. "Hey Carl," she said, letting a smile touch the corners of her mouth. "It's good seeing you."

"You look a bit like a drown rat yourself," he shifted the truck back into gear and nudged it off the shoulder onto the road. "Saw that bar I dropped you at wasn't 'round no more, glad to see you're alright. I was a bit worried for my little runaway."

"Long story," Marissa shook her head and patted the bag in her lap.

"So where to this time?"

"What?"

"Assuming you need a ride someplace? Hospital to get that shoulder looked at?"

"Can we just do east again?"

"You sure," he kept his eyes on the rain-sheeted windshield but nodded at her shoulder, "looks kinda rough."

"Ya, I'm sure."

"Well, there's a first aid tin in the glovebox. Might wanna get some ointment on that."

"In a bit," she leaned her head back against the seat and closed her eyes.

"If you say so. Got a bag this time. Get that thing taken care of?"

Marissa didn't open her eyes, but she patted the bag again, tucked safely inside were the strange book that Father McMurray had found in the hunter's shack, the Bible he'd given her when she was released from prison, and the money she'd taken from the pub's safe. "You could say that."

"You sure you want to head out? What about your family or that priest guy from the bar? What was his name?"

"Father McMurray."

"Sure. What about him?"

"He's dead," saying it aloud made it hurt, made it more real for her, and she felt the tightness forming in the back of her throat.

"Tough break," he said, turning his full attention back to the road. The rain had lightened up some, but visibility was still pretty limited. Marissa watched Carl holding the truck steady against the developing wind as they approached the town proper. She felt comfortable with him, more than she should be, having only met him twice, but his grandfatherly demeanor and easy smile helped.

The truck rumbled across the wet pavement, past Father Maria's parked car, and toward the church parking lot.

"Lot of people there for a Thursday," he said. "Y'll having a party or somethin'."

THE LOST

"Something," Marissa said, looking at the lit windows of the church. She could make out shapes that seemed to move and fade, but she couldn't make anything from them at this distance.

"Should I drop you here?" Carl slowed the truck down as the rain swallowed the church again, "With your folks, maybe?"

Marissa imagined the reunion, how her parent looked so confused when they'd seen her at the church, how they'd hugged her. The tightening in her throat came back as she watched the rain. She thought of the years her father didn't talk to her and her mother's tears at Mikey's funeral. She tried to remember a time when she'd felt welcome when she felt like they wanted her, but nothing came to mind, nothing since that day in the woods. She knew they probably loved her in their own way, but it wasn't enough. Her view of the rain began to blur, and she tried to muster up the courage to make a choice. She tried to evoke some sympathy for them, what they've been through, but she'd been through it too, and they had no sympathy for her. Finally, she just shook her head and turned back toward the window.

The road was empty, more so than was typical this time of day, and the two of them drove in silence for a time. Marissa fell asleep, lulled by the rocking track and the draining stress of the last few weeks as the miles fell away behind them. By the time she'd woken up, the sun had risen to burn off the last of the clouds, and the truck was on I 81 north. She looked out the window as they pulled into a rest area.

"Nature calls," Carl said with a smile.

Outside the cab, the air was still warm but not as oppressive as it had been in town. Marissa stretched and yawned. Her shoulder hurt, but not as severely as it had earlier. Her clothes had managed to dry off mostly while she'd napped in the truck's cab, and they were only slightly uncomfortable. She'd have to get something new, but not here. Carl came back a few minutes later with two coffees and two McDonald's apple pies. Marissa smiled and accepted the offering. They walked over to a picnic table in the sun to let her clothes dry off some more.

"So," Carls started, "anything more idea about where you want to go?"

"I thought that the coast would be nice," Marissa said, watching the cars steam along the interstate. "I've never seen the ocean."

"I'm on a run that's taking me up to southern Connecticut," he put the last of his apple pie in his mouth and chewed it thoughtfully. "Wouldn't mind the company, to be honest. Gets lonely on the road all the time."

"Nice up there?"

"Nicer than some," he nodded. "Like boats?"

"We had a lake in the town that my folks would bring my brother and me to when we were younger. Dad had bought one of those little two-person sailboat things. He and Mikey loved it. Lake was way too small for it, but I guess it was fun."

"Ocean's a bit bigger than that."

"I'd be disappointed if it wasn't," she laughed.

"Well," he said, standing up and putting their empty cardboard containers in the recycling barrel, "shall we?"

"Mind if we stop someplace where I can pick up some new clothes," she looked down at her tank top and jeans. The rain had washed away some loose dirt, but she was sure that the tank top would never be white again. "These've seen better days."

Carl's smile lit up his eyes, "Sure thing, kid." The engine rumbled to life, and he maneuvered the back onto the interstate. They took the next exit and found a Walmart so she could get some new clothes, then pulled back onto I 81 north. The sun was directly above them as they rumbled down the road. Up ahead, a blue and white sign hung from an overpass above the road

THE LOST

proclaiming Pennsylvania Welcomes You, State of Independence. Marissa looked at the garrulous man who drove the truck wearing his blue mechanic's overalls as he energetically told a story about some funny thing that had happened to him on the road, and she laughed a warm and happy sound.

Epilogue

Sitting behind his desk, the man held the phone to his ear and repeatedly tapped on the oak top of the desk while listening to the ringing through the receiver's earpiece. His eyes were closed, and his jaw set. He knew this was going to be unpleasant. He let himself hope there would be no answer as the ringing went on uninterrupted. His shoulders dropped when it came to an abrupt stop.

"Yes," the voice on the other end was quick and unfriendly.

The man took a deep breath before responding, "You said to call you if–"

"I told you not to underestimate her, you idiot," the condescension over the line was evident. "You said you had this covered."

"I did, I mean I do," he stammered and silently cursed to himself. This wasn't how things were supposed to have gone down. "The plan is still in place. The old man is out of the picture, and the rest are back under our control."

"Control? Is that what you call that disaster over there?"

"We didn't anticipate–"

"Of course not," the voice interrupted him. "I'm sending another representative who will hopefully be able to help you to *anticipate*."

THE LOST

"That won't be necessary. I have things under control here."

"Try not to get his one killed too, will you?"

Before he could answer, the person on the other end of the line hung up. The man slammed the old corded phone into the base and glared at the phone. He was not used to being talked down to, especially by someone so young, but his plans were more extensive, and he needed them to help carry it out. For now, at least.

He stood up and pushed the soft leather chair back. Walking around the desk, he went to a small table in the corner with a new crystal decanter filled with an amber liquid. He took one of the glasses and poured some of the liquid into it. The oaky smell warmed his nostrils, and he took it down in one quick drink, shuddering as it burnt his throat. He'd never been much of a drinker, but it was now the only way he could quiet the voice in the back of his head. He opened the door to the anteroom and motioned the three boys that sat there into his office, then returned to his chair behind the oversized desk.

After he'd settled back into his chair, he looked up at the three young men standing in front of his desk. They were about high school age, each with slightly bloodshot eyes, each waiting patiently for his command. He knew they'd do whatever he'd ask of them. He just hoped it would be enough.

"Find her," he said, looking at each of them in turn. "Find her and bring her here."

The tallest of the three, a skinny kid in a black teeshirt with some band's logo on it, gave a curt nod and then headed for the door. The other two, more athletic, followed him without comment. The man watched as they closed the door behind them and smiled. Soon.

Eric Johnson

The Second Coming is not done with Marissa yet. Join her as she meets new allies and confronts more insidious rivals in BOOK TWO:

The Found

Until then, sign up for my mailing list so you don't miss the updates, or my other books and stories!

www.ericjohnsonwriter.com

About the Author

Eric Johnson spends his days chasing after one of those diabolically bipedal entities we often refer to with the innocuous moniker of "Pre-Schooler" or waking in the wee hours of the morning to quiet someone's nightmares or weave them a pleasant dream. Otherwise, he is correcting papers, planning lessons, climbing trees, remodeling his home in the woods, reading in the groggy wastes of the middle of the night (since those aforementioned entities don't sleep), or drinking black, dark roast (or something with a little more bite). Sometimes he even gets some writing in there too.

You can also read his poetry in a full-length collection titled *The Conditions We Live*, published by Unsolicited Press.

To find out more about Eric and his work, or sign up for the mailing list at:

www.ericjohnsonwriter.com

OTHER BOOKS AND SERIES

Poetry:
    The Conditions We Live (Available Now)
    Transitions (September 2021)

Young Adult:
    Dreamweaver Diaries
        Book 1: Under the Shadow's Eye (Available Now)
        Book 2: Depths of the Rebels' Stone (June 2021)

New Adult:
    The Second Coming Trilogy
        Book 1: The Lost (Available Now)
        Book 2: The Found (Coming Soon)

Made in the USA
Columbia, SC
22 February 2025